FADE

BY

EV NEWMAN

NCI

Published by Nubus Creative Ink LLC

An Independent Idea Lab

Copyright © 2017, 2025 by Ev Newman

Library of Congress Cataloging-in-Publication Data

Names: Newman, Everett, 1973-author

Title: Fade / Ev Newman.

Description: First Edition. | New York: NCI, 2025

Identifiers: LCCN 2025926358 |ISBN: 979-8-999-4369-0-0
(Hardcover) | ISBN: 979-8-999-4369-1-7
(Paperback) | ISBN: 979-8-999-4369-2-4 (ebook)

Jacket and Symbol art by Ev Newman

Jacket design by Prime Publishing Studios

Dedication:

For my father, my hero!

Prologue

July 10, 1982

His life was worthless. He begged for it, but he didn't know why. The thought gnawed at the young thief as he lay face-down in a dumpster, blood pooling in his mouth, gunshots from a .357 still ringing in his skull.

Little Man made him kneel before pulling the trigger. He didn't want to die a pathetic addict, surrounded by the stink of ketchup, rot and an old boot. The taste of blood dragged him back to the day he lost his first tooth, when his sister whispered stories about the Tooth Fairy. He longed for her comfort, her voice. But memory betrayed him. He couldn't recall the last time he had seen her, or the last time he had teeth.

The dumpster door slammed shut, killing the moonlight. The alley had once sheltered him. What had been his safe haven had now become his coffin. No one would grieve when he slipped away.

The pain wasn't as sharp as he expected. Numbness crept in, more terrifying than the wound itself. Laughter echoed from outside the dumpster. Little Man and his crew. His last tie to this world would be mockery. Poetic injustice. He wished he could rewind, fix what he'd broken and see his mother one more time. For a moment, he imagined her reaching through the dark to take him home, but the light never came.

Where is she?

Shame seared through him as he begged for forgiveness. Tears cut through the grime on his face as he wept for the ruin he had become. Something inside him wouldn't quit. The boy who once dreamed of showcasing his creations with ink and paint still clawed for daylight, still believed he could escape the chains of dope and booze. He prayed, though he'd buried his faith with his mother long ago. The words caught in his throat, strangled by the fear of Little Man hearing him.

A cough ripped through him, blood splattering his chin. Gunfire cracked again. Shouts followed. The echo inside the metal box was deafening.

Did they hear me?

Am I already dead?

The laughter stopped. Silence thickened. His tears returned as he searched his mind for the childhood prayer his grandmother had tried to teach him.

Our Father, who art in heaven...

The dumpster lid screeched open. Light cut through.

Hands grabbed his leg and shoulder, hauling him out. His back hit the wet ground. A shadow leaned close.

"Take it easy, my friend," a raspy whisper said, pressing cloth to his head.

A savior? Or another trick? His thoughts blurred, stumbling between memory and blood loss. Could it be his father?

"I'm not sure how bad it is. Don't move. Ambulance is coming."

Darkness swam across his vision, but one thing burned clear: the eyes, the ones from the rumors.

"Your eyes..." His cracked voice broke. "It's you."

Sirens howled in the distance. The whisperer stood, retreating.

"I've seen your work. You are more than this."

The words stuck in his chest as the figure faded into shadow. Blood filled his mouth, drowning his gratitude, but he forced it out, anyway.

"Thank you."

He tried again, louder, desperate.

"I'll spread the good news. Tell them we have hope."

 **1**

Chapter

July 10, 2007 - 25 Years Later

Only when death stares us down do we grasp the weight of a human life. Every second with the ones we love becomes priceless.

Jacob "Jake" Johansson watched the cast of mourners at his father's grave. Penrod Johansson had fought illness for five long years and left explicit instructions for his end. He didn't want anyone attending his burial.

Yet here they were.

Jake stood in a loose semicircle with six others. His uncle, Father Colin Duffy, held a small book at the foot of the grave. A polished black coffin rested on a plywood platform beside the hole. Penrod wanted to be buried alongside his wife at sunset, with the Manhattan skyline silhouetted in the background.

Father Duffy's voice rose in his thick Irish brogue. "Ashes to ashes, dust to dust."

As the words hit, Jake shifted his weight on the artificial grass matting the edge of the plot. He wondered whether the movement had interrupted the prayer.

To his left stood Rosetta Jones, the nurse who cared for Penrod during his final years. Jake only spoke with her a few times during Sunday visits to the nursing home. She always wore a scowl, like she'd rather be anywhere else, making small talk with anyone but Penrod's son. The scowl came with her to the funeral, but at least she had shown up. That held some weight for Jake. The stethoscope around her neck was ironic at a funeral.

I guess you can never be too sure, Jake thought.

Beside her stood Cook, a tall, wiry old man in blue jeans and a pinstriped shirt. Instead of a cane, Cook leaned on a mechanical claw used for picking up trash. With his white hair slicked back with care, Jake understood this was Cook's version of dressing up.

Among the residents, Cook was one of the nursing home's long-timers. The medical professionals reached a consensus and gave him a diagnosis of dementia. He always called Jake's dad "Young Man" and addressed Jake as Jacob, but never seemed to get his own family's names right.

Jake watched him sniffle and shake, emotions pouring from him. Then Rosetta, in a rare show of warmth, reached over and caressed his shoulder.

Cook sneezed like a cannon blast.

"Whoa! Sorry, Rabbi! My hay fever's killing me this season!"

Father Duffy cleared his throat and slammed the book shut. "Ah, um, no problem! Just finished up here."

Jake's eyes slid toward a man whom Jake had only met twice. R. Ronald Ratner, the nursing home director, stood with his arms crossed and eyes on his watch. The guy was not someone Jake held in high regard. Ratner reeked of tobacco and looked like he had shaved with rocks. Two tiny Asian women stood at his side, each holding a plastic shopping bag with their arms linked like best friends. One of them appeared to be asleep on her feet. They were total strangers to Jake. Maybe they were other residents. Or maybe Ratner brought them along as part of some twisted field trip that he advertised in the brochure.

Father Duffy spoke the final blessing: "May God look after Penrod Johansson's soul with love and mercy. Amen."

Jake crossed himself and waited while the odd ensemble drifted off. "Always a pleasure, Jacob. Hope to see you soon," Cook said.

Rosetta walked past Jake in silence as Cook ambled toward the Econovan with Stanley Miller Nursing Home stenciled on the side. "Wake up, Sue. It's time to return to the château," Cook hollered.

The Asian woman roused from her upright slumber and gave Jake a half-hearted smile. "Well, that was a lovely affair," she said. "The bride looked exceptionally stunning."

Jake blinked his eyes and did not respond.

Ratner approached, skipped the handshake, and mumbled, "You have two days to pick up your father's belongings before we start charging storage."

"I am aware. Thanks for..."

Ratner had already walked away.

Advancing from the group was a man in a dirty white sea captain's cap, yellow "scrambled eggs" embroidered across the bill. Jake remained still, not moving an inch, and stared.

Poopdeck Pappy, Jake thought, *right out of Popeye.*

The old seafarer took a deep pull from his corncob pipe. "A wonderful evening indeed," he said, as he blew the sweet smoke into Jake's face. "Most enjoyable."

"I suppose. Thank you for coming. Mister...?"

The man saluted, his beard blowing in the Greenpoint breeze, and walked off.

Jake chuckled as he glanced at Ratner arguing with the sailorman near the nursing home van.

Jake shook his head. "Weird."

Father Duffy placed a hand on Jake's shoulder. "You ready, boy?"

"Who was that guy?"

"No idea." The priest exhaled. "But now it's time to raise a toast to your dad. I'm picking up the tab."

Duffy grabbed Jake's arm to steady himself, and they began the long walk to the parking lot at the far end of the cemetery.

There it was: a spotless 1970 black Cadillac with whitewalls bright as porcelain. Jake slid into the passenger seat and smiled at the plastic Jesus on the dashboard. The figurine's one hand gave a thumbs-up; the other pointed right at him.

"The church still has you driving this old holy boat, huh?"

"Yes. Only use it now for funerals and shuttling nuns to their appointments," Duffy said as they rolled toward the Williamsburg Bridge.

"At least you cruise with the ladies."

Duffy gave him a sideways look. "You watch that blasphemous tongue."

"Yeah, yeah. You've said worse."

They pulled up at a meter in Tribeca. Duffy popped open the glove box and pulled out a placard:

CLERGY:
The Church of Saint Francis Xavier

He set it on the dash.

"Going for a beer isn't church business," Jake muttered. He couldn't resist. Not with the man who had taught him everything: manners, friendship and how to drink.

"On behalf of His Holiness and the Catholic church, I'm here to offer comfort to a fellow Catholic in need."

Jake pointed to the street sign. "That's quite fitting. We're on the corner of Church Street."

"Grace fills all places, boy."

 **2**

Pontiff's Pints used to be a church. Now, it served as sacred ground for clergy of every denomination. Remodelers had converted old pews into deep booths and softened the lighting to a warm, amber glow.

The bartender looked as ancient as the city itself. Wearing an open white tuxedo shirt beneath a black vest, he wiped down the nicked oak bar like he had done a million times before.

The place buzzed with laughter and casual noise. Middle-aged regulars gathered around mismatched tables, toasting with jokes, sipping drinks far too colorful for their age. Off to one side, a rabbi and an imam sat hunched over a chessboard, locked in battle.

"Timothy, me lad," Father Duffy said. "How're ye?"

Humph. The old bartender grunted as he polished down the shiny bar top.

"This strapping young man is my nephew, Penry's son, Jacob."

"Pleasure. What'll be Duff?" Timothy's growl was barely audible over the din of revelers darting to and from the bar, toting drinks with names like "Dirty Virgin Mary" and "Sin and Tonic."

Duffy kept it simple. "Jameson's tidy with a lovely warm Guinness on the go."

Humph.

A small man in a black shirt and Roman collar shuffled over, cradling a beer mug and a glass of wine. His thick glasses sat crooked on his face, and he walked with a joyful wobble.

"Duff, is that you?" he yelled, slurring the words.

Father Duffy rolled his eyes in mock pain. "Aye, Benny." Then he mouthed along with the man's following line.

"Well, then, how the HELL are ya?"

"Doin' grand, doin' grand. You're drinkin' for two?"

"Oh no. These are for Dave and Moishe in the back." He turned to Jake. "And who might this be?"

"This be me godson, Jacob Johansson, the son of Penry. Jacob, this here be Father Benjamin Franklin."

"No relation to the forefather," Benny said with a laugh. "It's all in the Lord's work. I offer you my condolences. Your father was a good man. May the good Lord bless his soul." He raised both glasses in a lopsided toast.

"Thank you," Jake said.

"Benny lives at the rect'ry wit me."

"Yes, and Duff and the good sisters look out for me. I don't see that well anymore."

"Just got back from the Greenpoint cemetery, so we did," Father Duffy said.

Benny nodded. "Ah, then you would be sharing libations in ole Penry's memory. Now I should get back to those reprobates. So happy to meet you, son." He stumbled away, somehow keeping every blessed drop in the glasses.

"'Tis a character, he is. Your father an' I lifted many a glass with Benny."

The ordered drinks came to the table. With a swift motion, Duffy lifted his shot glass into the air. "Sláinte!"

Jake echoed the toast.

"Jacob, what have ye been at? Are ye still lendin' a hand to keep the city goin' clean?"

Jake sipped his whiskey and answered, "Yep. Still picking up other people's shit."

"We're all mighty grateful for it. How's that wicked wrist shot of yours?"

"Not as nasty as it used to be, but I still manage to hit the twine."

"Ah, it's been a good while since I popped by to see ye play a bit of hockey. I apologize for that, to be sure. No real excuse, life's been keepin' us busy, y'know?"

"Boy, you said it. Complications...ever since Dad got sick, I've been feeling kind of strange about life and what I've become. I feel a bit guilty that I might have let him down."

"Ah, so? You were his shining light, you were! That man was dead proud of ya, he was. All he ever wanted was for ya to be happy. You've turned into a fine man and never got into any bother, did ya?"

"My dad always wanted me to be a cop or a lawyer or something like that. He always talked about taking those civil service tests or law school."

"'Twas his dream, so it was. He wanted to serve the public with the NYPD, the FBI, or in a similar role. Penry had a great love for helpin' others. He was good at it, and as loyal as they come, he was..."

"Why didn't he ever go for it?"

Father Duffy shrugged. "He always said he would, an' then, in the same breath, Penry would be claimin' he needed to work an' never had the time. 'Tis a shame. He had so much to offer. He was never the same after that godforsaken war. Many a Vietnam vet fell into that hole, and then my sister!"

"Yeah. I can't shake the guilt, though."

Jake excused himself and walked to the bar for another round. He wanted to catch his breath. Father Duffy recognized Jake's uneasiness and let him be.

A beautiful pixie-like woman with a nose ring drifted toward The Pour Box and slipped a bill inside. Her bare feet peeked from under a light, flowing dress, toes painted a chipped metallic gold. She spun once, soft and effortless. Her eyes locked with Jake's. There was a warmth there. A mischief. The kind of boldness that made people forget their own name.

"What type of divine character are you?" Jake asked.

She tilted her head. "Magic," she said, smiling like it was a secret she was letting him borrow for a moment.

"Most definitely," Jake blurted before he could stop himself.

She stepped a little closer. "You know, they say people like you can see angels."

Jake blinked. "People like me?"

"You're cute," she whispered. "Your eyes, silly. Two different colors. That means you can see angels."

Something fluttered low in Jake's chest. He didn't know if it was grief, whiskey or this barefoot fairy spinning in front of him. His brain tried to warn him to back away, but his mouth had already taken the shot.

With the puck on his stick, Jake saw an opening and fired off the fastest one-liner of his bachelor career. "Well, I'm looking at you."

Her smile deepened, teeth catching the bar light. "Smooth," she said. "Chaotic, but smooth."

"Works on nuns too," Jake said.

"Oh, you flirt with nuns often?"

"Only the nice ones."

She laughed, bright and round. "Tell me your aura color," she said.

"I didn't know I had one."

"You do. But yours changes. That's rare."

Jake gave a helpless shrug. "Figures. My whole life's a mood ring."

She grinned, then traced a tiny circle in the air around him with her finger. "Majik," she said, deliberately spelling it out. "With a J and a K. The old way...the Wiccan way."

He didn't know what she meant, but the words settled in his gut like a warm flicker. A pull. Something waking up. For a half second, he forgot where he was. Then a fresh wave of uneasiness tugged at him: his father, the funeral, the day's weight pushing through the cracks. The room tilted.

"I should get back to my uncle," Jake said softly.

She gave him a slow, knowing nod. "You will," she said.

The implication in her tone almost tripped him.

"Eventually." She added.

As he walked away, he felt her watching him. Not in a clinging way, but like she had seen a thread tied to him...and knew it would pull them together again.

"Still carryin' that stress stone I gave ye?" Father Duffy asked.

Jake reached into the front pocket of his pants and rubbed his thumb on the flat, smooth surface of a dark-colored stone. "Yeah, of course."

"A well-respected and world-renowned Buddhist monk right here in this lovely spot gifted that stone to me," Father Duffy stated in a matter-of-fact tone. "Helluva card player, too."

Jake suspected a story was about to come on.

"We were in the thick of a poker game, so we were," Father Duffy said, eyes brightening as he leaned back. "That monk had the best poker face I've ever laid me eyes on. Calm as a breeze. No tells at t'all. I told him he was makin' me nervous, I did. The monk just smiled and handed me a rock. Said it'd help keep me peaceful and focused. After that, he cleaned up the entire pot with a straight flush."

Jake laughed, shaking his head. "Come on."

"Oh, it happened, boy. Don't doubt me."

Jake's smile lingered as he took a sip of his drink. The story warmed the space between them.

Father Duffy continued, but this time Jake noticed the shift in tone, softer and more honest. He had heard bits of this over the years, but never the whole thing, or maybe he just never paid attention enough.

His uncle explained how Penrod had helped him quit smoking after Jake's grandfather died of lung cancer. Father Duffy had been puffing away since he was fifteen back in Cork, running with the local toughs. Penrod had wagered him a year of Sunday Masses if he quit. Father Duffy pretended to think it over, having zero intention of stopping. Just another bet between old friends.

"That's when somethin' strange happened," Father Duffy said, slipping back into dialogue as he tapped the table once with his knuckle. "Later that night, I opened a fresh box of Marlboros and that very same stone must've slipped inside and smashed all the smokes, it did. Every last one. I took the rock and rubbed me thumb over it every time the urge hit. Did that for six months. Haven't touched a cigarette since."

Jake raised a brow. "Did Dad keep his promise?"

"Every Sunday for a year. Holy days, too."

Jake rolled the flat rock between his fingers. "I keep it because you gave it to me, Uncle Duff. I never use it," Jake lied.

"Ah, give it a go, why don't ya? Especially now! I reckon tossin' in a Hail Mary for good measure wouldn't hurt a bit."

Father Duffy took a sip of his whiskey, letting the quiet settle.

"Yer father always believed in doin' the right thing, he did," Father Duffy murmured. "He was a man of his word. Had a real knack for bein' there when you needed him the most. A good friend...the best, I tell ya. I miss him dearly."

Jake sat back and took a deep breath as his uncle lifted his glass into the air. The memory pulled at something deep and tender. Only a long exhale kept him from breaking down in the middle of the bar.

Yes, his father had a knack, an impossible one. Hockey games, math homework, late-night talks, keeping him fed, keeping him safe. His father had always been there.

"How the hell did he do it all?" Jake whispered, voice cracking under the noise of the bar.

Duffy reached out to grab Jake by the neck, still holding his whiskey high. "Here's to Penry! Me best mate, brother and the man who gave me a halfway decent godson."

 **3**

Jake had just turned ten, and the summer of 1987's sun shone bright above the busy streets of Greenpoint, Brooklyn. He rode his brand-new, dazzling green Mongoose GT bike. Its shiny frame sparkled like a jewel in the sunlight. With rotary handlebars spinning like a whirlwind and foot pegs ready for movie-worthy stunts, unstoppable Jake sped down the Greenpoint sidewalks. The bike was a gift from Uncle Duff. It fulfilled his greatest dream at that age.

With every pedal stroke, adrenaline surged through his veins. Jake popped effortless wheelies like a pro, the front tire spinning triumphantly in the air, the wind rushing past like applause. Older boys slowed their bikes to admire the gleaming machine and the kid who commanded it.

"Whoa! That's the new Mongoose!" one shouted.

Jake couldn't hide the proud smile that spread across his face. Now, high on neighborhood glory, he decided this day would stand apart from the rest.

Riding on the street was forbidden, though he never understood the exact reason. It didn't matter. Jake did not give his mother a reason to worry or push against his father's temper, even when Uncle Duff told his parents to stop raising the boy soft. After the arguments cooled, Jake and his father always found their way back to common ground.

With his fresh bicycle beneath him, Jake felt he could tackle anything, even the Bobby Sims gang that loitered across McGuinness Boulevard. There they were, on spray-painted BMXs, trading Garbage Pail Kids outside the Amigo Bodega. Jake rode to the opposite corner, waiting for his opportunity.

Bobby Sims wasn't the biggest punk, but he was their leader. He had the best bike, factory paint, four pegs and the biggest stack of cards. Bobby pushed his bangs from his eyes and scooted his front tire off the curb. The rest of the gang followed like infantry.

"Hey, why'd the chicken cross the road?" Bobby shouted.

Jake tensed.

"Cause it wasn't scared like Eerie Eyes Johansson!"

The gang erupted with explosive laughter that bounced off the glass storefronts and brick facades along McGuinness.

"Come on, boy, come on," Cal Grabowski mocked, puckering his frog-like lips and making kissing sounds.

Jake's front tire edged from the curb, causing the gang to freeze. The traffic light cycled through green, yellow and red, but the walk signal stayed on hold. Jake's forehead glistened as sweat gathered on it.

The signal switched. Jake pushed off.

The crowd across the street erupted in cheers. Jake streaked through the crosswalk, faster than he'd ever ridden. Near the opposite curb, he pulled off a perfect 180 powerslide, kicking one foot down and whipping the rear tire forward. The move stopped his back tire inches from Bobby's front tire.

The gang surrounded him with applause and pats on the back. Jake grinned from ear to ear.

Bobby dismounted and extended his hand. "It's about time."

Jake shook it, short but firm, just as his uncle taught him.

Miles Orsky stood next, his bike cobbled together from half a dozen others, including one Jake suspected had once belonged to him. Dirt stains covered Miles's face and hands. His torn jeans and dirty Chewbacca shirt suggested contagious disease.

"I like your bike. Can I try it?" Miles asked.

The group swarmed, forming a circle around their target. Jake paused, unsure whether to agree, knowing everyone would want a turn. The act of sharing can be a fundamental building block when people are forming friendships.

Hadn't I gone out of my way for them?

With a simple gesture, Jake turned over the bike.

Miles bolted down the street with an exaggerated grin, gone. Jake felt his stomach turn as his gorgeous green Mongoose disappeared around a corner.

Bobby patted his back. "Don't worry. Miles would never steal anything," he said, though Jake stood rigid and unconvinced.

Sixty seconds sank into a suspenseful crawl. Finally, Miles reappeared, barreling toward them, cackling like a crazed Sasquatch.

Jake gasped as Miles screamed, "GHOST RIDER!" before leaping from the bike and launching it unmanned into the heart of McGuinness Boulevard. The Mongoose shot across the road and into traffic.

It might make it! Jake prayed.

It did not.

A white box truck turned the bicycle into mangled art. The entire group vanished without a trace.

A man sprinted from the truck, shouting for police. The driver yanked Jake off his feet, shaking him. "You crazy little shit, you're gonna kill someone!"

Jake lost consciousness.

When Jake awoke, he was on the couch with his uncle sitting by him with a cool, wet cloth. "Jacob. You're all set, aren't ya?"

"My bike, my bike, it's not fair, please. It's not fair!" Jake cried as he hugged Uncle Duff tight.

"Right, me lad. All's well now. Mr. Alvarez, down at Amigo, filled me in on what happened and had a word with the coppers. No one's hurt. You're going to be..."

"Where's my bike?" Jake whimpered.

"I got it in the basement. It 'tis pretty banged up, though. Your dad will have to look at it when he gets home. I'll be honest, lad, it doesn't look good. I shall try to get you another one, but it will take a while."

Father Duffy patted his head and sat back on the couch.

"T'was a right awful fright ye gave me when I was called 'round the corner to find yerself with the coppers. Penry would've been mighty ticked if ye got pinched throwin' bicycles at movin' vans on me watch."

"Dad won't be home from work till two in the morning, and Mom promised to wake him at eight for his job interview. Dad will never have time to look at my bike."

"I reckon he won't," Father Duffy conceded. "Have a bit of patience, Jake. It'll all work out, I promise ya. Someday, you'll have a brand-new bicycle and be zoomin' around the town again. In the meantime, keep yer chin up and say a few prayers. Your dad will get to see that bike, but it might take a wee bit."

The defeated boy moped around the house for the remainder of the night, plotting his revenge against the Bobby Sims gang. The boy realized he would need an adult to buy a steamroller and blowtorches. After yet another spontaneous crying session on his mother's shoulder, Jake went to bed with no new battle plans, deciding to talk to Dad when he got home in the morning.

The alarm clock blared its irritating buzz at 8 a.m. Jake slept right through it and woke up an hour later. Jake sprang from his bed. Disheartened, he found his mom cleaning a frying pan in the kitchen. The smell of bacon and eggs still lingered in the air.

"Hi, Mom," Jake greeted.

"Good morning to you, Jacob. How d'ya sleep?"

"Okay. I have to see Dad. Be right back."

"Oh, your father's already gone, honey. Got'n early start and let you sleep in. He forgot to disable yer clock. After getting home so late, I wonder if the man slept at t'all. Said he'll see ya later."

Jake sat at the table, resting his head on his hands while his mother prepared his breakfast. He ate, then left the table. Dressed in his usual blue jeans and Denis Potvin t-shirt, Jake began his nerve-racking walk around the building to the basement to assess the damage.

As he entered the cool, damp basement, his bicycle was at the superintendent's workbench. Jake did not expect this at all. Instead of the mangled metal motif of a Picasso painting, the bright green Mongoose GT stood on its kickstand. Its two wheels were intact and looked rideable. Sure, there were still a few scratches, dents and a bent handlebar, but it appeared poised for cosmic travel. Upon further inspection, Jake found a piece of paper taped to the seat.

Hey Jake,

I did the best I could. DON'T CROSS THE STREET! Be home tonight.

Love, Dad

* * * * *

Father Duffy and Jake were close to finishing their drinks. Jake's eyes glimmered as his thoughts drifted back to Pontiff's Pints.

"He really was my hero," Jake stated and emptied his glass.

Pontiff's Pints became crowded. The pair decided it best to wrap up the day with happy memories, so they walked each other to the door.

"Do ya need anything, me boy? Anything at t'all?"

"I'm fine, Uncle Duff. Taking care of a few things before moving on. I promise to stay in touch more."

"Hey, Jacob, what happened to that old bike?"

"Stolen a week later."

"Why didn't ye ever tell me that?"

"It seemed too much trouble having the best bike in the neighborhood. I figured the person who stole it would have to deal with it."

Jake hailed a cab.

"You going to Brooklyn?" a squeaky female voice asked.

Jake turned around and saw the cute, self-proclaimed Wiccan witch walking toward him. "Yes," Jake and Father Duffy answered at the same time.

"Mind if I share the cab?" she asked.

"Sure." Only Jake answered.

Jake looked hard at Duffy's parked Cadillac and back at the inebriated priest with his clerical collar half off.

"Uncle Duff, how are you getting home?" Jake inquired with deep concern as he opened the cab door for the lady and followed her into the back seat. Jake rolled down the window to hear Father Duffy's response.

"Don't be worryin' about me. Benny's drivin'."

Father Duffy snickered upon turning around and stumbled back into the pub. Jake and his newfound fairy friend gave the cabby their respective cross streets.

Chapter 4

A woman screamed. Not a scared-of-a-spider scream, but an earth-shattering, bloodcurdling, "get me out of Jeffrey Dahmer's kitchen" scream. Jake's head lay buried in a pillow. He opened one eye. That is when the pain began. His head throbbed like it was slugged with a sledgehammer. Stupid hangover. Jake swatted at his "alarm off" button to silence the screaming woman, who he named Mrs. Hitchcock. The shrieking alarm clock was the best thing he ever bought himself. Regular alarms never worked.

Jake lifted his head in curiosity. Another woman's voice, screaming, vied with Mrs. Hitchcock's, and she added curse words. The pretty brunette with a nose ring jumped out of Jake's bed and ran around his room in the nude. She pinballed off every piece of furniture until Jake finally silenced Mrs. Hitchcock.

"What's wrong with you?" she exclaimed.

The gorgeous wizard girl gathered her things and left without looking back. Jake wasn't sure she had left his apartment fully dressed. At first, he found it convenient. He had no intention of seeing her again. She seemed clingy. Besides, all she talked about was Majik even during sex. Jake got up and shuffled to the bathroom.

He examined his reflection in the mirror to see if he needed a shave. The pinball wizard girl liked his rugged look.

She said it complemented his messy reddish-blond hair. Jake decided to keep it for a while.

As Jake continued to look at himself, he checked his eyes for any signs of a hangover. One of his eyes was green, and the other was blue, a trait he had inherited from his father. The eye doctor informed him that he had a condition called heterochromia iridum, which is rare in humans but common in some animals. Although his eyes were a little bloodshot, they would clear up after a hot shower.

Jake's father explained that having two different colored eyes meant they were part werewolf after some kids teased him about it. Jake realized how cool it was after watching the movie, *Teen Wolf*.

Two Advil and a good teeth brushing were a good start to feeling better. Jake hit the shower. At six feet tall and 190 pounds, he was still in decent shape thanks to years of hauling trash. But the slight bulge in his stomach reminded him that fall hockey season would help trim the fat. Jake had joined a thirty-and-over league this year, now the youngest on the team instead of the oldest.

Jake scavenged for clothes and found a pile inside his laundry bag near the leather recliner.

After his father moved into the care facility, Jake took over the two-bedroom, rent-controlled apartment he'd grown up in. He added a flat-screen TV and a fancy chair but left everything else the same, including his father's oil painting of the Brooklyn Bridge.

Jake threw on jeans, a New York Islanders tee and beat-up Pumas. Before leaving, he checked on Mrs. Daschle across the hall.

Knock knock

"Be right there." Jake heard Mrs. Daschle's soft shuffle through the door. She opened it with a smile. "Good morning, sweetie."

"Hey, I keep telling you to ask who it is before opening."

"Of course it was you. Who else knocks like that? How was the funeral?"

"Some residents from the home came. I wasn't familiar with many of them. Uncle Duff ran the service."

"That Colin Duffy. Was he sober?"

Jake grinned. "Mostly."

"Coffee?"

"No, thanks. I'm running late. Need anything?"

"Milk, if you remember."

"I will. I'm heading to the nursing home to get Dad's stuff."

* * * * *

Jake parked his silver Honda behind the Stanley Miller Nursing Home, a plain five-story brick building with a semicircular driveway and an awning. He walked up to the reception desk.

"Excuse me?"

"Yes?" the less-than-friendly young receptionist said, barely looking up from her National Enquirer paper.

"I'm here to pick up my dad's things. He passed away a few days ago."

The girl quickly looked at the computer screen before nodding toward a long hallway. "Elevator's on the left," she snapped.

Jake stood in silence near the world's slowest elevator, praying that no patients or staff would join him on the ride up. He wanted nothing more than to distance himself from the haunting memories of the dreary nursing home. The doors slid open with a whoosh, thankfully with no one on the other side.

Maybe I'm being dramatic.

The ride up began with a jolt, and Jake's moment of relief turned to dread as he feared what lurked in the common area on his father's floor. When the doors opened, three elderly ladies sat in their wheelchairs, hunched and crumpled like forgotten relics of long ago. They smiled, revealing decayed and missing teeth. Their eyes gleamed waiting for a visitor to break them out. Jake stepped off the elevator and a thin ribbon of cold slid between his vertebrae. Their movements were jerky and unnatural, like puppets on strings waving at him.

"Visiting today?" one patient chirped.

Nope. Not too dramatic at all.

"Kind of," he answered in a rush.

There was an urgency to Jake's brisk pace, but halfway down the hall he came to an abrupt halt. Terror flooded his senses. Fight-or-flight circuits in his brain twisted, unleashing a panic storm coursing through him like ice water. He had not foreseen this happening. An abomination was blocking his path to his father's room. This was the very monster that had stolen his solace, prompting him to skip too many visits to his father. It left nightmares and guilt in its wake: an anxiety-busting juggernaut, a fearsome behemoth of despair. A demonic presence filled the air.

Jake usually prepared for moments like this, plotting escape routes and backup plans. Every detail served as a lifeline against the suffocating grip of this fear. He had even stooped to bribery, doing anything to avoid this gut-twisting confrontation. But there it stood, the embodiment of his worst nightmares, beckoning him closer to hell.

A staredown between Jake and the most fearsome creature he had ever encountered began. Perched on a tray attached to an old wooden wheelchair was a cat on a leash. A short leash at that. The evil spawn of Wilford Brimley. Dame Bernice maintained an arthritic grip on the other end. She never seemed to move or make eye contact with anyone. She donned a bedazzled, turban-like headpiece from her probable flapper days and an elaborate lace robe with fur trim. Her makeup looked like she had applied it with clay. The Dame's angry snarl paled in comparison to the nameless feline staring at Jake with deep, thieving eyes.

"For fuck's sake! What is that thing doing up here?" Jake's F-bomb slipped out louder than intended and startled the nursing staff.

"Excuse me," Nurse Trudy called out. "Where are you going?"

Jake cleared his throat and stuttered his answer, "I'm, uh, going to room 510. Da...dad's stuff." The cat's paralyzing gaze fixed on Jake's eyes.

"Oh, Johansson, right?"

Jake nodded.

"There's a box on the bed. Don't take too long. We've got a new resident moving in a few hours."

Jake found himself frozen in place. Small beads of sweat appeared on his forehead. Nurse Trudy rolled her eyes and wheeled Dame Bernice away. Before the Dame's exit, she turned to him with a snap of her head, brought two knobby fingers to her eyes, and pointed them back at Jake. The cat hissed, and Jake bolted down the hall. He swore he heard laughter from all the nurses.

The air hung with decrepit despair as Jake hurried past multiple rooms. Moans of the forgotten echoed behind closed doors. Jake's father never appeared like this, not physically. Penry suffered from a mental disorder, talking to himself, drifting away, but never showed physical deformity.

Cook's familiar voice emerged from one of the rooms. He was singing along to the Frank Sinatra standard "The Summer Wind," and doing it his way:

She passes wind

It came blowing in

From across my seat

It lingered there, a fart in the air

How ripe was she...

Jake thought it best not to disturb Cook while he belted out his solo. He tiptoed past his room like a ninja on a stealth mission. And just like that, Cook's vocals remained undisturbed. Jake peeked into his father's old room. The room looked gutted, the mattress bare except for a small cardboard box sitting dead-center like a forgotten offering. Inside were scraps of Penrod's life: a pair of socks, a knitted blanket, a black ski cap and a laminated memorial card with a name Jake didn't recognize. Jake picked up the box and noticed a crucifix hanging above the bed.

Probably from Uncle Duff.

"Good morning, Jacob. Nice to see you," Cook shouted from outside the door. He hobbled in, balancing unwieldy steps with his trusty claw.

Jake figured the encore performance had ended. He slipped the crucifix into the box. "Hey there, Cook, what's shaking?"

"Well, they cleaned out the young man's things. Getting ready for the next victim."

"I guess."

"Won't be the same without him," Cook said, shaking his head. "Except for his yelling. Kept me up half the night."

Yelling? Dad hardly spoke intelligible words toward the end. It must have been the nightmares.

Jake edged toward the door, eager to leave, and took his cue once Cook resumed his Sinatra tribute with a unique twist on "It Was a Very Good Year." He carried the box down the hallway, past the nurse's station, and waited for the elevator. He dashed past the three elderly women and jumped in, punching the door-close button. With relief, Jake exited the elevator on the first floor and rushed to the entrance. The receptionist reminded him to sign out, but Jake ignored her. He had no intention of returning.

Chapter 5

A few days after his father's funeral, Jake resumed his routine. He certainly didn't miss picking up trash in the searing July heat. Even at 5:30 in the morning, the white garbage truck burned like a rolling furnace through Brooklyn Heights. One pickup into their route, Jake and his partner, Miles Orsky, the childhood ghost rider of Greenpoint, leaked sweat through their green jumpsuits and onto the sidewalks of Montague Street's trendy storefronts.

"The richest block in Brooklyn, and it smells worse than a Port-a-Potty at a music festival," Jake remarked.

The final pickups on Columbia Heights went smoothly. Jake stopped the hauler to help Miles carry a heavy load to the rear of the truck. A broken-footed dresser filled with children's clothes and prayer books still in its drawers made it heavier.

"Annoying rich people," Miles huffed.

They delivered the load to a Manhattan garbage barge docked at a pier, destined for a New Jersey landfill. Despite the busy rush-hour traffic, they arrived back at Pacific Street Station sooner than expected. Because sludge caked the inside of the truck, Jake and Miles used a shovel and a power washer to clean the bed. Deep in the muck, something gleamed back at Jake as he readied the shovel for another lash. It seemed impossible for such a twinkle to emerge from revolting filth. Jake sank the shovel beneath the item and carefully levered it up out of the grime. He bent into a squat for a better look, then hooked his finger through the delicate chain of a gold necklace. A heart-shaped charm swung from dirt-caked links.

"Hey Vile, check this out. I found a returnable," Jake said.

Miles approached and inspected what Jake was holding. "What're you gonna do with it?"

"Send it to Lost and Found."

"Nah, hold on to it. Those guys down there will keep it and pawn it for beer money."

"Yeah, you're probably right. Want it?"

"Nah. Give it to one of your girlfriends," Miles snickered.

Jake shrugged his shoulders and headed for his car, where he could at least think of his next move with the air conditioner on full blast. It blew nasty summer air for a bit, so Jake ducked below the vents and reached under the seats in search of something. A half-filled bottle inside an empty coffee cup had just what he needed. It crunched in Jake's grip as he unscrewed the top and poured hot water over the necklace. It shone even brighter, an inscription of "Hope" revealed on one side, the phrase "A Waking Dream" engraved on the other.

Miles was right about the Lost and Found, and this necklace looked too valuable to be traded in for a 12-pack of Molson Ice. Instead, Jake decided he'd take it to the nearby 77th Precinct, no matter how much those cops hated this kind of paperwork.

"Yo! Schwartz, you're studying for the next sergeant's exam. What do we do with found jewelry?"

Officer Schwartz provided a sharp reply. "File a complaint report and voucher it as found property. Then notify..."

"Great, you got this?" the first officer asked, not expecting an answer.

Schwartz pulled the documents and sighed, "Hair-bag."

The term was familiar to Jake. His father was knowledgeable about police culture and taught him that "hair-bag" was slang for idle officers. The term had even entered their household. Jake remembered his father using it to scold him for not cleaning his room.

A growing restlessness took hold of Jake as Schwartz asked questions. His anxiety spun faster with every slow *clack clack* of the officer's ancient typewriter. Schwartz finally handed him the receipt and a half-hearted thank you. Jake was proud. He managed the situation well. Now he could go home, guilt-free.

* * * * *

Arden Friel, senior supervisor of the Administration for Children's Services, poked his balding head into Theresa Sheehan's dingy office doorway. The investigator refused to look up from the paperwork on her worn-out desk.

"Hey, Terri, I wanted to say, great work today on the Britt case," Arden said.

"Thank you, Arden."

"I heard the mother was a real piece of work. Doesn't feed her three kids but drives a new Lexus. Are the kids doing okay?"

"No, Arden. They're not. I took them away from their mother and her disgusting apartment."

"I'm sure they're going to do better now. No need to worry," Arden said.

"It was their mother and home," Terri grumbled, signing forms. "Not sure they'll be all right. Two have chicken pox."

"Our job is to keep these children safe and give them better opportunities when their guardians fail. The removal was necessary."

"I get that, I removed them," Terri replied.

The supervisor rubbed his neck. "I called the precinct. Sheila Britt's arrest process is underway. She'll appear in Family Court soon after answering criminal warrants."

"Pregnant?" Terri asked, still not looking up.

"The test was negative. She informed officers that she was expecting, which would cause a delay in the processing. She probably wanted to inconvenience the officers as well."

Terri searched for a specific form and ripped it to shreds. "Good. One less thing I have to do."

"Well, one more thing," Arden said, adjusting his glasses. "I assigned Mary to help with the children's temporary placement so they stay together."

Terri, with a sudden surge of interest, directed her gaze upward. "That's good. Thanks," she said. Her relief was clear.

"Don't mention it," Arden replied and left. Terri heard him mutter, "I would have never heard the end of it if I didn't."

She leaned back, stretching. The reflection in her mirror-plated "Investigator of the Year" award showed her tired, worn face.

Stress ages you fast if not managed, Terri thought.

At twenty-nine, she carried herself like someone already in their forties, or at least how she imagined forty would weigh on her. Stress clung to her no matter how many mornings she jogged or how much water she swallowed between cups of coffee. Her business suit sagged with wrinkles, its style a couple of years out of date, and a brown stain still marked the collar, as if it had settled in for good.

I used to be so pretty, Terri daydreamed.

Boys and girls often stared, left love notes and bought her drinks. Every relationship ended with a great guy breaking her heart.

Poetic, like the day I was born and abandoned at a fire station.

She let the persistent thought slip in.

Married to her job, they'd say.

She often ruminated on her self-deprecation, a cycle she couldn't escape. The ringing phone interrupted her inner pain.

"Child Services...Sheehan speaking."

"Terri, it's Monty. I think I found Hope's necklace." Terri could hear the eagerness present in his voice. "Gold with a pendant that says Hope and something about a dream."

"Where?"

"A sanitation worker turned it in last week at the Seven-Seven, after finding it in his truck."

Terri thought she would vomit. Her mind spun the most nauseating sounds and images. Hope's fragile body, abandoned and mangled in a landfill, haunted her.

"Did you canvass the dump?"

"The worker said he dumped the garbage onto a barge that took it to a Jersey landfill. It took three days for the search to be completed. Nothing came up."

"Three days! Why didn't you call me?" Terri shouted.

With a tone of measured reassurance, Detective Molina offered the simple instruction, "Calm down. Didn't want to call unless we had something. This is just a courtesy call."

"You should have called anyway!"

"Look, Terri, this is a police investigation. I wanted to get the preliminary details before calling. I'm doing this as a favor. She isn't considered missing yet. I'm trusting you, and you need to trust me, too."

Molina sounded reasonable, but Terri understood he cared more about his career than Hope's fate. He had over twenty years of experience, ten in the Missing Persons Unit. Monty Molina was a decent detective, but didn't work well with others, especially with the ACS.

"Don't pull police investigation tactics on me. This is my case as much as yours."

"You'll come with me to talk to the sanitation worker. It's at Pacific and Troy tomorrow. His shift ends at 10 a.m."

"I'll be there. Thanks, Monty." Terri hung up.

Terri leaned back on her chair and recalled her first assignment as a hospital social worker after completing her master's program. Baby Hope never had a stable life. An unknown mother abandoned her at a hospital when Hope was hours old. The hospital discharged the baby to ACS in short order because she was uninsured.

There was the heartless Meyerson couple, who were the first to adopt her. A special place in hell awaits them. Terri's nerves still twinge when she remembers them bringing her back to Family Court. She cries too much, the Meyersons complained. It disrupted their social and economic well-being. They even argued in court that the city agency misled them, as they had expected a healthy baby, and the infant "clearly" had a "disease" called "Colic." The judge ruled it appropriate to remove Hope rather than force the issue with the Meyersons because *"clearly"* the court expected a *"normal family"* to adopt her.

Ms. Hettie Turner was a kind older lady who cared for many foster children. However, she sometimes took on too many kids at once. Terri assumed it was because Ms. Turner received more government money the more children she took on. Although Hope seemed attached to Ms. Turner, the foster mother didn't even recognize the child's name, despite having cared for her for two years. Eventually, Ms. Turner lost custody of Hope after someone found the four-year-old wandering about a mile from home.

Terri strained to find Hope a suitable family. Several placements failed, but she remained the only trustworthy adult in Hope's brief life, demonstrating unwavering dedication.

Patricia and Edward Tanner seemed perfect. They wanted an older child, had steady incomes and were friendly neighbors. Despite their strict Christian beliefs, they treated Hope well. Hope was happy with them. She enjoyed her own room and new clothes. But after the placement, Terri could no longer reach Hope. Phone calls went unanswered, emails bounced back and knocks on the door at the Tanner house turned up nothing, not even a rustled curtain or a faint footstep. Her supervisors thought she spent too much time on Case I200005207310, neglecting her other cases. Within two weeks, Hope and the Tanners disappeared without a trace, with no signs of foul play or farewell. Something was very wrong.

Despite Terri's concerns, the ACS leadership assured her the Tanners would re-register at a new location. Terri found her supervisors' casual demeanor regarding Hope's disappearance weird, but not surprising.

Detective Molina was her only confidant. They had worked together on cases before. Terri suspected he had a crush on her, which is why the detective agreed to create a missing persons case. Whether he believed Hope was really missing didn't matter. Terri snapped out of her thoughts.

"Yo! Fuck y'all! I want my moms!" a child's voice echoed in the hallway.

A soft voice responded, "Now, Shante, I'm listening to you. Let's come up with a solution together."

"Fuck that..."

Another child's voice rose above the shout. "Shante, stop. You're making Deshawn cry."

"It's okay, Elijah. Shante is upset. We'll work this out," the gentle voice said.

Terri stood up and left her office. Mary Hollingsworth loomed over the dirty, bruised Britt trio sitting in the hallway chairs. Mary had been at the Brooklyn ACS office for what seemed like forever. Terri could always rely on her for advice. Over the past twenty years, Mary had trained almost everyone in the office. She instructed the passing children to call her Miss Holly. Mary had such a Southern charm about her. She never spoke a bad word about anyone and had a knack for managing any situation.

Mary looked ready for a gala. Terri often wondered whether Mary wore a different wig each week, transforming her look with a variety of colors and textures. Mary's caramel skin glowed with a flawless brightness, immaculate for a woman in her fifties, as not a single blemish dared to mar her beauty.

"Is everything all right out here?" Terri asked.

"You know it is, girl. Finish that paperwork. I'll take them for medical evaluations soon," Mary replied.

Terri's stare was blank and distant, as though she were in a trance.

"Terri? What's wrong?" Mary asked with concern.

"Yo. She be like a fuckin' zombie. Zombie Apocalypse!" the foul-mouthed seven-year-old named Shante shouted out.

"That's enough of that," Mary whispered. "Terri, what's wrong?"

As if shaking off a heavy blanket, Terri cleared her head fog. "I'll be out tomorrow. I have to follow up on another case."

"Which one? Need help?" Mary asked.

"Hope," Terri answered.

"They found her?"

"No. Just a lead. Probably a dead end."

"What lead?"

"Detective Molina recovered the necklace I bought her as a baby."

"Oh, Lord." Mary crossed herself. "A waking dream?"

"Yes. That's what Molina said."

"Where did he find it?"

"In some garbage." Tears welled up in Terri's eyes.

"Oh, Terri, that doesn't mean...Well, I'm gonna say extra prayers at church this evening. The good Lord loves to answer prayers when he can."

"Please cover for me tomorrow?"

"Of course. Don't get yourself all in a mess like last time."

"Cinnamon buns!" Terri said, acknowledging Mary's favorite compensation.

Chapter 6

Terri's heart sank in her chest like a fifteen-pound bowling ball. She couldn't escape thoughts of Hope's terror. Monty stood in front of the Pacific Street sanitation garage. His slicked-back hair and expertly fitted pinstriped suit made him look like he was prepping for a mob hit, not police work. She chided him about it in hopes it would calm her nerves.

Molina tried to think of a snappy comeback while cracking his neck and rolling his shoulder. He couldn't think that quick. "I already talked to the sanitation supervisor. She's having the two workers come out."

With a mechanical whir, the large bay door opened. Jake and Miles exited, still wearing their forest-green coveralls.

"I'm Detective Molina of the Missing Persons Unit, and this is investigator Terri Sheehan of Children's Services. We have a few questions for you two. First, please give me your names and dates of birth."

Jake thumbed the stress stone in his pocket. "Jacob Johansson. Eleven, oh one, nineteen seventy-seven."

"All Saints' Day," Terri commented.

The three stood in uncomfortable silence, staring at Miles, the gargantuan garbage hauler. He was on the receiving end of Jake's elbow.

"Miles."

"Just Miles?" Molina growled.

"Um, Miles Orsky."

"Do you have a birthday, big fella?" Molina teased.

"July the second."

"I'm not a dentist. Stop making me pull teeth," Molina spat. "What year were you born?"

"Um, 1975?" Miles answered.

"Is that a question?" Terri asked.

"No. I was born then."

"Who found the necklace?" Molina moved on.

"I did," Jake volunteered while Miles stood in silent stupidity.

"Where did you find it exactly?" Terri asked.

"It was in the rear of the loader."

Molina huffed. "You found a tiny necklace under hundreds of pounds of garbage. Really?"

"What on earth is happening? Am I a suspect in something? I'm just a sanitation worker. I turned in what I believed was something valuable that someone might have lost."

"The necklace was reported as worn by a little girl named Hope, who went missing about two weeks ago," Molina snapped.

"How would that necklace get in the back of my truck?"

Miles chose this moment to express some of his limited wisdom about the situation. "Somebody threw her in the garbage." Everyone wished he didn't.

"Did you see a body in the garbage?" Molina asked, already guessing the answer.

"No," Miles stated and looked down. Terri looked like her eyelids could slice the big oaf in half with a blink.

Jake whispered under his breath, "Shut up, Miles."

"Can you provide us with a list of the exact stops on your route the day you found the necklace?" Terri asked.

Jake hesitated. "Sure, but it would be easier to show you if you've got the time."

Molina interjected into the conversation. "I got other cases. Ms. Sheehan, do you want..."

Terri finished, "Sure, I'll take the trip."

"Okay. You two work it out. Keep me posted. And thanks for your cooperation, Mr. Johansson."

Terri pointed Jake toward the black SUV in front of the garage. "I'll drive."

"Hey, can I tag along?" Miles asked. "I got good eyes."

"Thanks, Mr. Orsky, but we must keep it simple."

Standing near Terri's SUV, arms crossed and one bare foot angled to the side, was a familiar, attractive brunette with a nose ring and a necklace that featured a pentacle.

"Ah, shit, the Pinball Wizard." Jake grinned as he thought of her bounding around his bedroom to Mrs. Hitchcock's ghastly screams.

"So that's why you're avoiding me. I've foreseen this. Mars said to be cautious with you, but the signs of the lunar altar said we connected, but I may have to work for it."

Her whiny, screechy voice irritated both Jake and Terri.

"I got you a new alarm clock. It tells you your daily horoscope instead of waking the demons in you," the little witch said. She pointed to a wrapped box on the hood of a black Ford Taurus.

"How did you even find out where I work?" Jake asked.

"I always follow the aural sapience," she answered.

"Now you're making things up," Jake said. "Besides, you ran out on me, remember?"

"Does your girlfriend know about our lunar connection?"

"Hey, relax. Don't get your lunar-tic signs all out of whack. She's my third cousin, once removed from my mother's side, and she's a Gemini."

Terri fell right into place. "Well, twice removed, and my mother was a Capricorn, but she switched to a Taurus two months ago, and we're in a real rush. He'll call you."

Terri drove off, forcing the spiritual stalker to the curb.

"Your girlfriend seems nice," Terri said.

Jake groaned. "She's not my girlfriend."

"Well, Mars missed the bulletin. Anyway, I would like to go over your entire route from start to finish. I'm looking to identify something that could assist in the investigation."

"It seems like more of a cold case."

"You watch too much *CSI*. A little girl has been missing for a couple of weeks. It's still an active investigation."

"Sure. Sorry about that." Jake paused for a moment. "It's a nice name...Hope."

"Thank you," Terri responded. "I named her Hope after my favorite quote from Aristotle: *Hope is a waking dream.*"

"That's the quote on the necklace."

"Yeah. I gave Hope that necklace when she was four, something to hold on to when the world had gone strange and she was scared. I wanted her to know I was always with her, even if she couldn't see me. Now it's locked away in some police vault, and she's God knows where."

"What about her parents?"

"Never found her birth mother. Left in the hospital's emergency room, where I worked as a social worker. She was cold, wrapped in a filthy towel. She was probably not even a few hours old. The doctors weren't sure she would make it through the night. Her vitals were poor. I was the only social worker on duty that night, having just graduated from college and finished my on-the-job training.

"After all the paperwork and police stuff, I checked on her. Her vitals improved, and one nurse asked if I wanted to hold her. She said it would be good for the baby. I fell in love the moment she looked up at me. It felt like I was dreaming. I stayed with her all night, never going home. For months, I held her every night. Doctors said that closeness to another person helped her recover. At the time of her ACS release, I begged to keep her."

"Why wouldn't they let you adopt her?"

"I've been to court a dozen times. I even hired lawyers. They stated that I didn't meet the required standards. I'm a single woman, never married, never had a child. Despite being hired by ACS to protect children, my low income prevents me from raising the child I saved. Bullshit."

"Sounds like the system is screwed up."

"You got that right. Now, where is the first stop?" Terri asked.

"Atlantic Avenue and Henry Street."

Terri drove through the streets of Brooklyn Heights and asked Jake more questions about the people on his route. He explained that he rarely saw people because of his early-morning shift. Terri halted and gasped when near the end of the route. She put the SUV into reverse and backed down Columbia Heights Road until she was next to a parked van. The black vehicle featured windows on each side. A white calligraphy-type font spelled out "Ministry of Salvation" on the side.

"Holy shit!" Terri exclaimed. The color drained from her face. "That's a church van."

"Am I supposed to know what it means?" Jake asked.

"Hope's foster parents were religious nuts."

"I don't see..."

"Wait here. I'll be right back."

Terri leaped out of the vehicle and dashed over to the van. She had to stand on the van's running board to look inside. Then she checked the door handles. Locked. The investigator pulled out a pen and her pocket-sized notepad to write the van's license plate. Back in the car, Terri called in to her office to have the plate run. After a brief wait, the voice on the other end of the line gave Terri an answer.

"That's what I figured," she said, disappointment clear in her tone. She dropped the phone into a cup holder and turned to Jake.

"It's registered to a leasing company in New Jersey. Mr. Johansson, have you ever seen this van before?"

"No."

"What kinds of churches are in this neighborhood?"

"Besides the Jehovah's Witnesses' Watchtower, there's the Pilgrims Church and Assumption Catholic on Cranberry and a synagogue on Court Street. Why?"

"No storefront churches?"

"In this neighborhood? They couldn't afford the rent."

"There's got to be a reason it's here."

"Maybe they like the bagels. Montague Bagels is around the corner."

"Please don't try to be funny. Just keep your eyes open."

Terri drove down the block, surveying each brownstone she passed, searching for any link to the van. Jake recognized the brownstone with the dresser from the day he found the necklace. A young boy walked by the house on the sidewalk and glanced at both of them as they passed.

"The day I found the necklace; we picked up this huge old dresser in front of that house."

"Which one?"

Jake pointed to the brownstone.

"Why didn't you mention this before? I asked you if anything stood out to you."

"Give me a break, lady. Look what I do for a living. Garbage doesn't stand out to me. I don't keep a running inventory of everyone's trash."

"Okay, you're right. What else do you remember?"

"It was hot, and that load was difficult to toss into the truck. The drawers were left inside, still filled with clothes and some books."

Without responding, Terri exited the car.

"At least she left the AC on," Jake said to no one as he leaned back in his seat.

Terri approached the metal front gate and looked at the brownstone to check for recognizable features. Maybe a family welcome sign or a nameplate. Anything that would draw a line to Hope. She climbed the steps and heard a high-pitched voice singing off-key from an open window. It sounded like a child belting out a praise ballad.

A brass cross hung beside the doorframe. Clean windows, no toys, no clutter, just order. Terri searched the mailbox. It contained nothing.

The singing stopped, and the front door of the brownstone opened.

"Can I help you, Miss?" a petite, short-haired girl asked.

Terri had to think fast. "Maybe you can. I'm from Con Edison. We have two customers listed for this location, and

I'm verifying which one is correct. Are your parents at home?"

"I could help you."

"May I talk to an adult, please?" Terri answered.

"I'm twenty-five years old."

"Oh, I am so sorry. You look, well...you look fantastic for your age." Terri was thrown off for a moment, but had to get back on track for the ruse to stay believable. Twenty-five? The girl's floral-patterned t-shirt and brown overalls shouted "middle school teacher's pet."

"Are you the primary resident?"

"Yes."

Terri pulled out her notebook and looked at the numerals affixed to the building's facade. "Is this...77?"

"Yes. Of course."

"What is the name on the account?"

"Devlin."

"Is that your name?" Terri asked.

"Yes. I am Mrs. Devlin."

"I see. Do you have a first name?"

"Chastity. Why?"

"I have another name on the account. It must be a mistake. Is there anyone else the account could be under?"

"Perhaps my husband?"

"May I speak with him?"

Chastity Devlin hesitated. "My husband is not home right now. He is at morning prayer."

"And his first name is?"

Chastity looked back into the house with concern all over her face. She turned back to Terri. "Mr. Devlin should be fine," she said.

"All right, then. Please tell your husband that our records will be updated. Sorry to have bothered you. Have a good day."

"Good day to you. Peace be with you!"

Terri turned and walked back to her truck. She never noticed the figure peering through a second-floor window.

"Any luck, Sherlock?" Jake asked.

"I think so."

"Can we get back now? I'm starving."

"Not yet. I'll buy you a bagel after we're done."

"I like it with lox."

"Don't push your luck. Where's the next stop?"

* * * * *

"Who was that, my dear?"

A lanky man in a thin, dark suit slowly approached behind his wife as she knelt before a large crucifix on the living room wall. Chastity Devlin jumped at the drawling voice and dropped her prayer book.

"She said she was from Con Edison," Chastity said, keeping her head down.

"What did she want?" Mr. Devlin asked.

"Something about record keeping."

"That was all?"

"Yes, Husband. That was all."

"Thank you, my sweet. Please continue with your prayers. I have a meeting with The Minister in about one hour."

"My father will be so pleased," Chastity said.

"I hope so, my dear. I hope so."

Mr. Devlin slipped into his study and removed a plastic ringlet from his desk drawer. He knelt before the wooden cross atop the desk and opened the hinged circular device. It clasped around his skinny neck with a snap. He cranked the rear dial until it became hard to breathe. He began with a wheezy prayer.

"Oh Lord, who holds dominion over all things great and small. You have the power to do what my spouse no longer can. I entrust our future to Your will, knowing You know what is best.

"Your Word says no good thing will You withhold from the blameless. If I abide in You, and Your Word abides in me, I may ask what I will and it shall be given.

"Bless my body in the name of Christ. Restore my seed, O Lord, that my wife may conceive. Purify our union, make it holy in Your eyes, and let a child be born not for our pleasure, but to bind us to Your kingdom.

"As Mary bore the Savior, grant us the joy of bearing a child in Your perfect time. In Jesus' precious name. Amen."

Mr. Devlin could feel the power of prayer working in his pants as his boxers became tighter. He dialed another two clicks on the ligature contraption. His erection was solid and healthy as he struggled to unzip his dress pants.

The doorbell rang, and Chastity Devlin answered the door. "Yes. May I help you?"

"Good morning. My name is Moonbeam. The harlot who was here earlier is trying to steal my spiritual soul balance. Once our kindred spirits have finally met, we must fulfill the cosmic prophecies of our natural world. Thus..."

"We must fulfill?" Chastity interrupted.

"Well. Um...me and..."

Mr. Devlin seemed to float above his wife as he guided her behind him. "How can I be of assistance?" he asked. Moonbeam's eyes widened at the tall man's omnipresence.

"I wanted to tell you that the woman who was just here is..."

"Con Edison?" Devlin looked at both the wacky witch and then his wife.

"I believe so, my husband," Chastity answered.

"Well, whoever she is to you, please tell her I am his angel. He told me so himself. He can see me. The Majik that is..."

"What did you say?" Mr. Devlin stated with heightened interest.

"He can see me," Moonbeam answered.

"No. No. Before that."

"He knows I'm an angel?"

"Angel. Yes. Yes!"

Moonbeam sensed that her blazing aura was about to dissolve. "I'm sorry to have disturbed you both. Sometimes, my spirit can't be tamed when Majik is in my veins."

"Disturbed us? No, my dear. Not in the least. Those who don't believe in magic will never find it."

"Roald Dahl," Moonbeam said under her breath. Mr. Devlin's statement eased her anxiety. "Are you familiar with Majik, sir?"

"I am familiar with angels, my dear. Yes, angels. Please come join me and my kind wife for some brunch."

Chapter 7

Terri pulled into the underground parking garage at her office. She clicked the car off and sat in silence. The quiet calmed her, briefly, until her mind revved back up, piecing together all that had been revealed along the garbage route. The van, the brownstone, her awkward take on a meticulous Con Ed worker. On her way upstairs, she waved to the guard posted at the security desk. Rodney looked intense, as if he were on a mission, and stood up as Terri entered the lobby. He picked up the telephone and motioned for her to hold there. He whispered something into the receiver.

"Ms. Sheehan, please wait there a moment."

Rodney never called her by her surname.

"Rodney, what's going on?"

"I've been instructed to stop you at the door and have you wait for a supervisor."

"What for?"

"Beats me. Mr. Friel told me to stop you before you got on the elevator."

The elevator's stainless-steel door opened. Terri's supervisor, senior investigator Arden Friel, exited and marched over to Terri, followed by two other senior investigators she recognized.

"Hey, Arden, what's cooking?" She did her best to sound casual and clueless.

"You," was his only answer.

"Excuse me?"

"We have placed you on unpaid leave while the ACS Office of Special Investigations looks into allegations of official misconduct and your failure to comply with a direct order. Please surrender your shield and identification."

"What are you talking about?"

"We've received information that you are harassing private citizens under false pretenses."

Terri stared in stunned disbelief. "Molina asked me to follow up. Evidence tied to a missing kid. You really want to shut that down?"

"I haven't heard that. The department got the complaint, and I have to act on it. We can't have our agents running around contacting people without authorization. If you want to challenge the suspension, take it up with the union. Now, you're suspended. Any further involvement in the investigation could land you in jail. Shield and ID, please."

Terri couldn't comprehend what was happening. Her hands were numb as she pulled her ID wallet out of her purse and handed it to Friel. "Talk to Mary. She knows what's going on. I'm following leads. That's what we do here, isn't it?"

"Don't bring anyone else into this now," Arden answered.

Did Molina fuck me over? she thought.

Arden provided specific instructions on where to report so the hearing process could start. Terri listened, then turned and walked out. Halfway to her car, tears streamed down her cheeks. She took a deep breath and dried her eyes. Then, she took out her cell phone and dialed.

"Molina."

"It's Terri."

"Hey, gorgeous. How'd the..."

"You fucked me over."

"What?"

"I got suspended because of my ride-along with the sanitation guy. The one you approved. Remember?"

"Terri, I never told anyone about it and I don't authorize anything."

"You're full of shit."

"Settle down. I never said a word. Tell me everything."

She explained the ride-along on the sanitation route, the van, her discussion with Chastity and the suspension.

"Johansson said he thought he might have picked up the necklace with the trash in front of this minister's house?" Molina asked.

"Yeah."

"Did you ID yourself?"

"How stupid do you think I am? I made something up about checking the utility billing address."

Molina paused. "Any security cameras at the front entrance?"

"I didn't look."

"If so, they have your image now. If it's the Tanners' church like you suspect, they'll know who you are. Or, what about the garbageman? You probably pissed him off. Any of them may have phoned in a complaint."

"Damn, you're probably right."

"Sit tight. Keep a low profile. I'll take over the investigation from here."

"Please keep me in the loop this time."

"You got it."

* * * * *

The Church of St. Francis Xavier was an imposing Baroque-style church. Like many historic churches, it required significant repairs but lacked the funds. Several cracks marred its ornate granite facade. Emerging from beneath the grand arch was a smaller, damaged arch adorned with stone carvings that needed cleaning. A statue of St. Francis Xavier, covered in pigeon droppings, stood to the left of the arch. He raised a cross high, blessing all who passed by the unassuming side street.

Jake almost considered it his second home. He spent much of his youth there with his uncle, as an altar boy. He thought about his mother, a devout Irish Catholic, who ensured he remained faithful to his religion.

Father Duffy's office was on the second floor of the rectory next door to the church itself. Jake knocked on the door, and Sister Marie answered.

"Why, Jacob, it's good to see you," she said. "You'll want to see Father Duffy, I suppose."

"Yes, Sister Marie. Is he in?"

"He's in his office." She pointed upstairs. "You know the way."

"Thanks." Jake climbed the rickety old steps and knocked on the door.

"Come in."

"Hey, Uncle Duff. You busy?"

"Not for you, son. 'Tis a good excuse to take a break. Sermon writing is hard work." He opened his desk drawer and took out a bottle of Jameson and two glasses.

"A little early, don't you think?" Jake said.

"I think clearer about the Lord's ways now, don't ya know." He poured a glass.

"Not for me, thanks."

Father Duffy paused and took a sip from his drink. "What's on your mind?"

"I got involved with a missing child case and feel bad for the ACS worker investigating it. I did my best to help, but there was nothing more I could have done for her. Still, I can't shake the thought from my mind."

"Tell me more."

Jake shared what he knew about the girl and the story from Terri.

"A sad tale, but alas, 'tis not uncommon. This investigator, Sheehan, sounds like she's got a good heart and is quite the expert at her job."

"Yeah, she is tough and dedicated to finding this girl. I want to help, but..."

"But what?"

"I wouldn't even know where to begin. I usually keep to myself. My anxiety and all. It's hard to stop thinking about it."

The priest looked at his nephew. "Part of yer obsessional ways. Thinkin' too much. Son, ye've got yer dad's blood in ye. He was always one to lend a hand, he was. Perhaps the good Lord's reachin' out to ye. There be no coincidences. God always has a plan for us. Sometimes, the signs are all there for ye to figure out. I reckon the term used by Walt Disney to explain this is, 'It's a small world after all.'"

"Not sure about that. I'm not my dad."

"Did I ever tell ya how he met yer mum?"

"Yeah...he was her cab driver."

"Well, you need to hear it again, and maybe you'll understand."

Jake sighed and got comfortable, knowing his uncle would not stop when he had a story to tell.

* * * * *

Manhattan was taking a beating. Rain hammered the streets, bouncing off the pavement like handfuls of thrown nails. Bridget Duffy darted to the curb, soaked cocktail dress clinging to her legs. She threw up her hand, waving down every yellow blur that sped past. Their taillights smeared in the downpour and she could not tell if they were full or just ignoring her.

Her umbrella buckled in the wind, offering about as much protection as a napkin. She cursed under her breath with her heels slipping on the wet pavement.

"Unbelievable," she snapped, water dripping from her no-longer-immaculate blowout.

She was already late for her meeting at Barbetta's for dinner with a rising Broadway actor she was considering for a callback. The rain had diluted the ink in her note, ruined her hair and left her looking like a soggy extra from a show she wouldn't cast herself in.

A cab skidded to a stop, tires hissing across the wet pavement. Not because she hailed it. Because the driver noticed a desperate damsel, seconds away from burning the whole district down, even in this rain.

Bridget let out a storm's worth of frustration, complaining as if the driver was the one running late.

Rain hammered the roof. Penrod Johansson flicked on the meter without ceremony. "So where to, Princess?" he asked.

Bridget inhaled sharply. "Barbetta's. And it's *Miss Duffy.*"

Penrod nodded. "Right. Princess Miss Duffy. Got it."

She leaned forward, horrified. "That is not what I said."

"Storm's loud. Hard to hear specifics." He pulled his cab into city traffic with the confidence of a man who trusted his instincts more than any rulebook.

Bridget crossed her arms, teeth clenched.

He noticed the Broadway district pass by her window and said, "You in theater?"

She hesitated. "Casting."

"Ah. That explains it."

"Explains what?" she barked.

"The attitude. The hair. The makeup."

She gasped, offended on a molecular level. "I don't have an attitude."

"You do. It's all right. I've seen worse." He flicked his blinker. "I've also seen better. Theater people tip good."

Bridget stared at the back of his head, eyes narrowing. Her fight with the storm had turned into a fight with this man, this unpolished, maddening cab driver who didn't know he was supposed to be intimidated by her.

And yet...something in the way he handled the wheel, the road, the chaos, something calm, steady, paused her aggression despite herself.

"Just get me there," she muttered.

Penrod nodded, rain streaking the windshield like a curtain. "As you wish, Princess." Penrod eased the cab to the curb in front of Barbetta's, wipers squealing across the glass like two wet city rats fighting.

Bridget gathered her things with royal indignation and stepped out into the storm. A figure waved her over, face obscured by the rain. She clicked her heels toward the person without so much as a goodbye. The cab door shut like a judge's gavel.

Penrod rolled his eyes. "A least she tipped well." He shifted into drive...then spotted it. Her umbrella. A fancy one. Black, sleek with a golden handle shaped like a lion's head. "Of course," he muttered.

He drove around the block, pulled up outside the restaurant and instantly regretted every life choice that led him to step out into the downpour.

As he approached the door, a sharp noise cut through the rain.

A whimper.

Then, "Stop it!"

His spine straightened. That wasn't restaurant chatter. That was someone in trouble.

He pivoted toward the alley beside the building. A shadow jerked back, followed by another muffled yelp.

Penrod didn't hesitate. He dropped the umbrella, rolled his shoulders and muttered, "Fuck it."

He sprinted across the sidewalk, splashing through ankle-deep water like a linebacker baptized in the Hudson.

"HEY!" he shouted, barreling toward the alley. "Let her go!"

The mugger spun, dragging Bridget backward by the arm.

"Back off, cabbie!" the man snarled, waving a knife that looked like it had tetanus. "Unless you want some of this!"

Penrod slowed, hands raised. "All right, all right...desperation looks terrible on you, pal."

Bridget, never one to wait for permission, shrieked, "Just take me purse and let me go, ye gobshite!" She hurled her purse with Olympic precision, hitting the mugger directly in the ear.

"OW! Lady, what the?!"

Penrod seized the moment. He lunged forward and tackled the man into a pile of soaked cardboard boxes that gave up their structural integrity immediately.

The mugger slashed wildly; the blade nicked Penrod's arm.

He grunted through the pain, grabbed the man's wrist and slammed it against the pavement until the knife skittered across the alley. The two men wrestled with arms grappling, legs tangling, Penrod slipping, the mugger cursing, and at one point, Penrod accidentally head-butting a dumpster with a hollow metallic *TWANG*.

"Jesus, Mary, an' all the saints!" Bridget gasped. "Are ye tryin' to knock yerself out?!"

"I'm multitaskin'!" Penrod barked. He shoved the mugger's face into the puddles until the man sputtered and gave up. Sirens wailed from around the corner, red and blue lights slicing through the rain. Two officers sprinted into the alley.

"Police! Don't move!"

Penrod, still pinning the mugger, lifted one finger. "Does bleeding on him count as moving?"

The cops cuffed the man and hauled him upright. He muttered something about suing.

"Add that to your list of bad ideas," Penrod growled.

Bridget stood a few feet away, drenched, shaking, mascara running like war paint. Yet she somehow managed to hold herself like she was still the most important person on Restaurant Row.

Penrod retrieved her umbrella from the ground.

He held it out to her.

She stared at it, then at him.

At the cut on his arm.

The rain on his face.

"You...came back for me umbrella?" she asked.

Penrod shrugged. "Was either that or watch everybody's weird faces when they sat on it." A tiny, involuntary laugh escaped her lips. A soft one, but real. And for the first time since he picked her up, Bridget Duffy didn't look irritated.

She looked...grateful.

Penrod nodded toward the restaurant door.

"Go on, Princess. You're late."

She swallowed, then said quietly, "It's...Bridget."

"Well," he said, wiping rain from his brow, "nice to officially meet ya, Bridget."

Dressed in a raincoat and an eight-point cap, Officer Napolitano addressed the hero and the victim. "I need you both to come to the station to make a statement."

"But I'm working."

"Aye, I've a dinner engagement, I do. I'm already late,"

"Sorry, folks. Police procedure. Follow me in your cab."

* * * * *

"Your dad was rightly let go from drivin' that taxi. His boss said he didn't want to be involved in any lawsuits or the like. That's how your dad ended up as a night broom at the Midtown precinct for a few years. The coppers had compassion for him. He loved that job too. Some grand stories he used to tell."

"So that's how he got that scar on his arm," Jake interrupted. "He told me he was peeling potatoes for Mom."

Father Duffy laughed. "It mighta been a dig at yer mum's heritage, or he was tryin' to be humble, so he was. The rest, like they say, is history. Me sister married yer dad, gave up her fancy ways, and settled for a quieter life, so she did."

"So, what does it have to do with this missing girl case?"

"Ye see, Jake, yer dad always had a knack for helpin' others. He couldn't leave a disabled motorist stuck on the street without lendin' a hand or givin' a free ride if nobody else was willin' to step in. Years later, when he got let go from the precinct, he picked up that hot dog cart. He worked through the night and made a bit more by risin' early to work at the bakery. And who could forget about the bakery?" Father Duffy paused for a moment to tap his belly. "Ah, he never made the big money, did he? Lost a fair bit of his profit helpin' the homeless and the hungry, he did."

With a steady hand, Father Duffy poured himself another swig.

"He was always working till he got sick," Jake noted.

"He was a humble fella, never one to boast or grumble. Like it or not, you've a chance to carry on his good work. God moves in mysterious ways, me lad."

"Then you think I should help out?"

With a subtle movement of his head, his uncle nodded in agreement. "Auld Penry would be proud, so he would."

"I'll think about it."

"Ah, but don't be thinkin' too hard now. Just go with yer heart and if you always use yer God-given talents, you will always succeed. That's why the Lord gave it to ya. Now, I've got to get back to my talents from God and write this sermon."

"Thanks, Uncle Duff."

"God bless ye, son, and keep me informed, will ye?

Chapter 8

A steady downpour lashed the windshield of Jake and Miles's truck as it lumbered down Columbia Heights. The brakes squealed, and before the truck came to a stop, Miles hopped off and stepped right into the center of a brown puddle. Not even a sidestep or leap to avoid it. His big boot splashed down, spraying water over the curb. It was a nasty morning, but Jake loved when it rained at work. Sure, it made the garbage heavier and more slippery, but it also meant that Miles took an unintentional shower. Jake pretended to gag as Miles got into the truck for the drive to their last block.

"Why are you always messing with me, man?" Miles complained.

"Every day, I try to help you by giving pointers and tips, trying to get you a girlfriend or boyfriend or something. I wouldn't say I like to hurt your feelings, dude. You should bathe every day, sometimes even twice. Occasional grooming is good for the soul. You'll feel better rather than constantly being sick."

"I'm a garbageman. It's what I do."

"A lonely garbageman," Jake corrected.

"You ain't got no girlfriend either."

"I don't have trouble meeting people. I struggle to keep long-term relationships."

"Maybe it's because you smell, too," Miles stated.

As they neared the end of their route, Jake stopped the massive truck short. He observed a group of children following a small girl in overalls to the Ministry of Salvation van. The girl held the side door open as five children climbed in. The young-looking girl checked to ensure everyone had clicked their seatbelts and that the youngest was secured in a safety seat. To Jake's surprise, the girl could reach the gas pedal of the large van and drove away.

"Miles, we're going on an adventure. You must promise to keep your mouth shut."

"We got like seven more stops," Miles said.

"We can come back to it."

"Where we goin'?"

"Hopefully, somewhere close," Jake said, following the van from afar.

Jake guided the big white truck down Atlantic Avenue, wipers slapping hard as the rain turned the windshield into a restless gray blur. The church van ahead of them drifted from lane to lane, its brake lights flickering like a nervous tic. The big trash hauler lurked like a hunting megalodon behind a goldfish, except there were seven or eight cars between them. The van turned into a long driveway between a hardware store and a medical clinic.

"Stay with the truck," Jake told Miles as he double-parked. "Move if you have to." He jumped out before his partner could ask anything.

The rain hit him sideways. Jake jogged toward the alley the van had slipped into moments earlier, puddles exploding under his boots. The city noise thinned as he stepped between the two buildings, giving way to the metallic echo of something heavy slamming shut farther inside. It wasn't fear that hit him, it was that old pulse tightening behind his ribs, the body's way of saying *You're being stupid.*

He slowed.

The van sat halfway down the alley, not hidden so much as parked, as if it hoped no one would question why it was there.

Jake scanned the hardware store's exterior: bare steel doors, no knobs, no buzzers, just a slab of gray that gave away nothing. The kind of doors that didn't invite visitors, didn't suggest business hours, didn't care if a man wondered what was behind them.

"Jesus was a carpenter. Wonder what he'd say about this place," he uttered as he walked around to the front and into Brooklyn Brick's Hardware Emporium.

Jake perused the cluttered aisles, pretending to look for something in home repairs. He made his way to the furthest part of the store when a peculiar, hyperactive clerk popped over.

"Hey. Hey. Hello. May I help you find something? Need advice on anything? Try me. I got whatever you may need. I can get you started with any project. No matter how big or how small. I'm Brick, Dominick Brick. You can build it brick by Brick, I always say."

The stout fellow bounced back and forth on each leg between syllables. Jake thumbed the stress stone in his pocket. Dominick's frenetic demeanor was making Jake anxious. But everything made Jake anxious.

"I...well...you see..." *Think Jake.* "I need um..."

"Hey. Hey. Buddy. I got you. Take your time."

"Yeah. I'm looking for something..." Jake glanced around the store, looking for inspiration.

Then he received a sign. A sign stenciled on a wooden door displayed the initials "MOS" above a cross.

"I'm looking for something in worship," Jake said with newfound confidence.

The curly-haired proprietor stopped bouncing and clasped his hands to contain himself. "Yes. Yes sir-ee. I may have what you need. Wait here, please. Be but a moment."

The hardware dealer bounded to a side counter, picked up an old-school wall phone and whispered into the receiver. Jake discovered a small religious section near the back door and examined some items to make his ruse convincing. His heart fired off like a machine gun as he waited.

"Good morning! How may we assist you?"

Two teenage boys in matching tucked-in polo shirts stood behind Jake as he picked up a make-it-yourself crucifix kit. He jerked upright and dropped the box.

Dominick brushed past the boys. "Hey. Hey. It's okay, brother. I got it."

Jake turned to the teens. "Hi there, fellas." Nothing. Not even a blink. "I need God. Probably Jesus, too. A little more than the usual." He immediately regretted saying that much.

"Are you sponsored?" one boy asked.

"Yes?" Jake lied.

"By whom?" the other pressed.

Jake pointed at Dominick.

"No. No." Dominick shook his head. "Not me, Mister...?"

"Miles." Jake lied again.

"Well, Mr. Miles, the boys are asking who sent you to seek salvation."

"Oh. Right. That." Jake latched onto the first name his brain spat out. "John."

"John?" The boy echoed.

A guy named Jonathan. I work with him." Jake looked down at his uniform. "He says your church's amazing. It helped him through a lot."

"Ministry," the left boy said with the faintest smile.

Jake stared blankly.

"We call it a Ministry," the other clarified.

"Great. Well...I definitely need some saving."

"We will see if The Minister is accepting guests," the right boy said.

Both teens turned and slipped through the steel door. Jake leaned, trying to catch a glimpse inside, but the interior swallowed all light.

"The Ministry of Salvation is a congregation of miracles," Dominick gushed, bouncing again. "We make a difference in people's lives. We save lives. Children's lives. We give them a chance when families fail. Those two boys? You should have seen them when they first came to us. Now they work hard. Smart kids. Everyone has demons that can be exorcised here."

"Well, that's why I'm here," Jake said.

"You know, I built the chapel myself."

"Brick by Brick?" Jake teased.

"Oh, don't you believe it, Mr. Miles! I also built the classrooms and the sanctuary offices," Dominick boasted. "My life's best work."

"I hope I get to see it."

A smug whisper came from behind Jake's ear. "My apologies, Mr. Miles, but today will not be that day."

Jake jerked, nerves firing down his back.

"Easy, friend," the voice hummed. "I did not mean to startle you."

Jake turned. A tall man in a well-tailored suit stood inches away, hands folded neatly behind him. His gaze was fixed and unblinking.

"Man, you people know how to sneak up on someone," Jake muttered.

"My apologies," the man said. "The Minister is quite busy this morning. Perhaps you can remind this Jonathan of yours that he must complete the proper sponsor request. Then we may schedule an appointment."

Jake felt the man's disbelief like a hand tightening around his neck.

"We welcome all into our congregation," the man continued, "but procedures must be followed. Have your friend come to see me, and I'll give him the form myself."

"And you are?"

"I am The Elder of the Ministry."

Jake blinked. "But you look so young."

"It's a title, I assure you," The Elder said flatly.

Jake swallowed. "Right. Understood. Thank you. I'll...speak to Johnny right away."

The Elder didn't blink, didn't shift, didn't breathe out of rhythm. Dominick, meanwhile, bounced in place like a caffeinated altar boy.

Jake bowed slightly, unsure why, and slipped out to the street as fast as he could. To his relief, Miles had not moved the garbage truck. He argued with a female traffic agent who demanded that someone move the double-parked hauler.

"I'm here. Sorry, officer. Moving it right away," Jake shouted. He pulled the heavy door open and jumped into the driver's seat.

The agent frowned. "Your partner here almost got you a ton of tickets."

"Yeah, yeah. I'm movin'," Jake said. With the hardware store disappearing from view, Jake turned to Miles. "Why didn't you move? I told you. We needed to be off the radar."

"I fooled her so we could keep the truck close to you."

"Fooled her?"

"Yup. I told that meter maid I don't speak English," Miles said with pride.

"You don't speak any other language."

"I know, right?"

"You are a lovable, stinky idiot," Jake said, unable to suppress a chuckle. "Let's go finish our route."

Chapter 9

Terri sat at her favorite coffee joint, looking for any Ministry of Salvation tags on the internet from her laptop. The unexpected ringing of her mobile phone disrupted the search. She did not recognize the caller ID.

"Sheehan!" she answered in her usual business tone.

"Hi, this is Jake Johansson. You know, the garbageman."

"Yes, Jake. How can I help you?"

"The thing is, I think I found the church you were looking for."

Terri swallowed hard. "What?"

"The church. The Ministry of Salivating."

"Salvation."

"Yeah, that one. It's here in Brooklyn. Inside a hardware store. Atlantic Avenue west of Pennsylvania."

"Do you have an address? The name of the store?"

Jake paused. "Brick's. Brooklyn Brick's Hardware."

"Great. How did you get this information?"

"I saw a bunch of kids get into that van while I was doing my route. I followed it."

"Hope!" Terri said aloud. "Were any of them girls? What did they look like? How old were they?"

"Um, there was one girl. She was the driver. She was short and looked too young to drive a big van. I think the rest were boys."

"How old were they? Six or seven, perhaps?"

"Can't tell? One was young, like a baby. He was in a car seat."

"How do you know the church was in the hardware store?" Terri asked.

"I went inside," Jake said.

"What? You went in?"

Jake told her about the alley, about Dominick and the creepy cast of characters who tried to help him find religion. He thought she'd applaud his clever "something in worship" line that made the encounter happen, but the investigator was way too focused on details to hand out any praise.

"What did you see?"

"A hardware store. I couldn't get into the church part. It was in the back. I think The Minister or some administrator suspected I was lying."

"Not sure why you helped me, but thank you. Thank you so much. You should have called me before taking any action. I don't want you to get hurt or in any trouble."

A wave of satisfaction and confidence that he had done the right thing coursed through him. The speech his uncle had given him earlier played back in Jake's head like a catchy song.

* * * * *

Mrs. Daschle greeted Jake in the hallway just as his keys slipped from his fingers and clattered to the floor.

"Good afternoon, sweetie. How was work?"

Jake winced as he stooped to pick them up. "It was a day. First one in a long time."

"Even in this gloomy weather?"

"Yeah." He surprised himself with the answer. "It was a pretty good day."

Mrs. Daschle's eyes softened. "I'm glad to see you happy."

"Thanks," Jake said, though he wasn't sure why he felt the need to thank her.

She hesitated, fingers fidgeting with her sweater sleeve. "Sweetie...I need a favor."

"Anything."

"I need a hug."

Jake didn't hesitate. He wrapped his arms around the woman who had patched his scraped knees, fed him when his father worked late and held him together during the worst years of his life. Without thinking, he lifted her off the ground.

"All right, okay, put me down!" she wheezed. "I'm too fragile for that."

He set her down carefully, both of them laughing. "You're in great shape for a hundred and twenty-seven," Jake said.

"I'm seventy-five," she sniffed, straightening her blouse. "And I am in pretty good shape. You've gotten stronger since you were ten."

Jake kicked off his shoes and followed her toward the small kitchen. "So why so glum, chum?"

She exhaled slowly, the weight visible in her shoulders. "It's been fifteen years since I lost my Harold. And now Penry...I'm worried about you."

Jake didn't know how to answer that. Instead, he stepped forward and gave her another gentle hug. "I'm fine. Really. Let's just have some lunch."

"I already made it," she said, brightening. Her table was set with homemade chicken soup, finger sandwiches and neat rows of scones, like Martha Stewart had stopped by with an hour to kill.

They sat, pockets of silence interrupted by clinking soup spoons and muffled chewing.

"Jake dear," she said softly, "I need to explain why I didn't attend your father's funeral."

"You don't have to explain anything. I still love you."

"I know that. But I wanted to be there for you." Her voice trembled. "I couldn't break that promise, not after all these years. But I feel so guilty for trying to talk you and Colin out of going."

Jake stirred his soup. "You did exactly what he told you to. Dad always said he didn't want anyone to come to his funeral. I was the stubborn one. I needed closure. Uncle Duff said no one would send my dad to heaven better than him. That sealed it for me."

She nodded. "You probably made the right choice. Penry always did things his own way. So selfless. He didn't want your last memory of him to be in a coffin."

Jake bit into a sandwich. "Yeah...but the last five years, I mostly remember him suffering. At least he looked at peace in the box."

Mrs. Daschle's expression softened. "He was adamant about not having a military funeral. Penry deserved that honor."

"He made that clear after Mom passed. At least they're together now."

He was so protective of you. Do you remember how you used to have nightmares after your mother died? Told him you were lying in the coffin next to her?"

"Yeah. I remember. I was twelve."

"He didn't want you to relive that."

"I'm glad he hid how sick my mother was," Jake said quietly. "I don't remember her suffering. Just...the shock afterward." His voice faltered. "Why does death destroy everything for those left behind?"

Mrs. Daschle reached across the table, squeezing his hand. "I've lost my share too, dear. You never get over it. Nor should you. You learn different ways to carry it."

Jake swallowed. "How do you carry it?"

"I have you."

"Why waste your time? Get a boyfriend."

"Harold would roll in his grave. And you always go for snide humor when things get uncomfortable. That's why you need me. Someone has to whip you into shape so *you* can get a *good* girlfriend and take care of little ol' me for once."

"You chasing away my last girlfriend with a dirty toilet plunger wasn't helping."

"She had big hair and wore pointy shoes."

"That was the style."

"In the eighties. And that waif slapped you in the hallway over spilled ketchup."

Jake laughed. "What do you have against pointy shoes?"

"Feet aren't shaped that way," she declared. "You take a girl on a date, her feet hurt, the night is over. Comfy shoes keep magic alive."

"So...flat hair and sneakers?"

"Precisely."

Jake shook his head. "You have entirely too much time on your hands."

"And you need me," she said matter-of-factly.

He didn't argue. She'd earned that truth.

"I miss your dad," she said after a moment.

"You took good care of him."

"He was an amazing friend. Could fix anything. Always knew what to do."

"Dad had you and Uncle Duff."

"That was his choice too," she said proudly. "He picked the right people."

Jake reached for a vanilla scone and hummed in delight. Mrs. Daschle beamed. "They're not as good as those cookies your father brought from Zeyla's Bakery," she said.

"Those were made with the finest heroin," Jake deadpanned.

"Well, how else would they get customers to return? What happened to that place?"

"Not sure. Dad stored his hot dog cart there. I never went back for it after he got sick."

"That was five years ago!"

"I had more important things to do."

"Or you're just lazy," she quipped.

Jake laughed again, really laughed. And for the first time that day, he felt the apartment breathe with him instead of around him.

Chapter 10

Jake switched on the lights in his apartment. The box holding his father's belongings remained on the small kitchen table where he had left it. He opened the box and peeked inside. It held old socks, an electric razor, a memorial card, an old wallet and a Spiderman keychain.

The superhero logo on the back had a partial label, likely scrawled with a Sharpie marker. Jake could only distinguish the faded letters Z, Y and A. The keychain held an odd, antique-looking key. Crafted from dull metal, the long stem supported a round head adorned with pie-shaped notches.

Weird.

Jake searched through the wallet. Among his father's driver's license and military identification, a creased photo with a ripped edge was jammed behind a dried-out shred of leather. The photo, folded in half, showed his dad alongside a man wearing a chef's hat. Jake recognized the man as Mr. Jesus Zeyla.

The bakery.

Jake hadn't seen Mr. Z. in twenty years, but he still remembered the way the man shouted his name like confetti at a parade.

Does Mr. Z. even know my father has died? They were pretty tight. I wonder if the cart is still there.

The ride to the old downtown pastry shop zipped by. Friday meant sleep would wait with no shift scheduled later. The storefront on Livingston Street had its rusted metal security gate padlocked and appeared to have been closed for years. His father's key did not match any of the old locks. As Jake prepared to leave disappointed, he remembered the small alley that led behind the abandoned bakery. Jake thought again about his dad's old hot dog cart.

Perhaps the cart remains inside, or some money or personal items left by Dad.

Jake ducked into the alley, sneakers crunching through the gravel and broken glass. The air smelled like wet cardboard and something sour he couldn't name, exactly how he remembered this block from childhood.

He kept moving. No lingering. No overthinking. Still, his chest tightened anyway.

This was the same alley where his father used to pull the hot dog cart inside after a long night. Same alley where Jake waited in the car with a comic book while Penrod disappeared through a side door to grab "a tool" he needed. Same alley where Jake swore he once saw someone sprint out crying, though Penrod told him not to worry about it.

He swallowed and forced himself forward.

The long corridor narrowed, and he brushed past a half-fallen stack of milk crates. A rusted dumpster sat crooked at the end, with the same dent in the side, the same faded graffiti. It looked like it hadn't been moved since Jake was twelve.

A small rolling gate sat to the right, candles melted into the concrete below, a makeshift memorial. Someone unlucky, someone loved, someone gone. He didn't look too closely.

Three shallow steps led up to a steel door he had never noticed before. Maybe he had. Maybe he'd been told not to.

Jake's heart thudded in his throat. His palm sweat slicked the keychain in his hand.

He approached the keyhole, a strange circular thing, like it belonged on a safe more than a bakery. He exhaled, long and shaky, and slid the key in.

A perfect fit.

Jake froze.

For a second, his breath wouldn't move, realizing now that he wasn't just opening a door.

He was opening every unanswered question his father ever shut down, every odd look, every late-night "not important" conversation.

Jake tried turning the key.

It wouldn't budge.

Jake pressed harder.

Still stuck.

He leaned his forehead against the cold steel and whispered, "Come on, Dad."

Needs WD-40. One of Dad's favorite tools.

He tried again. With a determined resolve, Jake pushed against the door. The weight of the heavy steel surprised him.

Jake exerted more force. The hinges screeched, and the door shifted enough for him to slip inside.

Before going any further, Jake stopped ahead of the pitch-black expanse. He took out his phone to use the screen as a light. The faint glow failed to bring the space's features to light, but it did help him avoid falling down the steps leading to some garage. Jake hoped to locate a light switch near the entrance. Instead, he found red and green buttons for the bay door, but that was all.

Jake descended into the open garage. With his free hand, he swept the air beside him, feeling for anything recognizable like a pole, a counter, a power cord, a switch. Anything.

His sneakers slipped on something greasy. He froze; breath caught in his chest. Probably old cooking oil. He did not want to check.

Jake pushed on.

A flash of reflected light stabbed his eyes. Up ahead, a shiny steel panel bounced his phone light straight back at him. He knew that shape. He could never forget it.

His father's vending cart.

Standing upright.

Frozen in time.

A dark trench coat was draped over the top, the fabric stiff with dust. Jake's steps quickened without permission. He reached the cart and opened the compartments, each sticky latch clicking like a gun being cocked.

Inside: old NYC ski hats. Cheap umbrellas. Mold-fused pretzels. Stone-hard mustard packets. Warm soda cans floating in stagnant brown water. Nobody had touched any of this. Not in years. Not since his father stopped coming.

How had he never come here? How had no one checked? Why hadn't he asked more questions?

Guilt crept over him cold and heavy.

Here he was in a forgotten Brooklyn garage, surrounded by the remnants of the life his father never talked about. A life Jake never bothered to investigate. Penrod hadn't asked him to visit, and Jake never pushed. His mother hadn't pushed either. They'd all lived inside a comfortable silence.

Jake swallowed hard.

What secrets did you keep, Dad?

He scanned the perimeter in jittery arcs. As his eyes adjusted, the space took form, not a garage, not really. More like a shop. A workspace.

A long workbench stretched along one wall; machinery huddled against it like sleeping animals. The faint outlines of tools hung overhead: wrenches, cutters, something that looked like a soldering gun.

Jake shuffled forward, shoes whispering through years of dust. A thin string dangled above the workbench. He tugged it.

A fluorescent bulb stuttered, flickered twice, then buzzed to life.

Jake's heartbeat slowed, then stuttered for an entirely different reason. Three walls were lined with overflowing bookshelves. Hundreds of books. Stacked. Leaning. Overflowing.

Jake blinked hard.

Dad didn't read. Not even the newspaper. He always said he was too tired for books, too busy for stories.

Jake stepped closer, his hand shaking slightly. "Dad...what the hell is all this?"

All the books focused on criminal justice and true crime. Some looked like textbooks, while others were small paperbacks highlighting specific cases. Jake discovered FBI publications on profiling and victimology, books about police tactics, procedural techniques, traffic issues and evidence collection. The shelves held several law dictionaries and other related materials.

The cluttered wooden workbench displayed an array of tools and equipment. An old, ragged sweatshirt lay across a rickety stool. The pullover's unique material carried a strange texture under Jake's fingertips, like rubber mesh. Old batteries ranging from AAA to D, battery power packs and loose wires were scattered across the worn tabletop. An unusual pair of form-fitting black gloves with thin silver coils embedded in the rubber material hung on the pegboard wall behind the workbench, the coils wrapped around the fingers, thumbs and palms, extending to the forearms.

Next to that, a black balaclava hung on a hook. A molded ceramic plate was affixed over the mouth and nose.

Someone spread out and pinned newspaper clippings across the workbench and to the walls behind it. The headlines detailed crimes from around the city, most notably muggings and burglaries, spanning at least twenty years.

Notepads were everywhere, piled on the workbench and strewn among the bookshelves and floors.

"What was he doing in here?" Jake wondered aloud.

While exploring the workshop, Jake pulled an oversized shoebox from under the workbench shelf. When he opened it, he found a black handheld device. Jake thought it resembled a wireless electric razor, only with two prongs in place of the shaver screen. The shoebox included a black whip with similar coils and a bunch of thick black plastic tie-wraps.

Intrigued and growing more curious with each discovery, Jake picked up the razor device and pressed the button in the middle of the handle. Nothing happened. He checked the battery compartment and found that it used a standard nine-volt battery. After disconnecting the old battery, he touched the terminals with his tongue, but still nothing. Jake figured the batteries were long dead.

He turned to the whip. This contraption also had a button on its handle, but Jake decided not to touch it. He moved within the room, trying to comprehend what it meant. Something drew his eyes to the strange gloves on the pegboard. Jake pulled them off and examined them. They were soft yet rubbery, like thick surgical gloves. His fingers ran up and down the outside, along the ridges of the silver coils. He slid his left hand into one glove. *Wow, so comfortable.* A bulge on the inside of the forearm caught Jake's attention, and he ran his other hand over it. The designer integrated a few rectangular batteries into the fabric.

Running his finger along the seam from his forearm to his palm, a small wire protruded from the bulge. It ended at a small, round button implanted in the center of his palm. With his bare hand, Jake pressed it, and in an instant, a faint crack and an electric-blue current flickered briefly around the glove. The glove powered down, causing the blue light to fade into the silver coils from which it originated. Jake pressed the button again. Nothing happened.

No more juice.

Jake continued to search the workshop.

Was this all Dad's, Mr. Z's, or somebody else's place?

Jake couldn't piece all of this, *any* of this, together until he noticed a framed family picture. It sat undisturbed on the workbench amid all the tools and gadgets. His father and mother stood side by side, smiling, with young Jake, seven or eight years old, in the middle. Both his parents had a hand on his shoulder. Jake remembered the day they took the photo. His family visited the portrait studio at Sears. Bridget made the photographer take a ridiculous number of photos until she got the perfect one. Jake and his father were exhausted. It was the only time he regretted skipping school. This was indeed his father's workshop.

The place had waited for years, ready for Jake to arrive. Jake wanted to understand what this meant. He went to feed the meter for his car and stopped by the nearby bodega for coffee, a sandwich and batteries. Back through the heavy steel door and down into the garage, Jake dusted off the bookshelves and organized the clutter on the workbench to start making sense of everything.

A strange book beneath a pile of wires and an old newspaper dated October 10, 2003 caught Jake's eye. It resembled a large sketchbook with thick pages. The leather cover had a painted red symbol that appeared to be an upside-down anarchy sign. Jake opened it.

The diary brimmed with jagged notes and sketches of the brutal devices scattered across the table. Rubber-mesh gloves promised seventy-five thousand volts ripping through coiled wiring while keeping the wearer untouched. A black hoodie hung nearby, Kevlar threaded and sealed in the same sinister mesh, ready to deflect blades and bullets alike. The whip and other tools were all built to spit raw electricity, designed for one purpose: to drop an enemy.

Then there were the excerpts themselves: firsthand accounts of events and adventures that Jake's father experienced while working on the streets of New York City. His father penned them in his handwriting. In 1980, his father wrote about how much he missed being a janitor at a police precinct. He was angry at being fired for snooping through a detective's case file and leaving a note on how to solve the case. He advised the detective that he should check the room of a suicide victim for "trophies," which tied him to a string of dead prostitutes.

Countless pages contained notes and blurbs about robberies, burglaries, rapes and other "Index Crimes," as his father called them. Jake could not believe what he was reading. Many narratives concluded with "Apprehended and Delivered" or "AD." It hosted two decades worth of carefully recorded data. Penrod Johansson was a street vigilante determined to deliver justice for the everyday citizen.

Jake flipped through a few pages until he found one with the same logo as the front cover. A note read, "*I like this.*"

The next page explained how, in 1983, he saved a young graffiti artist named Sing X from a group of drug dealers. Jake's father grew annoyed with Sing X because he would sometimes appear while Penrod was lurking about in some drug den. As Jake continued reading, he learned that Sing X handled the symbol, painting it throughout the city wherever his father delivered justice to some wrongdoer. Jake sensed his father took pride in it. He delved deeper into the diary. Sing X was like a partner or sidekick, as far as Jake could tell, providing information and being tasked with various fact-finding missions. The journal entries contained various details; some were facts and notes, while others offered insight into his father's thoughts.

Case #1981–013

10/10/1981

Info from Sing X

Homicide

West 30th St / 9th Ave

Motive: Sexual Bias / Gang Infused

Victim: Santos Ulan M/H/17

Subjects:

30 Dirty Mutts Gang Members

A. Filipe (Philly) Milagros M/H/18 - AD

B. Dean (Tonto) West M/B/19 - AD

C. Israel (Izzy) Rivera M/H/19 - AD

Synopsis: A 17-year-old victim walked into 014 Pct on 09/01/1981 and stated someone sexually assaulted him in the

Amtrak bathroom / Penn Station. PO Netterville interviewed victim Santos Ulan, who determined he was a male prostitute and sent him away. Victim found unconscious West 30 / 9. DOA at Bellevue 10/10/1981. Stabbed left torso.

Witness: Aaron West M/B/17: Interviewed by detectives at Bellevue.

- He says he was the victim's boyfriend. He got caught kissing a victim by his brother Dean about a month ago.

- Dean was angry. Made Aaron break up with the victim

- Dean, a 30 Dirty Mutts gang member on 30 St

- Dean is known as Tonto.

- On 10/08/1981, Victim Santos told witness Aaron that a month ago, Dean and his gang dragged him to a Penn Station bathroom at knifepoint and made an unknown male pro / sexually assault him while gang members watched.

- Witness Aaron confronts his brother the same night.

- Dean calls witness his little faggot and threatens him. Denied any involvement.

- Witness has not seen brother since.

Leads:

- 30 Dirty Mutts are known to be on W30 St / 8 to 9 Ave

- Drugs

- Vandals

- Violent Street Robberies

Notes:

- Witness on the street says Vic no prostitute

- known pros at Penn did not recognize Vic

- Vic is a good student with no known criminal past

The flip side of the page gave his father's insight, and an attached newspaper article told the remaining details. Jake's imagination launched into orbit, filling any hole as he fell into the trance of an extraordinary story about his father.

Chapter 11

West 30th Street lay in eerie silence; whispers of past homicides now echoed in the night air. Moonlight cast dark shapes clinging to buildings, and the veil of darkness hid secrets. On rooftops, a figure stalked, cloaked in malevolence, waiting, watching, hunting. An electric tension crackled. The faceless shadow radiated primal aggression like a predator prowling its territory.

Something simmered inside him, sharp and urgent. A life was gone, and nobody seemed to care. No investigation. No grief. Justice had slipped through the cracks, leaving only a cold certainty that something was terribly wrong.

Had they forgotten? Will the city ignore the next victim, too? The wicked play without rules. The good pay for everyone. Evil is effortless; the good stand to lose it all. But when the good become nameless...the night finally evens the score.

He avoided being seen. He was not a cop. No rules to follow. Just a concerned citizen doing his part and doing what was right, in the wrong way.

So far, it went without issue. In the past six months, twelve miserable scumbags had been enjoying "three hots and a cot" on Rikers Island. It was righteous, euphoric. The vigilante craved more. Time to find "Tonto" and handle his dogs. Battling two-bit thugs no longer posed a challenge. It served as practice. The real test comes when you stand eye to eye with a killer. This campaign will define his purpose out here on the streets. It may bring him closure, or it could end with his death. Justice might finally be served.

The hooded stalker scanned the walls for fresh graffiti. Gangbangers always had to leave their mark; it was better to blast paint than piss on a corner like feral dogs. Some of them had talent, too, strokes and colors that cut deeper than crude vandalism. To the dark vigilante, gangland murals were nothing more than modern cave drawings, primal warnings scrawled in neon. The Mutts' stories mirrored their ancestors', trading caves for urban claims.

Someone tagged a wall on West 30th Street and 9th Avenue. They must have completed it in the last couple of months. A menacing-looking dog wearing an Indian headdress overlooked the spot on the sidewalk where they found Santos Ulan. The dog was biting into an oversized cartoon ass. The upper body of the unfortunate fellow was inside the Injun mutt's mouth. Still standing on the ground were the legs of the hapless character, pants down to his ankles. The tags around the dog collar read "Izzy" at the top and "Philly" at the bottom. From the collar, the letters "TNT" dangled like a name charm. The dog's eyes were billiard balls: the right was a red three-ball, while the left was a white cue ball. The most despicable part of the mural was a pool stick, which pierced through the half-eaten man's bare buttocks.

A pool hall was around the corner on 9th Avenue, on the second floor of a three-story commercial building. It had no name, just a small yellow sign with the word "Billiards" jutting out from the second-floor facade. The three front windows were smoky but glowed with a reddish light. Thirty Dirty Mutts graffiti decorated most of the brick establishment.

Four in the morning, and nobody was outside. The building had a convenient alley to the right and a fire escape in the back, allowing the hunter roof access. He watched, listening to the sounds of billiard balls clinking together amid music and laughter. A faltering figure exited through the front door. Alone and drunk, the guy slumped into the alley like a fish to a baited hook. The hunter slid down three stories of ladders as the drunk began urinating in the dilapidated corridor. As he approached, the hunter observed the large 3-0 tattoo on the drunk's neck. The gang member looked up just in time to see the eyes staring at him. Everything then faded to black.

The vigilante left "Trippy" tied up behind the alley. Somebody will find him, maybe. Alcohol is one of the best truth serums. Trippy told his tormentor where to find Tonto. He gave no further information about the murder, but he admitted that Izzy and Philly were also members of his gang. Tonto had been at the pool hall earlier that night. He left with a girl and was taking her to The Osgood Motel, nicknamed Oz, located two blocks down. The place was a seedy joint with hourly rates. Trippy said the girl Tonto picked up was a "human sperm dumpster," and they were staying in room #30.

Masked and ready, the Wild Hunt stepped into Oz. The cloaked sentinel stalked past the concierge slumped at the desk, nose buried in a crusted porno rag. The stink hit next: stale smoke and rotten booze. Torn linoleum curled underfoot. Yellowed wallpaper peeled from the stairwell like dead skin. Rats darted through the flickering light while roaches climbed the walls, scuttled like bellhops. Overhead, bulbs hissed and spat sparks, buzzing like dying bees.

The masked hero knocked on door #30, third floor.

"Hey! You fucking kidding me? Go away!" a female yelled from inside the room.

He knocked louder.

"Yo, motherfucker! Someone better be dead!" she spat back.

W *ell, somebody is,* the dark visitor thought to himself. He knocked even louder.

"Fuck this punk," the female voice said.

The door swung open, and the skanky redhead crumpled to the floor in an unnatural heap. She was wearing only a black tank top, and her bare buttocks stuck straight out. A tattooed male jumped up from a mattress. His greasy hair hung over his face, and only his gritted teeth were visible. The gangbanger smelled horrific and wore only dingy underpants. The two men charged each other, and the masked vigilante had the jump. As the sweaty thug cocked his fist back, the vigilante grabbed his foe's upper arm with his gloved hand and gave a squeeze. The fighting paused. For only a moment, the man with "TONTO" tattooed on his throat lowered his rock-hard fist. The vigilante gripped Tonto, glancing at his failed electric grip. Confusion marked his dual-colored eyes.

"What the fuck, you some kind of faggot?" Tonto exclaimed.

The vigilante widened his eyes in disbelief as the fight erupted. This would be a brutal encounter. Tonto delivered a punishing blow. Each strike landed like thunder, crumbling his defenses, and the would-be hero raced to comprehend the chaos unfolding. His thoughts jumbled in the face of Tonto's relentless assault. The vigilante crashed against a wooden dresser, which rattled and creaked under the pressure. A lamp wobbled atop a shaky dresser, its base quaking as the battered furniture withstood the brawl as best it could. Tonto, fueled by blazing fury, unleashed a brutal flurry of strikes that sent shockwaves rippling through the vigilante, amplifying the intensity of the battle. The vigilante sensed his stamina waning, his breath in ragged gasps. Driven to get even, his punches landed, but each strike was less powerful than before.

Why weren't the gloves working?

Tonto's mighty shove sent the intruder crashing. But in a heartbeat, the tide of battle shifted. A crimson whirlwind surged into the chaos, punctuated by a spine-tingling shriek that sliced through the air. Furious and determined, the redheaded skank launched her attack.

"Yo, I got this. Chill!" Tonto grabbed her by the waist. Red Skank was lifted as she continued to claw and kick.

"Get off me, Tonto. This fucker did some shit to me. I'm gonna fuckin kill 'em."

"Dude's a faggot! I got him!"

Tonto turned Red Skank away from the fight. She now aimed her disdain on Tonto.

"Yo, get off me, man. I feel..."

Out of nowhere she spewed hot, creamy vomit all over Tonto. The break refreshed the vigilante. He cracked the fallen lamp over Tonto's greasy, wet head. Tonto fell onto the mattress. The vigilante grabbed Red Skank by the throat and squeezed. He stared deep into her manic eyes.

"Don't you puke on me!" he groaned.

Red Skank stared back and asked, "What's wrong with your eyes?"

Blue lightning danced around the vigilante's gloved hand. Red Skank went stiff. The vigilante threw her onto the ratty mattress, her body slumped over Tonto's. When the two awoke, they were tied up. The vigilante moved close to Tonto's face, trying hard not to gag from the stench. He gagged Red Skank with a cloth as she tried to yell and curse. Tonto remained calm.

"What do you want, faggot?"

The vigilante whispered into Tonto's ear. "It seems your boys, Izzy and Philly, sold you out."

"Who?" Tonto played dumb.

"They told the cops that you stabbed your brother's boyfriend. They are telling everyone they are not going down for you."

"Wait...you're a cop?"

"Don't worry about who I am. You are the one with the problem now. Why did you kill that kid?"

"I didn't kill nobody. I didn't do shit. Untie me, mothafuck..."

The vigilante punched Tonto in his stomach. "I got all night to do this now. Why did you kill Santos?"

"Who? Man, I don't know any faggots named Santos!"

"That's what I thought." The Fade delivered a hard knuckle punch to Tonto's temple. "But, you knew he was gay."

"Yo! Fuck man, that fuckin hurt," Tonto whined.

The masked hero gave him another temple shot. Tonto looked like he was about to lose consciousness.

"Your crew sold out. How do you think I found you?" the vigilante half-lied. "Why did you kill him?"

Tonto committed the foulest deed a gang affiliate could do. "I didn't do shit. Izzy fuckin' iced him."

The vigilante got what he came for.

"Tonto...Mr. West...Dean-O...you did it. I understand you're not telling the truth. You killed him. I know why and I also know you are a closet homosexual. You were jealous of your little brother. You will have many boyfriends from now on."

Tonto stared into the strange eyes of the mysterious figure. "I'm not no fuckin' faggot...I didn't do shit. I'm not gay, man. I'm not into that..."

The Fade interrupted. "Your precious Izzy and Philly have no loyalty to you. Who do you think sent me?"

"Wait. What?"

The Fade was enjoying his little head game. He squeezed Tonto's arm again. Nothing happened.

Tonto stopped mid-thought. "Why do you keep squeezing my arm?" he asked.

Blue lightning danced around the glove once again. Tonto jerked stiff and fell back flat on the mattress.

Red Skank's fear came through in her eyes as she stared into the vigilante's dual-colored ones.

The last thing she said tried to scream through the gag was, "Wait, don't!"

* * * * *

The newspaper article, written a year later, described the aftermath:

Notorious gang members arrested in hate-crime murder

By James Fanelli, New York Post Contributor

NEW YORK CITY — Acting on a tip, cops busted into the Hell's Kitchen Osgood Motel yesterday and arrested Dean West, a notorious gang leader, for his role in last year's hate-crime murder of 17-year-old Santos Ulan.

West and a prostitute were found by police injured and hogtied inside a seedy motel room. The discovery led to the subsequent arrests of Israel Rivera and Filipe Milagros. The trio, all card-carrying members of the Thirty Dirty Mutts gang, quickly turned on each other and revealed key details about their roles in Ulan's murder last September. The three men will face murder charges and possible sentences of 20 years to life.

The report did not mention a street vigilante.

How in the hell was he able to hide this from everyone?

Jake's heart broke, and his head ached. He remembered his father didn't really talk much, but he could not understand how nobody was aware of his alter ego. He called his uncle.

When Uncle Duff answered, Jake spewed a cyclone of information in one breath.

"Slow down, son. Slow down," his godfather said.

"He was out there risking his life, fighting terrible people. Did you know what he was doing?"

"Jake, I assure you, I know nothing of the sort. Where are you?"

"I told you. I'm at Zeyla's. Well, the old Zeyla's. I'm around behind the shop."

"Jake, you are having a tough time. Please take a breath. You surely have stumbled onto something. I don't think your father is involved in a thing like..."

Jake cut his uncle off. "You should come here! Right now!"

"Jake, 'tis getting late. Maybe we can..."

"Now! You need to come here right now!"

The priest sighed through the phone. "Give me the location again."

Behind the old bakery, the silence was palpable, and Jake struggled to remember what it looked like when his father worked there. He did not remember entering the garage, but recalled many people being in the store when visiting his dad. Jake could never forget those giant chocolate chip cookies; the chocolate chips baked right on top. He could almost smell them as he daydreamed.

"This one's got your name on it," his dad would say. Jake could hear it now so clearly in the silence. Then his father would flip the cookie over, and food coloring would spell Jake's name.

To see a once joyful part of his life now engulfed in cobwebs and shadows, left to fade into sorrow, hurt his heart.

* * * * *

Terri stood across the street from Brooklyn Brick's Hardware Emporium. She wanted to get a feel for the place without too many people around. The area might be dangerous after dark, but Terri assumed that at 9:00 p.m., she was at least the one hiding in the shadows.

Suspension means I am just an ordinary citizen. I'm just taking an evening stroll in East New York, Terri justified.

The MOS van pulled out of the alleyway and turned onto Atlantic Avenue. Terri could not determine the occupants or operator. Her fingers shook as she pulled her cell phone from her back pocket and dialed a number while marching to her car. She passed a streetlight along the way, and with each step, darkness devoured the little light illuminating her path.

A painful, scratchy voice croaked, "You got a light?"

Terri almost jumped out of her sweatpants. "Uh, oh, no, I don't smoke."

The wheezy man leaned in a little toward Terri, but the poor lighting still prevented her from seeing his face.

"I didn't ask if you were a smoker. Why do you people always have to tell somebody you don't smoke? Great. You deserve a medal. *<cough>* Do you have a light?"

Terri wasn't comfortable with the man's arrogance. He was the one begging for a favor. "I already told you I didn't." She turned and walked away.

Wow, the freaks do come out at night.

Puttering footsteps from behind made Terri run.

She sensed the stranger's true intentions. Escape was impossible as she reached for the vehicle door. The man's wheezing breath became louder. Nobody was around to help her if she screamed. Cars were whipping through the intersection of Atlantic and Pennsylvania. Terri went full running back, dodging a bus, a moped and two cars. Her pursuer kept on until the last car. It struck his right flank, sending him tumbling across the road and into a curb.

The driver yelled, "Good for ya! You fuckin' idiot!" and drove away toward the Jackie Robinson Parkway.

Terri felt guilty, but understood she shouldn't. She tried to get the license plate of the fleeing vehicle as it sped through the traffic light to escape. Terri wanted to see the would-be attacker and didn't care whether he was alive or dead.

The chiseled-looking Hispanic man grumbled in pain. Terri stooped for a better look. His dark eyes seemed to penetrate her very soul.

"Mind your own business," he mumbled before trailing off and losing consciousness.

Terri screamed for somebody to help, then remembered her phone. She dialed 9-1-1, but before she hit send, she realized this would officially involve her in the incident. A curious crowd of people gathered.

"Please, someone call 911!" Terri pleaded.

Most people took pictures of the injured man with their cell phones instead. When Terri saw the approaching emergency lights, it showed that decent humans still exist in New York City. She slipped away unscathed and anonymous.

 **12**

Jake paced outside the rundown bakery, anticipating Uncle Duff's arrival. Thirty minutes seemed more like thirty days. Jake was elated when he saw the husky priest walking up.

"Where's the Caddy?" Jake asked.

"Took the subway," Father Duffy answered, taking a swig from a flask.

Jake brought him to the workshop and showed his godfather everything.

"Ah, Penry, what daft mess have ye gotten yerself into?" Father Duffy wondered aloud. "Bridget would've put a stop to this madness if she'd known what he was at."

"So, you didn't know?" Jake asked.

"No."

"So, you don't think my mother knew anything either?"

"Ah, sure, Bridget would've told me, wouldn't she? We both would've put a stop to all these shenanigans. He could've gotten himself in right trouble!"

"Well, my dad is dead," Jake muttered.

"The point is, Jacob," Father Duffy paused, looking to choose his words.

"He didn't die doing it," Jake said.

"Yes. That may be true. But..."

"I'm taking that as he was really good at it."

"At what? Besides keeping secrets."

"At bustin' bad guys!" Jake exclaimed.

"He is no superhero, Jacob. This is vigilantism. Dangerous and reckless."

"That doesn't strike me as a bad thing. He helped loads of people. He brought justice where the police couldn't."

"Yes. But at what cost?"

"Dad is dead. Mom's been dead. We're still standing. That's gotta count for something. We don't have any other family. At least not here in the States. Besides, we never knew this side of him. For the last five years, he had been sick with dementia. It's been years since he was out saving the city. So, it's a wash!" Jake hummed.

"Aye, I do see yer point there. I'm a bit of a pessimist by nature, I am. Always worryin' about New York City an' its long tentacles. Best we clean up all this shite, so it is. We don't want anyone else findin' it."

"Agreed. But Uncle Duff, I must do one thing first."

"What's that?"

"I need to find this Sing X."

* * * * *

Jake and Father Duffy arrived at the barren McCarren Park Pool. Closed since the eighties, its stone and brick arches stood graffiti-ridden and cracked. The city shut it down, allowing this neighborhood staple to drown in obscurity. Young locals later discovered the free-standing stone diving platforms and claimed the empty basin as their own amphitheater. Punk bands turned it into a feral little church.

Obnoxious music blared, as it should. The noise rose in a jagged wave, drowning thought, rattling bone, turning Jake's chest into a drum someone else was beating.

Father Duffy leaned closer, hand cupped to his ear, waiting for an explanation. Jake did not speak right away.

He thought of the journal's smeared ink, unfinished sketches and margins filled with frantic spirals. After the towers fell, his father's writing had changed, like someone had shaken the sanity out of him. Pages incomplete. Sentences collapsing mid-thought. Whole entries reduced to jagged scribbles. Notes for impossible devices...a man-sized mousetrap, a handheld glue cannon, blueprints that looked like fever dreams.

And the words...*The Jypsy* and *Evil* scrawled again and again, a hundred times, until the mantra twisted into something darker. The final line still haunted him: *The Devil is Dead.*

Jake exhaled hard, letting the music cover the tremor in his chest. He leaned toward Father Duffy, raising his voice over the blistering guitars.

Something broke in Dad. His later entries stopped making sense. But "Sing X" was the last name he wrote down while he was still himself.

Father Duffy's eyebrow arched. "And that's why it's worth me ears bleedin', aye?"

"Yeah," Jake said. "If Sing X was really here, then this is where the trail went cold."

"What're ye expectin' t' find 'ere among this chaos?"

"Not sure," Jake said, looking down at the basin. Layers of graffiti and a massive, chaotic mural covered the floor, but the crowd's stomping made it impossible to make out anything clearly.

"Ah, 'tis a grand plan, then," Father Duffy said with an eye roll as he followed his nephew into the pool area.

Beer spray hung in the air like humidity from hell. As they weaved through mohawked partygoers, people shouted "radical" comments at the priest. A hooded teenager spray-painted a skull on the wall; Father Duffy pointed it out. A small child darted past, and Jake caught it...the symbol from the journal flashed on the far wall.

"There! There it is!" Jake said.

They stood beside the red tag. "What does this mean, then?" the priest asked.

"Not sure, but if Dad wasn't hallucinating, this proves the journal wasn't all madness."

"Aye, you may be right."

Jake turned back and approached the hooded artist, who was walking away. "Hey, man, can I talk to you for a second?" Jake yelled over the music.

The figure turned around. The young girl's eyes widened at the sight of the priest. She tried to be discreet as she slipped the spray can into her front hoodie pocket.

"Whoa, sorry 'bout that, you had your hood..."

"Excuse me? We have a quick question fer ya," Father Duffy said.

"Yo, not interested in what you're dealing, pedo," she said, then walked away.

"He's not a podiatrist." No one was sure if Jake was joking.

"Get the hell away from me! Fuck off! Stranger Danger!" she screamed.

Jake lost his temper because of her disrespectful attitude toward his uncle and godfather. He ran up to the hooded girl's face.

"Hey, a priest asks you for help, and you tell him to fuck off?"

"What! Do you feel left out? Fuck off!"

"Cut the tough-girl attitude. He's a priest, for God's sake. What's your problem?"

"A real priest? Really? A real live, honest-to-goodness priest?" she asked, lowering her hood.

Her youth surprised Jake. She could not be over fifteen years old. "Yeah. He's a real..."

"Fuck off!" she screamed and walked into the crowd of revelers.

"Leave her be, Jake. 'Tis fine," Father Duffy said.

"No. You can't let that punk talk to us like that." Jake fast-stepped to the young girl as she bumped into several bouncing partygoers.

"Listen, you little shit!" Jake shouted, his finger aimed at her nose. "We are only asking about some graffiti."

"I didn't do no graffiti."

"Cut the crap. Not worried about yours. That one over there. The red symbol looks like an upside-down anarchy sign."

"I didn't do it. Now go..."

"I got it. I got it. Fuck off. What does it mean?"

"How the fuck should I know?" she answered.

"Do ya know who Sing X is, lass?" Father Duffy asked.

The girl's body language and facial expression shifted. She hesitated while glancing down at the concrete floor.

Now that they were lower, the floor mural emerged, a bright, sprawling cartoon landscape half-destroyed by years of foot traffic. The girl pointed to a specific section. Jake and Father Duffy stepped around a cluster of dancers until they reached it.

There, on the shell-top sneaker of a cartoonish child, was the signature:

Sing X.

"Who is he?" Jake asked the girl.

"Only the greatest street artist that ever lived," she answered.

"Do ye know where we can find him?" Father Duffy asked.

"Her."

"Sing X is a girl?" Jake asked.

"Maybe she is. Nobody knows. Nobody's ever seen her."

"We need to find out who they are," Father Duffy said.

"Forget it. SHE might not even be real," the girl shot back.

Jake was almost out of patience. "Look, this is important now. Whoever Sing X is, we need to have a word with them."

"Who are you guys? Cops?"

"Umm. No." Jake nodded toward his uncle. "We are obviously from the church."

"What church?"

Jake gave his neck a rub. "Latter Day Saints."

Father Duffy looked down and shook his head in disappointment.

"This Sing X may be in danger," Jake lied again.

"What kind of danger?"

"Dangerous danger."

That was enough for Father Duffy. "Here now, young lass. Where might we glimpse more of his or her art, then?"

Through her sidelong glance at Jake, she answered, "Asphalt. It's a gallery in SoHo. I will get my work there one day. The only place where we street artists can showcase our work without the cops or you ass hats bothering us."

When they reached the car, Jake said, "Nearest public library. Need a real computer if we're gonna dig up anything on Sing X."

Father Duffy cleared his throat. "Asphalt Art Gallery is on King and Varick Street."

Jake froze mid-step. The priest was thumbing through a BlackBerry, the little trackball glowing like the Pope himself had blessed it. "Uncle Duff...where did you get that?"

"Shh," Father Duffy said, eyes never leaving the tiny screen. "Modern technology is proof that miracles come in strange forms, so it is."

Jake squinted at him. "Yeah. Or social media's just another way the government or the devil keeps tabs on everyone."

"Ah, the old dance 'tween heaven and hell," Father Duffy murmured. "A never-ending jest."

He tapped again. "I seemed to have found Sing X's Myspace account."

Jake blinked. "What pray-tell is *that*?"

"And I'm the old one?" Duffy muttered. "Social network."

Jake pointed a warning finger. "Probably invented by the devil. Or the DMV. Same thing."

"Aye," Duffy chuckled. "But even devils leave clues. Now look here..." He turned the screen toward Jake.

"It's more of a tribute site than an account. But it tracks the legend. Says Sing X is an anonymous street artist...never photographed, never verified. Their murals vanish and reappear across the boroughs like ghosts. Collectors pay millions, but no one knows who or what they really are."

Jake leaned closer. "So, they're a phantom with a spray can."

"Exactly." Duffy flicked the trackball. "And here's the bit that matters: Asphalt is hosting a ceremony tomorrow night. A company named Info Group Inc. will auction off a World Trade Center barricade painted by Sing X. Proceeds go to the Widows and Orphans of 9/11."

Jake nodded slowly. "Well...so much for being anonymous."

"It doesn't say whether the artist will appear," Duffy added. "But someone representin' 'em likely will." With that he clicked the BlackBerry shut like it was a relic too powerful to stay exposed.

Chapter 13

The hardware store, the attacker, his body sprawled out on the Atlantic Avenue pavement, it was all primed to leap from Terri's tongue by the second unanswered ring of Molina's phone. Two more rings passed, separated by what felt like a taunting silence. Terri balled up a piece of paper and threw it at the wall.

Pick up the goddamn phone.

Finally, she heard a click on the other end, followed by a hurried voice rising above the chatter.

"Detective Molina speaking. Hello? Hello?"

"It's Terri. I got a lead."

Molina's silence was either anticipation or a terrible connection. Terri banked on anticipation.

"Hardware store, East New York. Atlantic Avenue near Pennsylvania. Brooklyn Brick's..."

"Slow down, Terri. Hold your horses. Give me more details."

"There is a church toward the back of the store. It's real cult-like stuff. It had to be them. The Tanners were devout Christians."

"Since when does being religious automatically make someone guilty?"

"Look at the facts. It adds up," Terri said.

"Not always the case. How did you get this information?"

"The garbage route, a church van was parked near a brownstone. I checked into it, and a religious leader lives there. They threw out a dresser full of children's clothes."

Molina cut her off. "Terri, please. I get it. But that does not prove anything. There is nothing really to go on."

"Jake followed the van to the store." Terri knew she had made a mistake and stopped talking.

"Who the hell is Jake?" Molina asked.

"The garbageman."

"Why the hell is he following..."

"He did it on his own. I'm telling you. I didn't know he would..."

"Terri, look, I intend to look deeper into this. It's just that..."

"I was almost attacked by one of them," Terri said.

"Attacked? By whom?"

"Almost attacked. By one of the cult people."

"When? Where?"

"Last night. Located across from the hardware store. I was staking out the place."

"By yourself?"

"I'm a big girl."

"What exactly happened?" Molina asked.

"He ran at me. A car hit him. Lucky timing, maybe divine intervention."

"Are you sure it was related? A pretty girl walking alone in East New York at night is almost an invitation to trouble."

"First off, stop the pretty girl shit. Second, he told me to mind my own business."

"Were the police involved?"

"Yeah. I think so. I left."

"Why did you leave the scene of an accident?"

"Sticking around would probably get me hurt."

"Who hit him?"

"Hit and run. It seemed random. The driver took off on the Jackie Robinson Parkway. The guy was chasing me. Ran into traffic. Fuck'em. I doubt he was hurt too badly. Bump on the head."

Terri's encounter did nothing to sway Molina. She pulled her hair back with a sweaty, tear-smeared palm while he droned on about a fresh case he just picked up. Something about the Chief of Patrol's missing daughter. A favor. Big stakes. Terri didn't give a shit. She stayed silent and let the dull whack of her fist against the table say what she couldn't.

"I'll look into the church thing. But that's all I can promise right now," Molina said. "It's the best I can do."

"Your best sucks."

* * * * *

People queued outside the art gallery, with a red carpet lining the sidewalk, flanked by velvet ropes and a bouncer checking invitations on a clipboard. Jake's anxiety grew as impatience and coldness engulfed him.

"These people seem to have an invitation," he said to his uncle.

"Aye. Follow me lead," the priest said with a wink.

"Good evening, gentlemen. May I have your invitations, please?" the man-tower asked.

"Aye, pardon me, me lad. It seems I've misplaced it," Father Duffy said. "I reckon it's in me other coat."

"Your name?" the bouncer asked.

"Ah, indeed. Father Colin Duffy, I am here to carry out the invocation for tonight's gathering."

"You are not on the guest list, Father."

"Ah, well, me son, common sense will tell ya I'm not a guest but part o' the festivities, don't ya know."

"And who is this with you?"

"This be my ward, so it is."

"Ward?" Jake whispered through the side of his mouth.

"What does a ward do?" the bouncer asked.

"Like an altar boy who's got his driver's license, so he has," Father Duffy answered, flashing his steel flask inscribed "*Holy Water*" inside his pocket.

The guard gave his blessing with a head nod to go inside.

The gray cinderblock walls stood tall, transformed into a vibrant canvas as vivid artwork and eclectic sections of raw building materials adorned their surfaces. Miniature street lamps cast a warm golden glow over every display, creating an inviting atmosphere that beckoned onlookers closer. Jake and Father Duffy wandered through a whimsical maze of bubble letters and colorful cartoons, their senses captivated by the playful creativity surrounding them. They ventured into a section featuring a graffiti-tagged number 7 subway car, a striking contrast to more refined pieces nearby.

Countless attendees, dressed in tuxedos and evening gowns, mingled amid the exhibits. Their voices were a symphony of awe and admiration. Some guests traded whispers over flutes of champagne, the bubbles catching the flicker of fake streetlights like stars. Suddenly, a voice echoed through the space, announcing the gathering in the main gallery.

"Ladies and gentlemen, thank you for attending this year's Asphalt Showcase," a young man wearing a turtleneck bellowed. "We have traveled the five boroughs this past year in search of the brightest and most prolific artists in New York City. To give them recognition and a voice in our modern world."

Jake tuned out most of the master of ceremonies' chatter and name-dropping until the MC introduced an Info Group representative; he did not catch her name. She was stunning in a shimmering, fitted gown and with perfect, braided red hair. Her lipstick sparkled with every word she spoke.

"Sing X regrets that they could not make it here tonight."

A tremendous amount of laughter followed the statement.

"I was instructed to tell you that it was because of, now I'm quoting, a personal matter."

More laughter. The graceful speaker gave the crowd a warm smile. Jake did not understand the joke.

"But more important is the reason you are all standing here."

The MC pulled a white sheet at the far end of the stage and revealed a wooden sawhorse; a police barricade used to section off parade routes. The artist painted it a depressing gray and stenciled a silhouette of the city skyline across the beam. Each World Trade Center tower had blue, red, and green ribbons, which represented first responders.

"This simple design captures the love of the American hero. Sing X will donate all proceeds to the Widows and Orphans Fund for our 9/11 heroes. Thank you, and God bless."

The representative walked off the stage without saying another word, leaving everyone to scream out questions.

"I bet you she is the real Sing X," Jake whispered in his uncle's ear and slipped away into the crowd.

He pushed through a knot of tuxedos and sequins, eyes locked on the shimmer of her gown as she disappeared down a side hallway. By the time he reached it, he only caught the flash of a shiny high heel stepping into the ladies' restroom. He was sure they were the same heels the redheaded orator wore. Father Duffy caught up with his nephew in the hallway. Jake was propped up against the wall, thumbing his stone.

"I think some sort of crime goin' on here, lad," the priest said.

"She went in here. I want to ask some questions."

"I know ye do. But it might put the lass off a bit, ye stalkin' outside the jacks."

"Jacks?"

"Toilets," his uncle clarified.

A blonde woman stepped out and gave the two a polite nod as she walked down the hallway. It was not the same woman. She seemed shorter and dressed in a business suit. Jake noticed the same shiny heels sticking out of a tote bag.

"Miss? Miss? You dropped something," Jake said.

She shifted, glancing down, then toward Jake.

"I don't think so," she said.

Jake held up his phone with a picture of The Fade's symbol, keeping his eyes wide open.

The woman looked less than interested. "Um, yes. Very nice." She turned to walk away.

"Don't you recognize this?" Jake asked.

"Why? Should I?"

"You spray-painted this. Aren't you Sing X?"

"Oh. I see. Goodbye now." The woman turned and walked away.

"No. Please. Wait. I'm not some artsy, stalker guy. I don't even own a turtleneck."

She waved her hand and kept walking.

"The lad's in a bit of a spot, Miss. He's not tellin' you porridge," Father Duffy called after her.

She stopped. "I assure you. I am not Sing X."

"Where can I meet with him or her?"

"Sing X is anonymous. Or possibly it is a concept. There is no way to meet with him or her or anything else."

"It's about this symbol and what it represents," Jake said.

She turned around and made eye contact.

"Again. I assure you. I have no idea what you are talking about. Good evening to you."

Jake turned to his uncle for more advice. Father Duffy shrugged his shoulders and took a swig from his flask. When Jake turned around to the hallway, the woman was gone.

"Oh, miss? Ye dropped something," the priest mimicked Jake in a cutesy voice. "I'll admit it. I was fairly impressed with that one, I was!"

"I needed to get her attention. It worked."

"Ah, it did. It worked a treat for Ted Bundy, too."

"You think she thinks I'm a serial killer?"

"Without a doubt."

"I still think that lady is Sing X, and she knew exactly what I was talking about."

"That's why yer still single, me boy. Ye don't know how to read a lass," Father Duffy teased.

"Says the celibate one."

"Touché."

* * * * *

Jake returned to his father's hideout, his heart racing with the thrill of his new obsession. Thoughts of his father's fear and determination swayed in his stomach like the pirate ship ride at an amusement park. Jake was proud but also felt like throwing up. He spent some time organizing the surrounding clutter, the air thick with anticipation. Though he intended to pack everything to take home, something held him back. A sense of foreboding lingered as he prepared to leave. Darkness dropped over him like a curtain. He walked toward the door, his hand trembling as it hovered over the cool handle. A sound shattered the silence: a footstep in the alley. He froze as a stranger emerged from the shadows, removing a blue ski cap and lighting a candle.

The stranger slipped from view, but Jake's pulse quickened as he caught the unsettling sounds of rustling.

Was the man bending down, inspecting something?

Time dragged on as Jake's heart jackhammered in his chest. When he finally dared to breathe, the stranger reappeared, strolling away with an unsettling calm. Jake stayed rooted to the spot, mind racing to catch up with what he'd just seen.

Jake found it odd that the person before him didn't look like a homeless person. The stranger wore an LA Dodgers baseball jersey and dark, baggy jeans. He walked a few feet toward the street, then spun around and locked eyes with Jake. Although Jake wanted to slam the door shut, he couldn't move. The stranger rubbed his goatee, looking nervous and confused, then reached into his pocket, pulled out peanuts, and broke open the shells. He walked toward the door, bobbing and weaving as he ate one after another. He kept sucking his bottom lip between bites.

Panicked, Jake departed that entrance and then slipped from the step's edge. He tripped down the three steps to the dusty garage floor, too numb from emotion to sense pain.

Jake watched the mysterious man scrutinize the crack in the doorway, each second dragging with ominous weight. An icy dread crept along his spine; his eyes remained riveted on the gap, unblinking. His hands trembled uncontrollably. His mind raced for escape, but the stranger, now near the metal door, seemed to sense his fear. Every muscle in Jake's body felt frozen, his legs like stone, rooted to the ground as darkness closed in.

The trespasser slipped through the narrow opening, and Jake's adrenaline surged. With a fierce battle cry, he leaped onto the platform. Jake charged at the stranger, who let out a high-pitched scream as he tumbled to the ground. Falling peanuts crackled through the garage as the men collided, limbs thrashing.

They slammed to the floor, the impact rattling through Jake's ribs. Moonlight slashed through the doorway, spilling silver across their faces. Jake's pulse thundered, his breath sharp, every nerve screaming. The intruder froze for a beat; eyes locked on his. A grin split the stranger's face, too wide, too knowing. A jagged, nervous laugh broke the silence, echoing in the dark like a promise of something far worse to come.

"You're back. Oh dang, I knew it. Yes! Yes! Yes! You're finally back!"

Jake's words caught in his throat. Fear gripped him as he hesitated; his hold on the stranger slipped. In a struggle, they wrestled, grunting. Jake locked eyes with the looming figure.

"Oh. I'm happy to see you, man! It's been a long time!" The man jumped up and stomped around in a fit of excitement. "Yo, man. I kept watch for you. I kept you up in this dang city. This is great!"

"What in the world are you talking about?" Jake snapped.

The animated stranger seemed to deflate. "What'cha mean, man? It's me!"

"What?" It felt to Jake that the circus had set up its big top in his brain, complete with carnival music.

"It's Sing. Sing X, man? It had to be you looking for me."

Jake was indeed dumbfounded. His eyes darted around as if the logical response was scrawled somewhere on the filthy walls.

"Yo, man, what's wrong with you?" Something dawned on him. "Oh, dip man. Sorry to bust into your crib like that. You haven't been around in years, and I saw the door open a little. I wasn't sure if. Oh, and your mask. I didn't see your face or nuttin'. Just your eyes. That's how I recognized you. I didn't see anything, man. Sorry."

Sing backed up toward the doorway, looking down.

"Hey, listen. I'm not who you think I am."

"Yo. It's alright, man. I didn't see your face. You always trusted me, man."

"I'm telling you, man. I'm not him."

Something seemed to click with Sing, and he froze in place. "Then what are you doing here?" he asked in a little more articulate voice.

"It's my father's place. I'm not sure why I'm here."

Sing became very serious and stared into Jake's eyes once again. "You shouldn't be here then."

Jake had become more defensive now. "Who the hell do you think you are, telling me?"

"You got it wrong, cat. You really shouldn't be here." Sing's demeanor transformed, and Jake was preparing for another grapple. "You have his eyes," Sing whispered as he looked at the floor. "Is he gone?"

Jake was so taken aback by the question that he let his guard down and answered.

"Yes."

The two men both jumped when Father Duffy tried poking his head through the half-open door. Sing gave another little high-pitched squeal and raced to slam the door, but Jake grabbed his wrist.

"Wait! He's with me."

Sing X backed off and became more vocal again. "You shouldn't be here. You've got to leave."

Father Duffy pushed open the door a little more and slid himself in.

"Jake? Are ya alright?"

"I'm all right. What're you doing here?"

"Of course ye'd come here. Ye really shouldn't have to do this alone."

"Really?" Jake asked.

"I'll admit it now. I'm also a wee bit curious and a touch worried about ya. Is there a bit of light in here, or what?"

Sing X answered, "Let's keep it dark. I don't need to see you, and you don't need to see me. Trust me, it's better this way."

"Jake, are ya bein' robbed, are ya?" Father Duffy asked through the corner of his mouth.

Sing X erupted. "What, motherfletcher? A black man asked to keep it dark, and you, white folk, immediately assume someone's being robbed. Ain't that some dip."

Jake jumped into the mix.

"Everybody, stop! I'm not being robbed. This is Sing X, apparently."

Sing X interrupted, "Listen. I doubt that he'd want you here. You shouldn't get involved."

Father Duffy asked, "Who'd he be then?"

"The Fade," Sing whispered and looked around as if someone else was watching.

Jake looked around in the dark and asked, "The what?"

"The Fade. From what I guess, your father."

"What does that even mean?" Jake asked.

"That's what we call him on the streets. I've already said too much. Y'all got to go. You don't want to know nothin'."

Sing X appeared to have tears in his eyes as they glistened in what little light the doorway provided.

Father Duffy stood beside Jake and touched his shoulder, sensing his tension. Although shaken and lost, Jake tried hard to keep the conversation going.

"The Fader?"

"The Fade," Sing corrected.

"He couldn't have come up with anything better than that. It sounds like a bad haircut or something."

Jake tried to maintain a conversational demeanor.

"We named him."

"Who's WE?" Father Duffy now showed interest in continuing this latest revelation.

"The street. Everyone knows The Fade, man. Where in the hell have YOU been?"

"Not there at all, I promise ya," Father Duffy expressed.

Sing now looked as if he had missed something.

"Hell. He wasn't there in hell," Jake needed to clarify. "He's a priest."

"Oh. Damn. I mean, Dang. Sorry, Padre. It's dark. I..."

"Aye, it's all right, me lad. I've a good sense of humor, I do."

Sing turned preacher-like, head tilted skyward. "This could be a sign."

"Sign?" Father Duffy asked, curious that Sing was now talking more in his language.

"I prayed every day that he would return. The people in this city need him more than ever. News is spreading that The

Fade hasn't been around in a while. It's starting to get ugly again. Now, it seems the Holy Father has sent you as an answer. Praise Jesus, Allah and Moses, or whoever it was that answered."

"Oh, um, yes. Praise Jesus and the like," Father Duffy responded, feeling that he needed to confirm an answered prayer with a fellow believer. A little help to lean into what Father Duffy saw as the right direction couldn't hurt.

"My father has been sick for the last five years. He hasn't been here for at least that long," Jake said.

Sing gave a crooked smile. "I have been keeping him out here. Well, in a manner of speaking."

"What! What's that supposed to mean?" Jake spat.

"I'm like his personal calling card, letting the people know when he's been around. It reminds them that they have a guardian angel, a savior. Hope, man. There is always hope."

"Them's some mighty strong adjectives ye've used to describe someone, isn't it?" Father Duffy stated.

Sing became solemn. "There is nothing but the truth in the words I speak."

"If it is the same fella we're both talking about, I'm completely with you on some points," Father Duffy said in the same solemn tone.

Sing X continued, "He was what this city needed and embraced. He was a champion among the people. He brought hope to everyone he encountered. It least the good people, anyway. I couldn't let that virtue wither into disappointment and despair. I continued by notifying the residents he served that he was still out there. This maintained order. It kept the denizens of discontent guessing and kept hope alive. I assumed he would come back someday."

Sing bowed his head.

"I've been doing it for so long."

He reached into his pocket for another peanut.

"A calling card, huh? Oh God, in heaven, please give me a clue to what the hell, I mean, what the heck, is going on here?" Jake figured prayers were working for everyone else present today.

Sing appeared to have snapped out of his gloomy mood, but his anxiety wore on his face like a dirty stain.

"The Fade wouldn't want you to know about him. I suggest you leave it alone. I've already revealed too much, my friend."

Sing then headed toward the door.

"He's my father, damn it!"

Sing turned to Jake.

"The Fade has no family, boy!"

Jake flung himself at the self-proclaimed calling card. Sing let out another high-pitched squeal. He spun around, caught Jake's arm in an arm bar, and pushed the front of his body into the heavy steel door.

"Yo. I'm telling you. The man may have been your daddy, but The Fade is a ghost. They will come for you. He's got a lot of enemies. He's a ghost. Got it? Just a ghost!"

Jake was surprised by Sing X's strength and understood the warning: someone threatened his father, and Sing X was protecting him.

Father Duffy confirmed Jake's suspicions by touching both men's shoulders.

He then said, "Ah, don't worry, lads, I reckon I've a fair idea of what's goin' on here."

 14

"Oh, Penry, what daft mess did you drum up?" Father Duffy wondered aloud as Jake led him into the workroom area.

Jake reached into the darkness, grasping for the dangling string. The fluorescent bulbs buzzed to life with a gentle pull, illuminating the surrounding space. Sing X stood awestruck, his gaze fixed on the mask, the same one that had stared down monsters in alleyways and watched them fold under their own sins. Memories flooded back as he noticed familiar items scattered across the workbench. Recognizing the impact this revelation had on Sing, Jake stood silent and empathetic, giving him the precious time he needed to work through his swirling emotions.

Sing spoke out, his low voice heavy with solemnity.

"I've been following him for years and have never been inside The Fade's lair. Always curious, I imagined it would resemble the Batcave, filled with high-tech gadgets. Now I see he kept everything stored in his mind. He had a talent for being in the right place at the right time. I take that back. A higher authority sent him."

Jake grasped Sing's intent; he couldn't resist, as usual. "He had a boss?"

"Now cut it out." Father Duffy couldn't help himself. He flicked Jake on the forehead. His nephew was unraveling again.

"He was a handyman. I'll even go with the street vendor thing. But running around the city in a rubberized tunic and a *Phantom of the Opera* mask, curing the city's static-cling problem, is not something he would do. He's my dad, a regular guy. I can't believe this is all happening. This is all some kind of sick joke."

Sing let out a passionate yell. "The Fade was a *hero*!"

"Yeah? Where's his cape?" Jake snapped.

"He wore a black trench coat."

Father Duffy stepped between them like a referee tired of watching toddlers fight with knives. "Ah, enough now. Jacob, we have a situation here, an' ye need to make it easier. So, as nicely as I can say it...shur tyer trap and listen to the man."

Jake dragged his fingertips across the stress stone in his pocket, a habit now pushing like a second heartbeat. His silence was graceful; grudging, strangled, held together by stubbornness and the faint authority of his uncle's voice.

Sing drifted toward the shelves, eyes wide with something approaching reverence.

"This is some library in here." He murmured, running his hand across a row of cracked spines. "You think The Fade read all these?" Jake watched him thumb through yellowed pages, pause over entries about fingerprint powders and blood-drop trajectories. A tug of memory tightened in Jake's chest.

"I didn't even know he could read," Jake commented.

His uncle shot him another unhappy look.

"What? I'm just kidding. I just don't remember ever seeing him read, well, anything."

Sing X continued. "Everyone loved or feared him. For over thirty years, he ripped the 'Kick Me' sign off the backs of the residents of this city. The Fade stood up to the street-level bullies that plague our society," Sing boasted.

"Over thirty years, is it?" Father Duffy exclaimed, clearly taken aback. "Penry never said a word. Not a peep. He's just my..."

"Yeah, it's been at least that long since I started to hear about him."

Jake was not following and asked, "What do you mean, heard about him?"

"Oh man, only a few of us playas heard of him back then. He didn't even have a name yet. Thugs only described his eyes. Two different colors. They were getting jumped by this unknown specter that seemed to come out of nowhere, and before they passed out, they could only see his eyes as he faded away, like a ghost. That was a long time ago. Now, everybody knows he is out there watching over them. He's a legend."

"He's just my dad, just...my dad."

Sing X lunged for something of note on the bookshelf. "Ah! He kept it!" He handed Jake a paperback entitled *The Chronicles of Chronic Christmas*, written by Hornsby "Christmas" Holiday.

"This motherfletcher wrote a stupid book detailing all his misdeeds. It was mostly made up, but it mentioned The Fade in a chapter. I left it in the dumpster for him to read, as a gift."

"Why the dumpster?" both Jake and Father Duffy asked at the same time.

"That's where I would leave him information. I told you we never spoke. Anyway, he got some justice for some unfortunate souls in the stories, the true ones, at least."

Jake turned to his uncle. "Have you ever heard of this?"

Duff looked pale. "I'm afraid not, lads. Never would've thought Penry might've been some vigilante."

Sing's voice jumped all over Father Duffy's. "No names! I don't want to know anything about names. That's how he has stayed successful all these years. Everyone knows not to question The Fade's identity. This ain't no comic book. There are evil men out there who would use personal information like that to destroy him and everyone close to him. It's one of the few things he had ever said to me. Keep his identity anonymous, and we'll be straight. I never questioned that."

"So, you did know him?" Jake asked.

"Man, I told you. The Fade never spoke to me, and I never spoke to him out of respect."

"You said one of the few times he spoke to you."

"Motherfletcher, don't read too much into this. It's bad enough I'm even talking to you. Go now. You said he's dead. Go so that I can keep my word to him. I will tell everyone he's a hero." Sing took a heavy sigh. "And tell no one The Fade is gone."

Jake put his hands on his head and grunted out of pure frustration. "Now, what is that supposed to mean?"

"Look, man, it's not like I don't understand that you're upset, but trust me, the less you know, the better off you'll be. It can be a tremendous burden to know who your father was. Trust in why he never told you. That's all I can say."

Sing looked into Jake's eyes again. Jake stared back and realized Sing was much older than he first thought. The staring contest let each participant know they were both serious about their stance. Father Duffy broke up the match by stepping between the two men.

"The lad's dad has passed on. It's right that he should know who his dad was and what he stood for. A man's son can only be guided in this life by the footprints of his dad's shoes. They were as thick as thieves. I can see why he never told a soul, especially his only son, but sure, that's how it is now. Let the lad decide how his dad's memory should unfold."

Uncle Duff's words moved Jake. A large lump formed in his throat, making it difficult for him to talk.

"I couldn't go by my mother's footprints; they were much too small."

Father Duffy slapped Jake's head playfully and said, "Honor thy mother and..."

"Yeah. Yeah, I got it. I got it," Jake remarked as he stepped away. His quip did not impress Sing.

"This isn't a joke, boy."

"All right. I got that too. Look, X-Man..."

"It's Sing X. MY MAN."

"Yeah. That too. I'm a big boy now. I must know what he was doing. I can't help it. What would you do if you found out your father was this crazy Don Quixote type? He's all dressed up in a Halloween costume and trying to joust all the city's skyscrapers with some electric shaver?"

Sing gave a quick answer. "I suggest taking advice from someone who knows a little more about it."

"So, I just walk away?"

"Yes, I'm not saying it's not hard to do, but it will probably keep you and everyone around you safe."

"Safe from what, exactly?" Father Duffy asked.

"I told you. The Fade had a habit of pissing off the real dregs of society. To be sure, there are numerous prices on his head and other body parts. He was smart, though. He kept them at bay. Well, until now, I guess."

Sing bowed his head.

"What do you mean, until now? He's been sick for years. He hasn't been your Darth Fader since...for five or six years." Jake was exhausted. He realized how whiny he sounded as the words came out of his mouth, but he was much too tired by now to care.

"How did he die?" Sing asked.

"I believe that is none of your business," Jake snapped.

"Probably not," Sing agreed. "Please tell me nobody got to him."

"He was sick. Let's leave it at that."

Father Duffy rubbed his head. "How do ya fit into all this, Mr. X?"

"I told you. I'm The Fade's voice on the street. I keep him in their hearts so there's no chance of compromising his identity."

"And how'd ye do that, then?"

"With my art."

"Oh, you must explain that one, of course," Jake stated.

"A symbol. Look around. It's everywhere. Whenever I can confirm a Fade story, I paint a symbol at the incident location. It's my way of letting the public know he's watching." Sing displayed a spray-paint can from under his shirt. "Now I read police reports, and if a thug is arrested, I mark the location. Keeps him around. Get it?"

"A marked territory," Father Duffy stated, to show he was paying attention.

Jake smirked. "Oh, graffiti. I get it!"

"No, motherfletcher. It's called art. Graffiti is what the white man calls a young black urban expressionist's work. It's meant to criminalize their First Amendment right to freedom of speech. Keep the young black man in his place. He can't have no writing on the wall. It might start a revolution or revelation or something."

Jake had the feeling he could not win that argument.

"We can't have that in America, can we?" Sing X's sarcasm again oozed.

"Why were ya doin' this if he wanted to keep quiet an' stay anonymous?" Father Duffy asked.

"Every city needs a hero, hope," Sing X stated.

"And it just so happens that it was my father." Jake was proud but apprehensive about accepting the idea. "What's in it for you?" Jake asked.

"What? Does a brother have to get something out of this? Yeah, I got something out of all this. Thanks to him, I got righteousness, dignity, faith...and my life."

"How?" Father Duffy asked.

"No disrespect to the cloth, Padre, but I'd rather not divulge my info. I don't go around asking why you became a priest!"

Jake let his curiosity get the better of him. His voice conveyed innocence. "Listen, Sing. I'm starting to like these stories. How did you get involved with all this? How did my father become this Faderman?"

"I honestly don't know how he became what he was. He was already making a name for himself before I met him for the first time. My path was quite different then."

Sing's voice softened to a whisper, creating an uneasy stillness that hung in the air. Jake and Father Duffy exchanged worried glances, aware of Sing's need for space. They stood by in silence. Sing took a moment to gather his thoughts, preparing to share his story with them.

"There was this stone-cold crackhead named Jo-Jo..." Sing began. "The worst kind, too. He robbed, stole, scammed...hell, he even came close to suckin' the pink rocket once. He did some runnin' for a local dealer named Little Man in Vinegar Hill back in the day. Little Man ran the Farragut Houses. Two-bit thug. He used to bully all the crackheads around, but he would give them rocks for what he called 'missions' when they had no greens. He also had two-fer Tuesdays."

Chapter 15

"Where's the money, you little shit?" Little Man asked.

"Yo, I'll get it. You know I always get it. I'm good for it, man."

"Fuck it. I got a mission for you."

"I'll do anything," the crackhead said.

"I got this cache of uncut groceries coming in from Virginia. Don't need to get busted by no pigs while holding the stuff in case of a snitch. I'll give you ten yellow tops to go with me to the Port Authority for the exchange."

"Yeah, yeah, I can do that, man. I got you."

Little Man proceeded to beat the living hell out of him with a baseball bat. "Cops do not like searching bloody, messy crackheads and then babysitting them all night in a hospital," he explained.

"Please, man! Please stop. I can get it," Jo-Jo pleaded.

Little Man kept laughing as he continued the beating. "Stop crying and walk it off, you little bitch."

Mixed up, alone and scared, the teenage addict struggled to walk as Little Man dragged him by the neck to the subway. Bystanders on the train stared in horror.

"Mind your fuckin' business. I'm taking my puppet to the hospital. He'll be fine."

Some people kept to their own business as usual. Some even laughed as Little Man continued to taunt and humiliate the born loser.

Who cares about a skinny, bleeding nigga junkie anyway? Jo-Jo thought.

The two arrived at the Port Authority, and Little Man oversaw the exchange as planned. As Jo-Jo walked away from the supplier, Little Man came up from behind and kicked him square in the ass. The two jovial dealers had a good laugh as the weak, pathetic crackhead lay crumpled on the floor in front of everyone.

The drug-riddled kid couldn't take it anymore: the withdrawals, the humiliation, the cowardice. Most of all, he could not take the laughing.

Jo-Jo remembered when he found his mother dead in their disgusting apartment when he was twelve. She was sitting on a soiled five-gallon bucket with a rusty needle sticking out of her arm. She must have been there for at least three days, surrounded by used condoms and maggots. When the cops came and lifted her stiff body and put her on the ambulance gurney, she was still in that sitting position. They laid her on her back so her arms and legs hung in the air like some dead cartoon animal.

The cops and the investigators all laughed. They laughed even harder when they saw she released her bowels into the bucket when she was shooting up. One of them gagged and choked from the smell. One insensitive officer threw up on the living room floor from cackling so hard. He then threw some garbage over his vomit and left it while everyone howled in hysterics. Jo-Jo stood there, stripped of all faith in anything, amid their laughter. His mother's empty eyes stared at him from that ambulance gurney. Empty as his heart. Empty as his life.

"There would never again be laughter from this child." Sing X sighed and shook his head. The story continued.

Jo-Jo lay on grimy tile in the dirty Port Authority. The dark, depressing hulk of 8th Avenue heaved body odor and bus exhaust. It was the kind of place where two low-life dealers could nearly beat a crackhead to death without drawing attention. Jo-Jo couldn't get any lower than that rancid floor.

I made shit decisions in this shitty life. I'm going to die anyway. Fuck it. Fuck Little Man. Fuck that laughing.

The boy picked himself up from the floor, grabbed the package and ran. "Laugh at this, motherfuckers!" he shouted back, limping away.

Jo-Jo remembered that Little Man had no gun on his person and ran into the subway tunnel. They tried to pursue him, but Jo-Jo was agile despite his injuries. He ran on pure adrenaline. Besides, the dealers were slow and fat. He doubted they would even enter its opening.

The A train's headlights came fast up the tunnel. Jo-Jo found an indented section of the tunnel wall and flattened himself against it. The rushing train screamed inches away from his nose. When the train passed, Jo-Jo couldn't believe his luck. He survived. Little Man probably figured he was dead now.

Jo-Jo's heart thumped hard as doubt and fury mixed inside him. His destination didn't matter anymore, only the revenge. He had secured the package, stolen Little Man's precious money rock, and now Little Man's laughter was gone, replaced by shock and rage. The thrill of victory burned within him.

* * * * *

"So, what happened next?" Father Duffy asked with intense interest.

"The kid surfaced back in Brooklyn a few weeks later, completely strung out and wasted on Little Man's devil rock. He spilled half of it onto the tracks and half into his lungs. He went back to hustling the streets, and Little Man got word from the regular snitches that Jo-Jo had been seen in the Fulton Mall area. Little Man and his crew found him in this very alley, which at the time was his home. It was hidden out of the way, and nobody bothered him here until then. They surprised the poor little fletcher as he sketched out a black man in chains on a pad."

Sing became teary-eyed and choked up as he continued.

* * * * *

"Get on your mutha fuckin' knees, you thieving bitch!" Little Man grunted as he aimed the .357 Magnum at Jo-Jo's head.

"Please, Little Man. I'm sorry. I'm sorry. I was sick. I fucked up."

One of the gangster's thugs chimed in, "Yo, fuck this sucka junkie," before another shouted, "Ice him, man. He was disrespectful."

"I'll make it up to you. Please, God. Oh God, please. I promise. All of it," Jo-Jo begged.

Little Man rolled his chin, cracking his neck, and asked, "Do you believe in God?"

* * * * *

Sing X looked up at the ceiling and continued. "Do you have any idea what that stupid mother fletcher said?"

"No?" Jake answered.

"He said YES! Why the fletch would he answer yes to such a ridiculous question? Of course, he didn't believe in God. Why? God hasn't done anything for him. God didn't save his mother. There was no God. We are all animals. Survival of the fittest. No heaven! Jo-Jo would have ended his life years ago if there were one. No hell, or was he in it already? What does a clumsy outcast of society want with a God, anyway? Why the heck did he answer YES?"

"Your God can't help you now," Little Man said, pressing the gun to the kid's head. "Tell your God, I said, fuck you!"

Sing X continued.

"Little Man passed judgment on that boy as if he were God. He executed that poor, selfish crackhead. The world was indeed a better place now that there was one less junkie on this planet, desecrating the good earth's soil.

"His useless body was thrown into a dumpster and left for the maggots. They say when you are about to die, you should say some last rite prayer or something. He prayed for the first time in his now shortened life and he died alone."

Jake winced his face, "Um, you're standing right here."

"Don't interrupt me, motherfletcher!" Sing snapped. "Now, where the heck was I?"

"Dead," Father Duffy answered.

"Yeah, dead! That's when it happened. A rebirth. An answered prayer. I'm talking salvation on a major scale. God sent him, the eyes. I heard about 'em. Some saw anger, others gratitude. His arrival was mysterious. A ghost, a spirit, an angel sent by the Holy Father to save one forgotten child.

"I was reborn that night. A believer. Maybe that poor crackhead was right to have answered yes. Perhaps the man upstairs appreciated that. This was my calling. I needed to share my faith, a righteous answer to prayers. The Fade pulled me out of that metal crypt. How could anyone know I was there? There was an ambulance. They said an anonymous caller reported a male shot in this alley. Police were everywhere. I lost a significant amount of blood and was at risk of bleeding to death. Transfusions became necessary to save my life. The Fade was responsible for calling the ambulance."

"What happened to Little Man?" Jake asked.

"I messed that motherfletcher up self-defense style. There were like three of them. They tried to rob me in the alley and shot me in the head. Somehow, it didn't hit major parts of my brain, but it cracked my skull pretty good. Before I fell unconscious, I had enough adrenaline to fight them off. I knocked them all out, too. Cops found them lying right on the sidewalk outside the alley. Gun and all. Motherfletchers spent like ten years in Attica for that dip."

"'Tis a miraculous tale altogether. The Holy Father was surely keepin' an eye on ya that night," Father Duffy stated with a smile.

"It was the least that motherfletcher could do after my dippy childhood. Still, it had to come with a price." Sing paused to grab a brownish pill bottle from his pocket. He unscrewed the top and fished out one of the pills. "I get seizures when I'm excited. Some fragments had to be left in the dome."

Jake smirked. "The cops bought that story, that after being shot in the head, you beat up three drug dealers and knocked them all out?"

"Nah, not at first. The three woke up and said I'd shot myself and they were trying to stop me. Then, they described what happened after that. Some ghost came in and robbed them. Po-po and the jury figured my version was more believable."

Father Duffy rubbed his chin. "Why didn't ye tell the truth, then?"

Sing looked grim as he answered, "They would look for him. Cops aren't as dumb as some people might think. They understand a lot more about the happenings out here. They are out there, day after day, searching for answers to all kinds of things. So, with that experience, cops get good at catching people. I didn't want them to catch The Fade when they should have embraced him. So, I told them it was all me. The jury bought it."

"Surely the cops know about him if he is that famous," Jake attempted to point out.

"Some seasoned cops followed the stories about him throughout the years. Word on the street was that some cops were looking to bust him, and better ones were happy to turn a blind eye. Still, others chose not to believe the stories at all. All the better. The street kept him hidden. We need him. We need his spirit of hope."

"Hope," Jake said aloud. "The ACS lady could've probably used Dad."

Sing X interrupted. "I'm checking out. I got to go see a lady about a cat. You appear to have an overabundance on your silver platters, and I'm not here to serve you any additional dishes. I hate to leave you high and dry, so take my card."

He handed Jake a shiny black metallic business card, which read:

Hell's Kitchen X Show Card

"What's this?" Jake asked.

"If you ever need hard-to-find information," Sing answered.

"Well, isn't that what we are doing here now?"

"Don't use the card for yourself. Please pay it forward. I can't help *you* any more than I have."

"Who is The Jypsy?" Jake blurted out.

Sing looked paler than a winter morning. "Another name for The Devil." His delivery was hushed and apprehensive.

"What? What does that even mean?" Jake asked.

"I've got to go."

"Yer more than welcome to join me and the congregation at St. Francis Xavier on 16th Street and 5th Avenue. Don't hesitate to look me up. It'd be a grand thing for some to pray with a true witness."

Sing paused. "Saint Francis X? L.O.L. Rain check, Padre."

Before Jake could ask any more questions, Sing X walked out of the garage with a quick sign of the cross to Father Duffy. The cleric observed him sign himself wrong, but there was no use trying to correct him. Sing X was already halfway to the street.

"Well, that was entertaining, huh? He gave you a Laugh Out Loud. That was funny," Jake said.

"Yes. I suppose you would think so."

"Why did you come here?" Jake asked.

"I was thinkin' 'bout it after ye dropped me off, this whole vigilante business. I feel like a right eejit that I never knew what me best mate was up to. How could he keep such a secret? I'd never have suspected somethin' so mad. He was always obsessed with the news and the local papers. Things are finally makin' sense to me now."

"What things?"

"Well, after your dad was admitted to the care facility, I went to see him a lot, y'know. Most times, he wouldn't say a word to me. But now and again, he'd be spoutin' off gibberish. It was almost like he was havin' a proper chinwag about bein' robbed, findin' drugs or scrappin' with someone. I believed he was talkin' about his imagined dealings with the other residents or PTSD from Vietnam."

"Yeah, I've had those moments too with him."

"Ah, but lookin' back on what we know now, I reckon yer dad was tryin' to tell us somethin'."

"Tell us what?"

"I'm not sure. About what he may have been doin'?"

"So, you wanted to come here and look again for yourself?"

"Like I told ya before, boy. I know ya. I saw you were obsessed and figured you'd return here. I had to come back to tell ya somethin' else."

Jake's heart skipped two beats as he swallowed hard.

"Yer dad's next-door neighbor..."

"Mrs. Daschle?"

"Ah, no. The older fella at the care facility. The one that sings the songs, he does."

"Cook?"

"Aye. Him. He once told me it was a pity that yer dad was a proper superhero. Figured he was auld and addled like Penry."

"Don't let that crazy old guy fool you. I believe he's full of shit most of the time," Jake said.

"Ah, sure. Then he went on about somethin' more interestin'. He told me to always look out for the boy. I reckon he meant you. The old coot even made me promise Penry. And of course, I kept me word."

"Shit. I'm not sure I want to fall into this rabbit hole."

"Jake, me lad, when ye stumble into shite, ye splash a belly flop," Jake's godfather said with a smile.

"Call it a talent."

Chapter 16

T erri hadn't slept. Not really.

Every time she closed her eyes, Hope's face flickered in the dark like a broken bulb. The little girl who chose her, the one nobody wanted her to love, the reason she was sitting on forced leave while the city spun without her.

She lay in bed, staring at the ceiling, bruised by a night that refused to let her go. Her thoughts kept circling the same drain:

The hardware store,

The cult van,

The man who barreled at her from the shadows,

Molina brushing her off like gum on his shoe.

She rolled onto her side. Then on her back. Then into a fetal curl.

Nothing helped. Peace was a rumor people with normal lives talked about.

Around dawn, exhaustion finally dragged her under, not sleep, just a thin, haunted drift.

Her phone shattered it.

Ring, ring

"Hello?"

"It's Detective Molina."

Terri sat up, pulse spiking. "What's up?"

"Listen. I need you to come to my office ASAP."

Her voice sharpened. "Is it about Hope?"

"No," Molina said. "Something else."

She got dressed and was out the door in ten minutes.

Terri stood at Molina's desk, surrounded by celebrity photos, waiting for a sign that he was ready to host a female guest. He studied his reflection in a desktop mirror and smoothed his greased-back hair. Then, like Jay Leno, he invited her to sit in the guest chair. Terri noticed Molina glance at his arms, which tensed as he spoke.

"I got a call from our Technical Assistance Response Unit while at Dumbbells."

"Did you say Dumbbells?" Terri asked.

"Yeah. My gym."

"Wait, you go to a gym called Dumbbells?"

"It's a legendary place. It's a chain. Many celebrity fitness enthusiasts go there. They're in all five boroughs. You need a sponsor to get in. If you're interested, I can..."

"No. Not interested. Why am I here?"

"Well, anyway, I need you to look at this surveillance footage."

Molina pecked at his keyboard. A grainy video popped up on the monitor. The two men in the video were walking on a sidewalk. A cab pulled up, and a third person, a woman, stepped onto the screen. All three had a brief conversation. Then one of the males, accompanied by the female, got inside the taxi.

"Okay. Sooooo?" Terri asked.

"Do you recognize any of these people?"

"Not really. No."

Molina paused the replay and spun the mouse wheel. The image zoomed in on the male entering the taxi.

"Holy shit! That's the garbage guy!" Terri said.

"Yep."

"What's going on?"

"I believe the girl in the video is Chief Beame's daughter, Monica. She's been missing since this video was taken."

"Holy fuck."

"Exactly my thoughts. The other guy seems to be a priest."

"When is this footage from?"

"A little over a week ago," Molina answered.

"When was she reported missing?"

"The day after we met the garbage guy at his garage."

"Damn it," Terri said under her breath.

"Well, spit it out."

"She showed up at the garage after you left. I think she is the garbage guy's girlfriend."

"Tell me more."

"She was intense. A bit obsessive. The guy looked like he wanted to get away from her. It was an unusual exchange. How did you manage to get this footage?"

"Monica used her father's credit card for her bar tab. There was a camera on a bank across the street. One of those new 360-degree ones."

Molina stood and took a coat off a stand-alone rack.

"Where are you going?" Terri asked.

"Going to find out what he knows."

"I'll go with you. I have a better rapport with him."

"I disagree. This is NYPD business. Besides, that asshole is probably the one who dimed you out. Best to let us real detectives handle this."

"Really, Detective? Seriously, do you intend to pull that card?"

"Really, social worker?" Molina retorted. "Unless you want to come to the gym with me one day. They have an incredible health bar."

"Oh my God! Are you joking with me? Are you really going to bribe me for a date? And at a gym?" Terri was proud of herself for calling Molina out.

After a fit of stuttering and stammering from the self-conscious Dick Tracy, Terri walked out of Molina's office, laughing to herself. She had him on his heels. Now it was time for the knockout. "Duh, duh, what was it you said...*spit it out?* I'm coming with you."

"I got his address from a friend in the Sanitation Police Department. Let me do the talking this time," Molina said.

"Don't worry. I don't intend to talk at all."

* * * * *

Jake had the perfect plan to unwind after a long, uneventful shift on the truck. Hot shower, mushroom egg foo young with brown gravy and dumplings from Wo-Hop, NHL '94 on an old Sega and whatever garbage the TV decided to cough up. Probably no pants. It would all be a perfect diversion. The whole thing felt like a peace treaty with life. Maybe he'd grab a mini Junior's cheesecake; game-time decision.

When Jake arrived at his lobby, bounty nestled in his arms, he caught sight of his apartment door hanging open, lock twisted like a broken tooth. The day collapsed.

"Shit."

The hallway hummed its usual fluorescent hum, but everything inside him went quiet. He edged closer. From the doorway, he saw his life overturned; cushions gutted, drawers yanked like dislocated limbs, lamp on its side as if it tried to crawl away. Nothing stolen. Just...

Violated.

He drew two slow breaths and nudged the door open with two fingers.

Darkness waited for him, thick and wrong. His palms were slick with sweat. He eased inside on careful steps that somehow still sounded too loud, each footfall thudding like he was wearing concrete shoes. He scanned every shadow, every corner, bracing for the shape of some tweaked-out stranger crouched and ready.

The apartment breathed around him, settling wood, humming appliances, but no intruder revealed themselves.

Kitchen cabinets were flung open. Silverware scattered like fallen shrapnel. Refrigerator door ajar, leaking cold air.

He moved to the living room. Books tossed. Remote cracked open on the carpet. Couch cushions were torn off and thrown aside in a pattern that felt too deliberate to be random.

A tight, rising frustration began to stifle his ribs. Not quite anger, something sharper. He stepped into the bedroom. It looked like a storm had paused here to admire its own chaos. Sheets were dragged halfway to the floor. Closet door off its track. His alarm clock dangling by its cord, radio mode sputtering static like an insect trapped in glass.

He steadied the clock back onto the nightstand, mind racing.

Should I call the police?

He hesitated. After the missing-kid fiasco, he'd had enough police for a lifetime. The idea of giving someone else control of this moment made his stomach turn.

And then he thought of Mrs. Daschle across the hall. Seventy-five. Stubborn as stone. What if she'd heard something? What if she'd tried to help?

He reached for the alarm clock to shut off the static, only to trigger Mrs. Hitchcock's blood-curdling scream. That shriek ripped through the room like a machete.

A heavy thump answered it from the closet.

Then a low grunt.

Jake froze.

Another breath, another inch of movement. Suddenly, a familiar blade of a hockey stick exploded out of the dark and cracked into his ribs, hurling him against the wall. The room spun. Pain bloomed hot and sharp under his arm. He struggled to catch his breath, and he realized with growing horror that he was not alone.

A man's voice, deep and gravelly, as if he had inhaled lung cancer itself, croaked, "Mind your own business."

As Jake staggered upright, the room still tilting like a rink after a bad line change, he caught only a shadow of the intruder. The guy was already darting toward the door, leaving behind nothing but the thud of heavy steps. Jake's eyes locked onto the only clear detail he could grab: Doc Martens with red laces, cutting through the dark like a warning flare. Everything else about him was swallowed by the apartment's wreckage.

Jake lunged after him, adrenaline making promises his legs couldn't keep. His foot snagged on the same hockey stick that had cracked his ribs, a perfect, humiliating can-opener takedown, the kind defensemen use when the ref's looking the other way. He went down hard, face-first, tasting dust and outrage.

The front door slammed.

His pride hit the floor a second later.

Jake remained sprawled out in confused silence, disgusted that he had taken the slash and trip from his favorite stick. He snapped himself back into the moment and ran to the street, looking in all directions for signs of the escaped intruder. Nobody was around, so he reentered the apartment building and pounded on Mrs. Daschle's door.

Mrs. Daschle reassured Jake that she was fine and saw nothing unusual. Jake returned to his apartment and saw Terri's card still on his kitchen table.

"ACS Friel speaking. How can I help you?"

"Can I speak with Investigator Sheehan?"

"Investigator Sheehan is on leave. Can I help you with something?"

Jake hung up the phone, contemplating his next move, when he heard someone knocking on the front door. It was barely open halfway when Terri pushed her way through, grabbed his shirt and pinned him against the wall. It was the second unexpected attack Jake endured in a matter of minutes, in his own home no less. This one sent a surge of pain through his torso. He didn't know if the pain was from Terri's hit or the earlier beating with the hockey stick.

"What the fuck?!"

"Give me your cell phone."

"What? What for?"

"I said, give me your cell phone!" Terri snarled.

"Whatever. It's in my front pocket."

Terri jammed her hand into Jake's right front pocket.

"Be careful. That tickles," he said.

She pulled the phone out and kneed him hard in the groin. "Does it still tickle?"

Jake stared at Terri for a second, lost for words. Then the aftershock hit his stomach, and he leaned up against the wall, breathing hard. Jake noticed his stress stone on the floor. It must have fallen out when Terri pulled his phone from his pocket. He picked it up and rubbed his thumb up and down along its side.

Terri opened the phone and spotted her office number among his outgoing calls. "You bastard! Why would you do that?"

"What? I didn't do anything!"

"How could you tell them?"

"Tell who what?"

"That I was investigating Hope's case."

"I didn't tell anybody anything."

"Yeah, well, how come I'm suspended, and nobody else knew I was out there? And, your call history shows you called my office."

Terri turned to an amused Molina as he walked in behind all the commotion. "You were right. He did call," Terri said.

"Well, so much for me doing all the talking," Molina countered.

The theme of *The Incredible Hulk* danced around Jake's head. He realized he was now standing upright and backing Terri into a corner while pointing his finger at her face. Terri's eyes widened in recognition of the impending danger. She clenched her fist, ready for the scrap, but backed away in pure instinctive common sense.

"Who do you think you are? Busting in here, assaulting me and making bullshit accusations?! Unless you got a warrant, get the fuck out before I call the real cops."

Molina stepped between Jake and Terri. "I am the real cops! Put your goddamn finger down before I rip it off and shove it straight up your..."

Mrs. Daschle appeared in her doorway, holding a can of hairspray and a lighter. She sparked the lighter and held the aerosol can behind it. "You'd better get out of this building, you animals, or I'll light you up like a California wildfire."

The flame of the lighter reflected in her stormy gray eyes.

"Jacob, call the police. I'll hold them back."

The elderly woman's voice was serious, a seriousness only a caring mother could convey. The sight of a five-foot-tall, seventy-five-year-old woman in a pink housecoat threatening trespassers with a homemade flamethrower brought Jake's anger back to normal levels.

"Don't worry, I got this one. That guy is the real police, and they are leaving."

"So, I shouldn't call the police?" Mrs. Daschle lowered her Aqua Net blowtorch.

"No, we'll probably both end up locked up in the end."

"But she broke into your apartment and wrecked the place," Mrs. Daschle protested.

"No, it wasn't her."

"Wait," Terri jumped in. "Someone broke into your apartment?"

"Whatever," Jake dismissed her. "Nothing taken. Now get out."

"Why did you make a complaint about me? What do you know? And where the hell is your girlfriend?"

"I didn't call to complain about you. I called to tell you about my break-in. Someone answered and told me you were on some kind of leave."

"So, what did you say?"

"Nothing. I hung up. That's it."

"Oh, you just hung up, huh?" a skeptical Terri asked.

"Yeah, I hung up on him when you tried to beat the shit out of me. I mean, really, what's that gonna do for my Manley Men's Club membership?"

"You just hung up the phone? Come on!"

"I'm not answering any more questions without a lawyer," Jake said.

Despite Mrs. Daschle's muted tone, Jake heard Mrs. Daschle say, "I'm your lawyer. It's been many years since I practiced. I was a damn good attorney in my day."

"Oh, come on! This is ridiculous!" Terri shouted. "I want some answers. Give me your damn phone again."

"You don't have to give it to her, Jake. Cops need a warrant for that sort of thing."

"I'm not a cop. Miss...?" Terri paused for the elderly attorney to identify herself.

"Daschle...Mrs. Evelyn A. Daschle. Attorney at law."

It gave her pleasure to state it once more, though she was confident this case was going nowhere. It had been quite a few years since she had used the title.

"I'm an ACS worker investigating a missing child who, thanks to Mr. Johansson here..."

"Please call me Big Jake." After getting beaten up by a girl, he needed to restore order with some of his familiar sarcasm. Especially if it pissed Terri off. But she ignored it.

"I have some evidence that would lead me to believe a foster parent kidnapped her, and now his girlfriend is missing. This big dope calls my office and gets me suspended."

"You have a girlfriend?" Mrs. Daschle asked Jake.

"I told you, I didn't say anything. And for God's sake! I don't have a girlfriend!"

"Why would you get suspended for doing your job, Miss...?" Mrs. Daschle paused for the return identification.

"Sheehan, Terri Sheehan, suspended ACS investigator."

Terri committed the worst possible thing a professional investigator could do. She showed emotion, tears fell. The tiny cough and quick wipe of her sleeve were not enough to fool the other three standing in the hallway. She loved her job and Hope. However, her direction became confusing, and the situation was falling apart. She was not sure why she was standing in Jake's hallway anymore.

"Look at the phone." He handed it over to her.

It showed Terri that he had some compassion. After another fast wipe with her hand, Terri re-examined the outgoing call log that she damned him for. He was telling the truth. He did call moments before. She scrolled down and checked his other past calls.

Who ratted me out? Who knew I was out looking for Hope?

Now, Terri was even more dazed. She took a deep breath and composed herself.

Jake turned to Molina, but he was nowhere to be seen. Terri looked just as confused. Mrs. Daschle nodded her head toward Jake's open apartment door. All three walked in as Molina stepped out of Jake's bedroom.

"Apartment's clear," he said.

Terri meant to speak again. Molina interrupted.

"Mr. Johansson? Would you mind coming down to my office to answer a few questions?"

"Regarding what? I found a necklace in my truck, turned it in to the police and found a weird church cult in a hardware store. That's all I got."

"I'm here regarding a missing young lady named Monica Beame."

"Who the hell is Monica Beame?" Jake asked.

"Pinball Wizard," Terri clarified.

"What? The girl from the other night?" The realization smacked Jake with full force. "She's missing?"

"Best you come with me to my office and answer some questions," Molina said.

"Is she okay?" Jake asked.

"That's why we need to talk. Here is not the place," the detective stated.

"Is he a suspect?" Mrs. Daschle asked.

"Officially? No," Molina answered.

"Well, then, I'm going with you as his attorney."

"Not with that hairspray," Molina quipped. "An evidence collection team will respond here to try and pull some prints or something."

"I guess that would be okay," Jake said.

Molina made a radio call to the dispatcher. Two uniformed officers responded in short order.

"These officers will keep your apartment secure while they wait for evidence collection. A complaint report will be filed for you at the nine-o precinct," Molina stated.

Terri and Molina walked ahead of Jake and Mrs. Daschle.

"You are going to help him even if you suspect him of doing something to that girl?" Terri whispered.

"No. I'm helping my investigation by looking for any evidence linking him to her disappearance without a warrant. It would be too time-consuming. I wish to find her alive. The opportunity presented itself, and I'm taking full advantage."

"So, wait. You took me along to distract him?"

"Sure," Molina said.

"So. The date at the gym."

"No, that was real. I really do..."

"Forget it, Detective. Don't say it," Terri warned as they got into the car.

Chapter 17

Jake and his new attorney followed the detective's car to the Downtown Brooklyn office on Gold Street. Traffic was abysmal on the three-mile trip. The slow crawl past graffiti-tagged garage doors and elevated-highway pillars gave him plenty of time to bring Mrs. Daschle up to speed on the missing girl and the necklace he had found in the bed of his truck.

"Jake, this is not a joke. He will twist your words. He is not one to listen carefully. That's how detectives work. I don't think he will give you a fair..."

Jake interrupted. "It doesn't matter. It's in God's hands. The truth is the truth. Every little detail helps. I owe the Pinball Wizard that much. Whatever it takes to help her."

"I know you will, Jacob. I'm going there with you to advocate for fair treatment."

Every type of police car surrounded the Gold Street office as two cops directed Jake's car into the parking lot. At least fifty law enforcement officials occupied the lot when Molina approached. As Jake opened the door, Molina reached in and pulled him out without any restraint. He slammed Jake hard against the hood and began searching his body for something. Of course, Molina found nothing. The detective reached behind his back, pulled out a pair of handcuffs and secured

Jake's wrists. Jake remained silent, stuck in a blank stare as if lightning had struck him.

Mrs. Daschle jumped out of the car as fast as she could, and Terri stormed to Detective Molina, her eyes flashing with rage. She berated him for his overzealous behavior. Terri demanded to know why he had handcuffed Jake. Mrs. Daschle, trembling with concern, approached and asked Molina if Jake was under arrest. Molina gave a firm and simple response. He assured them they were not arresting Jake but had handcuffed him for safety reasons.

Molina's longtime partner, Detective Liz McColgan, was determined to keep the situation under control. The pretty blonde stepped between Terri and Molina, then escorted them all to the office. Jake remained compliant and silent throughout the ordeal.

Anxiety coursed through Jake like bad electricity. The interview room did nothing to help. It was too quiet, too clean, too square. A shoebox built for panic. The mirrored window stared at him, a cold, unblinking eye pretending it wasn't watching. Every time he tried to look away, he caught his own reflection instead: tired, bruised, confused. A guy who just wanted Wo-Hop and no pants, now sitting in a room where people confessed to murder.

He rubbed his thumb along the stress stone, trying to anchor himself. It didn't work.

The silence pressed on him from all sides, thick enough to chew. His brain wouldn't stop. Monica Beame's face. The hardware store. Terri's kneeing in the balls. The cult. His busted apartment. His father's mask. Sing X calling his father, The Fade, "a ghost."

Everything tangled.

He unscrewed the cap on the water bottle and took a sip. The cold did nothing for the dryness in his throat. It felt like the room was drinking it faster than he was. Jake swallowed, stared at the metal table, and wondered when his life had stopped belonging to him.

Jake kept envisioning the Pinball...Monica Beame, hurting herself or meeting some psycho-killer stranger. The thought of the pretty little witch crying, *Why don't you like me, Jake? The Astro-Time Continuum...*

"Sit up straight, boy!"

Jake did not realize he was even slouching. Like a battering ram, Molina stormed into the room, interrupting Jake's macabre visions. Molina sat on the chair backward and leaned forward.

"Is this necessary?" was all Jake could muster.

"I'll sit any way I feel like it," Molina snarled.

Jake could tell the detective worried he overplayed the macho-man chair routine, but figured he'd take a different approach. "No, I mean the dramatic police TV show stuff. I think you are trying too hard to impress someone."

He regretted it the second it left his mouth.

"What are you talking about?" Molina lost himself for a moment.

"Investigator Sheehan?"

Molina leaned toward Jake, and Jake stared right back into his eyes, waiting for the detective to fly off the handle into a tirade. But Jake was the one flying. He hit the floor with a bang. He never saw it coming. Molina let go of Jake's tipped-over chair.

"I now have your undivided attention!"

Jake was a little stunned as he sat on the floor. "I'm not sure you can do that," Jake whined.

"I'm so sorry, sir. I believe that the chair may be broken. Please, take mine." Molina stood up and tossed his chair at Jake. Not too hard. Enough to prove a point. Molina was following no actual rules now, and Jake was terrified.

Detective Molina informed Jake of his Miranda rights.

"Where's Mrs. Daschle?" Jake whined.

"Who?"

"The lady I was with. My attorney."

"Yeah, the old lady is busy at the moment. How do you know, Monica?"

"I met her at a bar," Jake huffed.

Detective McColgan led Mrs. Daschle into the room.

"Are you okay, Jacob?" she asked.

"He's fine. We are just getting started," Molina answered before Jake could.

"How the fuck did Polaroid photographs of you, Mr. Johansson, get into a police chief's department car?"

"How the fuck would I know?" Jake said.

"What is going on here, Detective?" Mrs. Daschle asked.

"An unmarked police vehicle was found unoccupied on the center span of the Verrazzano Bridge. The car was assigned to an NYPD chief whose daughter was reported missing."

"The Pinball Wizard is a police chief's daughter?" Jake asked.

"Glad you're paying attention. Why are you calling her the Pinball Wizard?" Molina growled.

Jake's gaze moved from Mrs. Daschle to the mirror. He knew the police chief had to be watching. "She said she was a wizard, uh, at pinball," Jake lied.

"Really?" Molina huffed.

"He answered your question," Mrs. Daschle said.

Having the lawyer present complicated Molina's interrogation. Ninety minutes of twisted scenarios, retraced driving routes and cab-ride conversations shattered everyone's patience. Molina's voice was hoarse from the strain of this futile interrogation.

Jake told him most of the truth. Molina could get nothing incriminating. Jake was innocent; Molina might have realized that now. Would he allow himself to believe it? That was a real challenge. Molina's career was at stake in this case. He asked to speak with Mrs. Daschle outside the room. Before the detective exited the room, he seemed to pull a folder from thin air. He threw it down on the table, took the water bottles and left.

Jake found himself alone with his imagination and thirst. The silence was louder than any voice. He was unsure whether Terri believed him.

She was there and saw Monica Beame. She knows nothing happened. Was she watching the entire interrogation? Did she believe me? Did she catch on that I was about to break down in tears after how much time...like ten hours? Is someone else yelling at her and Mrs. Daschle? Where is Monica Beame? Molina kept hinting at terrible scenarios about her disappearance. Did she kill herself over me?

Morbid thoughts swirled like a tornado in his head.

Is this normal? Do regular people think like this? Do innocent people have visions of people dying? Oh God, am I innocent? Could I be capable of...? Is that what guilt feels like? Or is it something worse?

Jake looked through the folder. It included photos of him with Father Duffy at the bar and the cab he took the night he met Monica. Other photographs showed the car she drove when she visited him at work. Even the alarm clock resting on the hood of her car. It must have been from the sanitation depot's security cameras.

This would prove that I am innocent.

Then Jake saw the photos of the car on the Verrazzano Bridge and Polaroids of himself spread out on the passenger seat.

Detectives had affixed the photos to cardboard backings and sealed them in three separate evidence bags. Each photo was of Jake doing random stuff. Things like driving his garbage truck, going to the store, coming out of his house, walking into the nursing home and sleeping in his room.

Oh my God, she's a goddamn stalker. Holy shit! Did she kill herself? Is this what this is all about? Is this my fault? Did she kill herself because of me? Was I so selfish that...

Molina, with Mrs. Daschle, returned inside.

"What are you thinking about right now, Mr. Johansson?" Molina asked.

"I'm confused." Jake leaned his head back. "Why would she jump? She's a sweet girl. She didn't have a mean bone in her body. I wasn't thinking about her. I was selfish. We could have been friends. I would never want anything bad to happen."

Jake looked at Mrs. Daschle, and tears dropped from his eyes. "I'm so sorry. I didn't know she was..."

"You're sorry for what, Mr. Johansson?" Molina said. His tone had a forceful edge. He had his subject on the ropes. The detective's muscles tensed in anticipation of breaking the case wide open.

From the other side of the one-way glass, Terri swore she could see Molina's heartbeat through his suit jacket. She sat beside Chief Daryl Beame. Both sat with clenched fists, awaiting Jake's answer.

"I didn't mean to hurt her feelings. She was nice, and to be honest, I get overwhelmed when I'm around too many people. That makes me nervous about what to say, or it causes me to talk too much. I sometimes wonder if I could have been a good boyfriend because I tend to mess things up. When I met her, I took her home because she said she had nowhere else to stay that night. I was drinking, which wasn't smart, but I felt sorry for her. She loved discussing magic, and it was never my intention to make her feel so bad that she thought about killing herself. She even visited me at work and gave me a gift while I was helping Ms. Sh..."

Something shifted in Terri then, subtle, but unmistakable.

Jake wasn't a threat. Not even close. She'd sat across from liars, abusers, manipulators, people who could turn their guilt into a weapon. Jake wasn't one of them. His shoulders carried worry the way other men carried muscle. His eyes kept darting to the hallway, like he was checking on invisible others.

He cares too much, she realized.

That's the whole problem. He cares so loudly he has to bury it under sarcasm just to function. Returning the necklace wasn't some fluke, it was who he was when nobody was looking.

Terri felt an ache rise in her chest she hadn't invited.

God, she knew that kind of anxiety. That kind of heart. The kind that made you hold the world up even when it wasn't your job.

Why am I thinking about this now?

Focus, Sheehan.

She pushed the thought back down, hard.

"What are you whimpering about?" Molina scoffed. "You saying she killed herself?"

"Well, yeah. You said her car was found on the bridge's center span," Jake said.

Mrs. Daschle nodded in confirmation.

"Yeah. All right, smart guy. But she was not the one who had left it there."

Chapter 18

Jake exited the building with a burst in his step, moving with as quick of a pace as his trusted neighbor-turned-attorney could handle. Given his anxiety, he wisely focused straight ahead at the car door to keep from absorbing the death stares emanating from a line of uniformed and suited officers.

"Let's get to the car," Mrs. Daschle said. "Look down, don't give them anything else to get worked up over."

Her voice was comforting, and Jake was grateful that he took her along as his newfound legal representation. Moments before, while trying to find somewhere to pee, Jake overheard Mrs. Daschle pushing Molina for his release.

"You certainly don't have enough to charge him with anything," he heard her say. "This interview is over. I demand that you let him leave right now."

Watching through the slightly opened interview room door, Jake saw Molina once again on his heels, trying to parry little Mrs. Daschle with talk of DNA and fingerprint tests. She was poised, not at all hesitant to stand their toe to toe with a seasoned detective. An arrogant prick, to boot.

He listened in as a second male voice joined the conversation. "Detective Molina, I appreciate your efforts here, but I'm afraid Mr. Johansson's attorney is correct. We don't have enough here."

"But, Chief? This is the best lead we have right now. I need a little more time. I don't want this scumbag disappearing or worse, disposing..."

Chief Beame tried not to gag as he coughed.

"Detective Molina, I trust your judgment and experience. I do. This is my daughter. I have to go with my gut on this one. Let him go."

Mrs. Daschle turned around and caught a glimpse of Jake eavesdropping on Chief Beame's command. With that, she broke her incredible poise for just a brief moment...to raise her eyebrows at her stressed-out client as if to say, "Bingo."

Now, in the parking lot, she switched back from legal expertise to motherly instinct. "Don't mind them, Jacob. They stick by one another. It's a good thing most of the time."

Terri stepped outside to talk to Jake. She was too late. Jake and Mrs. Daschle drove away.

Molina stood behind Chief Beame's backside. "Sir. I'm not trying to be insubordinate. It's just that the results will..."

"Detective. We don't have time to wait for results. Find my daughter."

"Sir. I..."

"Why are you still here, Detective?" Chief Beame asked. "Put a tail on him."

* * * * *

"It's a good thing the police left a key to your apartment under my door," Mrs. Daschle said, handing Jake an envelope.

He walked from room to room and ensured that Mrs. Daschle's apartment was safe, and stood by while she locked herself inside.

Jake tiptoed around his padlocked apartment. This time, no shadows lurked, no hockey-stick wielding lunatics in the closet. Just silence and overturned cushions. He set the intruder-free verdict aside and let the coffee pot burble to life while he sat at the kitchen table. He called in sick to work, his voice cracking like a teenager trying to fake the flu, and hung up.

His father's box still sat there, stubborn as ever. A memorial card slid loose when he nudged it, the glossy edge catching his thumb.

Katherine "Katie" Heitz

July 10, 1992 - December 6, 2001

Nine years old.

He paced. Back and forth. Scraped the dust in the hall with his heel. Tried to remember why that name felt like a splinter he couldn't see.

Finally, he dropped into the chair at his desktop, a chunky Dell tower that wheezed when he woke it. The monitor flickered on with a faint *pop*, bathing the kitchen in blue-white light. Windows XP blinked awake like it needed a minute to stretch.

Jake opened Internet Explorer 7, the browser grinding its gears while it climbed online through his cheap cable modem. Each pixel-loaded letter of the Google homepage appeared like it had to walk there.

He typed "Katherine Heitz," the clacking keys loud in the empty apartment.

The coffee maker hissed and sputtered behind him, filling the room with the comforting smell of burnt diner roast. He reached for the mug without thinking, took a sip he didn't remember pouring.

Google results crawled in.

One blue hyperlink...

then another...

and then another...

A small graveyard of headlines slowly assembled itself.

He clicked the first one, the rectangular cursor blinking like a pulse.

Jake braced himself.

And he read.

Manhattan jury begins deliberations in death of 9-year-old Katherine Heitz

May 20th, 2003 – Updated Archive (2007)

A Manhattan jury began deliberations yesterday in the year-long trial of Sean and Olivia Heitz, the Alphabet City couple accused of killing their 9-year-old daughter, Katherine "Katie" Heitz.

Prosecutors told jurors that Olivia Heitz, who had struggled with drug addiction, relapsed on the night of December 6, 2001. In closing arguments, Assistant District Attorney Marianne Keller said Olivia, "in a narcotic haze," beat the child, causing a severe neck fracture. Investigators contend that Sean Heitz, who they say has a history of alcohol abuse, attempted to clean the scene before calling 911.

Defense attorneys countered with a digital reenactment, arguing that Katie woke during the night and fell down the steep loft staircase in the family's apartment. Lead attorney John Reiss told jurors the death was "a tragic accident, not a crime."

Medical Examiner Dr. Christopher Grgas testified that the fatal injury did not initially appear consistent with a fall down thirteen steps. Under cross-examination, he acknowledged that such a fall could produce a similar fracture, though he maintained it was unlikely.

The parents' emotional outbursts during testimony forced the judge to pause the proceedings twice last week.

A verdict is expected later this week.

Jake dug through every corner of the internet wasteland he could find. Newspaper archives, half-dead blogs, and message boards that hadn't been updated since the Y2K panic fizzled out. At first, nothing explained why his father kept a memorial card for a girl he'd never heard of.

The Heitz case, though, was everywhere.

The acquittal sparked a media brushfire back then. Some outlets painted Sean and Olivia Heitz as monsters who'd slipped the noose. Others insisted they were grieving parents railroaded by an overzealous DA. Jake remembered the story vaguely, a headline glimpsed on the front page at the deli, maybe, but he never formed an opinion. He wished he had. His father clearly had.

Did Dad know something? See something? Do something?

A throb started behind Jake's forehead.

Then he found a grainy news clip, a local station's follow-up interview with Olivia Heitz, filmed six months after the verdict. Her husband had taken his own life by then. She stood on the courthouse steps, sobbing into microphones, insisting Sean was innocent. Her grief was so raw it made Jake sit up straighter.

And then he froze.

Because just over Olivia's shoulder, half-blocked by a reporter, was a face Jake knew. A shape. A presence. A flash of green from one unmistakable eye.

His father.

Penrod Johansson, lingering in the background like a ghost who hadn't learned he was dead yet.

There for one second. Swallowed by the crowd, the next.

Jake lurched forward and dragged the rewind bar back with shaking fingers. His lukewarm coffee sloshed as he replayed the clip again and again, trying to catch more than a phantom outline.

Olivia's voice cracked through the speakers.

"He loved Katie."

Jake whispered into the glow of the monitor, "Dad...what the hell were you doing there?"

Jake awoke on the couch the next morning. He stared at his father's haunting painting of the Brooklyn Bridge. The painting was different somehow, a masterful depiction of shadows and secrets. The artist had captured the landmark in its most captivating state, at night, shrouded in mystery. For the first time, Jake examined the intricate details of the oil painting, feeling an inexplicable pull toward it. With chilling clarity, he understood now why his father was obsessed with it. From this couch, his father had spent hours staring at it, his gaze intense and wild. Jake remembered that his father would bear a slight smirk, curling his lips like he knew something Jake didn't.

The signature leaped out at him, almost slapping him in the face: J. Sing. It felt like a cryptic message, a dark invitation beckoning Jake to unravel what lay beneath the surface. A shiver coursed through him. He grabbed his keys. A sense of urgency gripped him as he rushed to his father's downtown lair, ready to uncover the shadows that lurked behind that canvas. This wasn't just a visit; it ignited an adrenaline-pumping pursuit of the truth.

Chapter 19

Terri hoped to zone out and forget about investigations and garbage trucks and garbagemen on her hour-long ride home to the Long Island suburbs. She was not often intimidated, but the winding Southern State Parkway, which collected commuters from the outer boroughs and snaked them east through Nassau County, commanded her full attention. Her driving instructor from back in the day would be proud. She was a classic "ten-and-two" driver on the parkway, hovering near the speed limit as the road plunged around sharp curves and beneath ornate stone-arch bridges.

The dirty looks and middle fingers didn't bother her, but the roadside memorials did, when she would foolishly allow herself to catch a glimpse of one. They were hard to miss. Every half-mile or so, a small cross appeared along the roadway's shoulder, a family's attempt to keep the memory alive of someone lost too soon. Balloons, photos and memorabilia of a favorite sports team usually filled out the shrine, and sometimes family and friends could be seen paying their respects on the side of the road. As she slowed down to exit toward home, Terri gazed upon a newly built memorial to her right. The cross was surrounded by pink candles and a baby doll. Her brief mental respite from the investigation was over. All she could think of once again was Hope.

Landon Talbert put down his clippers as Terri pulled up to her home. The landlord was out front trimming the hedges that lined the two-story house. "Hi there, Terri," the jovial property owner said. "I didn't know you had a boyfriend. Sure was a noisy fellow."

"What? I don't have a boyfriend."

"Who was the gentleman in your apartment this morning? You must have given him a key. He even locked up when he left?"

Something was wrong. It had been over a year since she had any kind of boyfriend. She was sure she hadn't given her key to anyone.

"Oh, that was a friend. The kitchen sink leaked. He's a plumber. I didn't want to bother you with it when it was so easy to have him stop by to take a look. I got a call, and everything's resolved."

Terri wanted her landlord to remain ignorant. Besides, she adored her apartment and did not want to be asked to leave. She also didn't want anyone else, even him, to have access to her home. "You know what? Can I borrow your key to the apartment? I forgot to stop by Jake's to get it."

"Do you think your friend could look at my clogged bathtub drain?" Mr. Talbert asked.

He charges me enough for rent. Now he wants me to get him free plumbing? Terri smiled at her landlord. "I'll see what I can do."

Mr. Talbert gave Terri a spare key and asked her to return it before she went out again. It struck Terri that the landlord had the key right there in his pocket. Now she definitely did not want him to have it, and she had no intention of returning it. The thought of her landlord snooping around her home brought on a special queasiness. She viewed Mr. Talbert in a peculiar light now. Terri made a mental note to search every inch of the apartment for hidden cameras. She hoped he didn't have any other keys. She loved her apartment and its beautiful location. Moving would be sad and an enormous hassle.

Terri felt nauseous as she stepped into her apartment. Its silence was unsettling. She scanned the room with mounting anxiety. Her belongings lay in disarray, strewn across surfaces, while drawers gaped open as if inviting her to peer inside. Her heart raced as she approached the kitchen table, where her laptop flickered in standby mode. She knew she turned it off and folded it closed that morning. Her nausea grew more intense.

She touched the pad with reluctant fingers, and the screen came to life. But what greeted her was terrifying. Someone had arranged the desktop icons into the shape of a sinister cross.

Her eyes darted to the wall, and dread coiled tighter in her chest. There it was, the photo of her and Hope. The sharp cut-out of Hope's image left a disturbing void. It whispered warnings of an unseen presence lurking about in her once-safe haven.

Terri looked closer at her computer and found the Hope case file icon missing. Upon further inspection, she discovered everything related to Hope was gone; someone had deleted even the recovery and backup files. Terri tried to make sense of it all. It didn't seem possible. Hope was gone, every sign of her erased, leaving only a hollow silence that clawed at her. They played on the fear of what mattered most to her. They didn't break in for money; they came for her soul instead.

Terri staggered into her bathroom, fighting for breath. Her vision was a haze of tears and shock. The world was closing in around her. She splashed cold water on her face in desperation, hoping to clear her mind and steady her pulse. When she looked up, her heart dropped. On the mirror, scrawled in crimson lipstick, were the words "Thess. 4:11." The chilling message deepened even further the sinister aura surrounding her violated apartment.

Terri picked up her phone and dialed Mary Hollingsworth's work number. "Mary, it's me."

"Terri? Child, where have you been? What happened?"

"What did you hear?" Terri asked.

"That you were suspended. Mr. Friel came to me asking if I had talked to you. They expected you to go to the central office, but you didn't show up."

"I'll get there. Listen, please go to my office. Go into my computer and find the Hope file. The password is Aristotle. See if you can create a backup. There is a flash drive in my top drawer. Try to gather all of the case files from my cabinet and hide them in your office, or make copies."

"What kind of trouble are you in, child?"

"I am suspended, so I guess a lot." Terri was impatient, waiting for Mary to assure her she would do it. "Please do this for me now. I don't want to take a chance and lose those files."

"Terri, this should blow over. Get down to the central office and contact the union rep. Don't mess around with this stuff. You're a real blessing for these kids."

"Mary, please, I need this done like yesterday. Don't let them tinker with those files."

"All right, I'm on it right now."

"Cinnamon buns!" Terri said.

Terri cleaned up the mess, put on a coat, locked her apartment door and left the house. Mr. Talbert was still outside, caring for his arborvitae.

"Hey, Landon, did you see my friend today?"

"Only saw him on his way out. I tried to introduce myself, but he had headphones on," the landlord said while clipping a couple of branches. "I figured the guy was going for a jog."

"Yeah, sorry about that. He's shy, but what are you getting at by jog?" Terri was trying to keep up with her story.

"Well, he wore a sweatsuit and jogged down the street. He did wave, though. Didn't look like a plumber."

Terri couldn't tell if Talbert was getting suspicious or playing some sort of mind game. She didn't want to push the issue, so she said nothing but goodbye and got into her truck.

Now it appeared Jake's break-in was her fault.

How did they know where I lived? How did they know who Jake was? Maybe Jake had answers. Maybe he had none. But I can't face this alone anymore.

She had trouble keeping her thoughts focused.

Why did it seem that Hope would have a life of despair and torment just like mine?

Terri drove aimlessly until she ended up in front of Jake's building, unable to recall how she got there. She would apologize to him and get more answers to her nagging questions. The constant influx of questions without meaningful answers tormented her, making her feel sick inside, like a parasite nibbling at her organs. She rang Jake's doorbell, stepped back and thought she would faint. No answer. She rang again.

Behind Terri the lobby door opened slowly, and recognizing the ACS investigator, Evelyn Daschle peered through the crack and opened the door wider. Terri thought about ducking for cover.

"Well, you must have missed him, dear. I don't see his car out front."

"I'm very sorry for all that has happened." Terri wanted to make amends with the spunky counsel.

"I understand your situation. I would probably do the same thing." Mrs. Daschle gave one of her signature warm smiles. Jake perhaps updated her. Terri appreciated the support she now seemed to get from the elder attorney.

"I need to speak to him. I inadvertently got him into a bigger mess. My apartment was also burglarized."

"Sounds like an intriguing mystery to me."

"Please tell him to give me a call?" Terri handed Mrs. Daschle a business card. "Tell him to use the mobile number this time."

"I'm worried he won't. No matter the consequences, he tends to shut people out when flustered."

Terri detected a deeper meaning to the caring neighbor's insight, a hint. She thought Mrs. Daschle had a suggestion if she knew enough to ask.

"What would you think is the best way for me to help him?"

"Sixteenth Street in Chelsea. St. Francis Xavier Church. Ask for Father Duffy."

"Can't I call?"

"Colin Duffy never answers the phone either. God knows why," Mrs. Daschle said with an eye roll and closed the door.

Terri believed the abrupt end of their conversation served its own dramatic purpose—it got her moving. She took her truck down to Chelsea, watching the skyline for church spires as she hit a red light on 6th Avenue. She wasn't entirely sure what good talking to Jake would do, but she knew one thing for certain: he needed to hear the truth. His break-in wasn't random. Someone had targeted him. He wasn't going to take it well, but better he hears it from her than from the next guy to jump out of his closet.

Terri admired the three main arched entranceways above the stone steps. She drew a long breath, steadying herself before stepping through the middle arch. It looked like it would swallow Terri whole. The cathedral was enormous. Lavish stained-glass windows on either side of the rear wall let in splashes of sunlight, complemented by a few lit prayer candles. Their geometric shapes projected beams of light in various directions. Both sides of the prayer parlor's walls featured hand-painted scenes depicting Christ's crucifixion. Sculptures of biblical figures kept watch over the magnificent marble altar. Every footstep resonated like thunder as Terri approached the rear of the church.

The figures in the paintings followed Terri with their eyes as she walked. She found the empty church creepy yet peaceful. Her skin tingled with some unknown fear. Dark-stained pews were littered with forgotten Mass books, and the few elderly parishioners in attendance looked as though they'd been seated there since the varnish first dried. All five had their heads bowed in prayer or sleep.

As Terri turned to look closer at the somber audience, a nudge on her arm made her shudder. She spun around expecting a demonic attack but found a small, frail, dark-haired fellow with heavy-rimmed glasses and a white clerical collar.

"Good afternoon, young lady. How may I assist you?"

"Oh, hello, Father. I'm looking to speak with Father Duffy."

"Who may I ask is calling for him?"

"Oh yeah. I'm Terri Sheehan from...I'm a friend of his nephew."

Terri was nervous that the small white lie would be amplified in a house of worship. She stood ready to dodge a lightning strike.

"Oh, a friend of Jacob? How the hell are you? I'm Father Benny. I am a friend as well. Very nice to meet you," the priest said.

"Nice to meet you, too." Terri was trying to decide whether to bow, curtsey or shake his hand.

"If I may," little Benny said. He reached his arms up in a gesture that he wished to be carried. "I could guide you to Father Duffy's office if you don't mind carrying me on your back."

Terri turned red and panicked at the thought of walking around the passages of an old church while giving a tiny priest a piggyback ride. Father Benny took a step toward her. She took a step back. He laughed.

"Oh, come on, I'm only kidding. Your arm will do. Unless you really want to."

Terri let out a sigh of relief and gave a little embarrassed laugh. "The arm will be fine. I left my baby harness in the car."

Benny snorted at Terri's return shot. He guided the visitor through a maze of hallways and stairs that eventually led them to Father Duffy's office.

"Ah, Colin. I found a friend of Jacob's wandering around a confession booth, babbling about six of the seven deadly sins. All was forgiven, though. There's no need to thank me."

Father Benny walked away whistling "My Favorite Things" from *The Sound of Music.*

"Please, don't mind him. Bit of a daft idiot, that one is," Father Duffy said to his new guest.

Terri explained the reason for her visit and a little more about her situation than she intended. Father Duffy was a fine listener.

"What does Thess 4:11 mean to you? I think it's a biblical thing. It was written on my mirror in my apartment."

"Aye, it is indeed Thessalonians," Father Duffy said as he opened the good book on his desk. "Ah, sure, yes. The First Epistle to the Thessalonians is from the New Testament. The oldest book in the New Testament, 'tis."

Father Benny then added his take from somewhere outside the doorway. "Allegedly the oldest book in the New Testament, it was personal letters from Paul the Apostle after the death and resurrection of Christ. Paul's main purpose in writing them was to encourage and reassure the Christians in Thessalonica to persevere in their faith. All while hoping for Christ our savior's return."

"Benny? Why're ya eavesdroppin'?" Father Duffy asked.

Benny stood in the doorway, holding a tray of cookies and coffee mugs. "Was offering refreshments, Colin."

"Ah, it's God's will, so it is. Benny here knows all there is about religious text, he does."

Benny explained a little more about Paul the Apostle. "According to writings in the New Testament, a man named Saul was dedicated to persecuting the early disciples of Jesus in Jerusalem. In the Acts of the Apostles narrative, Saul traveled from Jerusalem to Damascus when the resurrected Jesus appeared to him in a glorious light. He was struck blind, much like me, but after three days, his sight was restored by Ananias of Damascus, a devout follower of Jesus. Saul was baptized and began to preach that Jesus of Nazareth was the Jewish Messiah and the Son of God. Saul is now better known as Saint Paul the Apostle."

Father Duffy assisted and turned to the page in First Thessalonians.

[1 Thess. 4:11] Make it your ambition to lead a quiet life, to mind your own business, and to work with your hands, just as we told you.

This was all Terri cared to hear.

"To mind your own business. Of course. That is what that creep said to me after he got hit by the car," she said aloud.

"I reckon the one that broke into Jacob's flat said the same thing to him," Father Duffy added.

"It's like their freaking catchphrase. God, so freaking pathetic."

"Ah, I'd say my nephew's more involved than he'd care to admit," the priest said.

"How can I get in touch with him then? So he doesn't shut down on me? He may be in danger."

After several tries on his cell phone, Father Duffy put on his black blazer. "I think I know where we can find him."

Benny picked up the tray and nodded to his colleague. "Contact me when you find your nephew Colin. This may be important."

Chapter 20

Jake looked through every piece of paper, book and newspaper article mentioning Katie Heitz. He found nothing. His mind drifted to his father's inventions. The notebook explained some items, especially the gloves. The simple setup of the gloves amazed Jake. They delivered enough voltage to knock an average person out cold without lasting damage through a punch or a grab. Jake compared it to modern police Tasers. After that, he noticed the notebook's 1980 date and wondered whether the police had Tasers. The basis for the shirt and glove's rubbery texture dawned on him.

"Oh! The shirt and gloves are non-conductive. No shock," he said to himself.

The text unveiled a thrilling array of devices, with the whip stealing the spotlight. Jake thought it was as an exhilarating tool, especially since it had a jaw-dropping twist. It could unleash an electrifying shock on its target with the mere push of a button. His father, the mastermind behind this invention, drew inspiration from Indiana Jones himself. Yet, his father noted the whip's drawbacks; not good in tight spaces and it caught on everything when clipped to his belt.

A small, hand-sized rectangular box housed a formidable duo of nine-volt batteries and a timer, ready to spring into action. As the countdown neared, an intense charge surged through the metallic box, jolting its holder with a shocking surprise. And during heart-pounding close encounters, the device electrified with the touch of trigger button. A bold notation on the side proclaimed that this electrifying contraption was a game-changer when fastened to a metal fence, zapping its reach to an astonishing six feet.

Jake fiddled with the shock box like a stubborn jar of pickles, then inserted new batteries. The metal door clanged open at the entrance, creaking like a horror-movie ghoul. Startled by the noise, Jake hit the activate button, which sent him tumbling into a bookshelf. Books and pages became ticker tape, plummeting and swirling around him in spectacular fashion.

Father Duffy heard the crash. Jake's worried uncle dashed into the workroom. He comically flailed his legs, followed by a confused-looking Terri.

"Jacob, Jacob, ah boy, what've ye gone and done now?"

"What happened?" Terri asked.

"He's been messin' with his father's things," the priest answered. "Jacob, are ya all right, Jacob?" Father Duffy gave Jake a solid slap in the face.

"Whoa!" Jake's eyes twitched. "Whoa! I think that hurt."

"What did ya do?" Father Duffy asked, as if speaking to a little kid with a scrape on his knee.

"I must have pushed the juice button."

"What exactly are you mumbling about?" Terri said.

Jake tried his hardest to clear his head. Books and papers slid off him as he tried to stand.

"Easy, Jacob." Father Duffy eased him onto a stool. "Ah, I reckon he might've accidentally given himself a shock, so he did."

Always observant, Terri began scanning the room. She looked with interest, at first, at the workbench, the bookshelves, the gadgets. By the time she turned back toward Jake, self-electrocuted on the garage floor, she was stuck in a mouth-agape stare of unfiltered bewilderment.

"What is this place?"

"It seems, me dear, that Jake's dad, well..." Father Duffy paused, unsure if Jake wanted to involve her in this. "His dad used this workshop to, well, get the job done."

"Oh, okay. I see that," she said. Terri scanned the room once more, then checked her watch. "When Jake gets done playing with Daddy's tools, can we please talk about your big plan?"

She was trying to be as polite as possible, but Terri knew how transparent her impatience was. After all, she was scared.

"I'd like to head back to the church if it's all right with ye. I have a notion that might be of help to Ms. Sheehan's situation," Father Duffy said as if in a trance, like he just had a dire epiphany.

Terri blurted out, "Let's get going."

"Ms. Sheehan, I hate to be rude, but it's best ye stay and have a wee chat with Jake. Someone with yer talents might do him some good. And Jacob, would ye mind lockin' the door behind ye when yer in here?"

"Wait, where are you going?" Jake asked.

"Ah, I just mentioned it. I've a notion that might help Ms. Sheehan out. She explained everything to me. I'll be takin' the subway back. I'll be in touch soon enough. Trust me now."

Jake and Terri followed the priest out to the alleyway.

"God, now I see where you get your weirdness from," Terri said.

Chapter 21

"So, tell me. How did you hook up with my uncle?" Jake asked.

"I'm a smart lady," Terri answered. "So, what is all this stuff?"

"I'll tell you if you tell me how you ended up here."

"I went to your apartment looking for you."

"Why?"

"Because Detective Molina is a dick, and I know you weren't involved in that girl's disappearance."

"Why is *Defective* Molina such a penis?"

"Because he is so desperate to impress a chief and get promoted or earn a medal or something. He's wasting time on you. That girl might be in trouble, and so is Hope!"

"Wait, you think Monica's disappearance is related to your missing kid's case?"

"I have a nagging inclination that it is."

"How could that be possible?"

"Too many coincidences. A certain dick-tective says that all the time."

"My uncle doesn't believe in coincidences. He believes God is the one laying down the path."

"Either way, I think there is some connection. They both may be right."

"Look, I feel bad for the girl. I do. Nobody wants her found safe more than I do. But let's face it: she went home with me after ten minutes of conversation. She doesn't have the best judgment. She could be anywhere or with anyone."

"Jake, are you victim-blaming?" Terri asked.

"Shaming, not blaming."

"A woman has the right to..."

"Yes, I apologize. I'm trying to get a sense of the situation."

"Well, I hope Molina will find her safe either way, for both your sakes," Terri said.

"So, how did you contact my uncle exactly?"

"Mrs. Daschle thought you might have gone to see him. Molina had a surveillance video of you, the priest and Monica Beame," she explained. "She told me you may have gone to see him at his church. Your uncle cares about you. He came with me to find you."

"Uncle Duff is the greatest," Jake said. He was unsure whether to fill her in on his situation. *What else am I supposed to do?* he thought.

While Jake went on detailing the things learned regarding his father's concealed existence, something broke into Jake's mind. He kept pausing and looking into Terri's big brown eyes. She was beautiful, way out of his league. Terri was staring back at him, hanging on to every unbelievable word, lost in a fantastic story of...

"Eww! What the hell are you doing?" she screamed as she stared down at Jake's lap.

"Wha...What? I'm ah..." Jake panicked. *What does she mean? What the hell am I doing?* Jake drew his eyes to his lap. *Please don't let me have my fly open or a stain or something.*

It was worse. Jake's hand was in his front pocket, and his thumb stroked his stone a hundred miles a minute. He looked up at Terri, who returned his horrified gaze. Then she laughed.

"Man, I knew you were fucking crazy, but Jesus! You come near me, and I'll cut your fucking balls off." Terri reached over to the workbench and grabbed a pair of scissors.

"It's not. I'm not. It's just my rock."

"I don't care what you call it. You back the fuck up."

Terri held the blades out and backed out of the workshop. Jake took his hand out of his pocket, holding the stress stone.

"I rub it when I'm stressed out." *Oh man, that wasn't good.*

"I don't give a shit what your malfunction is," Terri growled back.

"No! Look, look, the stone. Here!" Jake held the stone out in his palm.

"Oh! You are fucking crazy."

"You know what? I don't have to explain myself to you. Yeah, I've got issues. But I find a way to deal with mine."

"Yeah, rubbing one out. Way to go, sport," Terri jabbed.

"It's a stress stone," Jake said. He was too embarrassed to have any chance of winning a snappy comeback contest. "I rub my thumb on the stress stone when my anxiety is high. It helps me. I know it doesn't look good, but you gotta believe me. I'm not a creep."

"You've got to admit, it looked pretty sick there for a minute," Terri said as a peace offering.

Jake reached down to start picking his father's books off the floor. He gathered pages and notes and torn covers, trying but failing to sort them into neat stacks. Terri helped, another peace offering, though it came with a chuckle at Jake's expense.

"Please, I got it. Leave it alone." Jake stared fixated at the floor. He turned bright red.

"Stop it. Ya gonna take your balls and go home?" Terri poked.

"I got it. Leave it alone!"

Terri found the deep end of Jake's anxiety pool as she read through one of his father's notebooks.

"Leave that alone!"

"Jake, stop the shit. You don't have to be embarrassed. I realize now that you weren't touching yourself."

"Yeah, great. Thanks, sport."

"Oh, come on. I'm sorry." She bolstered her childish apology by grabbing a handful of books and placing them on a shelf.

"Listen. I'll clean this up. I'd rather do this myself," Jake said.

"I'm only helping. Relax!"

"You relax! As a matter of fact, relax right there on that stool! I don't want you touching anything!" Jake realized he had made things a lot more intriguing for Terri.

"Oh. I see, Mr. Man. Fine. I'll stay put." Terri sat on the stool, browsing through another notebook.

"I told you. Don't touch anything."

Terri ignored him. "This is what superhero stuff looks like, huh? I imagined it would be a little flashier. Where's the cape?"

"He has a trench coat," Jake mumbled.

She put on her best cute act and stood up, putting one finger on the workbench as she strolled a couple of steps across.

Jake fell for it. He cracked a sly grin. "Hey, come on over here. Hold this box for me," Jake said. In his hand was his father's shock box.

Terri was as sharp as ever. "I'll pass on that, Stroker Ace. Whoa! That's a scary mask. Was your father a superhero or a mugger from the seventies?"

Jake couldn't help it. He told her everything. Terri's face warmed at Jake's pride in his father. The way Jake told the story made him more attractive. He had a magnificent smile, and his eyes seemed to add sparkle to the room every time he said, "My dad." She dreamed of having a dad and a mother. Listening to his every word, she felt comfortable, not at all jealous. Terri noticed Jake had a small dimple on his cheek when he choked up, especially when he remembered his mother. Innocence danced about Jacob Johansson. Perhaps a shielded innocence. A breath of fresh air since the only people she associated with were the damaged, jaded and skeptical types. Like-minded people. Birds of a feather. The conversation ended on a melancholy note: Penrod Johansson's final years. Silence followed as the two finished cleaning up together.

"You okay?" she asked, for real this time.

Jake nodded. "No."

22

T erri picked up one book on the workbench titled *The Chronicles of Chronic Christmas,* authored by Hornsby "Christmas" Holiday. The cover was bright red, with the text plastered across the center in bold black typewriter lettering. A towering red-brick building stood in the background, surrounded by a wrought-iron fence, and an old red Santa hat hung on one of the posts. Terri turned to the back cover and read the reviews the publisher listed:

"A hot ghetto mess! A brutally honest journey into the Thug Life. Exciting, bold, and as entertaining as you would expect Hell to be."

Scott Granai - The New Yorker

"Dizzying and hypnotic! Keeps it as real as fried chicken wings and fries at the Chinese takeout window. Bone check mutha f@#ker!!!"

T to da B - Platinum Record Rap Artist

"As the saying goes, life on the streets is hard. This guy might be why. Christmas may be the reason for open season. Every paragraph is an absolute wild abomination of civil discord and villainy. This is the most important piece of literature from the ghetto since Boyz n the Hood."

Shorty Johnson - King Magazine

"This piece of human excrement writes about robbing, stealing, and destroying the very principles of our society's security in the hopes of another egocentric cash-money handout. If you must read this utter garbage, allow me to spoil the ending. It is a happy one. Do society a favor and do not buy this book."

John Walsh - America's Most Wanted

"Yeah, that book was given to my dad by that Sing X guy. He told me there is a story about my dad in it."

Terri handed the book over so that Jake could sift through it for any mention of his father. Occasionally, the holiday-themed debauchery and mayhem turned him wide-eyed, his dropped jaw gingerly mouthing Hornsby's passages. Terri sat silent and hung on every word.

The book started with the author introducing himself as "*One of the original ghetto superstars.*"

"Whatever that is," Jake said.

Holiday then stated he offered no apologies for what he had done or was "*going*" to do.

"Blah, blah, blah," Jake summarized. "The streets are for the most competent survivors. Blah, blah, blah. He is the most extraordinary thug in history. Blah, blah, blah, blah. The streets are his playground. Blah, blah," and finally, "blah."

Jake skimmed the beginning chapters. The book matched the advertisement. A criminal's unfiltered thoughts and actions. Articles varied in length from brief to several pages long; the layout seemed random. He found the story titles amusing.

One passage started "Christmas Comes Early," and told a tale of Chronic Christmas waking up extra early in the morning to catch a heroin addict he named Ed.

He found Ed shooting up under a bridge at 102nd and Park. That's where Christmas gave Ed a "*Pony.*" As Jake continued reading, he realized that "Pony" referred to a quick injection of more "*Horse,*" the street name for heroin. In this plot, Christmas aimed to assist the doomed derelict in overdosing. It would stop him from informing the police about the beating Chronic Christmas had given an old lady on Grandparents Day.

Christmas was disappointed that Ed lived but relieved that his brain damage prevented him from snitching. Chronic Christmas also boasted that he still had the old lady's dentures.

Another segment, "The North Pole," explained the Santa Claus hat on the fence post from the book cover. The red hat perched on the building's north fence post, which signaled to potential customers and residents that business was taking place inside. If someone lingered outside long enough, one of Christmas's "*elves*" would guide them to the right spot.

Christmas never chose the same apartment twice. Each day he crowned a new one his workshop, slipping in like a rumor with teeth.

The Christmas hat was the only warning he offered. Miss it, and his elves would beat you so badly you'd pray for a different ending.

Mr. Roosevelt did.

He lived anyway.

Heaven forbid anyone should touch the hat. The elves, all under fourteen years old, swarmed like a pack of killer bees. A young thug named Odd was immortalized in Hornsby Holiday's book. Odd became a pincushion for sharpened candy canes.

Jake and Terri wondered why Chronic Christmas involved young children in his operations. Holiday would later explain that his elves never get arrested by the police due to all the complicated rules and paperwork surrounding minors. Judges rarely sentence juveniles to jail time.

Jake discovered another section describing Chronic Christmas's audacity, titled "Mistle-hoes." In this piece, Christmas revealed his placement of mistletoe in prostitutes' hair to signal his ownership and deter disturbances. This led the girls to con the Johns instead. Jake and Terri laughed, realizing it likely hurt business since there seemed to be no repeat customers.

The entire Christmas theme struck Jake as absurd, yet he thought everyone needed their "*thing.*" Even his dad enjoyed dressing in black and parading around the city, shocking the public and making them believe he was Batman or something.

Jake skimmed through a few more stories until he found one that piqued his interest. The title was "Chestnut's Roasting."

Chronic Christmas began the passage with:

"*Let me tell you about the time I saw the eyes. They resembled two big Christmas balls; One blue and One green.*"

Jake dove into Hornsby Holiday's world, imagining himself narrating his father's adventure as The Fade.

* * * * *

The snowstorm caused it.

Christmas was busy working in his workshop in apartment 10E. Chester, his three-year-old chestnut-colored pit bull, growled and gnawed on a table leg.

"What the fuck is wrong with you, boy?" Christmas asked the steroid-laced canine.

Again, the dog grumbled, released the now-splintered stanchion, and stalked to the apartment's door.

"What? You got to go out? Damn, dog, I walked you an hour ago. What the fuck you been eating?"

"Small babies!" one of the Christmas elves blurted out.

"Yo, whatever, they must go right through him," Christmas joked back. "I need to get out for a minute anyway. I'll take him."

The strapping pit bull's ears rose in recognition that relief was on the way. He yelped in appreciation, accompanied by a kind of doggie dance. Christmas opened the door leading to the graffitied hallway. The drug dealer thought of letting Chester relieve himself right there. Then he decided it wouldn't be fair to the dog to have to piss or shit in such deplorable conditions.

"Come on, Chester, we'll go up to the roof."

Chester wagged his little stumpy tail in recognition as his master attached a short chain to his behavior-modifying spiked collar.

Upon reaching the rooftop, Chester growled. The heavy snowfall behind the elevator house produced whispers. Christmas pulled up on the leash, and Chester quieted down as the two approached. They followed the ever-disappearing footprints in the deep snow. The whispers stopped as Christmas got closer. He steadied his breath and reached for his nine-millimeter pistol tucked away in the small of his back.

He was only wearing a t-shirt, but forgot about the cold. Chester became unsettled and lurched forward as Christmas muted him, pulling tighter on his leash. Snowflakes seemed to shatter on Christmas's hair as they turned the corner. The dog grew frantic in his eagerness to unleash his rage on whoever dared to grace his outhouse. Christmas now stood tall and pointed his black pistol at a large, dark mass sticking out of the snow. He sighed and loosened the tight grip on the gun's trigger, but also loosened Chester's rein, allowing him to bark.

"Dopes, you stupid fat mutha-fucker! Get your ass crack out of my view!" Christmas shouted as he lowered his weapon.

Chester's demonic bark and Christmas's vulgar snarl sent the burly goon bumbling to his feet from under the snow where he had tried to bury himself.

"Dopes, what the fuck you doin' on my roof? Shit, what the fuck you doin' in my building?"

"We um, I rolled Old Julio's Bodega and somebody chased us. I, um, mean me, Ah, shit, Chronic C. You scared me so bad, I shit myself."

"No doubt, damn snow melted around your fuckin' fat ass. The whole fuckin' roof stinks like rotten fried chicken. Now, who are you with?"

"No-nobody man. I, I'm solo, yo!"

"You a large, fat lying sack of shit. Chester, he's yours."

Christmas moved to let go of the demon dog's chain. A pile of snow shifted. Dopes took a stumbling step in front of the collapsing snowdrift, followed by a choking gag. A tall, skinny, sullen-faced teenage boy jumped up from the pile.

"Yo man, don't be standing with that movie screen-ass over me. God damn, you fuckin' got chicken shit stank-ass." The emaciated male tried to shake loose icy snow that clung to his clothes and stood up next to Dopes.

"Who the fuck are you?" Christmas stood freezing, staring at the two trespassers while trying to keep Chester at bay.

"Please, Chronic C., please, he don't mean nothin'. He's following. He's my little brother, yo. It's not his fault. He followed me up here. I didn't think anyone would dare follow me in here. Please, man, let him leave." Dopes was sweating and producing more steam than a manhole.

"That's your little brother? Little Black Mikey-Likes-It? I haven't seen you round here in a minute. Shit, man, the two of you look like the number ten. No wonder he's so skinny. Mutha-fucker, let him eat some of your food. You stealing from your own brother's mouth? Look at him; he's starving.

I should let Chester here have Thanksgiving on your huge ass."

"Come on, man. Please, I know I fucked up, but my brother's sixteen. Let him leave," Dopes pleaded.

"Shut the fuck up! You said someone was following you?"

Dopes explained, "Yo, that was around the block. It was some other playa that wanted some action. He wouldn't follow us into the building. That's why I came in."

"What playa?"

"I never saw him. He was some stray cat who came at us between the buildings. We ran in here," Dopes said.

"There's two of you. You said you hit Old Julio's. Aren't you two pussies holding a burner? You couldn't drop one thug?"

Black Mickey answered, "Nah, Dopes don't even know how to handle one. He shot himself in the balls the last time he tried to roll someone. We told him we'd got one."

"Yeah, I remember. Dopey One-Ball," Christmas laughed. "Old Julio fell for that shit? Everybody has robbed that asshole. He knows the difference."

Black Mickey cut him off. "Some new kid he got working for him."

"How much you get?" Christmas put his hand out.

Dopes reached into his black snorkel coat and pulled out a fistful of dollars. "It's like seventy-five dollars. I haven't counted yet."

"That's about how much my fine is for using my building as your hiding place."

Dopes passed the cash to Christmas. "Does that mean we can leave?"

"I hate Old Julio. I like the way you stuck up for your brother. You'll fuck up again, then...Thanksgiving. I'm a patient man. Get!"

Dopes grabbed his brother's lanky arm and ran for the stairwell door, leaving a trail of hot brown mess.

"Yo, Dopes!" Christmas yelled as the pair reached the roof exit.

"Yeah?" Dopes gasped, out of breath from his ten-foot-long run.

"Only seventy-two greens here. You owe me three. Tomorrow by noon."

"Yo, I got you. Where will you be at?"

"You'll find me." Christmas turned to undo Chester's leash.

"Yo, Chronic C.!" Dopes called out while shielding himself by the metal rooftop door as Black Mickey ran down the steps.

"What the fuck do you want?" Christmas was now sounding impatient.

"Thanks, man. Thanks for not fuckin' us up."

"Chester, get um!"

The door slammed closed with a loud bang before the savage beast could process the command. Chester lunged for the closed door, barking and jumping up and down and clawing at the gray-painted metal. The scraping of the monster's sharpened nails stung Christmas's spine as he laughed. The sound of Dopes falling down the stairwell made him laugh harder.

"All right, Chester. All right. Now sit."

Chester obeyed the command but stared at the door.

"I always liked that nigga. He always showed me respect. Shame his brother seems to be as dopey as him. The whole family must be..."

A scuffle and a brief, sharp scream from Dopes interrupted the man-to-dog chat with Chester. The ornery pit bull went berserk once more.

"Easy, dog. It's the elves. They got our back."

The words didn't ease the maniacal mutt, so Christmas put the leash back on and pulled it extra tight. All was silent now. Too silent. Christmas couldn't help himself, so he whistled "Silent Night" as he opened the stairwell door. The stairwell's first landing had no light. Christmas swore they had been working when he came up. He could still see a puddle of piss glistening in the moonlight. Though his master held tight, Chester tried his best to get down those stairs.

"Come on, stupid, relax. It's just the boys. They got them. That's all."

Christmas let Chester lead him down to the first landing, and as they reached it, they could see down the stairs to the left. Dopes and his brother were lying in a heap, unconscious on the second landing. They were indistinct in the darkened stairwell, but Christmas knew that enormous mass anywhere.

"Ah damn! That dumb, fat bastard fell on his little brother. Good for 'em," he said aloud.

As he finished, a shadow crossed the stairwell's light. Though barking, Chester retreated up the steps. Sharp street instinct kicked in, and Christmas followed suit, backing upstairs toward the rooftop. The snow and wind intensified, making it difficult to keep his balance. Chester ran in circles, yelping and growling, creating space to move in the snowdrift. Christmas held his leash tighter, like a child clutching a blanket when scared. He watched the door to the stairwell open with the loudest creak he had ever heard.

The snowfall was a blinding curtain of white, obscuring everything beyond a few desperate feet. He squinted, trying to discern the dark silhouette of a figure cloaked in a long, tattered coat. The figure emerged, ready for a standoff in the tense air. The stranger's hot breath twirled in ghostly wisps, swirling through the large snowflakes that spiraled down like fatal projectiles. Christmas couldn't tell if the figure had a cigarette, but he craved one against the cold.

"Hey, man, got a smoke?" Christmas yelled out. He had nowhere to retreat now.

"No," the figure stated.

"Too bad. You lost or something?"

"Nope."

"What you want?"

"The money. The money they stole." The figure's tone was flat and even.

"What money?" Christmas's tone was unconvincing as he reached for the small of his back. Then, he let go of Chester's leash.

The dog sprinted at its target, but the mysterious man in the coat never budged. Not a flinch. Christmas drew his weapon and aimed at the darkness in the snow. The storm stopped him from getting a clear shot. And he was afraid of hitting Chester. Christmas opted to wait for his killer canine to sink its locking teeth into the stranger's throat, just as he had trained it. Then he would get closer and finish the phantom with one shot to the head to not alert any nosy neighbors. They would only call the police for multiple shots.

You have to think of these things when you're a criminal kingpin. Nobody cares about one shot.

Christmas stumbled forward in the snow behind Chester, his gun still aimed at the darkness. Chester leaped into Christmas's line of sight and straight toward the figure's throat. The shadow caught its prey with both hands. Christmas saw a flickering electric-blue light as the dog convulsed in the figure's grip. No more barking, no snarling. No movement of any kind. Chester hung limp in the stranger's grasp, smoking like a pig roast.

Perplexed at his predicament, Christmas punched his firearm out and squeezed the trigger. The dog's body slammed into Christmas. A deafening pop erupted. Christmas bells were ringing in his ears. Chronic Christmas tried to fire again but slipped, landing in the snow without his gun. Chester sprung back to life. He yelped, scrambled to his feet and jumped off the building. Christmas patted his hand around in the icy powder searching for his pistol as the dark figure approached.

"Yo, man! What you want?" Christmas's comfortable machismo dulled into a sad desperation.

"I told you already," the shadow answered.

Christmas found his pistol's handle under the snow and suddenly regained his confident edge. "All right, all right. Help me up, man!"

Christmas reached out his hand, prepared to grasp the stranger's and wish him a very merry death. The man reached down and pulled Christmas to his feet, returning the firm grip with a rock-hard strength that left Christmas startled. The two men were face-to-face. Christmas froze for a moment. He saw no face.

"Eyes! The Fade, right? Everyone's been talking about you."

"All good things, I hope." The Fade's voice stayed flat and even.

"It depends on your politics, I guess." Christmas raised the gun above his waist, ready to deliver a sucking chest wound.

His eyes were all that Christmas remembered.

Holiday wrote that his elves heard the shot fired and rushed to the roof, dragging their unconscious boss down to the apartment. This was before the cops arrived and arrested the Dopey Brothers, caught with the stolen money and a firearm. Nobody seemed to see anything. Holiday described the difficulties in proving to his elves that Dopes and Black Mickey did not outsmart him. Dopes only got caught because the clumsy oaf fell down the stairs onto his starving, skinny brother.

Holiday vowed revenge, stating The Fade was an ex-Navy SEAL from New Jersey and a rival drug dealer aiming to squash competition. He said he would not reveal The Fade's identity, so only he could eliminate him and defend his own honor.

Jake got a belly chuckle out of that one.

"That's my dad. I think."

Jake scanned through the book, craving more Fade adventures, but alas, there were none. On the last page was an epilogue:

To the reader,

After the publication of this book, a family member of one of his many victims shot and killed Hornsby "Chronic Christmas" Holiday, while he was waiting in line at a local Chinese food takeout window. This publishing company does not endorse the ideology or actions presented in these pages. Readers should refrain from emulating any criminal act described, as it may lead to significant jail time, serious physical or mental injury, and/or death. The Urban-American Defense League will receive all proceeds from this book. This nonprofit organization dedicates itself to helping young men and women accused of crimes in New York City. Every individual named in this book should be considered innocent until proven guilty in a court of law.

In Memory of Hornsby "Chronic Christmas" Holiday

12/25/1961 to 10/10/1995

Chapter 23

Jake and Terri picked the last of the papers off the floor and assembled them in frayed stacks on his father's shelves. He slid the books back into place, taking care to arrange them in some type of order. It was important to him that he and Terri leave the workroom the way he first found it, though he did not understand why.

"So, what do you think now?" Jake asked.

"I find this all a little hard to believe."

"Yeah, because your story is so bland and boring."

"You didn't bargain for this type of trip, and I am truly sorry. You have your situation with your family. I'm trying to get you out of my mess now, but calling Molina will not help. Jake, I apologize for putting you through this. As I mentioned before, I gained more valuable information from you in one hour than any professional could."

Terri was becoming emotional and attempted to hide it.

Jake struggled to say anything. He stood up and hugged her without thinking. Comforting her seemed like the right thing to do. Still, he braced for Terri's right knee just in case his judgment was off, but she didn't strike. Instead, she wrapped her arms around his waist and cried. Jake held a sobbing Terri against his chest. Her cry carried more than sadness; it was a release, with quaking shoulders and a heaving chest. They stood there as long as it took.

This woman's caliber surpassed Jake's previous embraces. It transcended comfort. For the first time, he understood what it meant to make a difference in someone's life during their moment of need. Jake was breathless, even though he didn't need air. His throat was dry, but he was not thirsty. Butterflies fluttered in his stomach like it was overtime in game seven. His hair bristled as Terri moved away from his chest. She looked into his eyes, her own shimmering with wetness. A small smirk played on her lips as she took a deep, calming breath.

"Again, I'm sorry for this. For everything," Terri said.

Terri leaned forward on her toes, permitting Jake to move closer to her glistening lips. He parted his lips to say that he would crawl through every cesspool in this city to find her child, scale every bridge to make her smile, and boldly go where no Jake has gone before and...ruined it.

"Is this when I'm supposed to kiss you?"

Terri did not expect such a question, which snapped her back to her senses. "You are kidding, right?"

"I think so?"

Jake shifted his feet, his face etched with stress. All his failed dating adventures swirled around his brain like an EF5 tornado. Jake tried, wanting finer words. He wanted to kiss her perfect face. Instead, Jake took a step back, not wanting to screw up more. He was good at walking away. It was easier than walking toward. But this was different. Terri was different. Jake knew it, but old habits are hard to break. He took a chance and stepped forward, swallowing hard. He closed his eyes.

"How 'bout we go for a drink instead?" Terri said.

Jake stuttered something.

"It's just a drink, Jake."

"Yeah, well. I really do want to."

"I'm over it. Let's get a drink and talk about our next step."

Terri knew she was being a bit harsh, but the truth was, she wasn't successful at relationships either. Her abandonment issues cleared away any fog that clouded her judgment. She was somewhat eased that nothing happened. Jake killed the lamps; gripping Terri's hand, they went toward the exit. Jake locked the door with the key and double-checked that the hideout was secure.

* * * * *

The plan was simple: Annie's Blue Moon on Montague Street, one drink, talk about what to do next, then home. Separate homes. As Jake rounded the corner of the Hanover Place alley, a brawny male spun Jake around and slammed him into the wall.

"What the hell?" Jake screamed.

Strong hands patted Jake's body.

"Monty? Is this necessary?" Terri asked.

"Yeah. And we are done. You trying to help this piece of shit?" Detective Molina spat.

"I told you! He has nothing to do with the girl's disappearance. Stop being so closed-minded."

"Yeah. You sure about that?"

"Yes."

"What are you two doing in the alley there?"

"None of your business," Jake said.

Molina sucker-punched Jake in the stomach. Jake fell to the wall, hunched over, trying to catch his breath. The wind shot out of his lungs. The already tender ribs from the hockey stick slash lit up like a live wire, sending a white-hot jolt of pain screaming through his chest.

"Holy shit, Monty! What on earth is wrong with you?" Terri said. She clenched her fists and went nose to nose with the detective.

"Stand down, Sheehan. This is an official police investigation. I have no problem arresting you, too."

"Fuck you, Monty. You are not going to bully us. You got nothing here. You're reaching for invisible straws. Stop wasting time with us and go find those girls."

"Again, Ms. Sheehan. I'm asking you one more time! What were you two doing in that alley?"

"Nothing. You, you dick!" Jake said. He managed to get to his knees, but he rose no higher than Molina's muscular chest before the detective made him pay up. With an open-handed chop, he struck a pressure point in Jake's collarbone like a snapping cobra. Then he wrapped Jake's wrist behind his back and followed with a leg sweep. Jake's face stayed pressed to the pavement as Molina dug his knee into the middle of Jake's back.

"Monty, stop it! You're hurting him!"

"What were you doing in the alley? Where is Monica Beame?" Molina growled.

"You wanna know what we were doing, Monty? You really want to know?" Terri asked.

Jake and Molina glanced up with interest.

"We were having sex," Terri said with a smirk.

"In the alley?" Molina asked like a hurt child.

"What can I say? I like it dirty."

"You had sex with this pussy?"

"Well, with this one, actually?" Terri gestured to her groin.

"Hey, just to clear up some things. I was the best fighter in my hockey league last season," Jake mumbled.

Molina looked as if his heart dropped a beat on a landmine. "I don't believe you," the heartbroken detective said.

"Well, I don't care what you believe. So, get your ass off my boy-toy, and leave us alone before I call internal affairs."

Molina freed Jake from his hold and made a final pathetic plea. "Seriously? You've got to be kidding me?"

Terri helped Jake up and gave him a massive kiss on the lips.

"Come on, seriously," Jake said, his wide grin displaying his boyish excitement while working to mask the searing pain in his ribs. "Let's go get that beer."

"And a cigarette," Terri added for good measure.

"Really funny, asshole! I got the *Airplane* reference!" Molina said, trying for some redemption.

The detective stood alone and dejected as he watched the two lovebirds twirl each other around the corner. Once they were out of sight, Molina stepped into the alley.

Chapter 24

A nnie's Blue Moon boasted an inviting ambiance characterized by bluish lighting and rustic decor. Warm light spilled across worn wooden tables where friends crowded in, trading laughs over plates of comfort food. The bar area featured an eclectic mix of vintage memorabilia. Its persistent aroma of bread and herbs made it feel like socializing in grandma's kitchen. Jake and Terri grabbed a high-top table on the second floor. The beer was cold and refreshing.

"So, boyfriend, huh?" Jake said.

"Molina's had a crush on me for a while. I needed him to stop hurting you. He's more predictable than most men."

"Aw, I can handle him. I was holding back because he is short."

"Ha, Detective Molina is like a 100th-degree black belt in Jerk-Jitsu," Terri said between sips. "All joking aside, I've seen him take on an entire apartment building by himself when I had to remove a child. He came out completely unscathed. He is very talented."

"I still can take him if we're both on skates."

"So, what's the next step?" Terri asked.

"Aren't you the professional?"

"Well, I have to get inside that cult church place somehow."

"My Uncle Duff seemed to have an idea. Let's wait for him."

"But in the meantime, what do you need to do?"

"Nothing, I guess. I would like to understand who this Jypsy guy was. Seemed like my father had a hard time with that person. It would have been about the time my dad got sick."

"Well, when I find Hope, I promise to help you find that information."

"Then, it's a date." Jake smiled.

"How was your father sick, if you don't mind me asking?"

"They said early-onset Alzheimer's or dementia. But never definitive. Dad went catatonic one day, followed by a series of mini-strokes. His eating and functioning ceased. Remained that way for five years until his organs failed."

"How old was your dad?"

"Sixty-six," Jake answered.

"God. So young."

"For the first couple of years, I fed him, washed him, changed him. Tried everything. Gave everything. But as his legs failed, he stopped walking. I couldn't handle it on my own."

"You took on way too much. No son should ever have to do that. There is so much help out there," Terri said.

"There are so many stories of patients being beaten, robbed and left to rot. I couldn't let that happen to him."

"Yes. But even your dad knew to get help. Mrs. Daschle, your uncle."

"You're right. So, I did have to put him in a nursing home eventually. I felt so goddamn guilty about it."

"I can't say I understand how difficult that was for you. But I am sure you made the right decision."

"What about you? Any family?"

"No," Terri said.

"Really? Nobody? Is that some teenage dramatics?"

"Nope. I'm pretty sure I told you. Left as a newborn at some firehouse. I was in and out of the foster care system till I was a teenager. Sometimes I had decent families, but they never worked out. Had some real shit ones too."

"Why did the good ones not work out?" Jake asked.

"One family I liked, the Sheehans. Lived with them through my elementary years. I was their only child. They were ready to adopt me fully. I was happy. We went on day trips and vacations all the time, had my own room, tons of toys and some friends. Then, Marc Sheehan died when I was in sixth grade. Heart attack at work thing. Erin Sheehan said she couldn't take care of me anymore."

"Wow. That sucks," Jake said.

"Yeah, well, she died a couple of years later. So..."

"I don't know what to say," Jake said.

"You said it. It sucked. Spent the rest of the time in foster care."

"Do you have anyone in your life?"

"You mean like an actual boyfriend?" Terri asked.

"Well, yeah, that too. But I also meant like friends, people you spend holidays with."

"I'm between boyfriends right now. Married to my work, I've heard more than twice. I have some friends, but they complain a lot like my past boyfriends. Hope is all I truly care about. That's the problem, I guess. She's all I've got. She is the reason I wake up in the morning. I probably won't have a job when this is over, so that most likely will not work out for me when I find her."

"Isn't there anyone better than Molina who can help you find her?"

"You're doing a pretty good job of it so far," Terri said.

"Somebody more qualified?"

"Mary. Mary Hollingsworth is my best friend and mentor, much like your Uncle Duff and Mrs. Daschle. She is working hard behind the scenes, for sure."

"Ever think about doing something else? Seems a bit traumatic, saving all the children of New York Shitty."

"It can be. But right now, it's crucial I find Hope."

"Hopefully, my uncle will have some information as well."

Jake walked Terri to her car. "Where do you live anyway? And don't say at work."

Terri laughed. "God, no. I wish sometimes."

"Really?" Jake asked.

"No, Jake, I don't wish I lived at work. I live on Long Island. Rockville Centre."

"Some fantastic bars over there."

"I wouldn't know. Always working. Love my apartment for the money. An okay landlord, I think."

"I'm not trying to be forward here," Jake began. "I don't think it would be safe for you to go home right now."

"I had one beer, Jake."

"I don't mean that," he said.

"Well, I'm not going home with you if that's what you are implying."

"I mean, it's legit though. You can sleep in my room, and I can sleep in my dad's room. Or switch. Whatever's more comfortable. I promise, no..."

She didn't roll her eyes or run away. Rather, her gaze was serious.

"I do appreciate it, Jake. I can stay at Mary's. She's here in Brooklyn. I have a drawer there."

Jake was disappointed but didn't press the issue. *I may be working tonight anyway.*

Chapter 25

A single bulb swayed from the ceiling, its light sputtering across the stark, square room. Monica knelt below on busted concrete. With every painful shift, grit and sand and jagged rock tore deeper into the bloody sores on her knees. A helpless groan rose from her chest through short, aching breaths, but she quickly forced herself quiet. Someone was watching, she sensed, listening and taking note of her sighs. Silence was elusive. The chains that anchored her to bolts in the floor gashed her wrists and rattled in what sounded like a sickening glee with every twitch.

I can't stand, I can't move, I can't escape. Helpless thoughts had barely evaporated when her head jerked up, pulled violently toward the sound of a haunting voice.

"You will learn from me, my angel. You will bear my fruit and rejoice in the joys of the Lord." As he spoke, Elder Devlin unlocked a hinged door at the front of her head covering, where her mouth would be.

Monica took in a deep, revolting breath. The elder's scent floated through the door and gagged her.

"Why are you doing this?" she cried.

"You dare ask me why? I am to be addressed as Elder. You will learn to respect me and mind your own business. You will work hard and do what you are told."

Light from the hanging bulb illuminated, ever so slightly, the inside of the wooden box that was locked over Monica's head. All she could see in front of her face was wood grain hiding amid darkness. Above her, out of view, a heavy chain extended upward from the box, fastening it to the ceiling.

"Please. What did I do to you? Please. I want to go home."

"But you are home, my angel. You are home. I am the way. Sent by the Lord our God, you will relinquish your will to my soul and complete my journey towards everlasting salvation. You are the angel meant for me."

"What are you talking about?" Monica screamed. Her body tensed, and the shackles ripped at her skin. Tears and sweat burned the wounds on her neck as she groaned once more.

"Silence. Or you will fast longer for your sins. You are to be reborn into the light of God's will as intended by the everlasting covenant that was made to me. You may not hear, see or speak until all of Eve's temptations are dissolved from your tainted womb."

"Please! Please! Please!"

"Please, what?" Devlin yelled.

"Please! What do you want me to do?"

"Please, what?"

"Please, Elder!" she said.

"Good, good. You will fast for one more day."

Devlin shut the head box door and locked it with a key. He stepped around to the rear of his kneeling subject and cut open her dress with a knife, revealing her bare back. He dipped his long, slender finger into a jar containing a black-ink substance and drew wings on Monica Beame's back.

* * * * *

Terri used a dumpster and a standpipe to scale the backside of the medical clinic. She navigated the moonlit rooftops toward Brick's Hardware's rear parking lot, careful to keep a low profile. An empty church van loomed ahead, an ominous reminder of what was at stake. She had no solid plan, only a fierce determination to reclaim Hope by any means necessary.

The back door of the hardware store creaked open. Terri stood at attention, hyper-focused, as adrenaline invigorated her muscles and limbs. Chastity Devlin stepped out, swinging open the van's side doors with an eerie calm. One by one, a line of three boys and a line of three girls emerged from the store, disciplined and silent. Terri's heart plummeted as she scanned the faces; none belonged to Hope. But the boys seized her attention. The danger was far from over.

"Holy shit!" Terri gasped.

Chastity searched to see which child spoke out of line. "There is no talking. You must all remain quiet until you are told to speak. Understand me, Shante?"

"Yes, Mrs. Devlin," Shante Britt said.

"Mrs. Devlin, Shante did not say anything," said one of the other boys.

Chastity smiled and spoke in a pillow-soft voice. "Elijah, you have spoken out of turn. Please follow the rules. We will all remain happy if we mind our business and do what we are told."

An atomic bomb named Guilt made a direct hit on Terri's heart. Terri froze as Chastity loaded the children into the van and drove away.

Terri couldn't reach the street fast enough to tail them. She sprinted to her car, yanked the door open and stabbed at her phone, calling the only person who still gave a damn. She prayed she hadn't left work yet.

"ACS. Miss Holly speaking. How can I help you?"

Hallelujah.

"Mary, it's me. Listen, do you remember those Britt boys? There were three of them. Elijah, Shante..."

Ms. Hollingsworth interrupted, "Yes, yes. Slow down, sugar. I remember them. What's up?"

"Who did you place them with?" Terri asked.

"Well, I didn't. The boys were brought to 1st Avenue, intake."

Terri raised her voice. "Where the hell did they send them?"

Ms. Hollingsworth stayed her usual easy self. "Sweetheart, I wouldn't know that. Intake does the placing once they are there. They assured me they would stay together, as a favor to me."

"Mary, you said you would take care of them."

"And I did. Per our procedures, they go to the 1st Avenue intake if other relatives are not found."

"You said you would find a way to keep them together."

"And I did! Josey, at intake, owed me a favor. She said that she will find a way."

"Mary, those boys are with the Ministry of Salvation. That is the same cult..."

"Terri, darling-girl, I know what the Salvation is. You never stop talkin' bout it. You have been down this dead end before. Honey-child, you must leave this alone. Your job is at stake here. The police are working on this. You need to mind your own business now. We have been through this so many times."

Terri swallowed very hard. "What did you say?"

"You must mind, well, child, you already..."

Tears ran down Terri's cheeks. She jabbed the end call button on her phone.

 **26**

The doorbell shrieked. Jake jolted from bed, stumbling barefoot to the door, praying it was not Miles dragging him to work. At the lobby entrance, Terri stood tense, eyes darting, scanning shadows like they whispered threats.

"Hey, what's wrong?" Jake asked.

"You were right," Terri said, voice low, trembling. "It's not safe at my place."

Jake pulled her inside, shut the world out and brewed coffee while Terri, hands wrapped tight around the mug, finally let the story spill.

Terri was staying the night. Her host attacked the mess like his life depended on it, stripping sheets, vacuuming every corner, folding clothes into shaky stacks. Even Mrs. Hitchcock fell silent, mercy-killed with a flick of the switch.

"I called in sick to work again tonight," he explained. "I'll sleep in my father's room."

Terri believed him. In the back of her mind, she felt it would be a test of Jake's actual intentions.

She awoke to daylight and two men arguing in the living room. Father Duffy yelled at Jake for not having breakfast for his guest.

"I don't know what she likes," Jake whined.

"It's not about what she fancies, you eejit. It's the effort a woman would truly appreciate."

"Oh, and Sister Mary Margaret likes that?"

"Don't be getting blasphemous with me, lad!"

"A little spam and eggs at the rectory?" Jake teased.

"Jacob! Do not...oh. Ms. Sheehan! Good morning to ye," Father Duffy said.

Jake spun around. "Oh, good morning, sunshine."

"Coffee, please," was all she said.

* * * * *

Father Duffy did not disappoint. The three sat discussing a plan of action.

"I've a connection that could help look into this Ministry of Salvation," the priest said.

"Sounds like there is a catch," Terri, the skeptic, added.

"Aye, there is. Indeed. We need to find someone on the inside who can spill the true intentions of that so-called church."

"Mary," Terri said without hesitation. "Mary is clearly on the inside. I can get her to testify."

"Well, this isn't a courtroom affair, Ms. Sheehan. It's more like a confession in church."

"How would the church be able to help without a courtroom? People need to go to jail for kidnapping."

"Ah, sure. That's a different kettle of fish from what me connections do. However, they can be quite influential with law enforcement when needed. You've got to trust me on that one."

"If your friend Mary is a member of that cult, don't you think she is far too brainwashed to help you?" Jake asked.

"I'm afraid the boy makes a valid point," Father Duffy said.

"You may be right. But Mary is an incredible person. I believe that she has been fed a load of crap. I can..."

"Save her?" Jake said.

"Fine," Terri huffed. "But I have to try at least."

Father Duffy turned to his nephew. "Do ya still have the Sing X card, aye? I've got another plan on top of Ms. Sheehan's notion."

* * * * *

Theresa Sheehan, a civilian, entered the ACS building.

"Whoa, Terri. Hey, what's going on?"

"Leave it alone, Rodney. Friel needs to see me. Should only take a few minutes." With determined strides, Terri made her way past the security guard and to the elevator. She pressed the up button with force. Her gaze fixed ahead, ignoring the guard as if he were a fixture hanging on the wall.

"Well, I think I'm supposed to call if you come into the building."

"Rodney, give me a break today. Mind your business. I won't get you in trouble." Terri surprised herself with that all-too-familiar phrase. It felt foreign, and it disgusted her. She glanced at Rodney to tamp down the fire she had started.

"It's been a wild few days. Rodney, I would appreciate it if you didn't call Friel or anyone else. I'm going to get my personnel file to contest my suspension. Promise. I'm not here to hurt anyone. I'll explain that I slipped in through the maintenance door. Friel is a spineless dipshit. You hate him, remember?"

Rodney smiled.

"Remember, you went in another way. These damn cameras don't even work."

"Rodney, you are one of the good ones. Thanks."

Terri stepped out of the elevator and headed straight for Mary's office. Her own door sat dark and shut, nameplate still clinging to the frame like a ghost. Terri didn't bother hiding. Let them watch. She stopped at the open doorway, staring at the woman who had once been her friend. Mary hunched at a desk, fingers striking keys like nothing between them had ever mattered.

"I guess you didn't bring me any more cinnamon buns, huh, sugar?" Mary asked.

"How could you?"

"What are you referring to? You understand you're not supposed to be here."

"Mary, cut the shit. What is going on?"

"Sweetie, you must listen. This is God's will, baby. Stay away from this now, and everything will be all right."

"You must be joking. Don't throw me that line of shit. How long have you been a member of that goddamn cult?"

"Theresa Sheehan. I'm not in a cult. I'm a church-going lady."

"Goddammit, Mary! You know I love Hope. I'm the only one who'll protect her! How the hell can you sit there and think those cult freaks are better for her? I looked up to you, trusted you. And you're blind to this madness! Is she even alive? Safe? What are they doing to her? Is she in school, eating, healthy or scared out of her mind, crying for me while you do nothing?"

Tears welled in Terri's eyes, her breath catching as the first sob slipped free. She tried to hold it back, but the hurt pushed through, trembling in her voice before spilling down her cheeks.

"Terri, you've got to stop. This is not the place, honey-child. Wipe your face and follow me quickly before anyone else sees you."

She looked older than Terri remembered. Or maybe smaller.

The two reconvened in a deserted bathroom on another floor, the one Terri sought out when she needed silence, where people couldn't find her. She gripped the sink, knuckles turning white, eyes focused on Mary's distorted reflection in the cracked mirror.

"Terri, you have to understand," Mary said, voice trembling.

"Understand? They stole her. And you helped them." Terri's stare sharpened. "That's a crime. She doesn't..."

Mary stepped closer, cutting her off. Her voice dropped to an icy hush. "The child belongs to us, all of us. She isn't yours. She is the hope. She is the answer. The new savior."

"Oh, you gotta be fucking kidding me!"

"Please, Terri, The Elder and The Minister have spoken to the Lord. She is of the light. Born of no parents. Created by divine..."

Terri slapped Mary right across the face. "Are you fucking insane?"

Mary pushed her rotund body into Terri, pressing her hard into the sink.

"Child, do not resort to violence to get your point across. Faith is the only way. I truly care about you and understand what you think is your loss. Give consideration to what I'm saying. What I can tell you is that the child is safe. She will be revealed to us all very soon."

"She is not theirs. Not yours. Not the Tanners'. It's all made-up shit, Mary. Please listen to me."

"Oh, sweet child. You know so little of the world, dear. I'm only telling you this now so you can rest easy. I love you like a sister, a daughter and a true friend, Terri. Nobody has worked harder at protecting children and their families. You are an authentic guardian for our Lord. I can't bear to watch you suffer anymore. I gave you this information to show you that I do care about you. Your heart is pure. I've seen that firsthand. You must, however, let God's will prevail. Please. This is the last I can say about this."

"Have you seen her? Does she ask for me?" Terri was manic.

"No, sweetheart. Nobody has. Nobody even knows she exists, exactly. I was tasked with protecting you from interfering with our savior's coming, is all. I assumed she was the 'Hope' The Minister and The Elder preached about. I make it my ambition to lead a quiet life, to mind my own business and to work hard just as I am told." Mary made the sign of the cross and kissed her hand up to God. She touched her heart in praise as tears fell down her cheeks.

"Protect me! From her? From her? Why? Why would you listen to them? You know me!"

"Theresa, listen closely. They are everywhere. We don't have the time. Listen to me. Hope is theirs. You don't wanna hear that, but she is theirs."

"Mary. Stop. You are not making sense..."

"Listen, child. Listen to what I'm telling you. She belongs to the church. I've spoken to the one who bore her for the Lord."

Terri became sick. "What are you saying?"

"The Elder would extinguish my light if he knew what I know. Excommunication."

"Mary, why? What?" Terri was losing her breath. Her legs quaked as if they were about to collapse.

"The child, the Hope. Hope. She was born to The Minister's daughter."

"Chastity? Chastity Devlin? Chastity Devlin is Hope's biological mother?" Terri huffed, waiting for the answer. She did not want to hear it, let alone believe it.

"I tell the truth."

"I don't understand what you're saying to me right now."

"Chastity Devlin revealed having the Lord's child to her husband on their wedding night. The Minister doesn't even know. She hid her pregnancy in shame from her family and dropped the baby at the emergency room. The Elder promised his wife he would find the child and bring Hope and salvation to our church and humanity."

"And, of course, he found you to help him find the child."

"It is God's will, sweetie. God's will."

"Who's the biological father?"

"Jesus, my dear. The child was born of his light."

Terri couldn't tell if Mary's tears were of joy or sorrow for what she confessed. "You're a brainwashed lunatic, Mary Hollingsworth," Terri said as she exited the restroom. "A *fucking* brainwashed lunatic."

Terri wiped her face and collected herself. Nearby, Arden Friel scrolled on his phone in a waiting area. Terri's unexpected presence caused him to do a double-take.

"Ms. Sheehan. Excuse me. Ms. Sheehan, you can't be here. You're trespassing!"

Irate and exhausted, Terri made for the back stairs, reserving just enough energy to give her former supervisor the finger. She didn't bother to look back at him. He didn't deserve that much respect. The stairwell door clanged shut as the words "Fuck you!" echoed off the cinderblock walls.

Mary emerged from the restroom, shaking and weeping. She wiped her face and headed toward the elevator with her head down, not noticing Friel, who had ducked into an office doorway. Friel monitored Mary until she entered the elevator.

Certificates hung above Mary's desk alongside clippings and photos commemorating past achievements and accolades. A "We Love You, Miss Holly" card written on a folded piece of looseleaf dangled from a thumb tack beneath a picture of Mary and Terri. It was taken at an office party, the two sitting side by side wearing novelty glasses and beards. Mary stared at this collage from her office doorway. Her desk was tidy and organized, and all her cases were up to date, but none of that offered any solace at the moment. Mary let out a heavy sigh. She grabbed an empty box that once held computer paper and began packing her things. Friel entered her office.

"Going somewhere?" he asked, trying to sound innocent.

"No, no, not really." Mary lied, "I'm redecorating. Less is more."

Friel let out a light huff.

Mary looked at Friel with watery eyes and said, "Tough day, is all." She had already answered Friel's next question.

The senior supervisor fiddled with his dark-colored tie and asked, "See you at the Ministry on Sunday?"

Mary gave the best smile she could muster. "Of course."

Chapter 27

Terri picked up her pace and exited the building from a different door to avoid seeing Rodney. She pressed Detective Molina's name on her call log and walked to Jake's awaiting car.

"Hey, Monty, it's Terri." It was troubling that he did not sound happy to hear her voice.

"What do you need?"

"I got some info on the Hope case."

"Really?" His tone was exaggerated; fatigue mixed with sarcasm. It unsettled Terri even further.

"Mary Hollingsworth at ACS is a member of the Ministry. She has been the leak all along. Mary purposely blocked me from Hope at the direction of the Ministry. She even funneled removed kids to the church so they could be indoctrinated into the cult's beliefs."

"How did you find that out, Terri?"

"She told me."

"And why would she tell you that? Besides, church groups foster children all the time. I'm sure there will be legitimate court orders and affidavits."

Molina's smug demeanor rubbed Terri's patience. "Okay, fine. Mary also told me that Hope is Chastity Devlin's biological daughter. Do you think there is a way to confirm that, like DNA testing or something?"

The detective sat up straight at his desk.

"Terri, I don't have time for this anymore. I have this Chief Beame case working right now. Everyone is breathing down my neck. Your asshole boyfriend and his father's goddamn ghost are haunting me. The brass is busting my shoes to find this girl that your freak boyfriend probably buried in his backyard and..."

"He is not my boyfriend, Molina. He didn't do anything, and what does his father have to do with any of this? How do you even..."

"Too many coincidences. As a professional investigator, you should know that too many coincidences equal the right trail."

"Monty, I'm calling you because I need your help. If anyone cares, it's you." She figured stroking his ego would set him straight. "We need to figure out how to get a DNA test done."

"Terri, are you ever going to go on an actual date with me?"

The detour threw Terri off for a moment, but her answer was direct. "No, Monty."

"I'm going to be honest with you. I like you. I help you because I have a thing for you. I always hoped you would come around and agree to give me a chance. But now, things are too serious for any games. I believe in your fight for Hope. I will give you a hand in finding her, no matter what. Right now, I also have to find Chief Beame's kid. No more jokes, Ms. Sheehan. No more little boys and girls crap. I will keep it professional, and I expect you to understand how patient you need to be. I'll call you when I find out anything. You have my word."

Terri's mouth was wide open. "Monty? Oh, uh, Detective Molina?"

"Yes, Ms. Sheehan?"

"You are so pathetic, but that's probably why I don't hate you," Terri chuckled. "I must say, I find it a little endearing."

"Goodbye, Ms. Sheehan."

Molina's partner and best friend for the past ten years, Detective McColgan, stood at Molina's cubicle.

"What's up, Lizzy?" Molina asked.

"Fingerprint analysis came back," McColgan said as she handed Molina a packet of paperwork.

"Damn it!" Molina growled. "Not a match for Johansson."

"Yeah, but look further. The prints found in the chief's car do match prints taken off that hockey stick in Johansson's bedroom."

"So, they belong to Monica. We know she was in both places."

"But look here. The prints don't match Monica's sample prints, either. There are no police records for whoever the prints belong to."

Molina rubbed the back of his neck. "So, whoever broke into Johansson's place is the same male subject who left the car on the bridge."

"How do you know it was a male?" McColgan asked.

"Verrazzano Bridge surveillance showed a dark figure walking off the Staten Island side. It was fifteen minutes after the chief's car entered from the Brooklyn side."

"Did the cameras capture this person leaving the car?"

"Of course not. That would have made the case easier to solve," Molina said. "I can never understand how these perps get so lucky all the time."

"Do you think this perp threw Monica off the bridge?"

"Your guess is as good as mine. There was no body recovered yet, and the Harbor Unit is still out there looking," Molina said.

"Hey, do you think Chief Beame did it?" McColgan questioned, her gaze like that of a thief.

"Fingerprints didn't match either. Look here."

"How do you figure it was a male again?"

Molina brought up a video on his desktop computer. "See. This shadowy asshole is a male. Look how he walks. See that little bounce in his step, like a limp. The broad shoulders. And the way he holds that cigarette."

"How many angles do we have?"

"Four. None of the cameras show his face," Molina added.

"Of course, they don't. So, what now?"

"I have the Technical Assistance Response Unit reverse tracing the path of the vehicle to the bridge through every goddamn camera we can find. I know that it will take some time and groundwork. It has to get done."

"How are these cases tied to one another?" McColgan asked, soft as if to herself.

"I tell you this...there are too many coincidences. We are on the right track. We will keep plugging away. I need a favor."

"Yeah, whatever you need."

"Go pick up this Mary Hollingsworth. ACS office on Jay Street. If she is not there, get a home address for her."

"Is she a suspect?"

"No. She is a possible witness right now. Use kid gloves. I would like to interview her here in the office. I don't want any of her bosses to know she's here, and I don't want her lawyering up or worse. I don't want any unions involved."

"You got it. I'll stay in touch."

"Hey, Lizzy?"

"Yeah?"

"Thank you."

"You're gonna figure this out, Monty. We got this."

 **28**

The sun climbed over the horizon, spilling gold across the Brooklyn Bridge as they sped across its sweeping arches. Sunday morning breathed rare stillness into the city that never slept; traffic thinned, and even the skyline seemed to rest. These moments of Manhattan calm were fleeting, and anyone accustomed to the city's relentless hustle knew these were moments that should be enjoyed.

Jake would have loved to sit on a park bench with a cup of coffee, gawking at high-rises like a farm-country tourist, flapping the sports pages of the *New York Post* before the quiet turned back into urban tumult. But that would have to wait. He had a strange card to play, and Terri's lead-foot speeding up Hudson Street left no doubt this was not a morning of leisure. She pulled into a spot near West 40th Street and 9th Avenue. The scent of sizzling street food greeted them as soon as they threw open the doors. Heat gathered on Jake's skin, sweat glinting on his brow, his pulse quickening with the promise of whatever waited in the restless streets ahead.

"What's wrong with you?" Terri asked him.

"Nothing, I'm a bit anxious."

Father Duffy smiled. "Have faith, and everything will work out grand!"

"I'm encouraged. Gee, thanks," Jake sighed.

Terri looked nervous herself, like the stress was contagious. "So, what are we looking for?"

Father Duffy answered first. "Damned if I know." He glanced over at the business card that Jake pulled from his pocket, then up at his nephew, waiting for some sort of explanation.

"It says *Hell's Kitchen, show card*...show to whom?" Jake said. "God, this is nuts. What in the *Hell's Kitchen* are we supposed to do?"

Father Duffy scanned the street, eyes moving over cracked pavement patched too many times to count. The morning calm had burned off. Now it buzzed with voices shouting over idling delivery trucks. Street vendors yelled prices over the hiss of grills. This part of Hell's Kitchen had cleaned up over the years, but the ghosts still clung to the bricks. Faded murals peeled on the sides of old tenements, and scaffolding hugged buildings like bandages on old wounds.

Jake hadn't walked these blocks since his teenage years. Back then, sirens and shouting rolled through the streets like background music. Trendy shops couldn't erase the neighborhood's brutal history. It still reeked of grease and exhaust. Neon signs buzzed above doorways, flickering in daylight that couldn't wash out the grime. Flower pots sat along the sidewalks, chipped and dented from years of boots and bike tires. A man in a sweat-stained cap nodded to Father Duffy, his city-weary eyes sharp, a small acknowledgment born of shared survival.

A thin boy with a bowl cut wandered past a homeless man by the rear entrance. Neither acknowledged the other. The kid didn't dodge, didn't look afraid, didn't even seem aware of the chaos around him. Jake felt the boy glance his way for a heartbeat, too calm, too steady, before disappearing into the crowd.

"Hey, let's talk to that guy," Jake suggested as he gestured toward the filthy man.

"He must smell great," Terri added with obvious sarcasm.

Father Duffy huffed and snagged the card from Jake's outstretched hand. He approached the homeless gentleman.

"Top o' the mornin' to ya! I'm hopin' ye can lend a hand. I'm a bit puzzled, to be honest. I've got this card here for a business I'm tryin' to find, but it hasn't got an address on it. Do ye think ye could help me out?"

Jake put his hand on his head in embarrassment, not thinking his uncle would take the lead on a streetside interrogation.

"You think you can help me?" the bum wheezed back.

"Aye, aye, I reckon I can."

The dirty fellow jingled his money cup. Father Duffy pulled his "Holy Water" flask from his black blazer and poured some brown liquid into the cup, which still had coinage.

"I'll take what I can get," the somewhat grateful man said as he sipped.

"Now, regarding this card." The priest flashed it.

"Here on 9th between 42 and 41. Follow the mark. Show the card."

"Thanks a million." Father Duffy turned to walk away toward West 42nd Street.

"Padre," the man's voice choked. "Don't lose that card. It's pretty valuable around here." His voice drifted off into laughter.

"Of course, he had to laugh after saying that," Jake said as he fell behind his two companions. "And a creepy Vincent Price laugh at that."

The three looked around. Terri volunteered to cross the street and check for any markings.

Father Duffy said, "Here," entering a bar tagged with a white "X."

The place was a dive even by Hell's Kitchen standards, a bar that looked like it had given up long before any of its customers ever did. The door swung open to a blast of heavy metal and the sweet-rot perfume of spilled beer, old mop water and cigarettes ground into the floorboards decades ago. Crushed peanut shells carpeted the floor, grinding under Jake's boots like tiny bones. A single guy lay passed out at the far end like part of the décor.

Two bartenders held court behind the counter, celebrating something or nothing, with a round of tequila. Their shot glasses clacked like tiny cymbals. Natalia, the short one with enough energy to power the jukebox, spotted them first.

"Aye! Hallo boys and pretty lady! What you drink today?" she chirped in her thick, melodic Spanish accent.

Her sister Maria, taller, toned and much harder to impress, leaned in with a sly grin and pointed at Jake.

"That one," she said, "is the most handsome man on 9th Avenue...today."

Jake blushed at the compliment. He caught Terri leering at the girls. She could take the pretty small one, but he doubted her chances against the taller one. She was jacked, with her muscles stressed by a tank top.

"I was wonderin' if ye could help me out," Father Duffy asked as he flashed the black card. The two Tequila Sisters straightened up in a snap.

The smaller one stated in her best English, "It's nice to meet you, Father. You may find what you're looking for toward the far side of the bar and to the right." Her partner motioned for the three to follow.

"Please come see us when you leave. We would love to have some drinks with you."

All three nodded and continued past the drunk patron toward a narrow door. The mangy man popped his head off the bar top. "Hey, you going to the door?"

"You don't bother them. Go back to sleep, or I'll kick you in your ass," shouted the muscular Tequila Sis.

"Oh, come on, Maria, maybe they want a deal," the drunkard said as he squinted his bloodshot eyes at Terri.

"No thanks, friend," Father Duffy said, eyes ahead at the skinny door.

The man pulled out a wad of hundred-dollar bills and displayed it with a toothless smile. Jake and Terri stopped and stared at the cash.

"What's your price, eyeballs?" His pungent whiskey breath trailed just behind the question.

"For what? Her?" Jake played it dumb at Terri's expense.

"No. The card!" the man said.

Father Duffy rebuffed the man's proposal with his own wisdom. "If he's willin' to part with that much cash for somethin', then this deal won't be doin' us any good."

Jake figured his uncle was right as usual, but questioned his insight. "Is that one in the Bible?"

"Aye," the priest replied. "The Irish one, sure enough."

Terri spoke up. "There is an Irish Bible?"

"Aye, it's called Murphy's Law. Jacob follows it more often than the holy one, he does." Father Duffy tried to pull on the door handle while Jake lagged behind, still eyeing the cash.

"Hey, maybe on the way out."

"Yeah, we'll see. Natalia, I want some Jamo. Make it the black bottle." Sounding defeated again, the man leaned his head back on the bar and started snoring.

"It appears that the door is locked." The confused priest scratched his head.

"Look, there is a small slot. It looks like the size of that card. Try it," Terri said.

Father Duffy slid the card into the slot in the center of the door. He felt a tug. Someone grabbed it from the other side. Not wanting to let go, he began a brief tug-of-war with his thumb and index finger. It slipped into the slot. Everything went silent for a hot minute. Then, the door clicked and swung open. Jake thought it was an automatic door until Father Duffy stepped in and nearly stumbled down a narrow staircase. Jake looked down at the source of Father Duffy's misfortune.

The guy was pint-sized, no taller than a barstool in a dive joint that served whiskey by the thimble. A purple top hat sat crooked on his head, tails to match, shoes polished black with white spats, trying way too hard. Jake stopped cold, staring like he'd found a rabbit in a trench coat.

This wasn't your carnival dwarf or fairy-tale munchkin. No, this guy was lean and tense, built like he'd crawled out of a jazz club's back alley after hustling the wrong poker game. Father Duffy held the door with one hand and tried not to smash the little person flat.

The guy's face twisted with rage, teeth clenched, eyes flashing like a cornered rat ready to bite.

Jake moved Father Duffy's arm from the door and asked, with genuine concern, "Are you all right, Squirt?"

Terri put her hand over her mouth.

His little helium voice rang out through the stairwell. "Something funny, jackass?" Jake did not expect him to talk. "Stop staring at me before I climb up your ass and eat your colon out!" The wrathful, dwarf-like fellow emitted growls.

"I'm so sorry about him. He's a bit dense. I'm Terri Sheehan, and this is..."

"Lady, I don't care if you're Mother fuckin' Theresa and her whole goddamn brood of starving children. I don't need your sympathy or your gawking. One of you can come in. One card, one entrance."

The Dynamic Trio exchanged glances.

"Jacob will go," Father Duffy decided.

"Look, Daddy Diddler! That retard ain't coming down here. It's you or Mother Theresa."

"What the fuck? Why can't I go?" Jake whined to the minute bouncer.

"Because I'm sensitive about my size, you fuckhead!"

"I'm not sitting here listening to midget mouth here. Let's go down." Jake took a step toward the rickety wooden stairway.

"I'm not a midget, bitch boy. It's called primordial dwarfism. Read a book. You're not coming down here." The little guy stepped from behind the door, revealing a rather large pistol strapped to his leg. If he were three apples tall, his firearm would be at least two.

"Oh my God!" Terri gasped. "You can't have that."

"I have every right to have this. It's called the Second Amendment, nunny tits."

"Yes, but you still need some kind of permit."

"Here!" The small guard produced a valid firearm-carry permit and a security license. "You satisfied, Gestapo Sister? Now, I won't stand here and discuss my shortcomings with you imbeciles. One card, one entrance."

"Listen, Polly Pockets, no more name-calling." Jake leaned over and opened his eyes wide to ensure the little guy could see them. "We need to see Mr. Sing-a-Song-of-Sixpence. It's important. He'll know us."

"You some kind of freak?"

"Oh, I got two different contact lenses in. I am crazy like that. Oh no, look out. I'm out of control. What is that supposed to be? Is that the latest fad for you raver kids? Get out of my face, freak."

The little guard became more agitated. Father Duffy lost his patience.

"Enough already, lads. I'm going. You two stay put here, all right? Don't be arguin' with Mister...?"

"Chippendale," the dwarf said.

"I beg ye pardon?"

"My name is Chippendale. Lilliputian T. Chippendale."

"Your name is Lilliputian?" Terri asked with puckered lips.

"You got a problem with that, priest meat?"

Jake rolled his eyes. "Did your parents love you?"

"That's it! I'm gonna shoot you now," the armed mini-guard said. Mr. Chippendale tried to pull out his pistol with incredible difficulty. He couldn't unsnap the thumb release and tugged at it until he fell over. Father Duffy had to catch him to prevent him from tumbling down the stairs.

"Easy, friend," he said, placing Mr. Chippendale upright like a little action figure.

"Rape! Rape! Help! I'm just a man in a little boy's body," the little guy screamed in his little guy's voice.

"Now that's quite enough," Father Duffy scolded.

Jake whispered to Terri, "I love little people. They make me happy." Terri shot him a look of caution. "Oh, come on, Oz, circuses, *Fantasy Island*. They're entertaining."

"Well, this one is obnoxious," Terri said. It echoed in the stairwell loud enough for Mr. Chippendale to hear.

"You talking about me, Toots?"

"Cool it, E.L. Fudge. We're all going in." Terri walked down the stairs, followed by Father Duffy and a sniggering Jake. "I don't like being threatened with a gun," she said.

"Can I keep him?" Jake asked his uncle.

The staircase creaked beneath their weight, and the passage narrowed to a one-person crawl, twisting downward into a hallway that devoured almost every trace of light. Bare bulbs swung overhead, sputtering weak glows that threw jagged shadows across the walls as the three pressed on.

A presence stirred in the darkness. Ten feet ahead, a shadow swayed with a slow, unnatural rhythm. Each movement landed with a dull, meaty thud that echoed through the tight corridor. They crept closer. The figure sharpened into view. A gaunt young man in his early twenties staggered backward two steps and slammed himself into the concrete wall. Head first. Blood streaked down his forehead, glistening in the dull light, a raw testament to whatever savagery had unfolded here.

"Are ye all right, me lad?" Father Duffy asked. His voice startled the young man.

"Oh, I'm sorry, I didn't see ya there. Good day, mate." He greeted them with a polite Australian accent and a smile.

Father Duffy glanced sideways. "Well met, but I have to ask, are ye all right?"

"I love this place," Jake whispered to Terri.

Confused, the young man evaluated the priest's query. "Oh, the head thing! Yes, yes, I'm quite fine. Motherway told me I couldn't come in. Says I was acting too hyper. She told me to come down the hall here and calm down. I'm doing quite well now. I need a few moments; that's all. Thank you for asking, mate."

"Who's Motherway?" Father Duffy asked again.

"Well, the host, of course."

"Host of what?" Jake now jumped in.

"Info! Are you guys all right?" the headbanger asked.

"What's Info?" Terri asked.

"What's Info? You guys do have an X card, don't ya?"

"We did until Baby Bouncer took it," Jake answered.

"You'll see when you get there. It's the bomb. It's what you'll need. It's...!"

The young man became excited. He bounced his head off the wall again, creating a bloody Rorschach pattern. Father Duffy placed his hand on the young man's shoulders.

"You need to stop this. You are doing more harm than good."

"I'm all right. It's important that I calm down. You'll love this place. Everyone does. I'll see you inside." He then took another header.

Jake grew bored with this and continued walking, trailed by the other two. The hallway stretched long and winding, its floor covered in sawdust. Jake's dragging feet tested Terri's patience as they moved forward. Soon, they encountered two large African American men standing shoulder to shoulder, blocking the entire corridor. They dressed in matching black suits with black t-shirts underneath their blazers. The men were similar in height and had physiques that broadcast to any troublemakers that, yes, they work out. A lot. They stood still like concrete barriers.

"Man, you guys have tiny waists," Jake said as an icebreaker that didn't break.

"Jake, these guys are a little more intimidating. Let's not start on the wrong foot this time," Terri said. The priest followed with a slap to Jake's head.

"Is there a problem here?" the enormous statue on the left asked in a deep bass.

"Because we were told that two of you pushed your way down here and insulted one of our employees," the other said in a similar baritone.

Father Duffy stepped toward the two behemoths. "We're sorry about that. We're here to see Mr. Sing X. We met recently, and it's mighty important that we have a word with him. He knows us, so if you could..."

The left interrupted him. "We don't do requests."

"And we don't allow disrespectful behavior toward our employees," said the other. Their coordinated hall-monitor volley continued.

"We are sorry, but you must leave."

"And you will apologize to the card taker on your way out."

"Also, please tell him his mother called."

"Have a nice day."

Jake let out his frustration. "What the hell is this shit? Alice in Wonder Oz?" He thrust his hand into his pocket and began thumbing his stone again.

"Jacob, please, you're not helping," Father Duffy scolded. "Look, would ye be able t' get Mr. X for me? He will clarify. I promise it'll only take him a moment," the priest pleaded.

Righty answered, "That is not an option."

They detected a humming behind them, coming fast. A Harpo-like horn honked as the hum approached, followed by a wild "Yahoo, bitches!" In no time, a raging lunatic drove between them in a golf cart, pressing the three rejected guests against the wall. He had wild blond hair that shot out from his giggling head, and World War II-style goggles covered his eyes. He donned a converted straitjacket as an overcoat. The two stone carvings stood their ground as the motorized cart stopped short.

"Yo! Tweedle-dee and Tweedle-smart. What's shakin', bacon?" the deranged caddie greeted.

"You, if you keep honking that stupid horn," Tweedle-Left stated.

"Delivery or pleasure, Beatnik?" Tweedle-Right asked.

"How about both?"

"Pick one. Make sure it's the right one," Lefty commanded.

Beatnik sighed, "The D one, man."

"What is it?" Righty inquired.

"Peanuts and that book, *Ten Ways to Sexually Please Your Mother.* The one you ordered last week."

Standing aside as thoroughly perplexed onlookers, Jake, Terri and Father Duffy cringed at the bold insult, expecting massive carnage. But the two goliaths only responded with laughter.

"Oh shit! He got you with that one," Lefty said to his twin.

"Yeah, man, and I had a good one lined up for him, too. I'll save it for next time. Man, Beat, you're a funny motherfucker!"

"Thanks, Mr. and Mrs. Cheeks, see ya soon." Beatnik honked his horn again. Righty swung his inside foot to the side as if on a hinge. Lefty stood still.

"Mr. and Mrs. Cheeks? Why are you calling us that?" Lefty asked.

"I'm saying if you two put your two bald heads together, it would look like one big ass." Beatnik moved forward.

"You are a funny motherfucker, man." Lefty laughed as he swung to the side, allowing the crazed manic to drive his cart past. A logo on the cart's back read *Nuts by the Cases.*

Horn blasts and Beatnik's carefree laughter faded down the hall. The two guards snapped back into place like a spring-loaded door.

"We are definitely not in New York, Kansas or Earth anymore," Terri stated aloud.

"That was corny," Jake quipped.

"Oh, look who's..."

Tweedle-Left interrupted. "You still here?"

"Oh, come on. We're nuts!" Jake shot back. Father Duffy slapped his head.

"This is goin' nowhere, it seems. But trust me when I say that Mr. X would want to have a word with us," Father Duffy said.

The two roadblocks began advancing toward the guests. The hallway was a tiny tube and the titans were a syringe plunger. They wouldn't stop pressing ahead until the unwanted guests were expelled onto the street. Ignoring the basic science of the situation, Jake continued to push his luck.

"You guys smell great!"

"Sir, we must warn you now. This will hurt."

Righty grabbed Jake by his shirt with both hands and lifted him. Lefty reached for Jake's hanging legs. Jake looked straight into Righty's eyes and offered a relaxed smile. Terri and Father Duffy stood frozen. Jake wrapped one arm around Righty's bulging forearms and kicked off Lefty's tree-trunk thighs. He knew he faced long odds against those giants, but he had clerical support.

Jake reached over Righty's shoulder and slid his hand down his back as far as he could, grabbing the bottom of his blazer. Lefty seized Jake's shirt and yanked him away, but Jake never let go of Righty's blazer. He pulled the blazer over Righty's head and arms. The man struggled, tangled in his formalwear, trying to free his arms. Terri screamed for them to stop. Jake lunged at the mobility-challenged Righty and struck him in the groin.

He let out an "*ohhhh*" with bulging, surprised eyes.

Lefty grabbed Jake as the priest jumped into the mix, pulling on Lefty's arms and pleading with him to stop the violence. Father Duffy's scream, "Is this how yer mother reared ye two t'be violent beasts?" halted the mayhem.

"What about his mother? Did she raise him to be a smart ass and never follow any rules?" Lefty asked while squeezing Jake in a heavy bear hug.

"Well, my sister did have a keen sense of humor," Father Duffy said.

Terri voiced her displeasure now as Righty shook himself out. "And his mother is dead, you insensitive asshole."

Father Duffy stated in concession, "Sure, that mad lad did say, together they make a whole arse."

The two giants laughed as Lefty set Jake down. "You guys are funny. Why do you have to give us such a hard time?" Righty asked.

Lefty added, "His mother, dead, your sister. We are a whole ass with an insensitive asshole. Man, that's funny."

"Oh, now I get it," Jake blurted out.

"Get what?" Terri asked.

"Why, that guy was banging his head against the wall back there," he answered.

An unfamiliar female voice now cut through the chatter. "Gentlemen, is everything all right here?"

The two laughing mammoths suddenly clammed up and stepped to either side, still chuckling through their noses. A redheaded woman in a dark blue pantsuit and white heels stepped between them. She sported a slight grin, but Jake couldn't tell if something had amused her.

"Holy..." Jake started.

"Shite!" Father Duffy finished.

"Oh, they are still here." The woman turned to Righty. "How come they are still here?"

Her strangely polite tone made her presence all the more intimidating.

Righty was still trying not to laugh but said, "We are working on it."

Lefty added, "They are leaving, Motherway, but they are funny."

She faced the puzzled trio. "I love a good joke."

Jake couldn't help himself, and before Father Duffy could throw another slap to the back of Jake's head, he let loose with, "Hey, you're Mother..."

Terri rushed her hand over Jake's mouth. Father Duffy let that slap loose. Righty and Lefty bent over, wheezing from laughing so hard.

Motherway smiled wider. Jake, bewildered, pulled Terri's hand away and finished, "...way! We met you at the gallery."

"Well, that is funny how things work out. I am Motherway, and you are indeed the two men I met at the gallery."

Her voice was pleasant and varied as her tone now seemed free of malice.

Father Duffy spoke up for the others. "Hello, Ms. Motherway."

"It's just Motherway. One name, like Madonna."

"Ah, sure, a proper introduction is in order. I'm Father Colin Duffy. This is me godson, Jacob Johansson and our mate, Theresa Sheehan."

"Nice to meet you all. These are the Brothers Twins. Donald and Robert Brothers." Motherway pointed from left to right.

"Friends call us Do-Do and Bo-Bo. We are twins, but we don't look alike," Do-Do added.

Jake again couldn't control himself. "Of course not. Bo-Bo must look like his mother."

The two guards began howling with laughter. Even Motherway was laughing a little as she continued the conversation. "Donald, does this mean you are all friends?"

Bo-Bo answered for his brother. "No, they are leaving," as he snorted out another chuckle.

"Well, that settles that. If you don't mind, I have other business to attend to. You are not permitted entrance. Take care." Motherway turned around to walk away.

Father Duffy called out to her. "Please, we need t' see Mr. Sing. He knows us; he does. I'm sure it was y'er who told him we were lookin' fer him. He came over an' handed us a card. He'll know how important it is, surely."

Motherway wheeled around to stand before the priest. She smiled, judging him. Without saying a word, she did the same to Jake and Terri.

"Father, you must not drink so much. It will catch up to you, so don't worry; you are making a difference for the better in many lives. Jacob or Jake, I take it. You must be a decent hockey player. You need to relax more, though. Your anxiety will get you quicker than alcohol. You will find your way one day. I have no doubt. Terri, if I may call you that, you are unfortunate. Yoga does you well, but your sadness is deep. Working with children tends to do that sometimes. You will need a break someday. Take care when that break comes. Vacation will do you good."

Jake was on edge now. "What, are you psychic or something?"

"No, Jake. I'm observant."

Jake looked down and saw that he was rubbing his stress stone again.

Terri scanned herself for any given tells, and before she could figure anything out, Motherway addressed her.

"Terri, I would like to try to help you. You may come with me. Donald, these two gentlemen may remain back upstairs till we return. No fighting, boys. We are all friends now. Got it?" Motherway instructed, but almost like a tease.

The woman left Jake and Father Duffy in a stupor. She presented herself as a regular, down-to-earth person, but her command was hypnotic, a quiet calm melded with an underlying power that left them fully disarmed and hesitant to resist. Do-Do and Bo-Bo Brothers seemed to soften their stance and apologized for the physical altercation. Afterward, they performed a comedy act filled with "your mother" jokes for their two guests in the hallway while Terri accompanied Motherway. She couldn't understand what had happened but went along with it.

 **29**

The two women walked side by side.

"How did you know I worked with children?" Terri asked.

"I can see it in your face. Teachers, pediatric nurses, doctors and even directors of children's television shows have that same look and aura about them."

"Yeah, but can you pick that up that quickly? What about the other two? How did you know?"

"Men are even easier to read; the hockey player's typical shirt-over-the-head move and the priest is a given."

Terri agreed and smiled back at Motherway.

"I analyze people. It's what I do; I study behavioral science as a hobby."

"A hobby?"

"And I may have earned a doctorate or two in the field."

Terri was impressed. "You should have been a cop or an FBI agent."

Motherway gave away a coy smile.

The two ladies came around to plain gray double doors with the word "Info" written above them.

"I welcome you to Club Info. Please enjoy yourself," Motherway said.

As the double doors swung open, the women stepped into a small room adorned with vibrant red carpeting that gleamed with warmth. Soft light shrouded the room, infusing an air of mystery. In the center, a solitary figure, a young man sitting on a simple wooden stool, captured their attention. His eyes bore an awkward, penetrating stare while his head tilted at an unusual angle, fixated on the floor beneath him. The pants, pulled up to his chest, accentuated his strange posture and the room's enigma. As the women moved inside, the heavy doors closed behind them, sealing them in.

"We call this the Screening Room, and this is The Screener. Do NOT tell him your real name, but what line of work or talent you offer. And your favorite drink."

"Favorite drink?"

"It is always polite to offer someone a drink, especially when you may need that person's assistance," Motherway explained.

She ducked into a partially hidden door next to the coat check window, leaving Terri with the one called The Screener.

The man appeared boyish as he rocked back and forth on his stool. His cartoonish speech did not soften his diagonal stare.

"Name, please. Give me a name. Name please. Name? Name please. Give me a name, please." He showed no sign of stopping.

"Oh, um, Terrrr...uh, Terrific. Yes, Terrific Mess."

Fitting, she thought.

"What do you do? What do you do? What do you do?"

Terri could see a pattern here. "Child Protection."

"Drink? Drink? What's your pleasure? Drink? Drink? What's your pleasure?"

"Beer. Sam Adams beer," she said.

"Good choice. Good choice. Brunette, ponytail, blue coat, child protection, drinks beer, Samuel Adams, Terrible Mess."

"Boy, you said it."

Motherway's voice sounded from behind Terri. "That's all we need. You may walk through the other double doors, please."

Terri spun, heart kicking hard against her ribs. She wondered if it was Motherway or a different person. The figure loomed taller than she remembered, draped in a pink sequined gown that caught the dim light like shards of glass. Golden curls twisted upward, pinned with deliberate precision. Bleached hair glimmered beneath the glow, framing a face masked in flawless pageant makeup. Dark eyes studied Terri in silence, unreadable, as if holding back secrets best left buried.

"That looked like it took hours to do," Terri said.

"Thirty seconds exactly," Motherway answered.

"Impossible unless you have a twin."

"Thirty seconds. Trust me, my husband loves it."

"How in the world?"

"Practice. You have no idea how difficult it is. I must keep everyone guessing. Part of the job."

"I need to be friends with you just to teach me that trick," Terri stated.

"We probably won't be friends," Motherway stated, walking to the doors.

Terri was unsure how to react to such certitude. It made her uncomfortable, but she walked toward the far doors as they opened. The beat of the house music on the other side punched Terri right in the gut. Smoke and lasers swirled around. People partied, danced, drank and smiled. It felt like any other club in the city, Terri thought. She looked around for whatever it was that made this one so unique, half expecting some dude from Hoboken to offer her a drink. Sure enough, a voice spoke into her ear through the raucous bass.

"What kind of information are you in need of?" Motherway said.

"I would like to speak with a man named Sing X."

"You will need to be more specific."

"I don't believe I can be more specific than that." The mystique had become more irritating than captivating, and Terri's impatience cut through in her response.

"This is Club Info. You paid a ton money to acquire our entrance card."

"I didn't, I was a guest of Sing X!"

"Not exactly the truth, is it?" Motherway said.

"I guess my friend Jake was given the card by a guy calling himself Sing X?"

"Better, and he did not use it for himself. What kind of information do you need? Tell me, and somebody will find you."

"What exactly is this place?"

"A club."

"During the daytime? What kind of club is this?"

"A club full of secrets," Motherway answered.

Terri was more curious and played along. "I'd like to talk to Sing X about a missing girl who a cult may have taken."

"Noted. Enjoy the show. You'll know when it's time." Motherway walked off into the crowd and blended in until she was invisible.

Terri meandered through the bustling club, feeling underdressed and insecure in the presence of such beautiful people who oozed confidence right into their drinks. A dashing man in a sharp black tuxedo approached her, offering a chilled Sam Adams on a silver tray. The condensation reflected the strobe lights. Taking a sip, she savored the familiarity of the rich, hoppy flavor, the only thing here that seemed in any way normal. The club was a riotous tapestry of revelers, each person a character in this lively scene. The music's bass vibrated, and the DJ invited guests to dance. Colorful lights pulsed with the rhythm as smoke swirled.

Terri recognized celebrities and politicians. Even Patrick Perri, the mayor of New York City, was talking to the Reverend Al Sharpton over cocktails and awkward dance steps. Another good-looking man with a short buzz cut, dressed in all black, appeared.

"Ms. Mess, may I draw your attention to your right side?"

Terri looked down at her side.

"No, Ms. Mess. Over that way. White golf shirt and black mustache. White Russian, as well as his drink."

The whole act left Terri squirming with embarrassment. Half of her wanted to laugh at the absurdity, the other half hated herself for playing along.

White Russian had an eerie smile, like Monty Molina's every time he saw her. He gave Terri the two-finger salute as he lay back on a loveseat with his legs crossed at the ankles. He draped his arm over the space next to him. Terri had already pegged him right.

Great, a real loser.

"Hey there, sexy!" He laid all the cards on the table. "What's a little cutie like you coming to this big, bad boy club for?"

Terri figured she was desperate enough to get this far, so she played along as the horribly fake Russian accent and hideous playboy act pushed vomit up toward her throat.

"I'm told that you have information that I may need."

"It depends on which information you need, yes? How do you score with a handsome, how do you say...stud like myself? That one is easy. Have a seat." The White Russian pointed to his lap.

Terri couldn't believe what was happening. "I think I'm good. I already got the information I needed. Thank you anyway." She started walking away.

"Wait a moment, baby. Do not leave yet. I'm just warming up to you."

"Oh, sweetie, you're on fire!" Terri made her way through a crowd of dancing girls.

Somebody grabbed Terri's upper arm. Not in an aggressive way, just light enough. She hocked up some phlegm and spun around, expecting to be overtaken by the smell of cheap cologne. Instead, she was almost nose to nose with a well-dressed, bald African American man who smelled of peanuts.

"Ms. Mess, I truly apologize for Mr. Russian's boorish behavior. However, I believe he is the most qualified to help you with your unique situation."

"Of course, he is," Terri said, dripping with sarcasm. "I'm not interested anymore. Thank you, Mister...?"

"Don't mention it. God bless," he said, then dissolved into the crowd.

Terri was now in total bewilderment. She finished the rest of her beer and looked for an exit. Upon scanning the club, she saw the bald gentleman talking to the White Slob. They seemed to argue, and then the dapper fellow walked away as the White Russian sipped the straw of his empty glass. Another of the club's employees startled Terri.

"Ms. Mess, this is a message from Motherway. She insists you take the advice given to you. If you choose not to, we will show you the way out, respectfully, of course."

"Of course," Terri answered. She glanced back toward where White Russian was sitting. He wasn't there. Neither was the couch. "I'll uh..."

That irritating fake accent whispered in her ear. "Looking for me, babushka?"

Terri was sure she was going to hurl on his tacky white shoes. "No. I was leaving. Respectfully." Terri looked to her escort for some guidance.

"No, no. Now, mily moy. Speak to me. You will find my skills to your liking, yes?"

"Was that a question?"

The Russian looked perplexed. "Excuse me?"

"Look, asshole," Terri addressed, losing her patience. "I am not interested in you or anything you have to say. I would have taken you seriously if you had talked to me like a mature adult. Please step away from my personal space before I snatch that ridiculous wig off your pointy head and smash my beer bottle over it."

Terri's threat prompted the young club employee to step back and raise his hand while twirling his wrist.

"Look, I mean no insult. I wish to help you. Please sit down and talk to me. You will see. The only advice I give you is to stay committed."

Something about how he said it caught her attention, as more prominent Club Info employees appeared through the crowd. Terri stared at him, silent, awaiting more details about why she should bother with him.

"I'm pretty good at finding lost people."

"Oh, good for you." Terri looked wide-eyed at the approaching bouncers.

"Yes. Much like your little girl."

Terri got it. "Go ahead, I'm listening."

"You must stay committed. These people use lots of, how you say...head games to control their subjects. Most of time I find person, but they don't want finding. I try to talk with them. Some go with me, some stay. I find them. The rest is up to, how you say...God?"

"Oh God, stop saying 'how you say'!"

The bouncers moved in. White Russian waved his hand at them. "Boys, please. I am having a, how you say...delightful conversation with Ms. Mess. Please, you may leave us to dance."

"So, how are you going to help me?" Terri asked.

"Please. Plenty of time for business. Let us dance, mishka." White Russian gave a light touch to Terri's arm.

"No. How will you help?

"I must ask for an endorsement."

"Well, how much are you asking?"

"Free for you."

"I'm not some fucking prostitute," Terri screamed.

"No. No. No. Mily moy. My services are always free for clients. Especially classy, beautiful clients like yourself."

"I'm not understanding," Terri said.

"I am financed by endorsements from different organizations with a vested interest in my client's case."

They stared at each other without words. The music pulsed. Terri tried to comprehend everything he had said.

"You must tell me about who took your little one."

"Ministry of Salvation."

"Where?"

"Brooklyn," Terri sighed. She lacked sureness in her actions.

"Why?" he asked. Terri looked confused. "Mouska. You surely know why? You were referred to me."

"Complicated."

"Try me," Mr. Russian said.

"She may be related to one of the members."

"Interesting. How?"

"Biological kid. But she was given up at birth," Terri explained.

"That is a difficult task."

"The church is a cult. Funnels foster kids into their ranks and brainwashes them. Seems that they get tons of money, and it keeps the Ministry filled."

"What kind of worship?"

"It is, I think, a Bible-thumping type. Christian, not sure. Real strict."

"It is not radical Christian church's style to go to such great lengths to kidnap a child. Must have other purpose. Anything else?"

"Like I said, it's this so-called minister's biological granddaughter. Possibly, he doesn't know it, but the crazy mother wants her back." Terri became nauseous. Her imagination swirled out of control. "They have her. She is alive. They are trying to make her into some Jesus figure."

"Description?"

"Thin, eight years old, blonde hair, four feet tall."

"Name?"

"Hope."

"Ah, very pretty. I HOPE I can help you, no? How you say...pun intended? Now, let us dance. Please, other women here will be jealous. Yes?"

"Definitely no. Now what?"

"I told you. I wait for endorsement?"

"So, this is about money?"

"Of course! To buy you many things. Diamonds, cars, vacations to exotic lands, yes?"

"No. No. And no." Terri folded her arms.

"You're not seeing big picture. My employer pays. Philanthropists, you say. You return favor one day. It won't take long to find out. Contact me at this number." He slipped a card into the inside collar of Terri's shirt. She pulled it out in disgust. It read:

Fehrenbach 1-800-CULTEND

She snarled back at him. "You are kidding? A one-eight-hundred number?"

"Please. I am professional."

"So, what's my part? What do you want from me?"

"Nothing but a dance with a beautiful lady."

"And if I refuse?"

"I help you anyway if my employer endorses case."

"Who is this employer?"

"No clue, but my employers pay handsomely for my services, provided they agree to case. Please, one dance."

Terri laughed out loud. "You are kidding. This is crazy. I'm not dancing with you, nor will you touch me again. I'm leaving."

"I require the address to start my work. Call me tomorrow. There is always another beautiful woman here. I am sure you will not find more handsome man than me."

Terri looked to any employee in sight for a respectful exit. A man in a slim black suit provided one. She emerged into the disorienting daylight from a sidewalk grate about a block and a half from the original entrance.

Chapter 30

The Tequila Sisters continued yelling at each other in Spanish while downing shots, as Jake and his uncle chatted about his father's exploits. Metallica's "Leper Messiah" played in the background. Father Duffy finished reading "Chestnut's Roasting" from *The Chronicles of Chronic Christmas* book Jake had brought with him.

"I tell ye, me lad, I never knew. I'm not certain I still believe it's really him."

Jake put his forehead to the bar. "I can't say I even like the idea. It all makes sense, though. The working late nights, the bumps and bruises. Especially the way he avoided my inquiries about how work was. I usually got a grunt, or sometimes a 'just fine.'"

"Hola, there's the pretty lady who beat the boys." Natalia lined up shot glasses. "Three cheers for women."

"By cheers, we mean tequila," muscular Maria added.

Natalia slid Terri three shot glasses before she sat down, spilling liquor. Much to Terri's embarrassment, Natalia looked right at Jake and back at Terri while batting her eyes.

"No. Not so much. Not my boyfriend at all," Terri huffed.

"Oh good, me then," Natalia garbled in Spanglish.

Maria interrupted. "Oh, don't listen. She's just kidding."

Jake gave a sideways smirk. "What time do you get off?" he asked Natalia.

Terri heard a slight slur in Jake's speech. "Holy shit! Are you two drinking with them?"

Jake and the two bartenders gave an emphatic "No."

Terri looked at the priest. Father Duffy dropped his head down and took a shot. He did not answer the question and smiled.

"Oh my God. You two are like children," Terri scolded.

Natalia laughed and batted her eyes at Terri. "You are such a pretty beech. I think I love you. We go out on date, I think."

* * * * *

The traffic dragged like it owed the city money. Oppressive clouds gathered overhead, heavy and gray with a purplish hue, a sure sign of the tempest lurking on the horizon. Father Duffy exited the car at his rectory. When Terri finally navigated through the congestion and reached the welcoming warmth of Jake's place, the air crackled with electricity. A deep rumble of thunder rolled through. Dramatic lightning flashes illuminated the Williamsburg Bridge, heralding the heavy rains poised to drench the borough.

"Well, now what?" Jake said after hearing all that happened at Club Info.

"I want to kick in the door of that freak church and get Hope out of there," Terri said.

"I'm game. Let's go do it."

"Yeah. But I doubt she's there right now. Probably at that brownstone in the Heights."

"Well, let's go get her."

"Come on. This is serious. What do we do when we have Hope? It will still be a crime if we force ourselves in there. Then there will be no way for me to see her again."

"What about Molina?"

"I told him. He might be working on it."

"Look, if what you're saying about your friend Mary is true, Hope is probably safe and not in any physical danger. Those freaks are likely taking care of her if she's going to be the next Jesus or whatever."

"Perhaps, but they will punish her harshly if she doesn't listen to the brainwashing. Hope is a tough kid. She is acutely aware of how these techniques work and the punishments."

"You are welcome to spend the night again. There will be bagels ready in the morning this time," Jake said. "I promise."

"There are also some things I must take care of. I need to head home before the storm gets bad. I need a change of clothes and a shower."

"You think that it's safe to be there alone? I can come with you."

"Jake, I appreciate all you are doing for me. You are an amazing human being. I have involved you way more than I ever should. Sorry for being so selfish. I had to..."

Jake grabbed Terri by the waist. "Shut up," he said and kissed her soft lips. Terri wrapped her arms around Jake's neck and gave in.

"You know I'm married," Terri said. Jake's eyes widened, and his heart stopped. "To my job," she added with a smirk.

"Didn't you just get divorced?"

"We're on a break."

Jake clung to the one person who made the world appear unbroken. In that moment, reason didn't matter. Desire never bargained with logic; it burned, reckless and undeniable. Outsiders might dismiss it as total madness. To Jake, it was the purest kind of crazy, the kind that stitched his heart back together.

"I'd better go," Terri whispered.

"I don't want you to."

"I don't want to screw this up."

Jake looked unsure. "What? Really?"

"I like this, Jacob Johansson. My life is not fair for you."

Jake was ready to take Brooklyn with his bare hands. All because she kissed him back.

"I won't get it right. Not now," she added.

"That's supposed to be my line."

"Beat you to it."

"I don't want anything to happen to you," Jake said.

"I'm a big girl. Besides, I got a baseball bat."

"Oh, a baseball bat!"

"Yeah. I was a pretty good ball player in high school," Terri said.

"I got a hockey stick. We can fight off the forces of evil together."

"Yeah, you do have your father's superhero costume."

"So, one day I can wear that for you!"

"Yeah, you went a bit too far there, sport," Terri chuckled.

 **31**

Chapter

Lightning split the sky beyond the window, throwing jagged shadows that crawled across the room. Mary Hollingsworth knelt on a threadbare prayer pillow before a hand-carved wooden cross above the mantel. Countless nights of whispered pleas had crushed the fabric flat. Thunder cracked like a gunshot, rattling the glass. Mary flinched but didn't rise. Rain hammered the roof, streaming down the panes in frantic rivulets. She clutched her rosary and prayed harder, her breath hitching in the dim, flickering light.

The storm reminded Mary of the severe weather she had faced as a child in Alabama. Southern storms were much louder, and the lightning was more menacing. The stormy sky would glow red during the summer. Mary found her life safer here in New York City, where the towering buildings stood as sentinels to shield her from nature's fury. No tornadoes or baseball-sized hail would dare to strike this place.

Mary thought she heard someone rapping on the door as she continued to pray. It was late evening, and she wasn't expecting anyone tonight. She lived alone and was not used to visitors, anyway. Mary assumed her cat, Nazareth, was playing with something in the kitchen. The door, however, knew things were different. The knocking was louder and more pronounced. Mary was nervous.

"Nazzy? Is that you making all that noise?"

Mary could see that her cordless phone was on the charger beside her recliner. She walked into her kitchen as lightning splashed again. The kitchen table revealed the silhouette of a devil. It could have been the shadow from one of her kitchen chairs with a high back. It could have been something more demonic. In a blink, it disappeared. Mary wanted to scream. She peered at her apartment door on the other side of her kitchen. The four-pane window displayed a wet and blurry view of the outside. Thunderstruck. The whole block seemed to shake. Another flash of lightning revealed a white floating object in the lower-left pane. Something Mary recognized. A white paper bag with a logo so near and dear to her.

"Tons of Buns."

Terri.

"Girl, I knew you couldn't stay mad at me for too long," she said out loud.

Her friend came to see her in this weather and brought treats. Mary hurried to the door, eager, as if God was listening to her prayers this evening. She opened it.

"Oh my! This weather is truly the work of the devil," Mary exclaimed to whoever was listening. She fixed her eyes on the Tons of Buns bag. What she did not expect was Elder Devlin holding it.

"Oh, Elder Devlin, please, please come in. You will catch your death out there."

"Thank you kindly, Mary," he drawled.

"What brings you here this evening, Elder Devlin? I didn't know you knew where I lived," Mary said, hanging his coat.

"I'll get straight to the point. I am here to inform you that you have been promoted to the Ministry's High Choir."

Mary couldn't believe her ears. "High Choir?" She never thought she would ever earn the privilege of being considered for the Ministry's High Choir. It targeted the more learned, as well as upper-class males within the Ministry. They assist in all decisions and lead various committees responsible for church business. Alongside The Minister himself and Elder Devlin, the members from the High Choir rank among the most respected individuals in the Ministry. The special pews also have comfortable padding.

"What else can I say, Elder Devlin? I must admit, this comes as quite a shock. I am a humble servant to the Lord our God. I work hard just as I've been told."

"I expect that you will continue to serve our Lord in a greater capacity now, Mary Hollingsworth." Elder Devlin laid the bag of cinnamon buns down on the table. "I brought these to celebrate. I heard a rumor that these were your favorite."

Mary smiled. "Oh, that's no rumor, Elder Devlin. That there is heaven in a bag!" Mary was so elated that she lost herself in the moment. They both sat at her little, round kitchen table. Mary opened the bag and removed six large cinnamon buns that were all stuck together. "Oh, my Lord, where are my manners? I must get us some plates and napkins."

Elder Devlin watched Mary pull the items from her cabinet. He also noticed that she took a small, thin syringe and a tiny, stout, clear bottle from her refrigerator. She then placed them on her counter.

When Mary returned, she sat down at the table and blessed thy bounty for which she was about to receive. Barely a second went by before Mary bit into one of the warm, gooey treats. With a quick, high-pitched giggle, Elder Devlin lifted a swirled bun with his gloved hand. He took a small bite, then put it down. He never lost eye contact with Mary Hollingsworth of the High Choir.

"Aren't they delicious, Elder Devlin? Jesus himself must have made the recipe."

"Quite delightful, Mary. Please, indulge in another."

"Oh, one is my limit, Elder Devlin. I do have the diabetes now. Too much of a good thing will do me in."

"Yes! Gluttony is one of the deadliest of sins. But one more under this happiest of occasions will be forgiven."

"Elder Devlin, you are surely enlightened. God be praised."

Mary bit into her second one.

Elder Devlin sat straight up in his chair, watching Mary eat. He sat rigid, both gloved hands placed palms down on the table. When Mary finished, lightning flashed once again. Devlin smirked as the lights flickered as well. The thunder rumbled after.

"Now eat another one," Devlin commanded in a calm voice.

Mary froze. The sound lingered, too faint to trust, too sharp to ignore.

"Pardon me, Elder Devlin. I didn't hear what you said."

"Please eat another one."

"Oh. Elder Devlin, I couldn't possibly eat another. I know I'm large, but we big girls have our limits too."

"Eat another one." His tone was still calm but darker.

"I can't."

Devlin stood tall and domineering. "Eat another one."

Mary did as she was told, her eyes now showing unmistakable fear. Devlin walked over to her counter and picked up the syringe and bottle.

"Diabetes. The glutton's disease. God's way of thinning out the sinners. Eat another one."

Panic enveloped Mary as she struggled to eat her fourth cinnamon bun, which caused her to choke. She kept apologizing in between bites while Devlin emptied the insulin bottle down the sink. Mary knew she needed to devise a plan, so she slowed her eating, letting the hot, sticky mess fall onto her chin and shirt. Mary clung to a single hope: stall long enough to think. Elder Devlin's eyes swept the kitchen like a predator sizing its prey. His voice cut through the silence, sharp and venomous, ordering her to swallow the fifth bun. Fury curled in every word, shaking the sweetened air.

Her trembling fingers closed around the dough. Instead of lifting it to her mouth, she let it slip, watching it *thwup* against the floor. The sound echoed, Devlin's shadow grew, and the room seemed to recoil.

"Pick it up and eat it now."

"I can't. Please. Why are you doing this? Please, Elder Devlin, I beg you."

"Do as you are told! Do as you are told!" Devlin dragged out the last instruction.

Mary leaned down to retrieve the fallen bun as Elder Devlin opened her fridge. He found another insulin bottle and dumped it down the sink. Mary noticed Devlin's eyes were drawn to the liquid circling down the drain. She jumped up from her seat and ran to the living room. The kitchen chair tipped over and fell back with a bang.

The phone. Must get to the phone.

Mary knew, somewhere deep inside her, this was no longer about obedience. This man was sick. And he wanted to hurt her.

Rushing forward, she made it to the threshold of the living room. She could see her cordless phone nestled in its charging cradle. She reached her hand out early to maximize her chances of grabbing it. Devlin coiled around her like a serpent. His gloved hand covered her nose and mouth with savage strength. Mary tried to suck in as much oxygen as possible. Alas, none existed. The rubber-like material in the palm of his glove was unbreathable. A quick, high-pitched giggle escaped Devlin's mouth. Mary could see an evil smirk on The Elder's face in the reflection in her decorative living room mirror. The same mirror that Mary often looked at herself in, because, to her, it made her look thinner. This man, whom Mary admired and revered, was the serpent from the Bible. The cinnamon buns were the apples of temptation. Devlin let loose another high-pitched giggle. Mary had failed God. She fell for Satan's tricks and lost to his temptations. Tears ran down her closed eyes.

Damn it! Damn it to hell! Mary thought as her light extinguished.

Devlin continued holding on for sheer enjoyment. He hoped Mary could feel the awesomeness that awoke in his tight black pants when he wrapped his legs around her.

A little bonus to suffocating the larger women, Devlin acknowledged in his mind.

He experienced the incredible sensation of not breathing for at least thirty seconds. He brought the doomed glutton on top of him as he constricted around her body. This was a high he needed to feel again. He snuck another giggle out of his grinning face. He let his grip loosen. Mary's body was limp as Devlin rolled her onto her side. Devlin stood up and brushed himself off. He giggled again.

Devlin surveyed the neat apartment. The storm was still pounding. Devlin stared at Mary's motionless body. A bit of drool dripped from the side of his scowling mouth. He stooped low and put his face right to Mary's closed eyes. He ran one hand down her cheek. The leather glove drank in her tears, leaving a quiet shine behind. Devlin licked the gloved hand slow and long to taste his sacrifice's essence. Then, Devlin pressed his fingers against Mary's throat. Without warning, Devlin slammed his other gloved hand down over Mary's mouth and nose again. He giggled like a maniacal lunatic.

Mary's eyes opened wide. They seemed set to pop out of her head, like corks. Devlin continued with his short, high giggles. Mary tried to kick and flail her arms. Devlin spun around on top of her. He pinned her arms with his knees and pushed harder on her breathing holes. Devlin imagined that his manhood rested between Mary's large breasts. His eyes rolled back, whites glowing like dead moons. A twisted grin carved across his face, straight out of a nightmare. Thick drool slid from his lips and splashed into Mary's open eye. She thrashed, blinking hard, then stopped blinking altogether.

This time, Devlin never loosened his hold. His hands clamped down with inhuman strength, knuckles pale, tendons straining. A thin, needling laugh bled out of him, too high, too eager, the sound of something unhinged savoring its work. The rancid heat rising off his skin made the air swim, and his boxers had dried into rigid, crusted ridges, the silent evidence of a monster who had thrilled at Mary's final breath.

Devlin rose and stalked through Mary Hollingsworth's apartment, reshaping it into his twisted canvas. Forcing her into the kitchen chair had taken effort, but now her lifeless face rested in the sticky glaze of the final cinnamon bun. The syringe on the floor and scattered insulin bottles littering the table framed the scene like trophies.

He slipped on his coat, ready to vanish into the night. Nazareth, the cat, slinked out from the shadows, brushing against his leg with a low, rumbling purr. Devlin stared down, lips curling into a smile. A shrill slipped from his throat, echoing off the walls like a cursed nursery rhyme.

Chapter 32

T erri woke up to her phone ringing next to her bed. She answered without bothering to check who it was.

"Terri, it's Monty Molina."

"What do you want, Monty Molina?"

"We need to talk. In person."

The somber inflection in Molina's voice made Terri jump up wide-eyed in fear. "Hope?" she blurted.

"No. Not about her."

Terri sat on her bed in disappointment. "Then what do you want?"

"In person would be best."

"I'm home on Long Island. It will take me too long to get there. Just tell me."

"Mary Hollingsworth was found deceased last night," Molina said.

Terri was in silent shock. All she could muster were faint questions that trailed off into breathless whimpers.

"McColgan was the one who found her. Looks like she had a diabetic emergency. I'm so sorry, Terri. I know she meant a lot to you."

Terri forgot about all that had happened. "No, Monty, please tell me this is a joke. Please."

"I am truly sorry, Terri."

Detective Molina described how McColgan discovered Mary's body slumped over her kitchen table.

Terri dried her face.

"What else, Monty? I can hear it in your voice."

"Something is nagging at me about this."

"What? How do you mean?"

"Too many coincidences."

"You think I'm involved with it?"

"No, no, not at all, nothing like that. It's not my case. The 7-8 squad is handling it. They are treating it as a natural cause investigation so far."

"So far?"

"It's my gut, Terri. Something's not right. Let's talk over lunch. My treat."

"Are you kidding right now?" Terri yelled into her phone.

"No, that came off wrong. I am concerned about a couple of things. There are no gimmicks here."

"Then what is your concern?"

"The medical examiner ordered an autopsy."

"So, isn't that protocol?"

"Yes and no. The M.E. rarely orders one if the person is over fifty and it's considered an obvious natural death with medical history."

"So, maybe they are being thorough," Terri suggested.

"Yeah, you may be right. Or maybe the detectives found something and don't want to jump to conclusions yet."

"Don't you detectives talk to each other?"

"I wish it weren't such a complicated answer," Molina said.

"Where can we meet? And don't say wherever I like."

"Bergen Diner, Smith Street. How's noon sound?"

"See you then."

Terri hung up and looked at her clock. It was 6:00 a.m. She got dressed and cried.

* * * * *

The heavy rain blurred visibility at best. For a few seconds here and there, Miles Orsky couldn't see a thing out in front of his giant rig.

"When did you last change the wipers?" Miles asked his partner.

"I don't change wipers, man," Jake said. "We have mechanics for that. I'll drive if you are having a hard time."

"No. I got it. You have been off for a few days. You can haul today."

"No good deed goes unpunished."

"What do you mean?"

"Irish Bible thing. Drive."

Jake got out and did his job. The cans were slippery and heavy in the rain. Jake was nose-blind to all the smells involved, but the sloppy muck made the day more miserable. However, being one of New York's strongest members, you learn not to complain. It makes the day go longer.

"Take it easy going by here," Jake stated as climbed into the garbage truck.

"That's the house you took the pretty girl to?" Miles asked.

"Yes, Lenny. I took the pretty girl here to play with the rabbits."

"They have rabbits in there?"

"Yes. And lots and lots of runaway children."

"I don't like rabbits," Miles said.

"Did you ever read in school?"

"I don't like reading either."

"Miles, that's probably a good thing."

Jake looked for anything unusual at the Chastity Devlin residence. He hoped for anything that warranted contacting Terri. But everything appeared normal. Even the garbage cans contained regular household refuse. Jake threw the garbage bags to the side and did not use the compactor. They finished the route soon after.

"Pull over here," Jake told his partner.

Jake exited, heading toward the truck's cargo space. He tore open the two garbage bags, smiled and took photos with his flip phone.

"Time to go home, Miles."

"What was that all about?" Jake's partner asked.

"I looked at the garbage from that house. It has an empty bag of Dino Nuggets, Pop-Tarts and Cap'n Crunch cereal."

"What? You're hungry?"

"No. It proves that a child is living at that address."

"I like Cap'n Crunch and Pop-Tarts. I'm not a child," Miles said.

"Okay, you're like a child. But Dino Nuggets. That's a dead giveaway."

The philosophical conversation back to the Department of Sanitation garage did little to change Jake's mind. However, he was sure Miles was going to the supermarket to buy a bag of Dino Nuggets. Whether he knew how to cook them would remain a mystery.

The rain did not let up. The two partners, in filth, made it back to the Pacific Street Station by 11:00 a.m.

"Stop the truck!" Jake shouted about a hundred feet from the garage.

The rain and windshield fog made it difficult to see, but Jake was sure of what he saw: a familiar figure leaning up against the garage wall. He was wearing a bright yellow raincoat and a matching rain cap. A pipe stuck out from his bushy white beard. The rain-slicked man stared at the stopped garbage truck. Jake jumped out and walked toward him. The man sauntered off with a limp.

"Hey!" Jake yelled. "Hey!" Jake trotted toward him.

The old fellow reached the corner long before Jake could catch up. Then, as if swallowed by the storm itself, he vanished into the downpour. Jake skidded to a stop, rain blurring his vision. He turned in every direction, breath held. The street had gone still. No footsteps. No movement. Not a soul in sight. Not a trace. Just the sound of water and the creeping sense that he'd imagined it all.

"Did you see that guy, Miles?"

"The Gorton's Fisherman guy?"

"Yeah. You saw him, right? I'm not crazy."

"Who is he?" Miles asked.

"Not sure, but he came to my father's funeral."

Chapter **33**

Terri didn't want to wait, but she needed to. At least for a few minutes. Exhausted, her heart broken, then broken again, she had to refill her reserve of patience before taking the next necessary step.

She left her apartment and walked into the rain. By the time she realized she should have grabbed an umbrella, she was already too wet to care. Besides, the Long Island Railroad trestle up ahead would provide a few seconds of cover before she ducked into her favorite local coffee shop for some much-needed caffeine.

"Medium coffee, two muffin tops," Terri said to a young girl behind the counter. "One corn, one chocolate chip."

Commuters lined up behind her, nearly to the door. For a moment, the aroma of coffee and pastry in the morning felt normal. Terri looked back at the line. Everyone was ready to start their day, catch their train, joke with coworkers. It was comforting. Then she reasoned that none of them were woken up by a phone call with news that their close friend was dead under mysterious circumstances. The comfort evaporated.

Near the front window, a woman sat at a high-top table with a young boy. Terri, coffee and muffins in hand, made her way toward the door, but stopped short. The boy had taken his cup of milk and spiked it right in Terri's path.

"Jesus, I'm so sorry," the woman said, frantically grabbing for napkins.

"It's OK," Terri said. "Let me help you."

As much as she wanted to help, the smell of the milk mixed with trodden rainwater gagged Terri. And the sight of the white liquid, she knew, was a sign. Her time was up, and she had to make the call. "You know what, I'm really sorry, I'm going to be late," she told the woman.

Walking back toward her apartment, Terri pulled out her phone and dialed 1-800-CULTEND. A wispy voice answered.

"Hello?"

"May I speak to White? I mean, Mr. Fehrenbach," Terri asked.

"Who's calling?"

"Terri Mess."

"One moment, please."

After a long wait, a real gem of a character spoke.

"Aye, this is Fehrenbach?"

Terri knew the bold Brooklyn accent belonged to the person who answered the phone, and to White Russian. The voice sounded like it floated out of a helium balloon and landed in a cannoli. Terri had zero interest in chatting.

"Do you have any information?" Terri said.

"Oh, baby, you bet your sweet ass I do. You have been endorsed. Where is this church located?"

Terri provided all the information she knew.

"Are you going to go inside and get her for me? Do you think it's going to be that easy?"

"Lady, come on. I'm a professional. I infiltrate cults. That's what I do. I get the subject out. My employer deprograms them. That's it. Oh, that is, if the subject agrees to leave. And the whole biological child thing is a challenge."

"How do you plan to get her out? Can you involve the police? You cannot, under any circumstances, use ACS. They are compromised."

"I am a master of disguise. Surely you realized this by now."

"Is this your real voice or are you trying to sound like a New York construction worker cat-calling my great-grandmother?"

"Ayyye, I don't need insults from no broad. My work speaks for itself. I'll get your little brat back. You get the paperwork ready."

Terri was confused. "What paperwork?"

"Look, sweet cheeks. You need to prove you are the munchkin's guardian. Have the paperwork ready in hand. We will be in touch."

"How?" Terri asked.

"Call me tomorrow night." He hung up.

Terri needed to ask more questions. She had to gather her thoughts.

Where am I getting any paperwork? How will I prove anything? What will I do once I have Hope? Run away? To where?

The new headaches started.

* * * * *

Jake drove around the area, looking for signs of the mysterious sailorman. After an hour, he gave up and went home. Mrs. Daschle opened her door before Jake could knock.

"Good afternoon, sweetie. I have your new keys right here."

"Oh, thanks for getting that fixed for me."

"Of course, dear. While I have you, I was getting the garbage cans this morning, and this man approached me. He said he was a friend of your father's. Weirdo if you ask me. He asked if Penry used to live here."

"Was he in a yellow raincoat?"

"Why yes. You know him?"

"Not yet," Jake answered. "What else did he say?"

"He asked how you were doing. I told him you were fine and that you were working. Then he asked what you did for a living. He wanted to know if you worked in, and I'm quoting, a law enforcement capacity."

"What did you say?"

"I told him you were a garbageman."

"Anything else?"

"Well, naturally, I asked him questions. He was very vague. He said he knew your father years ago, but they weren't friends. That's a bizarre comment to make. I told him that I had to go. He was very strange. Do you have any idea who he may be?"

"Not really. The guy was at Dad's funeral. Maybe an escapee from the nursing home."

* * * * *

Breath caught in his throat. Vision tunneled. The office walls closed in, pressing him into a suffocating box of heat and deviance. Devlin's body twitched, suspended by a crude pulley system bolted into the plaster above. His knees scraped the floor, toes brushing the carpet. Rope burned against his palms as he clung tighter, arms trembling. A sick, high-pitched giggle slipped out, raw, hungry. Blood rushed where it shouldn't, swelling with each grotesque sway. He imagined Chastity beneath him, helpless. He pictured every filthy act, every violation he planned to commit. Tonight, he would prove his power. He would perform. He would not fail this time.

Jonathan Devlin, Elder of the Ministry, the one. The only one who can bring her into breathless ecstasy, he thought.

Devlin's eyelids fluttered as his irises rolled back in his head, a satisfied smirk playing on his lips. He had taken a perverse risk, but it had paid off in spades.

Devlin collapsed, and his head bounced twice before resting with his cheek against the surface. Gasping for air, he lay horizontal and breathed, collecting oxygen like a vacuum.

Devlin tossed the rope to the side as he lay on his back. The emergency escape system he designed worked to perfection.

Just a couple more times today, and I will be ready for tonight.

He wiped the sweat from his forehead and did ten sit-ups, not for the exercise, but for the exhilaration it brought him. A sudden giggle escaped him midway through his set. Devlin stood and enjoyed the head rush before composing himself and adjusting his black necktie as he unfastened his noose system from the ceiling. The tall and slender Elder of the Ministry sat at his desk to review church-related matters. Soon, someone struck his office door.

"All are welcome," Devlin said aloud in his slow drawl.

The office door opened, and The Minister appeared with a shorter gentleman wearing a striking blondish-orange toupee. The man's wire-rimmed glasses were too large for his small head, but his bushy mustache and soul patch went well with his thick wool turtleneck.

"Good day to you, Elder Devlin. Allow me to introduce you to a new prospect for our Ministry. Mr. Jonah Richman Jr. Mr. Richman, this is the Ministry's Elder, Mr. Jonathan Devlin."

"Well met. I'm sure," Mr. Richman stated as he stood, looking around Devlin's office.

Devlin rose and gave a polite head bow toward the newcomer. "Welcome, friend." Words dragged. Devlin's demeanor radiated coldness.

"Elder Devlin," The Minister addressed, "Mr. Richman has moved here from Kalamazoo. He is of Christian faith and is looking for a welcoming place to worship and continue his work with children."

"Children?" Elder Devlin asked.

"Yes. I am a Bible studies instructor. I have taught youth Sunday school for the past twenty years," Richman explained.

"Mr. Richman has also made a generous donation on top of his initiation fees," The Minister praised.

Devlin stood stone-faced. "References? Sponsors?"

The smug Mr. Richman justified himself. "Elder Devlin. I have provided The Minister with my lengthy resume and a substantial donation to the Ministry. All references are listed alphabetically, and all contact information is current. The Christ our Lord has blessed me with the gift of enlightening our youth to the ways of the Bible. Blessed be thy name. I have found your Ministry in need of such a service as I have found a need for the Ministry's salvation. I look forward to your consideration and brotherhood, sir."

The Minister spoke next. "Yes, my daughter is needed at home now. The vetting process has begun, and I expect Mr. Richman's baptism into our family to happen shortly. As we have discussed, Mr. Richman, a process is involved in becoming part of our little Ministry."

"I understand, Minister. I look forward to working hard in the Father's name."

Chapter 34

Jake started throwing clothes around and looking repeatedly in every crevice of his apartment.

"Where is that fucking key?" he said out loud.

He reclined, recalling when he had last possessed it. He remembered locking the door to his father's hideout with Terri and then...

"Holy shit. Molina!"

Jake remembered being assaulted and patted down as he raced to the old bakery garage. The door remained locked, at least. He scanned the alley and the sidewalk but found nothing. He was more confident than ever that Detective Molina had taken the key.

Terri's phone vibrated. Caller ID registered.

"Hello."

"Terri, it's me, Jake Johansson." He sounded panicked.

"I know who you are."

"Listen, I've got to talk to Detective Molina. I think he stole my father's key when he attacked me the other night. He might have gone inside and seen everything. And some weirdo sailor freak is stalking me."

"What are you saying? He took the key?"

"He took it from my pocket. I know it!"

"And who is stalking you?"

"Some fucking Captain Ahab guy. He showed up to my father's funeral.

"This is so goddamn confusing," Terri said.

"I need that key back."

"Well, I'm on my way to meet him now."

"Where?"

"Bergen Diner, Smith Street at noon."

"Meet you there."

"Wait, he probably wouldn't want you there."

Jake ignored her last comment, but the anger inside him was rising fast, hot enough to sting. On the drive to the diner, the truth finally smacked him full in the chest:

Molina hadn't just frisked him.

He'd stolen the key.

His father's key.

The last link to his father's life, his workshop, his notebooks, his ghosts, all violated by some detective who thought a badge gave him the right to crawl through another man's history.

Jake's jaw locked. His stomach knotted. The betrayal throbbed in his chest like a bruise.

That is his place.

Jake's father's place.

Their place.

And Molina had touched it.

Walked through it.

Snooped through it.

Like Jake's family story was just evidence to be bagged and cataloged.

By the time he pushed open the diner door and spotted Terri waiting in the booth, he needed to take something back, even if it was small, even if it was petty, even if it was only symbolic.

So, when she looked up, caught off guard but not displeased, Jake leaned down and kissed her cheek. Not romantic, not sleazy, just loud enough, bold enough, deliberate enough for Detective Molina to see exactly what it meant.

A casual hello.

A private moment made public.

A clean, unapologetic *fuck you* wrapped in a smile.

Then Jake slid into the booth beside her, shoulder to shoulder, as Molina glared daggers from across the table.

"Good afternoon, Detective," Jake said.

Tone sugar-sweet. Eyes anything but.

"You look like shit, Monty," Terri said.

"Yeah, haven't slept much."

"So, why the meeting?"

"Why is he here?" Molina said, glaring at Jake.

"I need my father's key back, thief," Jake spewed.

Molina got right to the point. "Do you and your father think you guys would get away with being some crazy vigilante?"

"You son of a bitch!" Jake yelled.

"Wow! Monty. What did you do?" Terri asked.

"I'll do whatever it takes to solve this case. My job has become more complicated since you got involved with this guy."

"I didn't involve him. That was all you, buddy."

"How so? You took him on that canvas."

"You didn't want to go. Remember?" Terri stunned him into a brief silence.

"Look. I needed to see if Monica Beame was holed up in that crazy dungeon. Then I find out all this crazy shit. Look at the facts. An eight-year-old kid on your caseload is missing."

"Her name is Hope," Terri interrupted.

"There is no sign of Chief Beame's daughter. You and Johansson are the last two people to see her alive. You claim the Ministry is tied to Hope's disappearance, but your suspect is dead. Then, I find out that your knuckle-headed boyfriend..."

"Not my boyfriend," Terri again corrected.

"...has some secret chamber where he and his father play street *electrocutioner*."

"Is that even a real word?" Jake asked.

"It is now. The point is that all these cases are connected by one hell of a web. It certainly appears that Mr. Johansson is the spider weaving it."

"You followed us and then broke into his father's workshop!" Terri said.

"Don't you need a warrant for that stuff?" Jake added.

"What can I say? Bring the lawsuit against the NYPD. I have to find Monica Beame alive, if possible, by any means necessary. That's how you and your father operate."

"My father's dead, and I just found out about this vigilante crap. Are you accusing me of being like him?"

"Well, fresh batteries. Your hair fibers are inside the mask. Should I continue?" Molina said.

"Wait. You tried on the mask?" Terri asked Jake.

"Um, I can explain," he answered.

"Hello? Are you listening to me?" Molina interrupted.

"Look, man. I'm not him. This is new information to me. I never knew anything. But I need that key back. I got some stuff to take care of."

"Where's Monica?" Molina pretended not to hear Jake's plea.

"I had nothing to do with Monica's disappearance. I swear on my father's soul. I have not a clue."

"Monty, you're being unreasonable," Terri said. "You need to stay focused. You need some sleep."

"Don't tell me how to do my job," Molina snapped.

"Look, Detective, give me my father's key back."

"No. I'm not letting you go electrocuting some hood rats because you believe you're more capable than the police."

"Look. My father was a hero. If you read anything in that journal, you will see that he did it for the greater good against evil. He helped the police. My father loved you guys. He didn't follow the rules like you do. Oh, wait!"

"This ain't no comic book, son!"

"Yeah, and I have no intention of following in his footsteps."

"Monty, he is telling the truth. You and I have been friends for a long time," Terri said. "Trust me, please. Give him the key back."

"Why do you need the key so bad? What will it accomplish? The equipment there is dangerous, and those notes and journals may be tied to evidence from hundreds of cases."

"Look, I think a guy who knew my father is stalking me. And I think my father was involved somehow in the death of a child about six years ago."

"What child?"

"A nine-year-old named Katie Heitz."

"Sounds familiar. Murdered?"

"Maybe. Parents were originally blamed, but it was ruled an accident after the trial. My father seemed to be involved somehow. It was about the time he became sick, though."

"What about this stalker?" Molina asked.

"Some guy dressed like a sailor. He was at my father's funeral, and now I've seen him in my workplace, and he's been to my home."

"The break-in?" Terri and Molina both asked.

"No, that was a different guy. Different voice and bigger. Maybe related."

"Why didn't you tell me this while you were at my office?"

"I only saw him again this morning at my job, and Mrs. D saw him in front of our building, too."

"So, how do you think the two incidents are related?"

"I don't, but coincidence seems to be the common theme here."

"Speaking of coincidence, Ms. Sheehan. That is why I called you here. You said Mary Hollingsworth was involved in shielding you from Hope and a church member?"

"Yes."

"When did you last speak to her?"

"Friday."

"I did confer with the 7-8 squad boss. He does think this was a tragic accident. Did you know she had diabetes?" Molina asked as he started writing notes on a notepad.

"Yes. I did."

"They said she seemed to have eaten some pastries and was out of insulin. Her family is cooperative and not surprised. She was very overweight and had a documented heart condition as well."

"So, another coincidence?" Terri asked.

"Yeah, another one," Molina answered. Skepticism oozed from his lips. "Who else knows you talked to Mary on Friday?"

"Nobody."

"Where did you speak to her?"

"At the ACS office, we talked in a bathroom on another floor."

"Aren't you suspended?"

"I am. Any means necessary. Is that how that goes?" she answered.

"Nobody saw you there?"

"Well, Rodney in the lobby saw me come in, but he didn't know I spoke to her."

"Who else?"

Terri paused to think. "My boss, Arden Friel, saw me in the office but didn't see me in the bathroom with Mary."

"Did he say anything?"

"Yeah. Friel told me I was trespassing."

"And then?" Molina pushed.

"I gave him the finger and left."

"That's it?"

"Yes. I'm sure of it. I wasn't there that long. What's going on?"

"Ms. Hollingsworth's family requested that her church not be involved in her funeral services. It seems they have problems with them, too. Her sister made a special request through the Medical Examiner's Office for the NYPD's help enforcing the family's wishes."

"I'm sure that is common with families outside a cult-like MOS," Terri said.

"Not really, according to the M.E. I did ask that very question. It goes by the deceased's wishes. However, with no will found, the church is pushing for immediate cremation. Do you have any insight on that as her friend?"

"Definitely not. Why such an interest in this? What does this have to do with Hope?"

"I want to free Hope from that place, if she's even there. That's my job."

"What do you mean by that?" Terri gasped.

"I'm working on both cases here. I'll be in touch." Detective Molina got up and threw cash on the table for the coffee.

"Wait. I want my key back," Jake whined.

"No," the detective said and walked out.

Jake wanted to continue battling Molina for his key, but his phone rang. It was his uncle. He looked across the table at Terri and answered.

"Yeah, I'm actually with her right now," he said. He cupped his hand over the receiver and leaned toward Terri. "You busy?"

"Does it involve finding Hope?"

* * * * *

Father Duffy entered the office carrying a tray of coffee and a variety of bagels. Terri thanked him for his hospitality, and the two told Father Duffy everything that had happened.

The serious-looking priest sat back in his desk chair.

"I must admit, I was up all night ponderin' the situation at hand, Ms. Sheehan. I've concluded that this church might be quite useful in helpin' you. The Lord works in mysterious ways; there's no exception for you, dear. Ms. Sheehan, Theresa. I always say there are no coincidences. Only the path laid down by the Holy Father. I say it, but I'll be honest, I don't always believe it. But I do now. I'd like to reintroduce you to someone who you'll be keen to hear from. Jacob, stay here for a wee moment, will ya?"

"Where are we going?" Terri said, between bites of her sesame bagel.

"Right here in the church, it 'tis?"

Father Duffy and Terri walked down a stone corridor, the echo of their footsteps reverberating off the cool, rough walls. They soon entered a large room, a sacred library filled with the scent of old paper and wood. Tall shelves crammed with dusty tomes lined the walls, their spines of faded titles and ornate designs. Toward the end of the library loomed an unremarkable door, unassuming yet inviting, nestled between two towering bookshelves. As they approached the door, it creaked open, revealing Father Benny standing inside a spacious room. His warm smile welcomed them.

"Well, Ms. Sheehan. I remember meeting you the other day. A friend of Jacob's." Benny took Terri by the arm. "Please let me give you a tour. Welcome to the Lords of Loyola."

"A right intricate operation it 'tis. I must be insistin' that ye keep this bleedin' conversation, an' the whole place, hush-hush, even to Jacob, mind ye!" Father Duffy said.

Terri explored the round room, her eyes scanning the surroundings with curiosity. The walls and floor comprised gray cobblestones, which gave the space a rustic feel. A large green rug lay in the center, contrasting with the dull-colored stones and beckoning her closer with expertly detailed patterns. Religious artifacts were arranged inside the cases, standing like trophies of significance and history, like they were waiting for someone to admire their stories. Etched around the tops of the walls, Terri noticed words in an unfamiliar script. Their meanings eluded her, but added an air of mystery to the room. They were written in Latin.

Exodus 20:3 non habebis deos alienos coram me

As she continued to read the words around the room, she also came upon the translation:

Thou shalt not have strange gods before me.

The ceiling towered overhead, shaped into a grand, domed vault carved from polished stone. Light struck the surface and scattered in soft, celestial glimmers. Clean lines and bare walls framed the room with absolute intention. Terri welcomed the clarity. The design dismissed excess, favoring bold simplicity. Yet every element whispered reverence. Vastness hushed her thoughts. The hush carried a strange gravity, pulling at her chest until even her breath felt reverent. No part of the space asked for admiration; every inch demanded it.

"This room is the Commandment Room. We use this room for conferences and to safeguard confiscated artifacts," Father Benny explained.

"Is that a golden cow?" Terri pointed out one of the display cases.

Father Duffy chuckled. "Ah, so it is. From the film *Dogma*. I tell ya, it's one of my favorite bits in our collection and one of my favorite movies! It's a wee bit of a humorous take on what we do here. Just a touch of comic relief, y'know? Have ya seen that film?"

"I love Kevin Smith movies," Terri said.

"Ah, that's why we get along so well."

Terri wandered deeper into the room, eyes wide as they swept across the display cases. Her head tilted with every step, caught between confusion and wonder. The cases burst with strange artifacts, each piece humming with secrets older than memory. A voodoo doll leered through cracked glass, its twisted stitches carved menace into its fabric face. Beside it, a shrunken head rested in solemn silence, skin leathery and shriveled, lips sewn shut to guard forgotten rituals.

An obsidian swastika gleamed under the dim glow, shadows clinging to its edges. Dust-choked cobwebs veiled it like a relic best left untouched. A river-smooth stone lay nestled next to a blackened brass lamp, its spout bent, its surface scarred by time and misuse. Framed photographs loomed from the walls, preachers frozen mid-cry, eyes ablaze with wild devotion, mouths twisted in eternal sermons.

Terri stepped closer to a cloudy jar housing a coiled serpent, its skin pale and eyes milky white beneath the formaldehyde. Her breath caught. Wonder twisted into dread. The room didn't simply hold history; it pulsed with it, like a shrine to things better left buried.

Father Benny then continued the commentary.

"This room also reminds us of what we are here for." The little priest paused for dramatic effect. "Wait for it. Wait for it."

Terri rolled her eyes and crossed her arms.

"The Lords of Loyola are enforcers of the First Commandment!"

"Like in the Ten Commandments?" Terri asked to show that she was indeed paying attention.

"Exactly," Father Duffy said. "Well, to be exact, we enforce Commandments one, two and three."

"Who enforces the other Commandments?" Terri half-joked.

"Irish Catholic grandmothers and the police," Father Benny answered.

Father Duffy took up the explanation. "They're a secret society backed by the Vatican, stopping false idol worship, like cults. I don't mean your average traveling evangelist out fer a quick buck. The Lords of Loyola are there to stop any life-takin', mass suicide, an' even kidnappin'."

"What about other religions, Islam, Judaism and Protestantism?"

"No. No. Not like that," Father Benny interrupted. "All mainstream religions worship the same Almighty Father. It's how we worship that makes us different. The Old Testament is the same for all of us. If I may simplify it for you, it gets complicated about the New Testament."

Father Duffy continued, "The L.O.L. must remain secret to be effective. They focus on the removal and deprogramming of a victim to preserve their life. They will also remove a victim who cannot escape their situation. If the person truly believes in what the unholy organization is selling, Lords of Loyola cannot and will not interfere. Free will is a sacred promise from God."

"What about a child?" Terri asked.

"Complicated," Father Benny sighed. "Very complicated."

Terri was intrigued and asked, "You said enforce. Does that mean you take the offending party into some kind of custody?"

Father Benny took the question. "No, not like that at all. We can expose corruptors publicly or financially disable the organization discreetly."

The trio entered a doorway that led to another sizable room. It possessed similar stone walls, yet it was square. It had six mahogany desks, each with a computer and phone. File cabinets claimed the entire back wall. Above them, a massive map of New York City. Colored pins marked various points on the map.

"This is our command center. Everything we need as investigators is in here. There are five of us tasked with New York City's dealings. We are a worldwide group. However,

New York City is unique in size, population and dynamics. We are assigned to stay exclusively within this jurisdiction. We have a wealth of resources and an incredible sense of humor. Thus, our acronym, L.O.L."

Father Benny moved to the right side of the office toward another door. A large glass window overlooked a smaller room with a conference table, a folder on top and some chairs. Terri, along with Father Duffy, followed behind and sat down. Father Benny looked serious behind his Coke-bottle glasses. He leaned over and spoke in a soft, direct voice.

"Ms. Sheehan, do you know a man who goes by the name of Fehrenbach?"

Terri shifted in her seat. "What the hell?"

Father Duffy jumped in. "Aye, Father Benny knows him as well."

Terri answered, "Yes? Sort of?"

"Fehrenbach is an agent of ours. Sometimes, he is a bit of a flake, but he has been very successful for us, at different times."

"That guy is a Lord of Loyola?" Terri asked, concerned.

"He's a private investigator we occasionally hire. Known for his talent with disguises. He can convincingly pose as a follower of fake prophets. Fehrenbach's ability to quickly absorb the beliefs and customs of his targets makes him invaluable. One time, he even infiltrated a massive secular sports compound while tracking a teenager brainwashed by his soccer coach."

Father Duffy nodded at Terri as Benny continued.

"If I remember right, Fehrenbach was Mr. Victor Van Le Pew. Convinced everyone at that compound that a made-up deficiency caused his addiction to milk. The truth was that crazy son of a gun walked around there for weeks, always holding a milk carton with the missing child's picture on it."

"Did he get the child?" Terri inquired.

"He did."

"Well, he makes a terrible White Russian," Terri commented.

"Fehrenbach had come to us with information about a foster child taken by her biological mother, who is a member of a radical Christian-type church. We would not normally investigate such a case. We turned down Colin here when he asked for our help. I recognized the unlikely coincidence and did some digging. I found a past file on this denomination of Christ."

Father Benny patted the file on the table.

"It involved a teenage parishioner of the Ministry of Salvation. The desperate kid had somehow found us and implored that we investigate the Ministry, claiming that the lives of some parishioners were at risk and that there was a high rate of suicide within its sect. The boy, I recollect, desired to flee the Ministry, but he wasn't able to abandon his devout parents. He begged us for help. We explained that our organization was not authorized to intervene and recommended that the boy contact a more conventional authority. From what we understood, the boy ultimately left the Ministry of his own accord, according to some witnesses."

"What about his parents?" Terri asked.

"Christian and Marylyn Miller. They stayed. May still be worshipping there. I, we wouldn't be aware," Benny answered. "Troubled young man, he was. In hindsight, may have been on to something. We endorsed Fehrenbach to investigate your case and report any findings to us. He knows our protocols."

"What did Fehrenbach report?" Terri anticipated the answer.

"Nothing yet. That is not unusual. It takes him a while to fully immerse himself in an organization. Likes to prolong things because he knows we will pay. Ms. Sheehan, how did you find Fehrenbach exactly?"

"Club Info," Terri answered., though she was not sure if she should have disclosed that information.

"Is that some sort of website?" Father Benny asked.

Father Duffy chimed in, "No. Not 'tall. 'Tis some social club. One hell of an operation, that it is. 'Tis a place for extreme networking. You lot need to get in on this one, somehow."

Terri's eyes widened. "Wait, Father Duffy. You're not part of Lords of Lola?"

"Loyola," Father Duffy corrected. "Well, no, not exactly. I'm a trusted member of St. Francis Xavier, a sort of liaison, y'know."

Father Benny provided more detail.

"Colin kept poking around and asking too many questions about what we were doing. The insufferable man always seemed to be nearby, constantly judging and pointing out minute details of our comings and goings. His constant presence at Pontiff's made it difficult to conduct business without him overhearing something confidential. Above all, he is the most reliable, genuine pal anyone might request. Giving him a position would be the only logical move. Around here, they call him the Lock of Loyola."

"I am the keeper of their anonymity, I am. At times, I must guide church officials, me colleagues, and others away from knowin' about the Lords of Loyola."

"It is a complicated professional relationship, but we find it effective," Father Benny said. "If someone gets too close to this organization, Father Duffy gets them drunk. He convinces them that their suspicions of our super-secret missions are a crazy conspiracy theory. He told one curious Cardinal that the Lords of Loyola was a Dungeons and Dragons role-playing club for priests."

"Ah, that's the craic of bein' the Lock, isn't it?" Father Duffy laughed.

"What is Pontiff's, then?" Terri asked.

Both priests chuckled like two twenty-year-olds about to reach drinking age.

"It's a bar!" they answered.

"Oh, speaking of minding one's business, why is all this happening to Hope? She doesn't deserve any of it. She is shoved around from one bad situation to another. Maybe this is all my fault. Perhaps if I had let her be when she left the hospital. Goddammit, I was so stupid. Why didn't I listen? All this time, it was Chastity. Hope's biological mother. She has been the one trying to get Hope back. What if she was forced to give up Hope? Who am I to take a child away from their rightful mother? Who the hell am I to think? Mary is gone. She always knew what to do, but Mary betrayed me. Damn, she was right all along. I can't figure this all out without her."

"Theresa."

That was all the burly priest could say. He hugged the now-hysterical Terri Sheehan, who cried on his shoulder. They all laughed when Father Benny nestled himself between the two and hugged them both. Terri wiped her tears and regained her composure.

"Where do we go from here?" Terri asked.

"In light of the information we have," Father Benny paused. "We still need more evidence and information on the Ministry of Salvation."

Father Duffy interjected. "May I suggest Pontiff's Pints?"

Terri exclaimed, "Wait, the bar?"

The two priests laughed.

Chapter 35

Elijah Britt and his brothers sat beside an obedient, yellow-haired girl at their classroom table. The room mirrored a vibrant kindergarten classroom, bursting with the innocent charm that characterizes early childhood learning. The bright white wallpaper, embellished with playful illustrations of little lambs and delicate crosses, lent a whimsical touch to the space. In the center stood a large oval table, its smooth surface inviting collaboration and creativity among the young learners. Colorful books and a corner painted in striking red added a splash of energy to the otherwise soft palette. A central plush carpet showed a kind, haloed man watching men build a house. Children's drawings, vibrant and full of imagination, captured the essence of their joyful expression. The day's lessons and creative endeavors were listed neatly on a chalkboard. A talented carpenter handcrafted the furniture, making it unique to the school.

Chastity Devlin was reading a passage from the Bible, the story of Adam and Eve. As Chastity read on, Elijah tried to get an older girl's attention by pulling on her long braid.

"Why don't you talk?" Elijah whispered.

The girl in the paisley dress said nothing.

"Shhh, be quiet, Elijah. Mrs. Devlin is reading a passage," Shante said.

Then, he signed the cross, kissing his palm up toward God.

Chastity Devlin continued reading but nodded in approval to Shante Britt. Deshawn sat in silence between his brothers. He played with a children's book. The cover displayed Jesus upon the cross.

Elijah didn't feel like giving in yet.

"Wanna play?" he asked the girl.

She sat motionless, listening to the passage. Mrs. Devlin paused her reading.

"Elijah, please don't be rude. Sarah-Prudence is listening to the passage."

"Sorry, Mrs. Devlin. It's just that I heard this story before," Elijah bowed his head in defeat.

A deeper voice thundered to the child. "Elijah, please do tell us the story then."

Elijah looked up in fear. The Elder's presence coiled above him. Elijah always acted as if he were studying when The Elder was nearby. He seemed like a ghost, except scarier. Elijah couldn't speak. He could only look down.

Chastity spoke up to her husband in her kind and melodic voice.

"Oh, Elder Devlin. He is only a child. Elijah has been doing well in school. Just boy energy. Besides Silly-Billy, you need not be down here in the school. This is where women work. I'm going to get the children prepared for their pickup. Then we can go home. I'm to make you dinner. You do seem so tense, my dear."

"Wife, the child must assimilate into his new way of life. We wouldn't want Mrs. Corning to become unhappy with this arrangement, would we? The child must obey and do what he is told. Elijah, you must kneel in the red corner and sing Psalm 38:18."

Elijah sucked his teeth. "Oh, man."

Shante refused to look at his brother as Elijah stared at his big brother for help. Chastity reinforced her husband's punishment.

"Elijah, please start your penance now."

Elijah walked to the corner, petrified because he couldn't remember the song.

The Elder then spoke to the young girl. "Sarah-Prudence." The young girl stood up and ran toward the far side of the room. She slid open a hidden panel in the wall, climbed in, and closed it as the classroom door opened on the other side.

"Oh, Elder Devlin! Is this where the little boys' room is?" Jonah Richman Jr. walked right in. The situation did not amuse Elder Devlin in the slightest. He verified that Sarah-Prudence was hidden from an outsider's sight and turned back to Mr. Richman.

"No! And that door is always to remain locked," Elder Devlin said as he glared at his wife.

Chastity knew her husband had entered the door last. She dared not question him. Instead, she became nervous and rocked, muttering a prayer.

"Mr. Richman, please close the door. I need a moment, if you can spare. This is a woman's place of work. You must wait outside."

The visitor closed the door with an apology, as instructed. He remained within, observing, demonstrating a vacant interest. "Wow. This is a nice classroom. You build it yourself, Elder Devlin?"

Devlin stood in astonishment at the brazen Mr. Richman as he strolled around the room. He examined and touched everything with his index finger.

"You only teach young boys down here, Miss...?" Mr. Richman asked as if waiting for Chastity to introduce herself. But she remained muted. Devlin wished he could put on his gloves.

"Mr. Richman, we in the Ministry aim to mind our own business and do as we are told. We expect that of our prospects as well. A strict and simple life has served the Lord well. You must never come to this place of learning while the women work."

"Oh. I'm terribly sorry, Elder Devlin and Miss...?" Richman tried again.

"Mr. Richman, please, the restroom is upstairs, across from my office. Surely you can't miss it."

Devlin stepped toward the door and opened it. Mr. Richman left first, followed by the lanky Devlin. The door locked. A key secured it from the outside.

After a moment of silence, Elijah and Chastity caught their breath.

With a quick click, the classroom door swung open. Elder Devlin glided across the floor in one stride, right to Chastity's ear. He whispered through clenched teeth. "This will never happen again! Understood?"

Chastity's eyes welled up. Although Elijah couldn't hear the words, he could see that she was afraid. Fear gripped him as well.

"That door must always be locked. I alone will call for you when your work is finished. Tonight, you will learn not to defy my rules. Tonight, I am prepared to make it happen for us. You will feel this man tonight," he hissed in her ear.

Chastity wanted to cry, but knew better. Not here. Not with the children present.

Elder Devlin then stood up and spoke aloud. "Sarah-Prudence, you may come out." The hidden compartment opened, and the child stepped out without saying a word. She closed the door and sat at the table with her hands on her knees. Elijah caught her eye for a second. She did not smile, but nodded. She seemed to acknowledge his fear.

"The congregation is not ready to receive your grace, child. You have done well."

The Elder's exit from the room matched his swift entrance. The door lock activated. He walked up the steps of the sub-basement and into the hallway to his office. Lazaro Villamil was leaning against the wall at the entrance of The Elder's office. His trademark unlit cigarette was hanging out of his mouth.

"Good evening, Elder. Our Weekly Adulation has concluded," he said in a deep, scratchy voice.

"Good. Thank you, Lazaro. You may unlock the school, and the children may be dismissed to High Choir Corning and his wife."

Devlin entered his office. "Oh, Lazaro, come in for one moment, please."

The gruff man entered with a limp.

"Lazaro, I need your services once again. Watch over the new prospect, Mr. Richman. Report your findings to me. That is all."

Lazaro rolled his cigarette to the other side of his mouth. "Yes, Elder."

Devlin sat at his desk. He started reading some paperwork over the rustle of the children being led out of the hallway toward the church area. Someone knocked on his door. "All may enter," Devlin bellowed.

The Minster entered with his hands clasped behind his back, as always. He donned his familiar black robe, tailored from his waist to his white clergy collar. The lower half fell straight down to his polished black shoes. A single dark-red vertical trim ascended the center of the robe, secured with small red buttons. Both cuffs featured dark red crosses.

"Evening, Jonathan."

"Good evening to you, Minister."

"Jonathan, I have received your report for this fiscal year. I am once again impressed with the result. You have proven to be a godsend. This Ministry has never run so smoothly. We remained under budget again, and yet we doubled our profits."

Devlin seemed disengaged as he gazed down at his desk.

"Son, are you listening?"

"Minister, could you please excuse me? I am in the middle of another project." Devlin never looked up. His dismissiveness was cold and clear to The Minister.

"John, you seem very intense these past couple of weeks. You seem to be under quite a bit of stress. Ever since you...we adopted Sarah-Prudence. I don't mean to pry, but I know the trials of being a parent."

"The child will belong to the Ministry. She was never meant to be my child. I have no trials, Minister. The child will be revealed next Easter Sunday, bringing hope to our congregation. She will belong to the church's legacy. All will revere and look upon her as a prophet, the salvation. As for myself and my wife, there will be another."

"Jonathan. It would be impossible for Chastity to bear a child. You know that. It was God's will to punish her for her sins. This has been discussed many times. It was God's will that she be childless for the rest of her life. That is part of her penance. She sacrificed her only purpose for Jesus Christ."

Devlin's fists clenched under his desk. "It is also God's will that I may be rewarded for my forgiveness and charity to my wife. I had a divine vision. A waking dream. For God has sent me an angel."

"What are you saying? A miracle?"

"There is still much work to be done," Devlin stated.

The Minister chorused, "Praise be to God."

"The devil is lurking, Minister. I have seen him in many forms. All will be exorcised and returned to the depths of hell from which they came. That, Minister, is my purpose. Only then will God's plan be revealed."

"Heaven have mercy," The Minister said. "Son, I must say, my soul warms when you talk scripture with me. My daughter will finally be saved."

Devlin gave a cruel smile and spoke in a more relaxed manner. "Well, anyway, the vision, the angel, devils, miracles, all true from my perspective. We will continue to be guided by the Lord's light. I'm glad you approved of my yearly report. Next year's budget will be submitted for your approval in sufficient time. I shall see you at home. My wife and Sarah-Prudence will go with me."

Chastity and Sarah-Prudence then walked into Devlin's office right on cue. Chastity kissed her father on the cheek. The child stood stoic, with her hands clasped in front of her.

The Minister addressed his daughter. "My Chastity, seeing how happy you have been these last few days makes me warm. See you all at home, dear." He ignored Sarah-Prudence.

As The Minister left, Devlin stood and adjusted his tie.

"Please cover the child up as I get my car."

Chapter 36

Guilt was the only drawback for Jake skipping the bar with Terri and his secretive uncle, as he stood in the nursing home parking lot. The receptionist sat behind her desk, dressed in a buttoned white sweater. She held a folded copy of the *National Enquirer*, and a deck of tarot cards was spread across the desk.

"Welcome to our home. How may I be of service?"

"Is Mr. Ratner in his office?"

"Are you scheduled for a meeting?" she sighed, rolling her eyes.

Jake hesitated. "Yes."

"Well, Mr. Ratner is gone for the day. If you leave your name and..."

"That won't be necessary. I also need to visit Mr. McCloskey in room 512."

"Sign in," she instructed, returning to doing more exciting things.

Jake passed the reception desk to a rear hallway, bypassing the elevator. He opened the door labeled R. Ronald Ratner, Director.

The office was a chaotic jumble of papers and clutter, permeated by the stale scent of cigarette smoke. At the center back of the room stood a desk flanked by two sturdy chairs, providing a makeshift structure amid the disorder. An elaborate system of file cabinets stood along the left wall, brimming with folders and files that hinted at years of accumulated work. The display on the wall drew Jake's attention. Certificates seemed to yearn for recognition. Two prestigious master's diplomas, various healthcare licenses and heartfelt letters of appreciation, all framed to reflect years of dedication and achievement.

A warm photo of a woman and child sat on his desk near an ashtray filled with green matchboxes. Adding an artistic touch to the disarray, a striking bronze statue of a galloping horse stood proud, embodying freedom and vigor amid the surrounding disorder.

This horse's ass really loves horses, Jake thought to himself.

Jake walked out and took the elevator to the fifth floor. He was accustomed by now to the slow ride, and like a reflex, he sunk into his anxiety about what awaited him when the elevator door opened. Jake thumbed his stress stone. The fifth floor did not disappoint. The zombies were in full-attack mode. Their desire to go home with a warm-blooded human only trumped their thirst for brains. A resident heart-wrecker grabbed Jake's arm and told him she would bake fresh cookies if he took her home. Jake leaned down to her eye level. He told her she was cute and honked her nose. This frenzied the rest. Jake escaped to his father's old hallway and recognized a melody from *The Wizard of Oz*.

Somewhere...

Outside my window

Airplanes fly.

In there...is a club that I hoped for

One called The Mile High.

Jake paused, admiring Cook's golden voice, until he heard Josephine's walker starting up like a drunk robot trying to find its way home. The woman haunted the nursing home halls, searching for five dollars as if she were a ghost who forgot to take her wallet on the way out. Nobody knew why she was after that cash, but rumors swirled. Some suggested it was for bingo, while others suspected she was starting a retirement home casino. Jake pounced into Cook's room like Cosmo Kramer and shut Josephine out.

"Hey there, Cook! Missed me?"

"Oh, Jacob! Afternoon or evening, or is it good morning? Wow, what a pleasant surprise."

"How have you been?" Jacob asked, trying to catch a little breath.

"Pleasantly bored. Thanks for asking."

"Josephine still roams the halls, huh?"

"She's a pain in the ass. Needs to die already."

"Wow, Cook. That was pretty angry."

"Ah, yes. Yes, it was. So, I guess you didn't come here to discuss my many ponderings to the end of that miserable troll's time on earth."

"No. Of course not." Jake said. "My father..."

"Dead?" Cook finished Jake's thought as he aimed his trusty mechanical claw for a bag of pretzels on his dresser.

"Yes. He is still dead," Jake tried to continue.

"Good. Means the zombie apocalypse hasn't started yet."

Jake lost his train of thought as Cook fished out a pretzel rod and chomped it like a salted cigar.

"Jacob, as you can see, I'm not a busy man. I have plenty of time to listen to somebody's shit, with enough time left to dwell on it. So, spit it out. What is it that you need?"

Jake could not determine whether Cook was annoyed, happy or messing with him. "Do you know the patient here who always wears a sailor's outfit?"

"Captain Morgan! He's right here under my bed. Want an introduction?"

"Cook, I'm being serious."

"No, Jacob. I am serious. I received a fresh bottle from my contact the other day."

"Is your connection R. Ronald Ratner?"

Cook's demeanor turned glum. He turned away and whispered, "Did you bring my pills, doctor? Are you here to change my diaper? What did you do with my fish? Where's my fucking fish?"

Jake yelled at Cook. "Don't pull that act with me, old man. I know that game."

"Dirty sock?" Cook blurted.

Jake looked perplexed.

"Come on, smarty! What about the dirty sock?"

"Please stop the bullshit. I am not wasting my time on this." Jake tried to stand his ground.

"Good thing I'm wasting mine," Cook countered.

"Wasting your what?"

"Time, boy. I'm always wasting my time. Day in and day out, I think of new ways to do nothing. I'm wasting so much precious..."

Jake's frustration boiled over and interrupted Cook's rambling thoughts. "Time! Yes. I get it. Do you know who I'm talking about? The person was at my father's funeral."

"That was like five years ago. How the hell am I gonna remember that?"

"It was only a few weeks ago, Cook."

"Oh, yeah. The young man's funeral. He was a peculiar fella. He had that great-smelling pipe."

"Yes. That guy."

"I never saw him before. He's not a patient here, but I admit. I only know the people I know."

"Ratner seems to have known him."

"Sure, he does. Sounded to me like Ratner owed him money," Cook said.

"What do you mean?"

"They were arguing before the funeral. He was there when we arrived, now that you mentioned it."

"I didn't mention it."

"Well, my take is, the sailorman is a bookie."

"Why would you say that?"

"Mr. Ratner loves horses. He always has me pick horses from the paper. He thinks I have a psychic gift or something."

"So, you know the horses?"

"No, I pick the names I like. It's luck, I guess. I picked some earlier. I liked Rock'em Sock'em Robot, and Rum."

"Where does he go? Belmont? Aqueduct?" Jake asked.

Cook reached the top of his armoire with the mechanical claw and brought down a green matchbox with an address printed on it.

OTB

62-17 Roosevelt Avenue

Woodside, NY 11377

"Why are you looking to find that knucklehead, Ratner?"

"I need to find out who that sailor guy is. I think he was an enemy of my father, and now he's stalking me."

"So, ignore him. He'll probably go away," Cook said.

"I'm not doing that. I have to find out why this weirdo is looking for me."

"No, Jacob. You don't. It's all nonsense. Life is very short," Cook huffed. "You should not go around making it any shorter."

"If I can end this chapter of my father's life, I can move on with mine without all this stress," Jake said.

Cook lit a match and put it up to his pretzel cigar.

"You hear about some wahoo who believes he is the only one who has ever had that epiphany: life is too short! So, the asshole goes and lives life to the fullest. He jumps off a bridge with a rubber band, gets chased by rampaging bulls and attends a rap concert. Then the idiot quits his job, sells off his possessions, smokes truckloads of pot and dies of frostbite while hiking to the North Pole. Young and stupid, and he made his life shorter. This here is the way to prolong life."

"Cook, you are truly insane. Are you telling me you are only here so you can live longer?"

"Yes and no. I'm in here because I have no stress. No worries. They would wipe my ass if I wanted them to. Occasionally, I can muster a sponge bath from the better-looking nurses." Cook smirked and gave his visitor a wink.

"What about your wife?"

"Dead. Too soon. Too short."

"You do have a family. I've seen them."

"Yeah. One of those left-wing, save-the-trees, hate-the-humans type. Weak-minded and stressed out. That feminist communist wife of his brainwashed my son. He is so freaking afraid of her."

"Wow, a little tough on him, don't you think?"

"Have you ever lived with them?" Cook took a pretend puff. "Couldn't even sneak a slice of pizza without some gluten alarm blaring."

"So, you think you're better off here?"

"Yes indeed."

"Any grandchildren?"

"Ah, now there you go, Jacob. Right there is the point. I'm here, alive. Relatively healthy. I can watch my grandchildren grow, teach them and guide them. They will be my legacy, and I intend to stick around to see it through. I have no stress here. No responsibility. I'm on a specific diet, so I don't overeat. I take vitamins. Feel great...and occasionally, Chinese takeout for delivery here."

"Why the crazy malingerer act?"

"None of your business," Cook said. "The point is, Jacob, your father wanted that for you, free of fear and stress. He didn't have his epiphany. The young man died too soon, destroyed by his love, devastated by his compassion, and wilted by his benevolence."

"Wow. Did you get that from a Bob Dylan song?" Jake jabbed.

"Fortune cookie."

To drive the punchline home, Cook extended his claw once more and lifted a fortune cookie from a bowl on his dresser. He offered it to Jake. "I have a message from Bob."

Jake declined with a wave of his hand.

"I've got to hit the head. Then we can talk more." Cook got up and shuffled over to his bathroom. As Jake sat down on the bed, Cook used the claw to open the bathroom door. He could hear Cook singing from behind the closed door. The song sounded like a Jim Croce tune.

If I could spend time in a brothel

The first thing I'd like them to use

Some whips and some chains

Till I scream out in pain

As they wear black, thigh-high boots...

Jake looked at pictures of Cook and his family while listening to him sing. On Cook's nightstand sat an old radio, a coloring book and crayons. Jake noticed the room lacked a television. Only two things hung on the walls. Across from the bed, framed with cheap brass, was a proclamation from the City of New York. Firefighter **Jeremiah A. McCloskey**, awarded the FDNY's highest honor, the *James Gordon Bennett Medal for Valor.* Jake stood a little straighter reading it, the weight of a life saved or lost pressed into every line of the citation.

The second piece stopped him cold. A woman painted in electric colors stared back, her face split between beauty and decay, half vibrant flesh, half radiant skull. The signature in the corner pulled the air from Jake's lungs.

J. Sing.

"Ah, yes, Lola Montez. An exquisite piece of work, don't you think?" Cook asked as he shuffled back to his recliner chair.

"Her name is Lola Montez?" Jake asked.

"That's what I named her. She looks like she should be named Lola Montez."

"Do you know the artist?"

"Nope. But it was a gift from your father. He gave it to me a few years back. Your father strolled in and gave it to me. Never said a word. I don't even know how he got it. I figured he stole it from another room on one of his midnight wanderings."

"Did my father ever talk about the artist?"

"Nope. He barely spoke at all. Behind the painting, it read, Día de Muertos, whatever that means. I wasted plenty of time learning to pronounce that, thank you very much. I changed it to Lola Montez."

Jake called Cook out on his Fire Department medal. "I see here you were not always so lazy."

"Yes, life was getting shorter by the moment back then. It was a long time ago." Cook paused for dramatic reflection. "A hero, they say. I suppose that's true. What a proud day that was. But, much like the young man, there was indeed a cost."

"What does that mean? What price?"

Cook reclined back, kicking the footrest up.

"Sanity, Jacob. The price paid is sanity. It's very stressful being the hero. The earned title *HERO* means you have or will have to make a tremendous sacrifice. Good people always have so much to lose."

"That's what my uncle always says."

"Smart man, your uncle. A good man," Cook said, his eyebrows raised.

"You say that like it's bad."

"The price is bad, Jacob."

"Cook, are you saying you'd rather be a bad guy?"

"I won't lie to you, Jacob. Been struggling with that question for what seems like forever. I have no desire to be anything, not anymore. If I can give you one insight, please promise not to take it the wrong way."

"Okay. I'm listening."

"I think your dad was a hero."

Jake swallowed hard. "What? I mean, how do you, wait?"

"He had all the signs. Seemed tense and tortured about something. He would cry at night alone sometimes. Occasionally, he would come into my room, sit in this chair and stare at me. It could have been some homosexual mind reader. But when he brought me that picture, I realized he was trying to tell me something. His mumbling never made sense, but I could make out your name. I've seen that behavior in guys. It's called trauma or post-traumatic stress disorder. I've seen the toughest guys and gals fall to this.

"Most shrinks spend time behind desks, listening to all types of people spouting wild ideas, pushing hundreds of drugs their books claim will fix the problem. Bookworms study hypotheses and control groups. Rarely do these experts put themselves before others or see a truly suffering human being. The proper help is not there."

"So, you think my father had PTSD?"

"That's a proper question. What did your father do for a living? Maybe military? A vet, perhaps?"

"Yes. He was," Jake stated.

"Well, there's something."

"And you think you know more than a doctor?"

"I am mentally ill, aren't I?" Cook answered.

"You are faking it."

"Yes. Because I'm crazier than a shithouse rat."

"You're making my head hurt. Do you know what my father used to do? I mean, really used to do?"

"Jacob, I don't want to know. I don't care."

"Well, you were right. He was a hero," Jake said.

Cook's eyes widened. He sat upright and stared deep into Jacob Johansson's soul. Then, when the tension was just right, he unleashed his best Yoda impression.

"Heroes, the world needs."

A slim man with salt-and-pepper hair entered the room and set some grocery items atop the dresser. "Hi ya, Dad!"

"I'm not taking your crazy pills. Get out of here," Cook yelled as if someone had flicked a crazy switch.

"It's me, Dad," the man said while rolling his eyes.

Cook squinted his eyes to see a little better. "Matty?" Cook asked timidly.

"No, Dad, Alex. I'm Alex." He said it loud and slow enough for the old man to comprehend.

A waif of a woman wearing a sports bra and yoga pants came in from behind and announced their arrival even louder, even slower.

"Hi Jerry. It's Anna McCloskey, Alex's wife. We brought you tofu and herbal tea with ginkgo biloba to help with your memory."

"So, where's Matty?" Cook yelled out, staring at another individual standing in the doorway. A large male wearing a loose tunic, linen pants and sandals he had stolen from Jesus himself.

"No, Dad. That's Kimmo. He's our masseuse."

"I prefer a Holistic Therapist if you please," Kimmo corrected in a smug, deep voice.

Alex talked a little louder but faster. "Well, yes, massage therapist. Ah, hum, Matty was your brother. He died years ago."

"That son of a bitch killed Matty?" Cook shouted.

"No, Dad. We thought you might like a nice massage to help clarify your mind." Kimmo jumped back in with another smug correction.

"A Muscle Tissue Stimulation and Consciousness Cleansing."

"Jerry, it's Anna McCloskey again. Nine out of ten holistic healers say a hot stone massage will help your concentration."

Jake let out a snort while trying to hold back the tears. "Can we help you, sir?" Alex said, making no effort to conceal his pompous attitude.

Jake's first thought was to slap him flush across his red cheek. Instead, Jake snapped into character. "Good day. I'm Doctor Johansson. I was making rounds when I saw your father wandering the halls again. I was helping him to his room, and now I am leaving." He turned to his patient. "Good day, Mr. Cook."

"That's McCloskey," Alex spat.

"Of course it is. May I suggest giving Mr. McCloskey actual food, like a hamburger or a pizza? Nine out of ten doctors figured that at his age, nothing would make him younger now, so let him enjoy himself. Life is too short."

Jake trailed off, saying, "You're on your own with the massage thing," before walking out.

At that moment, he heard a snap that sounded much like Cook's claw, and Kimmo's voice, suddenly high-pitched without a trace of condescension: "Get it off! Get it off!"

 **37**

Pontiff's Pints was empty until Father Duffy and Terri entered, followed by the stumbling Father Benny. "You have a clergy parking permit, Colin. Why did I have to pay the meter?" Benny complained.

"Because, Benjamin, those godless ticket blokes would leave a summons on their own granny's wheelchair. And the deal's always been, if I drive, ye feed the meter."

Father Benny played along. "You're still mad about the last time I drove you somewhere!"

"Aye, Ben. It cost me a lot more than a few quid."

Father Duffy and the eye-goggled priest giggled at their ongoing gimmick.

The three sat at the ever-so-spotless bar. Terri wondered if the elder barkeep was still alive as he prepared a round of drinks. Benny acted as if he might utter a poor joke.

"This is Brother Timothy McEwen; he's the Skeleton of L.O.L.," Benny whispered.

Terri looked amused. "I can see that."

"Why are you whispering? There's no one here, ye dolt," Father Duffy pointed out to get the conversation on track. "What Father Benny is saying is true, though. Brother

Timothy's title is the Skeleton of Loyola, as in the Skeleton Key."

"Oh, I get it. And you are the Lock." Terri proved she was paying attention.

Benny gave an additional explanation. "Father Duffy deals only with the members of the church community. Timmy Mac deals with the community. The public at large. His mission is very different from Father Duffy's. Timothy is tasked with directly listening to and vetting complaints of First Commandment violations from public sources. Once the Skeleton deems a violation credible, he contacts the Lock. Then the ball gets rolling, so to speak."

"How does the public know how to go to Brother Timothy?" Terri asked.

Father Duffy took to that answer. "Word of mouth, so it is. Many of the clergy and the good folks of the church know Brother Timothy and his keen interest in the First Commandment. If someone feels they're in need of a bit of help with that particular matter, they'll be directed to the Pints."

"This bar," Terri added.

"Precisely," Father Benny confirmed. "And sometimes Timothy finds violations himself. He is an avid reader and a maestro of the internet. Isn't that right, Tim?"

Brother Timothy grunted in agreement.

Father Duffy then explained why they were there. "Timothy, me lad, Father Benny stumbled upon an auld case file o' yours. A young fella named Kevin Miller came to ye regardin' a congregation called the Ministry of Salvation. D'ye recall that?"

Timothy thumbed through the file. "Aye," he said in confirmation.

"Well, we have a belief that this group may be involved in a kidnapping of a child."

Terri believed she heard the barkeep grumble what sounded like "Probably." She didn't want to leave anything to guesswork. "Can you provide insight on that case or even the Ministry?"

"Bad news," Timothy grumbled. "Everyone there is of their own free will."

"What about the Miller boy?" Father Duffy inquired.

"Don't know," Brother Timothy muttered.

"What about this Ministry of Salvation makes it so bad?" Father Benny asked. "We sent Fehrenbach in for some reconnaissance."

"Not good," Timothy grunted.

"Not good? Then why haven't they been shut down or exposed or whatever it is you guys do?" Terri said.

"Free will."

Father Benny articulated his colleague's short answers. "Brother Timothy is a man of few words, but his knuckle game is tight." With that, Timothy gave a slight smirk.

"How did Mr. Miller come across you? If ye can recall, that is," Father Duffy wondered.

"God of 42nd Street," Timothy answered with a chuckle.

Little Blind Benny and Colin Duffy exploded into hysterical laughter, pounding their palms against the polished bar like they were keeping time. An obvious inside joke between them. Terri and Timothy just stared at them, stone-still. When Brother Timothy finally spoke louder, clearer and with more authority than Terri had ever heard, the priests froze mid-cackle, their laughter choking into stunned silence.

"The Ministry of Salvation is a hazardous organization. Fehrenbach needs to get out as soon as possible," he said.

Terri jumped in. "What was so funny about this 42nd Street God thing?"

"A right eejit," Father Duffy described. "An imbecile who calls himself The God of 42nd Street."

"Biggest and stupidest con artist in the city. Complete moron," Benny said. "Loves to play preacher, prophet or circus clown, depending on the day. He'd talk you into donating money for a cockroach farm if you listen too long."

Father Benny settled down and leaned toward Timothy. "This so-called Ministry, are they fanatical?"

"And deeply secular," Timothy stated. "They use very effective and archaic brainwashing techniques. They don't interact well with the police, child services or any authoritative organization. The Ministry follows its own rules and does what it wants. Tough to deal with, like most cults. They hide in plain sight behind their Christian faith."

Father Duffy went further. "The danger is fanatics in groups like this rarely report any wrongdoing done by their leaders, y'know."

Timothy grunted, "Worse."

"What have ye got on them?" Father Duffy pressed.

"Work of a devil."

Terri didn't flinch. She had seen that work before. And she agreed.

* * * * *

Jake paused outside the Off-Track Betting parlor on Roosevelt Avenue, assaulted by the ripe stench wafting from the alley. A guy in a ruined suit slept against the brick, one hand still curled around a paper-bagged bottle like it might save him. Jake tugged at his collar. Something about this block crawled under the skin.

Inside was worse.

Heat, sweat and stale frustration rolled over him like a physical entity. Televisions barked race commentary in rapid-fire bursts while bells chimed over losing bets. Crumpled wager slips carpeted the floor, soft as snow underfoot. A pair of gorilla-sized goons loomed over a trembling gambler in the corner. Bookies hustled between windows, muttering numbers, taking side bets they weren't supposed to take.

A pocket of winners whooped near the center monitors. A larger crowd groaned and cursed their luck. And in the middle of all that noise, one solitary figure sat unmoved, chewing an unlit cigarette, sipping from a flask, completely indifferent to the world disintegrating around him.

Jake threaded through the chaos.

"Hey there, R," Jake said.

Ratner looked like sleep had broken up with him. Purple half-moons dragged down his eyes. His shirt clung with booze from two different days, and his smell hit Jake before the man spoke, a thick cocktail of sweat, regret and whatever rot seeped from these walls.

"Do you know why I'm here looking for you?" Jake asked, dropping into the seat across from him.

"No, but I'm sure you're gonna tell me."

Jake leaned in. "Who is the sailor-looking guy?"

Ratner went pale. His throat jerked like he might puke. "What?"

"The sailor at my father's funeral."

"I don't owe you money. Leave me alone."

Jake's patience evaporated. "Why is he stalking me, R? Why the hell was he there?"

"I was booking a cruise," Ratner croaked.

Jake slammed a palm on the counter. "You think this is funny?"

"A joke? No. I'm just not in the mood to argue."

Jake grabbed Ratner by the shirt front and yanked him close. "Tell me what that sailor wants with me."

Ratner snapped back, wild-eyed, and grabbed Jake right back. "You have no idea what you're dealing with." His voice shook with a feverish rage.

Jake broke the grip with a sharp forearm twist, and finally did what he'd wanted since the day he toured the Stanley Miller Nursing Home.

He punched Ratner square in the jaw.

Ratner hit the floor. Security descended instantly. Two guards hauled him outside while another barked at Jake to leave. Jake didn't wait. He followed them out, grabbed Ratner by the coat collar and shoved him into the back of his own car before anyone could object.

"Start talking," Jake said.

"Oh, good. Kidnapping. This day keeps getting better." Ratner slumped against the door. "You gonna give me the cement shoes speech?"

"Knock it off. I want information. Tell me where to find this Navy guy."

Ratner's shoulders sagged. "You don't want that guy. He'll ruin your life. Your father is gone, accept it. Whatever business they had...you get what you pay for."

"My father had no business with him," Jake lied smoothly.

Ratner scoffed. "Captain Jay seems to think otherwise."

"Captain Jay?"

"Yeah. Some preppy kid came around last year asking about a patient with two different colored eyes. I told him HIPAA wouldn't let me say anything. Then? My whole life went to hell."

Jake smirked. "What a tragic coincidence, R. Full of so much rich detail."

Ratner glared. "Why do you keep calling me R?"

"Because it's your name. R. Ronald Ratner."

"It stands for Roland. It's a professional moniker."

Jake didn't blink. "I like R. What does this Captain Jay have on you?"

"Family," Ratner stated. "My friend killed himself last night. So, I guess you can say he has that too now."

"Keep talking," Jake commanded.

"Me being in the same zip code as you will probably get my family killed. I said too much already." Ratner's eyes were moist now. The fire was out.

"Well, I heard a *probably* in there. That means there's a chance he won't reach them. Puts the odds in your favor." Jake tried a Charles Bronson approach.

"And what makes you think you can?" Ratner asked.

"How did you get mixed up in all this?"

Ratner dismissed the question and looked into Jake's eyes. "Why did you bring your father to my nursing home?"

"You had a high rating, and you took Medicare."

"Captain Jay wanted information on your father. I never knew why. Why my goddamn nursing home?"

"What did he promise you? What was so worth more than my father's information?" Jake began to lose his temper.

"He got my family back," Ratner trembled.

"That is so dramatic. What's going on?" Jake asked as he clenched his fists.

Ratner finally gave up. A broken man told his story.

"My wife left me about eight years ago," Ratner muttered, rubbing his jaw. "We got a daughter. Rory. Nineteen now.

Back then...money was tight. She went back to work. Met some guy there. You know the type: nice car, nice teeth, nice everything. No gambling problem. No me.

"I come home early one day and...yeah."

He swallowed, staring out the window like he might jump through it.

"Long story short, she took my kid, started over, blamed it all on me. And my wife, man...she was everything. Smart, funny, legs that wouldn't quit. I didn't see it coming."

Jake gave him a nod. "Been down that road. Never married, no kid."

Ratner kept going, almost talking to himself.

"When Rory was eleven, she wouldn't even look at me. Hated me. I tried, man. I really tried. Worked out, therapy, meds, school. Paid off every damn bill. Sent gifts. Nothing mattered."

He paused, breathing slow like he might puke.

"Then our recreation lady at the nursing home hires this fortune-teller. Like full crystal-ball gypsy stuff. I sit in on a few readings. Looked stupid but...I was desperate. Asked her for one. Asked her if my wife and kid would ever come back."

His breath hitched.

"She tells me no. Just like that. Sixty minutes of...whatever the hell that was...and then no."

Jake stayed quiet.

"A week later some preppy kid with a beard shows up," Ratner said. "Says he's with a charity called the Squids. Wants unused meds, heart meds, psych meds, whatever. I thought it was some free-drug scam and tried to kick him out. Then he says something weird. Says my family *could* come back. Just...drops it like he's ordering lunch."

"So you gave him the meds?" Jake asked.

"No. I told him to get lost."

Jake raised an eyebrow. "So why didn't you call the cops?"

Ratner let out a bitter laugh.

"That night, my wife calls me. Says she wants dinner. Says Rory asked for me. I didn't sleep for two days. Couldn't figure it out."

"Why would she do that?"

Ratner ignored the question and kept going.

"Next day this old man walks into my office dressed like Captain Ahab got thrown out of a costume shop. Captain Jay. He said he knew about my call, like the ocean told him or some shit and his crew helps people in trouble. He wanted heart meds. Lot of them. Said it was a pay-it-forward thing."

He rubbed his temples, exhausted.

"And I caved. I love my kid. I love my wife. I told myself it wasn't narcotics. Just medicine. For a bad heart. And then...things got better. Dinner. They moved home. Squid people stopped by once a month for the meds."

Jake's eyes narrowed.

"And then?"

"One day he shows up again. Captain Jay. Asked how my family was. Then starts asking about a patient in 510. Mr. Johansson. Your father."

Jake clenched his jaw.

"And you told him?"

"No!" Ratner barked. "I told him I couldn't. And that I already felt sick about the other stuff. He thanked me, like we were pals. That night...my wife and Rory disappeared again. No note. Nothing."

Jake growled. "Why didn't you call the cops?"

"You don't think I wanted to?" Ratner snapped back, eyes wild. "Every time I stopped giving him the meds, they'd drop hints. About Rory. About her school. About where she was shopping. Just...little things to remind me they could get to her."

Jake threw his hands up. "Jesus Christ."

"I tried to cut them off again. Finally asked the Squid kid to pass along a message, wanted to meet the boss. A week later, the bastard ambushes me at a healthcare convention in Maryland."

"Still wearing his sea-captain costume?" Jake muttered.

"Yep. Looked like he crawled out of a shipwreck." Ratner rubbed his jaw again, wincing. "He tells me to stop caring for patient 510. I said no. He pulls out a picture of Rory. Says she's doing fine. I almost killed him right there."

Jake punched him again. Ratner sagged sideways in the seat.

"What did you do to my father?"

"Nothing!" Ratner cried. "I don't hurt patients. I just...kept giving them the meds. My daughter called a few weeks later. We fixed things. And then I didn't see Captain Jay again until your father's funeral. He said he was there to pay respects. For a 'job well done.'"

Jake's face went hollow.

"I told him to stay out of my life. And to leave my daughter alone. And he just smiles and says, 'Rory's grown up so fast. Shame if she stopped.'"

Jake froze, horror and fury tangled.

"What the hell..."

"I was circling the drain," Ratner said, voice cracking. "Couldn't breathe, couldn't move. I let him stand there, looking right through me, like he owned the air I was trying to suck in."

"Why all the self-loathing, you piece of shit?" Jake screamed.

"One of my nurses, Rosetta Jones, came to me the other day and said that something was weighing on her. She said your father's last few bloodwork results showed an abnormal amount of salt in his blood."

"So, what the hell does that mean?" Jake asked.

"In the last months of your father's life, she noticed he was rapidly weakening. He had nausea, vomiting. The only thing Mr. Johansson wanted was liquids. He drank gallons of water. Nurse Jones reported difficulty getting him to eat solid foods. These were signs of hypernatremia. Because of Mr.

Johansson's other medical conditions, his symptoms were quickly attributed to his dementia and organ failure. She suspected his food might have too much salt."

"Are you saying that somebody purposely poisoned my father?" Jake asked, his shaky voice tinged with fury.

"I talked to the resident dietitian, Manny Acevedo. He was also a friend of mine. We used to play poker on Sunday nights. In retrospect, he did look a bit pale and detached after I asked him about Mr. Johansson's diet. He told me everything was fine. He went home and hung himself last night. That fucking captain had something to do with this. All I can think about is my daughter. I can't begin to guess how Captain Jay knows I suspect him, but he does."

"What makes him think you suspect anything?"

"I haven't spoken to my daughter in a few days."

"Well, go see her then," Jake suggested.

"I can't! She is way upstate in Oswego. College."

"Have you talked to your ex-wife?" Jake pressed on.

"She doesn't answer my calls, and I have no idea where she's staying. The second time was easier to handle. We haven't spoken since she left again."

Jake didn't care. "How do I get to Captain Jay?" Jake asked through clenched teeth.

"He probably needs his medicine. One of those bearded Squid bastards is scheduled to come to the nursing home this Friday. There's no set time, usually in the morning."

"Thanks for making this completely painful," Jake told the sniveling drunk.

"What about Rory? What am I going to do? Can you help me, please?" Ratner was falling apart.

Jake instructed him to get out of his car.

"Please help me, please," Ratner begged as he stumbled onto the curb.

"I probably could help you," Jake said.

"Okay, okay, what do you need me to do?"

Without another word, Jake drove away.

38

Jake took a seat at the table and sipped beer from a frosty mug.

"Do ye think Penry was murdered?" Father Duffy asked after Jake shared what he learned about the sailor and his Squids.

"Yeah. We should probably call Molina," Jake suggested.

"I'm on it," Terri said.

Jake's uncle filled him in on their planned visit to Times Square. "Tomorrow night would be best. Our target will make no money in the rain tonight. You are welcome to join us."

"You and Terri?" Jake asked.

"Yes."

"I'm in."

Terri interrupted their conversation. "Detective Molina wants to speak to you, Jake."

"Listen closely," Molina said. "I did some digging on the Katie kid's death you told me about."

"I'm listening," Jake said.

"It does seem like an accidental death. However, I don't normally do this...the detective who worked the case is retired now. He owns a used bookstore in Queens, Austin Street. His name is Pfeiffer. Perhaps he can set your mind at ease. I'm sure you won't believe anything I say."

"Why would you give me that information? What happened to the Blue Wall?"

"The way I see it, I owe you one. I still have some integrity."

"Owe me? How about finding out who killed my father! Find this Captain Jay."

"Yes, agreed. That will take some time. We will certainly cross that bridge if the evidence takes us there," Molina said. "We will meet in person soon. You can give me the details then."

"So what, now that you believe us?"

"Believe is a tough word. A hypothesis may be a bit more accurate. I need to find Monica and close the Hope case. I wanted to give something of a peace offering to help Terri."

"Sounds like you want me to talk to this retired detective," Jake said.

"Look. It was a tragic accident. That's all I could find out. I wanted to put your mind at ease. Closure will help."

"Come on! Why the change of heart, Detective?"

"I'm good at what I do," Molina said.

"Why don't you talk to him?"

"Pfeiffer and I don't work well together." Molina ended the conversation.

"Damn it. That guy is so frustrating, even when he is being nice," Jake said.

"Well. What did he say?" Terri asked.

"Tell you on our way to Queens."

* * * * *

"MapQuest says there is a bookstore on Austin Street near Continental Avenue," Terri said. Jake followed the directions. It was New York City rush hour, and Queens Boulevard stagnated like a parking lot.

"I hope it's still open by the time we get there," Jake said.

Terri smiled. "It says till eight o'clock."

"Good. Gives us time to find parking as well."

The live music from Sergeant Garcia's restaurant provided a pleasant backdrop as the two walked down the sidewalk and stood before Inja's Rare Books.

The bookstore appeared nothing like the dusty, cramped shops Jake had pictured. Warm light spilled over rows of matching cherry-wood shelves. Worn and weathered spines begged to be touched. Potted greenery, carefully chosen and thriving, broke up the aisles. Their ceramic pots in earthy tones matched the shop's calm elegance. A newspaper rack by the door held over thirty publications, everything from glossy international dailies to obscure specialty prints. A polished "New Releases" display stood front and center. One side of the store showcased a pristine comic book section. Jake eyed the colorful covers through their crisp plastic sleeves. The comforting scent of paper, coffee and something sweet baking in an oven made Jake want to settle into a plush seat and linger until the shop flipped its sign to "Closed."

Beyond the register counter, a beautiful exotic flower unfurled its vibrant petals, radiating colors that seemed almost otherworldly in their brilliance. Intricate patterns of a dress danced under the soft lighting, drawing the eye like a magnet. Standing nearby, an Asian woman with long, flowing black hair flashed a warm, inviting smile. Her vivacity could melt the iciest glacier while cooling the fiery heat of a volcano. Jake, entranced by the enchanting woman, found himself lost in a wondrous reverie. She was a hand-drawn fantasy come to life, as if lifted from the creased pages of one of those comics and reanimated as an angelic clerk working the counter in this Queens bookshop. Only when Terri backhanded him in the stomach did he jolt back to reality, breaking the spell.

"God, you're embarrassing," Terri said through clenched teeth.

Jake stood there like a dumbfounded child at their first sight of Disney World.

"Jake, say hello," Terri instructed.

"Hello." Jake complied with the master's order but still stood there, motionless.

"Jake, say, I'm an asshole," Terri smirked.

"I'm an asshole." He again complied, remaining still.

Terri was ready to have more fun with boys. She surrendered and turned to the most attractive woman she had ever seen, who was now waiting for someone to speak up.

"Hi. I, I'm..."

She couldn't believe she stammered. This alleged human being was indeed gorgeous. She smelled of spring rain and mythic cherry bliss.

"I, I'm Sheehan, Mess. I mean ACS, Terri."

"What can I help you find today?" the woman asked. The words did not compute on Jake and Terri's biological computer. A glitch seemed to translate everything the goddess projected into a sound of paradise. Birds chirping in play, the gentle cresting of the ocean waves, and...

"Hello? Can I help any one of you?"

Jake spoke. "Yes," was all he said.

"Do you have to be so dramatic?" Terri scolded through her nervous smile. "Yes. I'm, we, are wondering if Mr. Pfeiffer was available." She found it hard not to stutter.

The woman's perfectly sculptured face expressed concern as she took some books off the register counter and put them on a rolling cart. "Do you need help locating a book?"

"Yes," Jake answered, not knowing why.

Terri continued, "Well, no. We need to speak to Mr. Pfeiffer."

"Well, I am the owner. I can help you with anything you need."

The woman's glossy sheen started to dull. She darted her eyes toward the back of the store.

"We need to speak with Mr. Pfeiffer, if we may?" Terri asked again.

"And who are you exactly?"

"I'm Theresa Sheehan; this is Jacob Johansson. We are investigators for the Administration for Children's Services."

Her warmth came back. "Is this in regard to a special order?"

Terri took the bait.

"What's the book title?"

Terri cringed as she answered, "The Chronicles of Chronic Christmas?"

"I'll see if it's in. Please wait here."

The bookstore owner floated by, drifting past Jake to the back of the store. He instinctively tilted his head in her direction as she passed through a backroom doorway. The enchantment shattered when she disappeared from his view. Now, Terri stood before him, angry and jealous.

"Seriously? I'll give you that she is breathtaking, but do you have to act like a drooling idiot?" she lectured.

"Hey, you're cute when you're mad," Jake shot back.

"God, if that is not the worst line you could have said." Terri rolled her eyes in disgust.

The room smelled terrific once again as the angelic owner returned. Her floral sundress fell about her wondrous curves. Jake fell under her spell once again. Terri stood impressed but maintained some composure. She couldn't even hate her. The woman was too perfect.

"Ms. Sheehan, I don't see that order. Did you order it online?"

Before Terri responded, the store door jingled. An older gentleman entered. "Hey," he began.

The owner looked up. Terri took notice.

"Oh, sorry," the man said. "I didn't see you people there. Miss, I was wondering if my order was in."

The stunning owner smiled and stated, "Oh, yes, I believe it is. If you give me a moment, I am helping these customers."

Terri had seen enough parents covering for one another over the years to recognize a collaboration. As she was about to call out the deception, the bald, gray-bearded man's striking blue eyes widened. He stared at Jake.

"Inja, sweetheart, you must go to the back room," he said, calm and collected.

Inja looked surprised. She seemed poised to rip Terri's face off.

She would still look incredible doing it, Terri thought.

"Arnie, what's going on?" Inja asked.

"Sweetie. Now's not the time. I assure you I'm okay for now. Please, backroom, now."

Inja still fluttered to the back room. Jake's focus remained on the fellow's glare. The man locked the store's door.

"How can I be of service?" the man said with a bite.

"We need some information on a girl by the name of Katie Heitz. We believe you worked on the case about eight or nine years ago."

"If you are from ACS, you should have all those records. You should leave now."

"Wait! You're Detective Pfeiffer?" Jake asked. Terri and the man turned to stare at him.

"I prefer Mr. Pfeiffer," the man stated after an annoyed pause.

"I, we, need, how did that little girl die?" Jake asked.

"See, son, that there is the problem. That case is closed. You need to leave it alone. Leave me and my wife alone." Arnold Pfeiffer looked out through the store's plate-glass window. "Anyone else with you? Anyone else know you're here?"

Jake shook his head, but Pfeiffer approached the two and began crowding them. His expression turned grim.

"You'd best be leaving now. I have a fuck ton of PTSD and no patience to bring up an old case. That young girl passed away from a tragic accident. That's it."

Inja appeared out of thin air, no longer carried by invisible clouds. This time she was sprinting, wielding a baseball bat like she was charging the mound. "How dare you come into my business and harass my husband. Get out of here before I bash your fucking skulls in!"

"No, honey, wait!" Pfeiffer held his arms up, blocking any assault on the investigators.

"Do you have any idea what my husband endured working on that case? Huh? The therapy, the medications, his goddamn heart? And you come in here bringing it all back to him? Goddamn it. Leave him alone! He's retired now!"

"We didn't know anything about that case!" Jake said.

"Then why are you here?" Pfeiffer asked.

"My father," Jake began.

Terri stopped him with a squeeze and continued for him. "His father was a friend of the little girl's family. He died. Natural causes. His father asked him to check on the girl's mother."

"Who's your father?" Pfeiffer rolled his eyes like he was just playing along.

Jake's eyes widened, hoping for some recognition. "The..."

"Penrod!" Terri blurted.

"The Penrod?" Pfeiffer asked.

Jake sighed. "Just Penrod. He was a friend of that family. I don't have much detail. I want to make sure Olivia Heitz is okay. That's what he wanted." He felt weird saying it, but he was catching on to Terri's little mind game.

"Well, you guys are professional investigators, or are you lying about that, too? You figure it out," Pfeiffer said.

"Look, we tried to look her up," Terri said. "We couldn't find anything. We don't even know if she is still alive."

Pfeiffer's breath labored and he turned red.

"Sweetheart, control your breathing, please slow down," Inja said. She turned to Terri and Jake. "You must leave now. This is torture. You insensitive motherfuckers!"

"Okay! Okay! We're sorry to bother you. We didn't realize that the case was that traumatic," Jake said.

"An accident where a child died is *NOT THAT TRAUMATIC?*"

"Well, yes, of course, any death involving a child is horrific. Accident or otherwise," Terri said.

Jake was sick with guilt. "I didn't mean to bother you."

"She's a nurse," Pfeiffer said. Everyone stared at the retired detective. "It's all I got for you. Changed her name. Moved to Long Island."

"Arnie? You're done with this. Stop. You need to move on from this," Inja said.

Pfeiffer spoke deep in thought. "Good Samaritan Hospital, I believe."

Jake remembered his last conversation with Cook. "I'm sorry. I'm sorry for coming here. It was very selfish of me. You have my word, you won't hear from me again," Jake said.

"Arnie, why are you telling him anything? It's over, remember?" Pfeiffer's wife cried. "It's been years. It was an accident."

Terri pulled Jake to the door. "We better go, Jake."

"Hey!" Arnold Pfeiffer said. "I do want to hear from you again. Let me know if Olivia is okay. And don't you ever mention your father's name again."

Chapter 39

Chastity knelt beside her made bed, her delicate hands clasped too tight. The soft, dark-colored comforter beneath her elbows provided a gentle padding. A flickering candlelight illuminated the room, casting dancing shadows on the walls. With each repetition of her fervent prayer, "Praise the Lord, my soul to keep," the weight of her devotion filled the air. It echoed in the muted stillness of the evening.

A scarlet sash draped over a floor lamp to help create an ambiance of passion and tenderness. Despite the dark hiss in her ear that promised to be the key to all her pain, she continued to pray.

"Praise the Lord, my soul to keep. Praise the Lord, my soul to keep."

"Praise thy body for what you are about to receive," the snarl countered.

"Praise the Lord, my soul to keep. Praise the Lord, my soul to keep."

Chastity could hear the dial clicking from her husband's neck as she felt her flannel nightgown begin to lift. She was trying to finish her night prayer, but the distraction made her forget the rest of it.

"Praise the Lord, my soul to keep. Praise the Lord, my soul to keep."

Jonathan Devlin continued his preparation as he could feel the air thinning with every dial of his homemade lariat collar. He continued his perceived sweet nothings.

"You shall learn to obey me as the Lord intended. Your place is in thy blood."

"Praise the Lord, my soul to keep. Praise the Lord, my soul to keep."

Chastity felt her husband's hand under her armpit. She rose and helped remove her nightgown, keeping her back to him. She could feel his wheezing breath at her ear as her husband turned another click of his dial.

"Turn around, my sweet whore."

The obedient wife turned to face her husband. The prayer stopped. It did not seem that the Lord was listening tonight.

"Turn my dial again."

Chastity's hand went up, circling the back of his narrow neck, as she hunted for the circular knob.

<Click>

Devlin pushed his petite wife into a velvet armchair next to the bed. Her shoulders were only halfway up the backrest. Her thighs now hung off the seat cushion with her legs bent. Chastity could tell that her husband's breath was shortening. It's the way he liked it. A thick bead of sweat trickled between Chastity's breasts to below her belly button. She hoped her husband didn't see it. He would like that too.

Devlin moved closer to his prey. He could hear her deep, heaving breaths now. It turned him on as he stared at his wife's bare breasts. He leaned in closer, his tongue flicking along the line of her panties, savoring the sweet nectar as it slid up her body. His tongue felt like the slither of a wet snake as he reached the back of her right ear.

"Turn the dial," he hissed.

<Click>

He now let his serpentine fingers find their way to Chastity's cotton panties. The floral print was faint in the low light. It reminded Devlin how childlike his wife could be. But he knew her to be different. He knew she was a diabolical slut. A sexual demon who tempted and tormented him like she has with one other. Using his long legs, Devlin pried open his harlot's thighs. He slid his slender finger into the tramp's scarred hole under her panties. Chastity winced and let out a moan. Devlin manipulated himself.

"Turn the dial." His voice was strained. "Do it."

<Click>

Devlin's finger and other hand moved faster.

"Again."

<Click>

His appendages moved faster.

"Again!" His voice squeaked.

Chastity screamed with each thrust of his finger, her cries echoing through the room. Each movement like a jagged shard. Consumed by a relentless fury, Devlin pressed on, driven by a primal need that fed on his closing windpipe, leaving him gasping for a pinhole of air. Chastity sensed the dark shift in his energy, a predatory slowness creeping into his motions. As he struggled to speak, the words became trapped in his constricted throat, filling the air with a suffocating dread. His lungs stopped moving as his eyes appeared to be going away. The grip on his flaccid penis loosened as his opposite finger slid painfully out of her dry vagina.

Chastity considered allowing the collar to preserve her life. She knew the afterlife would judge her. She had already sinned, and Jesus Christ would not forgive her when her time came.

What's one more mortal sin? At least the remaining time would be free of pain and fear, Chastity thought.

Eternal damnation promised by her husband, her father and God would be terrible, but at least she would see her mother again. The Minister always stated that God might forgive her if she spent the rest of her life as a servant to the Lord. It seems she is living in hell already, and her mother isn't here.

But, Sarah-Prudence. Yes, Sarah-Prudence has returned. Indeed, this is a sign of forgiveness. A second chance from Jesus. There is hope.

Chastity pressed hard on a button that released the collar. Her husband's soulless eyes returned after a gasping breath. Hell's fury raged as if one more soul had been ripped from its grip.

"You have disappointed me once more, wife." He dabbed at the sweat on his lips, removing guilt. But it stuck. Chastity sat straight up in the chair. Devlin threw her discarded nightgown at her. "Get dressed, whore! I have no need to watch you peddle your wares before me."

Devlin ripped the sash off the lamp, and the bedroom turned bright white. Chastity became stoic as she pulled the old, faded lamb and sunflower nightshirt over her head.

"Certain damnation is what I saved you from. I have provided. I have given myself to the church. I have toiled for your father and this! This is your gratitude!"

"I'm sorry! I'm sorry!" Chastity rocked her torso back and forth in the chair.

"You're sorry? You're apologizing to me for being a whore? Were you sorry when you fornicated with that reprobate? Are you sorry for conceiving that illegitimate child out of wedlock? Were you sorry for hiding her birth? Throwing her away?"

Devlin was manic.

"It is my fault, husband," Chastity cried. "She came back to us, though. You wanted a child. She was born for us, a gift. I told you! It's the only way. Please, my husband. I love you."

Devlin gritted his teeth. He clasped his hands behind his body to help him from slapping his sniveling, weepy wife.

"You love me? A gift? A bastard child as a gift? You should be bearing a child from my creation. This is not love. This is an abomination."

Chastity kept rocking back and forth and did not dare look into her husband's eyes.

"She is your child. Your daughter now," Chastity said. "What you wanted."

Devlin sneered. "Stepdaughter. Yes, and I will teach her not to be a repository of sin like her mother. But she will never be mine."

"I cannot bear you a child. You know that!"

Devlin smiled.

"Of course, that was your penance for your sin. It seems those knitting needles you used to mutilate your vessel were more pleasing to you than my flesh."

"I had to be punished. I had given in to Satan's temptations. I didn't know you would save me. I didn't know God would give her back to me."

"Excuses, wife! Yet again, I am unable to perform sexually for you. You have failed me once again. Ever since that child has come back, I must be reminded of my wife's disgusting sins."

Chastity kept rocking. "You got Sarah-Prudence back for me. You saved her. You saved me. Is this not what the Lord would want?"

"When you told me that the child lived, my heart died that night. To know that you bore a heathen's spawn. It made me fear for your soul. I choose you to be my wife, a commitment. I wanted nothing but to save you so that we would live together in the glory of God eternally upon our death. The child will forever remind me of your failures. I fear I may have been mistaken in finding her for you."

"Don't say that, husband. Please, I yearn to be a family. She can be yours."

"Never will she be mine. What's done is done. There is another way. An angel has been sent to me. Yes. This is a sign of things to come."

"An angel?" Chastity stopped rocking. "You have seen an angel?"

"Yes. All in good time. You will not disclose anything about this angel, my wife. You have lived in lies before. If you don't follow through with my plan, your father will be cursed to know that Sarah-Prudence is born of his tainted bloodline. Sarah-Prudence shall be introduced as a child born in the light of the church. And you, you will then bear a child again. A son. A legacy."

Chastity began rocking again. "Please, my father cannot be bothered with this. It will kill him. He has been through too much. My mother."

"Your mother chose to take her own life. She chose the ultimate sin. Your father is left to shoulder her burden. I agree that news of you having the child years ago would ultimately destroy him. Then you will both join your mother in the bowels of hell."

"I am true to you, my husband. I can do better. You can be pleased again."

"Tonight, will not be that night."

Devlin stormed off and slammed the bedroom door behind him.

Chastity Devlin sang a hymn and cried, still rocking in her chair.

* * * * *

The box showed light. It must be time to eat. The light hurt now. The young girl had learned to anticipate it. It's been dark for so long. Her eyes were not used to it. The Elder spoke. She knew his voice now.

"Good evening, my angel."

The girl shivered but answered, "Good evening, Elder."

Her voice was hoarse. She saw part of The Elder's shoes through the feeding slot near her mouth.

"Do you fear me?" Elder Devlin asked the woman who knelt before him, her head adorned with the headbox.

"No, Elder."

"Do you trust me?"

"Yes, Elder."

"Will you fail me?"

"No, Elder."

"Good. Good."

Elder Devlin fed a carrot through the open slot. The subservient female chomped on the nourishing stick, and she was thankful. It crunched like something holy. She chewed it like a prayer.

The man walked around his prisoner. He stepped over the chains that bound her wrists to the floor. She was still wearing the long, flowing skirt that covered her legs and bare feet as she knelt before her captor. Her mission. The skirt flared out around her like a protective circle. Her back remained bare. The woman's sweat made the black-inked angel wings run as if bleeding down her back.

"Are you menstruating?" The Elder asked as he continued to circle.

"No," she answered between bites.

"When?" he asked.

"I don't..."

Elder Devlin swooped down to the open slot. She could see his angry eyes. "You must answer the question now."

"Fifteenth...the fifteenth of each month," she whimpered.

"You have lied to me, angel."

"No, Elder. It's true."

"No, angel. You said you were not afraid of me."

"I am not, Elder." The woman shook even more.

Devlin put his mouth to the open slot. "Do you hear your chains? They tell a different story. You will learn not to fear me. Only then will I remove your headbox. You are here for me. The Lord, our father, sent you. You will fulfill his mission."

"Yes, Elder Devlin."

"Good, angel. That is good."

The slot slid closed, and she couldn't see or hear again. The slam of the door vibrated through her. She cried, but no one could hear her. She tried to remember her name. But all she could recall was "angel."

Devlin emerged from the squalid prison through a hole beneath a cement floor. He grabbed the handle of a rolling toolbox to pull himself out, careful not to grip too hard and send steel and aluminum cascading toward him. He'd already put himself through enough. The slender maniac dusted himself off and kicked the diamond-plate trapdoor shut. The metal toolbox rolled onto the plate with relative ease. Devlin spat a large wad of phlegm onto The Minister's prized Jaguar and walked out a side door of the detached garage.

 **40**

The Long Island Rail Road ride crawled by in its usual dull rhythm. After a long, uneventful shift, Jake slept for most of it, head knocking against the window in quiet surrender.

Terri wasn't with him. She'd gone ahead to Mary Hollingsworth's family memorial, insisting she needed to be there, no matter how raw it still felt. Father Duffy went along as her shadow and shield, just in case the Ministry decided to circle again.

Jake understood. It made sense. Didn't mean he liked it.

Somewhere between Jamaica and Massapequa, he stirred awake, blinking at the reflection of his own tired face in the window. The train rattled on, indifferent. He hadn't expected the empty seat beside him to feel like such a punch.

He already missed talking to her.

Missed her steadiness. Her fire.

Missed the way she made the miles feel shorter.

But today, he was making the trip alone.

When Jake got off the train, he spotted a taxi at a convenient stand in front of the Babylon station. He slid into the back seat and muttered "Good Samaritan Hospital" to the driver. The man pulled the cab into gear, and the old horse rumbled forward, heading east.

Nothing else, no small talk, was shared between the two until the cab squealed to a stop outside the brown-brick hospital building. "Good Sam," the driver said. "Twelve fifty." Jake slipped him a ten and a five and walked out toward a colossal marble statue labeled The Good Samaritan. It stood tall at the heart of the traffic circle. The sculpture depicted a bearded man rendering aid to a helpless person. Three children laughed and ran in circles around the shrubbery that surrounded the statue. Jake entered the hospital with a slight smile and a warm heart. The Good Samaritan reminded him of his father.

"Good morning," Jake greeted the receptionist at the Patient Information desk.

A woman with a nasal voice and a short supply of patience skipped a greeting and asked, "Patient's name, please?"

Jake knew she probably outmatched him in a sarcasm contest. He became anxious when he did not know the nurse's name he was seeking.

"Could you direct me to the Human Resources department?"

The woman adjusted her glasses to look at Jake with disdain. "Do you have an appointment?"

"Of course."

"Name?"

"Jake, Jake Duffy."

The receptionist pressed a button on her telephone and spoke into the receiver. She glared back at Jake while listening to the response. "My apologies, sir, but HR does not list you on their appointment sheet today."

"Wow. That's weird," Jake said.

"Is it?" The receptionist made eye contact with a nearby security officer.

"Could I at least speak to a representative from that department?"

"Regarding what, sir?"

"I wish to compliment a nurse who took great care of my father."

The clerk spoke into her receiver again. "A representative will speak with you in a few minutes," she said while pointing Jake to a waiting area.

"Thank you!"

Despite his pride, Jake panicked, not knowing what name to ask for. He cursed himself for not planning. He fidgeted in the lobby, hoping to come up with a solution. The children from outside ran into the lobby, giggling, and sat on a couch.

Where are these kids' parents?

Above them was a framed display of Jillian Kidd, Employee of the Month. Jake let out a gasp in recognition. A nurse from the intensive care unit with a bright smile, a pretty face and short platinum hair. Her green eyes seemed more mature than the rest of her features. He could almost feel the pain hidden deep in the person's gaze, a dead giveaway. This was the new Olivia Heitz.

Jake hurried to the gift shop to buy flowers. When he arrived, the representative from Human Resources was relieved he was there for a reason other than filing a complaint about an employee. She gave him directions to Jillian's unit. Jake had a deep intake of sterile air as he entered, concealing his face behind the flowers.

The air danced to a symphony of bells and whistles. Each tone served as a lifeline for the doctors and nurses tending to their critical patients. Amid this cacophony was the ominous, mechanical breathing of Darth Vader, a stark reminder of the situation's gravity. Clad in colorful scrubs, healthcare professionals moved from room to room, purposeful strides punctuated by rustling fabric. As they carried out urgent tasks, conversations flowed, weaving anecdotes about families, weekend adventures and the latest blockbuster films. Rare moments of lightness amid the intensity of their work. A young nurse approached him.

"Hi. What can I do for you?"

"Um, yes. I have a delivery for Jillian Kidd," Jake said.

"Oh. It sure is nice to get flowers at work," the young nurse quipped. "She is over there at bed ten."

"Hey, Jill, you got a visitor," the nurse added before dipping into a nearby supply closet.

A voice answered back, "Okay. Give me a sec!"

As Jake approached bed ten, he recognized Olivia Heitz's voice from the video. He held the flowers in front of him and peered through them at Nurse Kidd, who was hanging an IV pouch on a stand. The patient in the bed was an elderly man who appeared unresponsive, with a tube down his throat. The monitors in the room displayed his blood pressure, oxygen levels, pulse and other vital signs. Nurse Kidd, who had seemed taller in the video when she was Olivia Heitz, now looked shorter and much younger. However, her eyes remained cold, something Jake couldn't help but notice. He wondered if he was biased from knowing what she had been through.

Nurse Kidd looked up from her work. "Oh, is that for Mr. Schmauder?"

Jake stammered a bit. "Um, no. No. Um. I think they are for you."

"Me! Wow, what a pleasant surprise. Please give me a second."

Jake lowered the flowers and stared at Katie Heitz's mother as she worked. She was strong, confident and skilled, but uncomfortable with how Jake stared. She then looked up and stared back, right into Jake's dual-colored eyes.

Nurse Jillian Kidd became Olivia Heitz and fell backward. She kicked her feet on the floor to back away further. A tray containing a water pitcher and other nursing tools fell over, hitting the ground with a slight crash. She struggled to get herself up while beginning to hyperventilate. Jake ran to help her, but she lashed his hand away.

"Get off me. Get away from me. You can't be here!" she cried.

"Wait. What?"

Other staff showed up, probing the disturbance. The young nurse asked, "Jill? Are you okay?" Another doctor pointed at Jake and asked Jillian if the man had hurt her. In the background, an older nurse shouted for someone to alert security.

Jake struggled to make any sense and could not get himself together. "I'm not. Wait! I'm helping her. I got her flowers. I'm..."

Nurse Kidd was then able to stop the confusion. "I'm all right, I slipped. It's okay. He was delivering flowers."

The young nurse asked, "You sure, Jill?"

Nurse Kidd teared up. "I'm good. Really. I need a little air." She left the room and the unit.

Jake picked up the flowers and tried to follow her, but nurses and doctors who were running after her blocked him. He found them in the family waiting room outside the unit. Concerned staff surrounded the teary nurse. She assured them she was fine and tried to convince them she had hot flashes. Jake stayed outside, patient and nervous. The nurses resumed working soon after they became satisfied that Jillian was feeling better. The waiting room was empty except for Nurse Kidd, who stood alone, wiping her eyes.

"Jacob, you shouldn't have come here," she said aloud, sensing Jake was still outside in the hallway.

Jake entered the doorway but was careful enough not to go inside. "How do you know my name?"

"You have his eyes."

* * * * *

Search Continues for NYPD Chief's Missing Daughter -
More Tonight on Eyewitness News.

The hospital cafeteria TV was muted, but Jake didn't need sound to feel the sting. Up on the screen, a rapid-fire montage flickered: school photos of Chief Beame's daughter, then a jittery slice of surveillance footage, then a reporter's lips moving in urgent, silent cadence.

Jake's stomach tightened.

Monica.

Her face hit him harder than the lukewarm coffee in his hands ever could.

Jillian Kidd, now transformed from her alter ego to Olivia Heitz, sat across from Jake, holding a cup of coffee with both hands. Olivia's trembling hands accentuated her worn and pained face. A deep sadness hung thick in the air, and Jake could almost touch it.

Before he could offer anything, Olivia said, "This is such a bad idea, Jacob."

Jake squirmed and apologized. Her distress was overwhelming. "I didn't want to upset you," he said.

"Please, you have to trust me. Go home and live your life to the fullest. Whatever you think you need from me, I can't give it to you. I am trying to live my new life, and it's hard enough. I can't worry about or protect you if you stay here."

"What's your point? I'm only trying to learn more about my father."

"He was a good man who loved you so much."

"Loved? So, you know he is dead?"

Olivia sighed and said, "He must be if you came looking for me."

Tears rolled down her cheeks, and Jake offered her a napkin. The weight of her sorrow was unbearable as Jake struggled to hold up the conversation.

Olivia's face reddened. Her body shook in order to contain the raw emotions that could erupt again at any moment. "I can't believe you found me. Why would he tell you about us?"

"He didn't. I don't know anything. I wanted to learn more about my father. Since he died, I've uncovered everything I never knew about him. I also found out that he became very sick around the same time your..." Jake stopped himself short. How could he bring up the death of a child to that child's mother? He tried to word it another way, but now the softball in Jake's throat made it too difficult to talk. Olivia showed she understood.

"He tried."

They sat in silence for ten minutes. Jake wore his sadness on his sleeve. Olivia offered Jake a napkin from the dispenser on the table. Then, Jillian Kidd reappeared.

"Jake. Would you come to church with me?"

Jake found his voice again. "This Sunday?"

"No. No. Now. There is a chapel here at the hospital."

Jake nodded his head and followed her. Two large wooden doors off the lobby allowed access to the chapel. It paled compared to a standard Catholic church, with three pews lining each side of a center aisle. A small, waist-high altar was on a one-step stage. A stunning hand-carved cross hung on a stained-glass backdrop. The multicolored glass portrayed The Good Samaritan, similar to the statue outside the hospital.

"Jake, please pray with me."

Jake knelt beside Jillian on the cushioned prayer rail in the middle pew. She recited the Lord's Prayer, followed by the Hail Mary prayer, and thanked God for listening. She asked for God's blessing. All was serene as Jillian continued praying. Jake remained patient. Suddenly, two children ran into the chapel, laughing. Jake recognized them as the same kids playing tag earlier by the statue. He signaled to the first child to be quiet by putting his finger to his lips. The little boy stopped and smiled, mimicking Jake's gesture. The two boys then ran out. Jillian remained in her prayer trance, and Jake wondered again where the kids' parents were. Jillian finally turned to Jake and spoke. She told Jake a story.

"Sean was a good-looking man who went to church and lived a life of faith. He was a good person, and I felt lucky that he found me. I was a bad girl who loved punk rock and lived a life of sex, drugs and rock and roll. Hated everything, including my parents, school and the world. I had a home, but preferred being on my own and partying hard. Quit school and followed a punk band around for a while.

"Eventually, I landed in New York City, broke, hungry and drunk. I blended into the street folk there. We all hung together. Did anything for food, shelter and drugs. We all found work from a guy named The Jypsy, who assigned us tasks to deliver drugs, damage property or crash parties. I wasn't sure why I participated, but I enjoyed myself and ignored the consequences. The Jypsy felt like a myth. Nobody ever met him. He led the NYC underground, urging protests and vandalism. He always delivered his messages in inventive ways. I gave it minimal thought.

"To start a mini riot at a phone company picket line, I made a cool twenty bucks. I celebrated a successful deed by going to Katz's Deli. I heard they made a fancy pastrami sandwich. That is where I met Sean. I was covered in mud. My clothes were shredded from where I tore at them. The purple in my hair stuck out in messy, uneven chunks, like I'd lost a fight with myself.

"Sean looked at me and told me purple was his favorite color. I called him a dweeb and ignored him. After ordering, the deli clerk told me the sandwich order was twenty-one fifty. I began arguing because I had only a twenty-dollar bill. Sean came over and gave me the dollar fifty. He said I looked hungry. I spat at him but took his money."

"Good for you, I guess," Jake commented.

"While I sat alone eating, Sean slid into the seat across from me and did what my parents never could. He knocked me down a peg. His words cut me. I felt like trash. His blunt honesty shoved me in front of the sober wagon. I hated it. I hated that some stupid part of me wanted him anyway." Jake remained silent to let her collect more of her memories. She continued.

"I became fixated on him and started following him around. I started taking regular showers and wearing better clothes to impress him. We eventually began dating. I even got a job and earned my GED."

"That part's kinda sweet. In a shy-stalker way."

Olivia half-smiled, then continued, her momentum regained.

"I joined his church to show my commitment, but it was a challenging experience. The Minister was an oppressive son of a bitch who enforced strict rules."

"Yeah, that doesn't sound like a commitment. Sounds like a cage."

"Although I loved Sean, and he loved me back, we had to get married in that church." "Wait, had to?"

Olivia nodded. Jake shifted, uncomfortable.

"After a few years, I wanted to attend nursing school, but Sean insisted The Elder and The Minister had to approve it."

"Jesus Christ," Jake said soft, not blasphemous.

"Unfortunately, they believed that my place was at home and that I had to bear a child for Sean and the Church."

"What the hell?"

"Yes. Hell. I had a conversation with Sean about leaving the church we attended. It felt extreme, and I wanted to live our lives without it. However, Sean committed himself to the church and even moved up the ranks. Though he acknowledged that some church rules were strict, he believed they were necessary to maintain order, peace and prosperity. Brainwashed. I thanked God and Jesus daily for my new life and Sean. But, deep in my soul, I felt this Ministry was not what God intended for us."

"Sometimes I wonder what God intends," Jake said.

"But things changed when I became pregnant with Katherine. The Minister controlled every aspect of our lives. Sean's income went directly to the Ministry, and I couldn't take prenatal vitamins or eat certain foods. They restricted my walking outside and watching television, instead encouraging me to listen to Bible music and read prayers. I followed these instructions to begin with, but I needed to remind Sean that the wealthy members of the church did not need to follow these rules."

"That must've gone over well," Jake said.

"Sean expressed his concerns to The Minister, leading to a meeting with The Elder and several high-ranking church members. During the meeting, I sat barefoot and pregnant in a chair at the center of the room, behind the stage area. I did my best to meet The Minister's demands, but the more he yelled at me to expel demons and obey, the angrier I became."

Jake let out a sigh. "That guy wasn't a minister. He was a bully with a Bible."

"I was not possessed. I was pissed off. As I cursed and screamed, The Elder, whose name I think was John, approached me from behind, wearing black leather gloves. I felt like the palms of the gloves were rubber because his covering my mouth to silence me made me unable to breathe. Sean rushed to my defense and tackled The Elder, who fought back with the other members. Sean told me to run and protect our baby, so I did."

"Holy fuck!" Jake said.

"I contacted the police and explained what happened. They visited the church, but it was closed. I gave them my husband's cell phone number. When they called him, he claimed I was ill and required hospitalization. The police took me to the hospital. I was positive that The Minister had influenced Sean and that they would come for me. As soon as the hospital staff left me alone in the emergency room, I fled and went to my old haunts."

"I get it. You did what you had to do."

"I tried to contact Sean, but he refused to speak. I knew he was in trouble, so I contacted some old acquaintances. They informed me that The Jypsy would aid me in rescuing Sean if I agreed to a 'deed' at a later time. I promised to do whatever it took if he could get Sean out of there unharmed."

"Damn it."

"Being eight months pregnant, I hid out with the derelicts for about two months. I ate healthy and took vitamins. I even managed to get a few checkups in different emergency rooms under a fake name. One day, Sean walked into the bar where I was drinking water."

"Just water?"

"I was changed. I loved being pregnant. Nothing was bringing me back to the poison."

"Sorry, what happened next?"

"Sean was different. He was crying and hugged me tight. I held him for a long time. He claimed that the Catholic church rescued him by giving him an awareness of free will and showing him the manipulative strategies of the Ministry of Salvation."

Jake stopped breathing. "What is the name of that church?"

"Ministry of Salvation."

"I was afraid you would say that."

Jake felt the temperature drop. The chapel wasn't cold. But his father's ghost had walked in. He could not believe his ears. He looked at the cross. "Man, you really work in mysterious ways," Jake said out loud.

"You know what I'm talking about?"

"Of them, yes. I think they kidnapped my friend's kid."

Jillian looked perplexed. "Kidnapping, huh? It's not their usual thing. It is more of a voluntary kind of cult. But they are that evil."

"This Elder John, what does he look like?" Jake asked.

"Very tall and thin. Slick black hair. Always wears leather gloves with a dark suit."

Jake's eyes went narrow. "Goatee?"

"Yes."

"What happened next?"

"Jake, the Ministry is dangerous. Please don't mess with them. Your father wanted to keep you clear of all this craziness. I'm nauseous that you even heard about them. Please tell me that you are not involved with them."

Jake filled his lungs, then exhaled. "Well, believe me, I'm not interested in getting cozy with them or even being in the same borough as them. I'm trying to learn about my father and why this is all happening to me."

Jillian continued with her story.

"Everything was going well for a while. Our family lived in Alphabet City, and our daughter Katherine was born healthy. Sean got a job as a bartender while I took steps to attend nursing school and raise Katie. The Ministry never contacted us, and Sean never mentioned them. We were happy. Went to a Catholic church on Sundays and made our own choices."

"I wish this was the ending. I know it's not," Jake said trying not to sound choked up.

"But when Katie turned eight, I received an unexpected visitor who handed me a CD. An audible message from The Jypsy instructed me to accept a job for Patrick Perri, a mayoral candidate who was a city council member. The message specified that I was to work for him for six months and become friendly with him. After that, he would create a scandal to ensure he wouldn't get elected as mayor. I had forgotten about it until then. I had to claim a sexual assault or plant child pornography."

"That's insane. That would be great evidence."

"Yes. Of course, once I played it the disc erased. Some kind of self-destruct program."

"Diabolical," Jake said. "Just not really a cartoon though."

"Days later, the Perri campaign accepted my application and invited me to interview at headquarters. I got the job. I worked under Mr. Perri for months. He is as awesome as he appears to be. The man had a squeaky-clean background and loved New Yorkers. His policies were terrific. He was what the city needed. He still is. I would come home and tell Sean what a great guy Patrick was. Mr. Perri even let me take Katie to work with me and set up daycare for other workers."

"Yeah, he is an okay mayor. I could use a raise though."

"My job wasn't very difficult. I helped organize meetings, travel plans and recommended some great bars, one where a very handsome man worked. Sean also became friends with him. It paid well. I saved enough to start nursing school. When the time came to start the scandal, I was nervous but loyal to my word. Sean was furious. He convinced me to cancel it. Mr. Perri was a genuinely good person. I listened to my husband. He was right. I told you he was the best kind of person. There were no problems in Mayor Perri's election."

"And he is still our mayor," Jake said.

"The Jypsy was not happy. Katie didn't come home from school on December 15, 2001. We found another audio CD under our door. It conveyed that Katie's safety relied on us not contacting the police. The voice also instructed that Katie would return home in three nights and would need intense therapy. I was in a nightmare. Sean was losing it. The message ended by telling me this was my fault for not paying back my debt. Sean suggested we reach out to a street vigilante."

"The Fade," Jake whispered.

"Yes, The Fade. Street hero. He was quite feared."

"My dad."

"So, you do understand?"

"Just found out. That's why I'm here. He was never the same after 2001."

Jillian continued as Olivia.

"Word spread quickly through the streets that we needed The Fade. I was concerned that word would reach The Jypsy. Sean met all types of people while working at the bar. He was convinced that Jypsy would never figure out what we were about to do. The Fade appeared behind Sean's bar as it was getting dark. He told us he was aware of The Jypsy, and he was an awful person. He also said that he would bring our daughter home safe and sound. I had faith in him and trusted him. We had no other choice."

"He was your best choice." Jake wanted to show how proud he was.

Tears began streaming down Olivia Heitz's face. She was getting choked up and had a difficult time talking. So was Jake, but he only had to listen.

"The Fade brought her home three hours later. It was 10 p.m. He laid her down on my living room couch. I thought she was sleeping. I kissed her head. She was so cold. The coldness. I went to get her a blanket. Then I saw the eyes. The Fade's eyes. Your father's eyes. Your eyes. He was crying. My husband knew and screamed. I couldn't understand, couldn't figure out what was wrong. I wanted to get her a blanket. She was so cold. Sean grabbed me. He kept screaming for help. I told Sean she was okay. She is just cold. She's home now."

"Wait," Jake said. "I don't understand."

"Sean grabbed Katie. She wouldn't wake up. He kept shaking her. He wanted her to wake up. She wouldn't wake up. The Fade was on his knees. He was praying. I stood without another word, watching. It was not real. It was like I was watching a movie. A sick horror movie. The Fade then took off his mask and hood. He couldn't talk. He tried mouthing the word 'sorry.' Sean wanted to call an ambulance, the police. The Fade grabbed his arm. He told Sean not to. He told us the police won't believe any of us. It was crazy. Sean punched The Fade right in the face. The Fade didn't even flinch. He took it. As reality started setting in, I started hitting him as well. He sat there on his knees. Sean pulled me off him."

"No...no way. He would save..."

"Jacob, we had some honest personal conversations for most of that night. We needed to figure out what to do. He told me what had happened to my baby, and he told me something else. He told me who he was and who you were."

"What? That makes no sense."

"Jake, you must understand. I made peace with the decisions we made that night. By no means did it make sense then, and it was probably the wrong decision. What's done is done."

"What happened to your daughter?" Jake asked.

"She fell down our stairs in the middle of the night," Olivia answered like a programmed robot.

Jake understood that, and after a pause, he let Olivia continue.

"The Fade told us another story," she started.

Jake braced. Whatever came next, it would not be easier. It was going to be worse.

 **Chapter** 41

The Fade only heard of The Jypsy. This was from the mouth of a particular sex peddler from Times Square known as Rufus. The Fade came upon this piece of shit trying to lure a teenage runaway to work for him as a stripper.

"Rufus, I should rip your balls out through your mouth," The Fade grumbled.

"Ah, shit man!" Rufus said without even turning around. "What the fuck, Fade? I didn't know you were into threesomes."

The Fade slapped his gloved hand on Rufus's shoulder. Blue light emanated from the glove, and Rufus fell stiff onto the hard concrete on the desolate sidewalk.

"Young lady. This is not the exciting and profitable opportunity you think this is. I see you are scared and cold. This piece of garbage will destroy your life, from which it would be difficult to return."

"He only wanted to take my picture. He's from a high-end magazine and was about to pay me 200 dollars."

The Fade reached into Rufus's pockets and pulled out thirty-five dollars in singles. "That's all he has. Why don't you grab a bite at the diner down the street? A police officer will find you there and help you get back to Kentucky."

"I don't want to go back. My parents don't understand. I want to be a model. This is where I'm supposed to be. Wait, how'd you know I'm from Kentucky?"

"Lucky guess. How old are you?"

"Sixteen. I'm old enough."

"Drugs?" The Fade grumbled.

"No, never. I know what I'm doin'."

"Well, you almost did. Get to that diner and wait for the officer."

"I'm not going back home," the defiant teen stated.

"This is a dangerous place. You will die."

The young girl trembled at the severity of The Fade's tone. He lit his gloves up. "Diner is that way." She ran.

The Fade dragged Rufus's unconscious body to the corner and was relieved to see the runaway enter the greasy-spoon restaurant up the street. He made an anonymous call on a pay phone and slapped Rufus awake.

"Come on, Fade. You got it all wrong. I was protecting her."

"I should collapse your lungs so you no longer breathe my air."

"Seriously, man. There is this new guy in town. His peeps are scoopin' up runaways comin' off the Greyhounds. I can't say for certain what they want with her. This kid was young and too pretty to be getting involved with this gypsy king group."

"So, you thought she was better off workin' for your classy establishment?"

"Beats whatever those other assholes have in mind."

"What assholes?"

"The gypsy kids. Aren't you paying attention? They look clean-cut, but word is they hang around Port Authority and Penn, grabbin' runaways and such. Heard they turn them into mindless sex slaves by beating them with sticks."

"You could be a little more creative with your storytelling."

"I'm telling you what I heard. I saw her getting off a Greyhound, and this weirdo kid. She immediately offered her a job. I told the kid to get lost. I just saved her, that's all. I could have made that girl a star!"

"What were you doin' at the Port Authority?"

"Buying a ticket to visit my mother."

The Fade lost his patience and shocked Rufus unconscious again. Afterward, The Fade stood hidden and watched as police escorted the young girl into a police car.

* * * * *

"It was years later when Katie was kidnapped," Olivia explained. "Word on the street was that Rufus was making serious money by working for a shady syndicate. He even expanded his business a bit. Rufus was the only other person to mention the name gypsy. The Fade decided to start with him, as Rufus wasn't as stupid as people might have thought. He somehow seemed involved with everything since forming a new partnership."

* * * * *

The Fade slid down a pipe from the rooftop of the strip joint. It was garbage day tonight, and The Fade tore through some bags, looking for anything helpful. His heart skipped a beat when a torn-up envelope revealed "Squ" and "Jyp." He pieced them together with a few other scraps. It read:

The Squid in box #5 has a Jypsy message.

This is too easy.

When The Fade was about to enter Rufus's establishment, Rufus barreled out of the door, drunk and in a hurry. The Fade followed.

Rufus wasn't aggressively approaching tourists or promoting his "ladies," nor had he pickpocketed anyone in the last twenty minutes. He hadn't even tried to trick any women into thinking he was a talent scout for *Playboy* magazine. It was clear that Rufus was uneasy about something, making him the perfect target for questioning the whereabouts of someone named The Jypsy.

I should have believed him back then, The Fade thought to himself as he stalked his prey.

Rufus was perspiring, chain-smoking and constantly glancing at his watch. The Fade could not shake the sense of unease as he followed Rufus onto the subway and into Brooklyn. Something was unfolding. The Fade was resolute in discovering what it was.

Beneath the Brooklyn Bridge in DUMBO, darkness prevailed, and nobody else roamed. Rufus approached a shadowy figure concealed beneath an oversized trench coat. As the figure turned to greet Rufus, The Fade's eyes widened in shock at the sight of a young girl beside the mysterious rogue.

The peddler of lies was deep in conversation with the figure, their voices hushed and secretive. The Fade tried to listen, but the distance wouldn't allow it. With increasing tension, The Fade knew a major event was coming. He was dead set on finding the answer, no matter how much it took.

"You didn't say it was a child," Rufus whined.

"Why does that matter?" the figure whispered.

Rufus seemed a bit panicked. "It's a child. I'm not sending her in there. They won't even want her in there."

"That's why you will convince them."

Katie was whimpering. "I want to go home."

The figure whispered to the child. "Don't worry, kitty cat. You will be going home soon."

Rufus again protested. "She is a child, man."

"I'm going to be as clear as I can. You take her up there. Convince that freak to film the act. You don't have to watch it. Then, drop the brat on her parents' doorstep with the film. That's it."

"I can't. I won't. That's, that's too much. You're taking this too far." Rufus was shaking.

"It will be much worse for you if you don't." The figure's voice deepened.

"10 Jay Street. Fifth floor. Do it yourself!" Rufus ran as fast as he could.

The shadows twisted as they trailed behind the figure, whose purposeful stride cut through the night. The Fade, an eternal ally of the shadows, strained to catch even a fleeting glimpse of the enigmatic character known as Jypsy. Clutching a terrified child, the figure moved with unsettling calm. Something felt wrong.

The Fade, sensing a tragic culmination, took a powerful step into the pale moonlight. His movements were deliberate and urgently charged. Electric-blue currents crackled ominously around his gloved hands, illuminating the scene with a supernatural glow. He lifted his chin, meeting Jypsy's chilling, vacant stare, an eye devoid of humanity.

Time froze; the air thickened with impending doom. The menacing buzz of energy enveloping The Fade was the only sound that pierced the silence. Every instinct screamed at him to act and rescue the child ensnared in Jypsy's clutches. He hesitated, heart pounding, needing a meticulous plan to snatch Jypsy before chaos erupted, while protecting the innocent girl.

Katherine Heitz's body went limp with a sickening crack. Without hesitation, her young life ended in an instant. The monster had snapped her neck. He kept silent, retreating into the darkness. The Fade ran to the fallen child. He tried everything to revive her. Rescue breaths, chest compressions and electric shocks from his hands. He screamed for help. Nothing. The child's life was lost. The Fade held the child's body.

"I promised. Shouldn't have hesitated. No. No. I promised!" he repeated.

Darkness birthed a spirit-like sound.

"You're more known to authorities than I am. They will believe you did it. I'll make damn sure of that."

The Fade jumped up and searched the immediate area for The Jypsy. He was unwilling to leave the child's side either. It was hopeless. The Fade lost all hope that night. The Jypsy was gone. He then took Katie home, though it differed from what he had promised.

* * * * *

Jake sat in stunned silence, heart racing. He was accustomed to hearing about how his father had won battles and protected the innocent. Olivia Heitz looked more vulnerable than ever. In a moment of comfort, Jake embraced her tightly, feeling the weight of her grief on his shoulders.

"I'm so sorry for everything," he said softly, searching for words to ease the pain. "I wish I could say more."

Olivia sighed, her eyes glistening with unshed tears.

"Your father took off his mask, laying bare all the secrets of his life to Sean and me. He shared everything about you, the depth of his love, fears and regrets. It was an act of trust that I wish could have been different."

"But why would he do that?" Jake asked, bewildered by the revelation.

"He revealed everything because it had kept him safe all these years. No one knew who he was, and he felt indebted to us. We realized the police would likely turn against him if we sought help. And we knew that The Jypsy would hunt us down, seeking revenge for the secrets we held. He feared the danger would extend to you as well, Jake. By confiding in us, he entrusted us with the chance to reclaim our power and confront his failure. We could get revenge on him for failing us. It was both a gift and a burden."

"You didn't use it." Jake pointed out the obvious.

"It was too late. I had lost everything already. My husband always believed that we should keep you safe and prevent another child from dying at the hands of The Jypsy. He taught me that. Your father's secret and the memory of The Fade must be kept alive by us in the hearts of the streets that loved him. We must ensure evil is afraid of him and keep a little hope alive in this unforgiving city. We can still save lives. I admit I didn't care or understand what Sean saw in all of this. I wanted everyone and everything dead, including myself."

"What changed?" Jake asked.

"I loved my husband, but I loved my daughter even more. It wasn't until Sean's passing that I fully understood the significance of my late husband's message. The world still has goodness, and hope is the greatest virtue. Unfortunately, Sean lost hope because of the media, the negative people around him and the jobs he endured. Everyone blamed us, and no one believed it was an accident. We couldn't even live in peace. Sean still had hope."

"It seemed he lost his will, though," Jake said.

"My heart aches for Sean. He was worn down to the bone, yet he still climbed to be with Katie. He couldn't leave her alone up there. I pray they're together now, safe, whole and at peace. I stayed behind to fight for his soul, to ensure heaven takes both of them. Perhaps it sounds crazy, but I feel them listening when I pray. Every sin I've committed burns on my back. I'll carry that weight until my last breath. My vow to God was to prove my love for him or her. I pray for our family so that one day, we can stand together again in the afterlife. Sean asked me to protect you, and I will. I've told no one. My focus involves rescuing many lives. Every life I save offers a chance to shift things. I can't save everyone, but I will bleed myself dry trying."

Olivia gritted her teeth as she delivered her final words to Jake in the chapel, knowing she would soon return to being Jillian Kidd. Her words seethed with anger and pierced like a venomous snakebite. These words became the last thread in Jake's unraveling world. At last, he had a sense of direction, and the arrows pointed straight to hell.

"The Jypsy is still fucking out there. Would have bet that old bastard would be dead by now. But now I know he is not."

"What makes you say that?" Jake asked.

"Because you're here."

Chapter 42

Elijah was bored during the morning prayer before preschool, which exhausted him. His brother Shante was lucky because he attended a big boy school. Elijah couldn't wait to join Shante's school, where he would meet new and interesting kids and play fun games. However, he missed his mother terribly. Mr. and Mrs. Corning, who were taking care of him, were very strict and only allowed him to play for an hour before bath time.

Many women and young children attended today's prayer, and Elijah was excited to see other kids his age. However, they all sat still and did not play, listening to what The Minister said. Suddenly, Elijah needed to use the bathroom and started doing the pee-pee dance. Mrs. Corning noticed and asked him if he knew where the boys' room was. Elijah nodded yes. Mrs. Corning allowed him to go, but reminded Elijah to return directly after he finished. She promised to stay with Deshawn.

Elijah departed toward the vacant hall to the church's left. The boys' restroom was also empty. He used the small urinal that suited his size and washed his hands as Mrs. Corning had taught him. As he left the bathroom, he could hear The Minister's muffled sermon coming from the closed door of the congregation area. Elijah had a great idea!

*I can go down into the classroom and play with the toy
trucks before anyone else comes. That way, I won't have to
share. Well, at least not until later. And maybe Sarah-
Prudence will be in her hiding place waiting to play. That
would be really cool.*

He crept down into the sub-basement.

The classroom door loomed at the bottom of the stairs —
the same one Elder Devlin always locked from the outside,
like the whole place was a school built for prisoners instead of
kids.

Elijah froze. If he let that door click shut behind him, he'd
be stuck until the Elder decided he deserved to be let out. No
way. Not today.

He wrapped both hands around the knob, turned it slowly,
and nudged the door open just enough to slip inside. Before
it could swing closed again, he dragged a plastic garbage pail
across the floor. The scraping echoed, but he didn't stop. He
wedged the pail between the door and the frame with all his
strength. Still not trusting it, he tore a handful of tissues from
Mrs. Devlin's bookshelf and stuffed them deep into the latch
hole, the way he'd once seen an older boy do it to keep the
Elder from locking him in during a "prayer lesson."

The door stayed open a sliver.

Good enough.

He wouldn't be caged.

Elijah hurried toward the rows of trucks lined neatly on the
carpet. Then, halfway there, Sarah-Prudence flickered across
his mind. He turned, stepped toward the hidden panel and
gave it three soft knocks.

No answer.

"Sarah-Prudence? You in there?" Elijah whispered.

Again, nobody responded. Elijah figured out how the panel slid open. He heard footsteps coming down the stairs, which caused the boy to panic. He regretted coming down here, where he didn't belong. It must have been Mrs. Corning coming to find out why he hadn't returned from the bathroom.

Elijah jumped into the cubbyhole and shut the panel. It was pitch black, and he felt around. Sarah-Prudence was not inside. The box felt roomier than he had imagined, and a soft blanket was inside. He grabbed hold of the blanket and clutched it in fright. He could hear footsteps inside the classroom, smooth and slow. Someone was in the classroom now. The panel remained partly open. Elijah peered out from the crack.

If I don't move, maybe the monsters won't know I'm here.

Mr. Jonah Richman was back in the classroom. He pushed up his glasses and fiddled with the collar of his pink button-down shirt. Fehrenbach always kept up his persona. Reading the children's projects and moving some papers, he studied the classroom. Then he walked over to the panel. He patted around, listening for the hollow sound of the hidden door. Elijah sat still, unsure if he'd been spotted.

You should have minded your own business!

A deep, guttural voice echoing from the shadows shattered the oppressive silence, chilling Mr. Richman to the bone. Elder Devlin spoke; his unmistakable tone radiated malice as he declared Mr. Richman caught. Before Mr. Richman could even attempt to respond, a gloved hand clamped over his mouth and nose, plunging him into a living nightmare of suffocation. The palm of the glove was icy and slick against his skin, intensifying the horror of his predicament.

In a frantic and desperate bid for escape, Mr. Richman thrashed, his legs flailing as unrestrained panic consumed him. Yet, the grip was unbreakable, a cold vice tightening around him. His face transformed into a mask of terror, flushed deep crimson, while his eyes bulged in sheer horror, straining against the encroaching darkness that loomed. It felt as though he were drowning, not in water, but in a suffocating fog of his breath. Each attempt to inhale panicked him more. The world around him twisted into a nightmarish void, shadows slithering closer. With gut-wrenching despair, he realized that time was slipping away, leaving him in the clutches of overwhelming dread.

His round glasses fell to the floor. Jonathan Devlin snaked his long legs around the private investigator like a boa constrictor. They both fell to the ground. The more the smaller man struggled, the tighter Devlin's grip became. The last thing Mr. Richman would hear was Devlin's quick, sudden giggles amid his heavy breathing. His body went limp. Devlin's eyes rolled to the back of his head as he kept a tight wrap. Sweat soaked him. A high-pitched snigger would squeak out of Devlin's mouth as he reclined on his back with the former Mr. Richman's body covering him. He was enjoying himself. It felt invigorating. He was alive after taking another life. Something turned him on. It exceeded his recollection.

"This is how God feels," Devlin whispered in Mr. Richman's dead ear. "Tell him I said hello."

Elijah sat still. He quietly strained to hear the unnerving sound of something being dragged across the floor. He shivered more as the classroom door creaked shut. The child felt an insatiable urge to escape from his hiding spot. The Ministry turned into a prison with the monsters in charge. It was more terrifying than the late-night gunshots that would shatter the silence, rousing him from sleep when he lived with his mother.

With trembling hands, Elijah eased the panel open a crack. The classroom remained shrouded in darkness, amplifying his sense of fear. His gaze fell upon a pair of black wire-rimmed glasses lying forebodingly on the floor, glinting faint in the light. He stepped out of the cubbyhole, each movement deliberate, as if the air was watching him.

He paused, snatching up the glasses and putting them on. They were ridiculously oversized on his tiny face. He could see through them with horrifying clarity, but their presence felt like a haunting memory clinging to him. Quick and quiet, he left the classroom, removing the tissue that had blocked the latch hole, his makeshift shield against the unknown.

His heart raced, a frantic drumbeat echoing in his ears as he hesitated at the doorway. He ascended the silent stairwell toward the hall, each step fearful.

Elijah heard footsteps approaching from The Elder's office. Without a second thought, he dashed into the boys' bathroom and ducked into a toilet stall. His breaths came and went in short gasps. Overwhelmed with emotions, tears welled in Elijah's eyes, and he began crying silently. When the bathroom door burst open and the footsteps tapped just beyond the stall, Elijah's body went rigid with terror. He saw a shadow sweep across the space between the locked door and the tiled floor. A pair of women's feet in heels stood outside the stall. Elijah's desperately tried to hold his breath and stay as still as possible.

"Elijah? Elijah?" Mrs. Corning's voice called out.

He tried to hold back a sniffle.

"Elijah, please open the door."

The stall lock slid open with a loud click.

Mrs. Corning pushed on the door. She knelt to his eye level and gave the street-smart Elijah the excuse he needed. "Did you get lost?" she asked in an exaggerated tone.

Elijah nodded his head yes.

Mrs. Corning wiped his eyes with her thumb under the glasses. "My Elijah, where did you get these glasses?" He shrugged his shoulders. He preferred not to give them up. "Well, if you found them here, someone might miss them. We will ask The Minister if he could make an announcement. Okay?"

Elijah again shrugged his shoulders. He was calming down now. Mrs. Corning took the glasses off his face. "You shouldn't wear other people's glasses; you can hurt your eyes." Mrs. Corning then looked through them. "Well, they appear to be a weak prescription anyway. Almost like they are made from flat glass. Are these toy glasses?"

Elijah nodded yes. Mrs. Corning gave them back, and he put them on again.

Everything was fine until they exited the restroom. Elder Devlin was coming out of his office across the hall when he turned and faced Mrs. Corning. He looked down at Elijah. The child slid sideways behind his foster mother. The Elder was still sweating.

"Ah, Mrs. Corning. You must be aware that you are on the male side of the Ministry?"

"Yes. Elder Devlin. Elijah was having difficulty in the restroom. I came to retrieve him. It won't happen again. I mean no disrespect to our Ministry."

Devlin wiped his brow. His hands were bare.

"What kind of trouble did you have, young man?" The Elder addressed the child directly.

Elijah knew he had to answer. "I was lost."

Devlin leaned down. "I don't recall you wearing glasses."

"I found them."

Devlin stood up tall. "Where?"

Elijah's lungs lost their air. "In there," he said as he pointed to the restroom.

Mrs. Corning added, "They are just a toy, Elder Devlin. We will return them to their rightful owner."

"Mrs. Corning. The child can speak and answer questions. Those are the surface of his abilities. He must learn to be self-sufficient, or he will remain a puppet on your strings, endlessly dependent. He will never break free if you continue to mother him and swoop in like a guardian angel. He needs to roam on his own, even in the shadows, where he can discover his true self."

Devlin tilted his head to little Elijah. "Next time, you must not hide. God sees best in the light."

He snapped back to Mrs. Corning. "You must never stray into this part of the Ministry again. It is not meant for women. Good day to you."

Devlin locked his office door and walked into the congregation area. Mrs. Corning and Elijah followed. The Elder was pleased that they had found their seats to finish listening to The Minister's sermon. He slipped out of the room, every step measured, the silence heavy enough to choke on.

Chapter 43

On his way back to the city, Jake was hell-bent on revenge. He wrestled with common sense and irrational anger.

I'm no hero. I'm a garbageman. But Dad...Dad was the real thing. Brave. Sharp. Built from iron. That kind of person boys aspire to be. He had the tools, the mind, the grit.

The Jypsy wasn't some TV villain. Not a comic book thug. He was pure rot. Real, breathing evil. A child killer. A psychopath with other psychopaths on his leash. This wouldn't be a hockey fight. This was the kind of fight that buries people.

Uncle Duffy would lose his mind. Who the hell would even pay for my funeral?

If Olivia Heitz told the truth, The Jypsy had desperate men at his back. Where the hell do I start? Is Sing X tied to him? Does this sailor work for him? Do I dump what I know on the cops right now? Would Molina laugh in my face? Maybe I need more. Maybe I need everything.

Back home, he took a quick shower and a short nap. He checked on Mrs. Daschle before meeting Uncle Duffy and Terri at Rosa's Pizzeria in Penn Station. They caught up on what was happening over some delicious pizza slices and boarded the uptown A train.

* * * * *

As the sun set and night fell, Times Square became a spectacle of bright lights that dazzled visitors. Tourists strolled around, craning their necks to gaze in awe at the stunning display, while locals hurried past. Adding to the surreal scene at Broadway and 7th Avenue, costumed characters wandered about, trying to entice tourists to take pictures with them for a fee. It struck Jake that many of these superheroes failed to live up to their heroic reputations. They caused more trouble than good. Their costumes were often in tatters, cheap knockoffs barely pretending to be anything but crude, laughable impostors. And everyone knew Batman and Spiderman lived in separate universes, so uniting them seemed sacrilegious.

"Well, at least you'll have a part-time job when you retire," Terri pointed out.

Jake looked at her to clarify her statement.

"You can wear your father's Fade outfit and take pictures," she joked.

"If they don't pay me, I can shock the hell out of them," Jake said, joining the fun. "I may even go around taking out the competition."

Father Duffy jumped into the game. "Perhaps give the DC lads a bit of a shock. I've always had a soft spot for Marvel Comics."

"Father Duffy!" Terri shouted. She followed in a whisper, "Me too."

Jake scanned the glitz and rot, his ears catching a street sermon from three self-proclaimed Black Hebrew Israelites. They stood on the sidewalk in bright blue, black and red tunics, voices booming with hate. The prophecy of a Black, vengeful Jesus coming back to enslave and kill all white Americans didn't rattle Jake. The jeweled gold daggers glinting from their sashes did. He could not tear his eyes away.

The lead preacher, dressed in a black headdress and studded leather crown, gripped a heavy wooden staff and locked eyes with Father Duffy.

"You, Preacher of Satan. You are hereby marked for beheading upon the rapture's arrival here on earth."

Jake stepped forward as if to challenge the extremist in defense of his uncle. Then, his effort marked him for a gruesome death. Father Duffy stopped Jake, explaining that provoking a fanatic is pointless. He then pointed out that the only people standing around listening to the radical speech were Caucasian out-of-towners.

He then turned to get Terri's thoughts on the matter. She was no longer standing with him. A small child, trying to keep up with his parents, walked past Jake toward the southwestern side of 42nd Street. As the cursed priest turned to look for Terri, Jake saw her across the street, watching another street performer.

This one stood on a short timber platform. He had wild, shoulder-length blond hair with a hint of salt and pepper. Tall and gaunt, the man had a pot belly protruding from his untucked black button-down shirt. The dark five o'clock shadow gave the entertainer a subtle, rugged appearance. The man looked like half a stick figure because of his black skinny jeans and shoes.

Terri watched from the front of a small crowd that seemed captivated by the peddler's words.

"Gentle souls, I am Robert Keener, a psychic medium for many celebrities and politicians. I have spoken to relatives and friends of William H. Macy, director Kevin Smith, Susanna Hoffs of the Bangles and former U.S. President Jimmy Carter. This was confidential until now. I am promoting a new off-Broadway live theater show, the *Keen Sight Experience*, starting in a few weeks. I will reveal the stars' secrets, provide insight into many unsolved crimes and connect my audience to their deceased loved ones."

Keener paused for applause. To Jake's surprise, some people clapped, but Terri did not. He continued, "Tonight, I intend to prove my abilities to the most skeptical and turn you all into believers. There is another side, the afterlife. Yes, your loved ones are there. They are there, dying to communicate with you." Keener paused at his *dying* quip.

"I consider myself both blessed and burdened by the extraordinary gift of communicating with those who have passed. Through this unique ability, I carry their profound messages of hope, love and caution to those they left behind. A bridge between the realms of life and afterlife with compassion and understanding."

Keener pointed to a woman in her sixties staring desperately at the street medium. Other relatives accompanied her, all of whom were pulling wheeled luggage. "You, ma'am, what's your first name?"

"Mabel," she spoke, her tone unsteady.

"Mabel, would you like me to contact somebody from the other side? A child, perhaps, A close friend, a parent, a hus..." Keener stopped, closed his eyes and continued. "Yes! A husband. A departed husband!"

Mabel became elated. "Yes! Oh my God, yes! My husband passed a few years ago."

Keener continued to show off. "Yes! His name is, wait, I see an R, no S, no T. Oh yes, a T!"

Mabel's exhilaration grew.

"Thomas, Tommy, Tim, Timothy, Theodore."

Mabel gave it away. "Yes. Oh my God. Teddy! Is he really there?" The woman began bawling and heaving. She could not be a plant. Terri choked up and wiped forming tears from her eyes.

Keener laid it on thick. He stepped off his makeshift stage and approached Mabel. Her companions all put a supportive hand on the grieving widow's shoulder. Terri felt terrible for the woman, trying to avoid missing something through her deep sobs. That was until Terri observed Keener looking down at Mabel's luggage. Keener tried not to be obvious, but he was trying to read her luggage tag.

"Yes. Teddy is with us here. At the crossroads of the world. What would you like to say to him, Mrs. Roth from Biloxi, Mississippi?"

Some onlookers murmured, "He knew her last name," and "This guy is for real."

Mabel cried harder. "Teddy, I miss you. I miss you every day. I can't do this without you. I love you!"

Keener's voice rose higher and cut Mabel off. "He asked me to tell he is doing fine. He loves you too and he is watching over you. He must go now, but he says he will see you soon."

Terri choked out a quick snort at Keener's last statement as he pointed to a frail, meek-looking male staring with his mouth wide open.

"Oh yes, sir, please step right up," Keener requested. Terri grimaced as the man walked between other onlookers.

"All right. Mr. Lent? Mr. Vincent Lent? Is that you?"

The little guy confirmed by nodding his head. Terri had to admit she couldn't figure that one out.

"Ah. That's good. I received a message. Somebody asked me to find you," Keener explained.

"Who?" Mr. Lent asked in a shaky voice.

"I'm not sure. I see an R, S, T, L, N-N-N-N. Yes, N."

Terri surveyed the situation. Mr. Lent's eyebrows were raised. Keener went on with the Ns. "Nanny, Norman, Nancy, Niece, Ned, Nun, Nun? Nun?"

Mr. Lent livened up. "Yes. My mother. She was a nun! Well, before she had me."

Keener smirked at his new challenge. Within the next ten minutes, he revealed personal messages to Mr. Lent. People opened their wallets and fanny packs and dropped dollar bills into a box at the foot of Keener's stage. After a few more psychic readings and a new crowd, Terri decided it was her turn to engage with the con artist.

Jake and Father Duffy remained quiet in the background while Terri gestured toward the performer. She put on her most pleading doe eyes. She wiped her eyes again and moved even closer to the stage. Keener couldn't help himself. He froze mid-reading during another successful performance and turned to Terri. Keener turned on his thickest charm.

"Well, hello, pretty lady. Wait, let me try to guess your name. Please hold out your hand."

Terri did as he requested. Keener leaned over from his stage and kissed Terri's hand. His lips were dry. Something stale sweetened his breath. Terri kept smiling. He began his letter guessing. "I'm reading an R, No, S, No, not her, uh, T."

Terri exaggerated and raised her eyebrows.

"Yes! T, Tanya, no, Theresa, no, Tammy, Tiffany, wait, it could be Theresa. Oh yes, it seems like I'm seeing Theresa!"

Terri was a little impressed. She tried not to give a *tell*. She confirmed his suspicions. Keener was getting into his role, and Terri was improving at hers. She used her God-given talents as a woman to play on a man's primal psyche. With every fishing line Keener cast, Terri would counter with an eye bat or duck lips and a cute giggle. When the reading was complete, Keener was in touch with Terri's grandfather, who had died seven years ago in an accident involving electricity. The grandfather, Benjamin, is now in heaven with Terri's Aunt Lucy, watching over her because Terri had lousy luck dating men, Keener relayed from the afterlife. Some things were pure fiction. Grandpa Benjamin and Aunt Lucy were as real as the Tooth Fairy and the Easter Bunny. Terri was enjoying the game until it was time to call out Keener for what he was: a thief and a con man.

She was playing him like a fiddle. And Jake couldn't help but smile, because he knew the encore was going to hurt.

"Just one thing, Mr. Keener. My Grandpa Benjamin can't be in heaven."

Keener looked perplexed. "Why would you think that? I have spoken to him."

Terri shocked even Jake and Father Duffy. "Because he is a killer of little girls. He got the death sentence on twelve systems."

"She used a Star Wars quote," Jake said to Father Duffy.

"You must be in love," the priest answered.

Keener became uneasy. He stammered through the closing of his little sideshow. Terri accused him of using the "Common Wheel of Fortune Letters" to deduce names from his victim's behavior. He fumbled his tips into his front jeans pocket. He began lifting his homemade stage by the handle in the back. Father Duffy came into Keener's view as the priest whispered into Terri's ear that Keener was the one and only "God of 42nd Street."

Terri laughed at her luck. "Wow, I'm the real psychic one," she exclaimed.

Keener's foul-mouthed tirade halted her excitement. "Holy shit! Can't you fucking self-righteous assholes loosen your collars and leave me the fuck alone?" He dropped his stage onto the pavement.

"Now, son, we are messing with you. We want to talk to you about something," the honest priest said.

"No fucking way! Stay away from me!"

Keener walked westbound on 42nd Street without his stage. The small crowd dispersed as he stormed off, some waving their hands in disgust. Father Duffy and Terri, following Keener, started catching up with him. The hefty priest had trouble keeping pace, but Terri had the stamina to close in on the taller man's long strides. Passing 9th Avenue, Keener sensed Terri would catch up with him. So he jogged. But he was out of shape and quickly winded. Keener didn't know how long he could keep up even a light jogging pace, but he wanted to escape the two meddling agitators. The con man was sweating hard now and slowing down as he turned onto 10th Avenue, still looking behind.

"Oh, excuse me," Jake said.

All Keener saw was a male with messy blond hair and a New York Islanders t-shirt walking right into him. The bump was not that hard, but Keener stumbled into a city-owned garbage can. The clumsy pedestrian walked off in the opposite direction with his head down. When Keener regained his balance, Terri and Father Duffy stood beside him.

"What is the problem with you people? I have the right to be left alone," Keener sneered.

"My name is Theresa Sheehan. I am an investigator for the Administration for Children's Services. I am investigating a custodial interference case involving an eight-year-old child. Do you or have you ever known a teenager by the name of Kevin Miller?"

Keener struggled to breathe. "No. Am I under arrest? I have a lawyer, you know!"

Father Duffy inserted himself into the investigation. "Robert, is it?"

"Call me Bob." Keener became red-faced.

"All right, Bob. You know how me organization runs, and I won't be tellin' you any lies."

Keener spat, "The old bastard priest Timothy lies to me all the fucking time. Always finds a way to ruin my business opportunities."

Father Duffy remained honest. "Timothy isn't a priest and doesn't fancy ya."

"What do you want?" Keener asked again with more desperation in his voice.

"Answer Ms. Sheehan's questions an' give her a hand. Outta the goodness o' yer heart. Perhaps the Holy Father, the Son an' the Holy Spirit will forgive ye for yer sins." Father Duffy made the sign of the cross.

"Yeah. Yeah. Religious mumbo jumbo. What about the old guy?"

Father Duffy smiled and said, "Brother Timothy will keep his distance. You have me word on that."

"Well, never heard of a kid named Miller."

Terri asked another. "What about the Ministry of Salvation church?"

Keener gave himself away as Mabel had. He knew it. "Yeah. Heard of 'em."

"Talk," Terri commanded.

"They're crazier than the Catholics." Keener stared right at Father Duffy.

"Keep going."

"Come on. Really? I have to go."

Terri tried another tactic. "Look, Bob. They kidnapped this young girl. She is in obvious danger with them. You sent a teenage boy named Kevin Miller to Timothy's place so he could rescue his parents. What do you know? Is that so fucking hard to understand?"

"That was like ten years ago. Jesus Christ. How the hell would I remember that?"

"You knew it was about ten years back, so it was," Father Duffy pointed out.

"Maybe eight or nine, to be more precise," Terri added.

Keener leaned back against a car. He gave careful thought. "It was for a girl."

Terri needed clarification. "Meaning?"

"I remember the teenage boy who wanted to rescue his girlfriend and parents. Although I don't remember his name, I remember the crazy church. He was a skinny, short guy with glasses and somewhat of a nerd. I saw him hanging around the bus terminal for two days. He was clean-cut, and he didn't belong. I warned him about some derelicts who were about to mess with him and told him to go home to his mom. The kid was scared and nervous. He explained he was waiting for his girlfriend, who didn't show up. He said that his crazy cult was keeping them apart, like *Romeo and Juliet* or *West Side*

Story. The kid was running away, but the girl didn't show up as planned."

"So, what about his parents?"

"They were real Bible thumpers, according to that kid. He said they were brainwashed. They believed everything that the cult said. He couldn't go back with them. I felt bad for him. He was upset and scared. He reminded me of how I was when I first came here from Bum-fuck, Kentucky," Keener said.

"You did have a real heart back then?" Terri asked, showing her disdain for the present.

"Yeah. Things were simpler for me once upon a time. I've had my share of heartbreak."

"So where does Brother Timothy fit into this tale?" Father Duffy asked.

"I was a pretty, well-known face around this part of town."

"The 'God of 42nd Street,' as I hear it," Terri interrupted.

"It's been a long time since I was called that. Let's say I had a few misunderstandings with the Catholic establishment cause of that name. I sent the kid to the only religious guy I knew of."

"Timothy," Terri stated.

"The same. I never saw that kid again. I'm telling you the truth."

Keener appeared to relax now. Terri was almost satisfied. Father Duffy put his arm on Terri's shoulder as a sign of leaving.

"Oh yeah. I also remember. The girl. She was like the head preacher's daughter or something. They got caught having sex. That's why the cult people were mad. The kid said that they were in real danger and that the cult tortured people when they got in trouble. They were gonna run away. That's it. It's all I got."

"So now, how did you know that Kenneth guy's name? I couldn't figure that one out," Terri asked.

Keener chuckled and rolled his eyes. "I overheard him talking on his cell phone while we were both in Starbucks earlier."

"Thank you," Terri said.

Jake stepped up into Keener's face. "Hi there, Bob. I have a question for you as well."

Keener looked perplexed. "Who the fuck are you?"

"Where can I find Rufus?" Jake's inner rage was boiling over.

Keener's tell was his nervous laugh. "Who the hell is that?"

Jake lost it and grabbed Keener by the shirt. Terri and the priest grabbed Jake's arms.

"Come on, Jake, this isn't necessary!" Terri yelled.

Jake's anger was intense. Keener looked scared. "Where can I find Rufus?"

"Jacob, stop this right now!" his uncle said. Father Duffy was pulling Jake's arm as hard as he could. Jake would not let go of Keener. Jake broke free of Terri. He raised his fist.

"One more time! Where can I find Rufus?"

Keener put his hands in front of his face to block the impending doom. "Peep-show place. On 44th and 8th, I think. New Town Girlz," he sniveled.

"How do I know he will be there?" Jake asked.

"He runs the joint. I promise, man."

Jake released his grip and walked back east toward 8th Avenue. Terri and Father Duffy followed.

"Jacob, I'm right disappointed in ye. Threatening behavior never solves anything, does it now?"

"You're right. Kicking their ass does!" Jake sneered.

Terri laughed. "He has a point, Father."

"Aye, God, there are two of 'em."

Chapter 44

R evulsion washed over the trio as they climbed the staircase to New Town Girlz on the third floor. The crimson light warped the room into something crooked and uneasy, shadows bending along the walls like they were trying to crawl away. A chemical tang clung to the room's haze, stale beer, mop water and something unnamed stewing in the corners, a smell that didn't just hit the nose but barged straight into the gut. Five stalls stood before them, each a dismal testament to neglect and depravity. Jake shuddered at the thought of the sinister possibilities lurking within, imagining unspoken horrors hidden inside the boxes. The entire place cried out for a deep, thorough scrubbing, but clearly the people running the joint had long forgotten such intervention. Sticky surfaces crusted with an unappealing film, deepening their discomfort and seeping into their very essence. In every way imaginable, the atmosphere was as repulsive as a public restroom in Downtown Hell.

"Holy fucking shit. What's with you guys?" a fat slob in a dirty Hawaiian shirt said behind a sticker-laden counter.

Jake stared hard at the degenerate.

"What?" Terri asked the man-thing.

"It's like the third reverend I've seen here this week."

"I promise ye, we're not here to indulge in any of Satan's temptations," Father Duffy said.

"Look, collar man, there's no judgment here; it's company policy. Pay me twenty bucks, and remember to tip the girls or the he/she thing in cabinet three."

Jake stepped to the counter, never breaking his stare.

"Hey, you fucking freak. I don't want any problems," the man told him. "I got a fuckin' shotgun here with three goddamn slugs. Pay or get the fuck out."

Terri tried to intervene. "Are you Rufus?"

"Who's askin'?"

Jake widened his eyes and growled, "What's the matter? You don't recognize me?"

The slob looked directly into Jake's dual-colored eyes. He seemed to lose his breath as he screamed a little. He backpedaled a few feet.

"You, uh! What? How? Mask! No mask!"

"Miss me?" Jake growled in his best Penrod Johansson voice.

Rufus hyperventilated. "Where did you go? Why are you?" <cough cough>

Jake got right up in his face. Rufus was shorter, but Jake could still make cold, direct eye contact. "Who tried to poison me?"

Rufus stammered. "I, I, I, don't know! I didn't think you were even around an any m, m, more. P, please, man, p, p, p, please don't hurt m, m, me."

"Where would I have gone?"

"Come on, man. Pleeease!" Rufus was panting in fear.

"So, who would want to kill me then?"

Rufus looked crooked at his tormentor. "Lots of people want you d, d, d, dead."

Jake had to think about that one. Rufus had a point. It was a dumb question. Jake figured he was new at interrogations and tried another angle.

"You knew what The Jypsy did. You are the only one who knows."

"W-What? No! No! Please!"

"Why couldn't you have saved her?" His anger and hate took over. Jake went full Darkside Sith. "You could have pretended to take her into the building that night. You could have called the police. You could have told the truth. You let her die at The Jypsy's hand," Jake added.

"No. No. You! You don't understand! He, he, would have killed me. He would have killed my kid." Rufus was coughing, fully panicked.

"Well, now, what's gonna stop him from killing you or your kid now that I'm back in town?"

Rufus looked bewildered. "But you killed him. Remember, The Jypsy is dead."

Jake's knees buckled. "I what?"

"The Jypsy's dead man. You killed him at the basin."

Jake was in shock. "Tell me," he commanded.

"Come on, man. Don't you remember?" Rufus rolled his shoulder in discomfort. "What's wrong with you?"

Terri lost some patience. "Tell him the story now!"

Father Duffy joined in as the three approached the counter and crowded Rufus. The priest got the shotgun, emptied it fast, then tossed it.

Jake imagined he was in a black-and-white film as Rufus retold the story.

* * * * *

The homeless commune looked abandoned. It was a rainy, foggy night. The patched-up rags of the various shelters looked dirty gray in the poor light. It would be easy to stay hidden in the shadows of the tent city under the West Side Highway at the 79th Street Boat Basin. Rufus started living there to hide from the monster. The Jypsy found him somehow. Rufus knew he was there because the son of a bitch whistled a tune as he searched for him.

Rufus spotted The Fade moving, hunting. No attempt to hide. No shroud of mystery. His eyes swept the street, then locked on Rufus crouched behind a shopping cart piled with cans.

The Fade's hand shot out and grabbed Rufus with a steel grip.

Out of thin air, a brick smashed into the side of Rufus's skull. Pain rang in his bones, but he kept his gaze fixed on The Fade's raging eyes.

The unhinged hero cackled behind his mask, drinking in the chaos as Rufus hit the pavement, blood pooling under him. He hadn't thrown the blow, but he claimed the moment. Then he vanished into the dark like a hunting lion. The Fade knew whoever hit the sniveling pervert was a target to bullseye.

Orange light flared, throwing the carnage into sharp relief. Screams tore through the air. Smoke rolled in heavy, stealing breath, burning eyes. Rufus clawed at the ground, forcing himself up, lungs screaming for clean air, legs dragging him toward anything that wasn't death.

The Fade was relentless. He seized a fleeing resident engulfed in flames, his eyes ablaze with urgency. With a primal instinct, he leaped onto the burning figure, working madly to douse the fire and save the hapless soul from certain doom. The chaos swirling around him only fueled his determination, transforming the scene into a heart-pounding battle against time.

* * * * *

Jake snapped out of the story. His visage showed both shock and bewilderment. "He, I, did that?" The childlike innocence betrayed his act.

"You fuckin' saved ole Butch's life, man. Come on, you don't forget shit like that."

"Maybe I like to hear about myself," Jake snarled.

"Or maybe you aren't him."

Terri slapped Rufus across his slimy, hairy face.

"You should likely wash yer hands now, Ms. Sheehan," the priest said.

"Fuckin bitch!" Rufus yelled.

"My turn," Jake said and raised his fist.

Rufus cowered back and coughed, rolling his left shoulder again. "All right, all right!" Rufus continued his story.

* * * * *

A few of the ragtag residents were now awake, scurrying in circles of sheer panic. Another set of tents erupted into flames, illuminating the night with a sick glow. Someone hurled a bucket of water onto the inferno, but it did not help, a doused flicker of hope as another tent caught fire. The Fade surged forward, shoving people aside with a fierce urgency, driven by a singular purpose: finding The Jypsy. He knew he was close.

The Hero of the Streets was gone, burned away, leaving only the thing that replaced him. His head hung like a predator stalking from the shadows, dual-colored eyes gleaming with cold, feral hunger. The black hood swallowed his face, but the glint in those eyes cut through the smoke like knives.

Gloved fingers writhed and curled, warped into claws itching to tear. He moved through the fire and choking smoke with the ease of something born in it, stalking the scent of his prey. Breath rasped. Words slithered from his mouth in broken fragments, mad, guttural mutterings from a mind splintered and rotting under the weight of obsession.

"I can't hear you! Where are you? What the hell is going on? Find the water! Mommy? Mommy, help me? Katie? No! Katie! The eyes, Damn my eyes! Help me!"

The Fade could not discern genuine voices among thoughts. He was trying, searching, swinging at the air and hitting nothing. Many others shouted for help. He couldn't focus.

* * * * *

Rufus interrupted Jake's vision of the story.

"You! The Fade shouldn't have come for The Jypsy yet. It was too soon, man."

"What? Who the hell are you to tell me?" Jake began.

"Take it from a loser with his fair share of nervous breakdowns. You were falling apart. I could tell that even with the mask on."

"What happened next?" Jake changed the subject.

"Pure hate came next," Rufus said, now clutching his chest.

Jake stepped back into the story.

* * * * *

Rufus hid behind a burned-out car near the bulkhead and watched. The Fade stood staring at the Hudson River, trying to put puzzle pieces of his brain back together. A solid smack of a baseball bat came across The Fade's head. Silence grew when someone struck his head hard once more. The blow should have knocked him dead. The Fade stood there. Human adrenaline can turn a mortal into a machine, but only for a short duration. The Fade turned around, slow and deliberate. He faced the figure known as The Jypsy, an older man with messy white hair and gaudy earrings. He wore a knit cap and long silk scarf. He held a metal baseball bat.

"Are you some kind of pirate?" The Fade asked, calm and casual, as if someone hadn't tried crushing his skull with a bat.

The Jypsy's eyes widened. He couldn't understand why his adversary didn't drop from the heavy blows. He swung again. The Fade caught the bat mid-swing with one hand and seized

The Jypsy's slender neck with the other. The Fade started talking to himself again.

"Squeeze the life out of him. Let him go and follow him. Let him ride the lightning. Fuck this little piece of shit. You're wasting time. Mommy. Mommy, where are you? Take me home."

The Jypsy spoke up through the chokehold.

"What's wrong with you, Fade? You look a little bit unhinged, huh?"

The Fade drew The Jypsy closer, lifting him off his feet.

"Jayson Basco Vascones!"

"I'm impressed. Thought I did a good job of killing that name off. I guess not."

"Narcissistic Sociopath, Chosen Method of Operandi: Blackmail, Political outcast, Basque Region of Spain, Social Syndicate, Terrorist, Murderer, Also Known as The Jypsy."

The Jypsy took his turn as he held on to the vigilante's outstretched arm.

"The Fade: Shining Prince of the Night, The Good Guy, Broken and Annoying."

The Fade held The Jypsy over the water.

* * * * *

Jake watched a sweating Rufus slouch to the floor.

"Then that's when you lost it." <*cough cough cough*> "I know what you did. That's why you're really here. I haven't told anybody nothin'. That piece of shit got what he deserved." <*cough cough*> "I'm not telling anyone if that's what you think. It's been years, man. I haven't said anything to anyone. Why are you here bustin' my balls now?"

<cough cough>

"What happened next?" Jake's pulse pounded like war drums.

Jake imagined the basin again as Rufus coughed through the remainder of the story.

* * * * *

"You won't kill me because you are a big, sappy imbecile. You don't have it in you because you were made to help people. Besides, I did something awful, and if you kill me, you won't find out till it's too late. Time's a-wastin' big fella."

The Fade sent electric currents through The Jypsy's body without hesitation this time. He held the villain by his neck for a moment before sending more lightning through the villain's convulsing form, outlining a dancing skeleton. A satisfied Fade threw the old man's lifeless body into the river.

* * * * *

Rufus clutched hard at his left arm, now in obvious discomfort.

"That's it? The Jypsy is dead? Just like that?" Jake questioned.

"Thank whatever God you want," Rufus added. *<cough cough>* "The real shit went down when you walked away."

"What's that supposed to mean?" Jake asked.

"The gigantic explosion, man. The Big Bang. You must remember that. The propane bottles." *<cough>*

At first, Jake felt puzzled. "Okay, yeah, The Jypsy did it. He was an evil fuck. I get it."

"Yes. But he tried to warn you. People died. Those people were good, trying to find their way. My friends! So, fuck you very much!" <*cough cough*>

"You know that wasn't his fault." Jake started to lose his grasp on the ruse.

"It was your fault!" Rufus screamed back.

"He tried to save you and all those people! He tried to save that little girl! He was a hero!" Jake screamed.

"Ha, oh, fuck man, you're not really him. Damn it!" <*cough cough*>

"I'm as much him as you're ever gonna see you fucking scumbag!" With spit dripping down his chin, Jake grabbed the smut peddler by his mucky shirt.

"What are you gonna do? Huh? Kill me? Huh? You look like him, but are you a killer like him?"

Jake ignored the hideous coughs that erupted right in his face. "So, who is Captain Jay?"

"What? Why?" A deep wheeze broke up Rufus's coughs.

"Who is the white-bearded guy that runs around in the sailor suit, calling himself Captain Jay?"

<*cough cough*>

Rufus's heart was failing him. He fell on his back onto the sticky floor. He was trying to talk. Father Duffy and Terri kneeled to him.

Father Duffy slapped the back of Jake's head. "Did you just shock him, boy?"

"No, I think it's a heart attack." Jake kneeled. "Okay, man, calm down. Take it easy," Jake said. His panic accelerated.

Father Duffy suggested that Jake should try to shock him.

"I don't have the gloves! Why would I have the gloves?"

Terri stepped back and called 911. Father Duffy went into prayer. Rufus was spread out on the floor, mouthing words that Jake tried his best to decipher. He thought the ailing scammer was saying "medicine." Jake went through Rufus's pockets and found a prescription bottle with the name Rufus P. Newton III written on the label. He opened it in haste. Some pills spilled out onto the floor. Jake picked up the closest one and raised his hand to Rufus's mouth, but the man grabbed Jake's wrist and squeezed with whatever strength remained.

"Captain. He is The Devil. Reborn. He will kill you."

Rufus stopped breathing.

"What does that mean? You fucking coward! Don't stop there. What the fuck do you mean?" Jake said while he began chest compressions. How Jake knew CPR was a mystery. Possibly Boy Scouts, or perhaps from television. He kept on giving him compressions. Terri screamed out directions for Jake to give rescue breaths as well.

"I'm telling you right now. There is no fucking way I'm putting my mouth on this asshole."

Father Duffy rolled his eyes. "The lad has a point, to be sure. The fella talks a load of shite."

Jake's mind was in a frenzy as he continued to perform chest compressions on Rufus P. Newton III. Sweat dripped down his forehead. He needed to keep Rufus alive until the ambulance arrived. Father Duffy paced and prayed and wondered how they had gotten into this mess. Sirens blared from down below, and emergency medical technicians rushed in to take over the rescue. Jake stood by, waiting for a kick, a raised fist, something to show that Rufus's life was saved. Father Duffy gave his statement to the police, his voice shaking as he recounted the events that led to Rufus's collapse.

As the medical team confirmed that Rufus's medication was for treating heart problems, Jake's questioned himself.

How had Rufus's condition deteriorated so quickly? Was it something we had said or done?

Everyone followed the medics to the awaiting ambulance, the flashing lights and screaming sirens echoing through the streets of New York. A small crowd of tourists gathered to watch them load Rufus into the ambulance, their faces filled with concern and curiosity.

Jake was on edge as he heard an EMT shout to his colleague, "I got a pulse. Let's roll."

The EMT shut the ambulance door, and a girl tried to look inside. Jake felt cold; the oddness felt bigger.

Jake traced and retraced his steps through everything that happened since he and the others climbed the stairs to the seedy peep-show joint. Guilt consumed him. Father Duffy suggested he take a mental break for the night, but Terri refused to leave Jake alone, knowing he was in danger. Jake convinced her that his bodyguard, Miles Orsky, would keep him safe at work. He invited Terri to stay at his place if they received new information. To sweeten the deal, Jake promised her that Mrs. Daschle would make the most delicious pancakes and coffee she had ever had.

 # 45

The Monica Beame case had gone cold. Six in the morning, and Molina had barely slept. Sitting on his twin bed, he decided it was time to start reconnaissance and run a preliminary interview on the Hope case. He pulled out his phone and called the office.

"Hey, Lizzy, it's Monty. Please do me a favor and sign me in for case #310 outside wire. I'm heading to 610 Columbia Heights here in Brooklyn. I'll let you know if I need anything. Put me down for surveillance only."

Detective Molina parked a block from the subject's address, sipping coffee and munching on a coffee roll. He listened to the news on 1010 WINS, the continuous *clack-clack-clack* of a radio newsroom offering calm background noise while he waited for leads on his cases. After two hours, a minivan pulled up near the brownstone's driveway. A Caucasian woman and three African American children got out of the car. The woman instructed the kids not to run and to act like gentlemen as they ran up the steps to 610 Columbia Heights. A young-looking girl answered the door, and then she allowed the three children inside. The woman thanked her from the porch and left to return to her vehicle as the front door closed. Molina waited for the minivan to drive away before walking up to the entrance of the home.

* * * * *

Jake drove the garbage truck down Columbia Heights. Knowing he would come to the Ministry people's house. He was anxious.

"You're killing me, Miles! We should have been done an hour ago," Jake complained as he inched his garbage truck closer to the next house. Miles placed two residential garbage pails back on the curb. He ignored Jake's complaint and waved him to the next house. Jake couldn't believe his eyes. Detective Molina was walking up the steps to the Ministry house. His hands were shaking. He wondered whether he should call Terri or confront Molina. Jake stopped the truck short with a squeal.

"That motherfucker!" Jake said aloud.

Miles walked up to the driver's side, curious why the truck had stopped.

"What. What did I do now?"

"Not you, Miles," Jake said. "Pull the truck over at that hydrant there."

He cleared the way for other vehicles, exiting his.

"I bet that asshole is part of that freak show cult. That's why Terri is getting nowhere with getting Hope back!" Jake exclaimed.

"I don't get it?" Miles asked.

"Forget it. Nothing. Let's hang here a bit."

"Oh, is that the house you and that lady were investigating, with the necklace and all?" Miles asked.

"Yes, Miles. Yes, it is. I wanna see what that guy does."

"All right. Let's get some cans and bring them to the truck. Make it look good."

"Good thinking, Miles. You go do that," Jake said, his frustration amplified by sarcasm.

Molina approached the front door and paused, glancing at the garbage truck and the large sanitation worker dragging cans to the back. Jake could have sworn that Molina smirked and winked. The detective pressed the doorbell. Though it was a sunny morning, everything felt gray and dark. The exterior lacked any decor like plants or a welcome mat. The gothic porch light appeared more like a warning than an invitation.

A petite, youthful girl opened the door. She was wearing overalls and pigtails. Molina introduced himself and showed his detective badge.

"What may I do for you, Detective?"

"Is there an adult here I can speak with?" Molina asked.

The childlike lady kept her smile. "I am an adult."

"And you are?" Molina gave his signature fake charm.

"I'm Chastity Devlin."

Molina fumbled for kid-friendly dialogue and produced the verbal equivalent of a mugshot. "How old are you?"

"I'm twenty-five. Is that old enough?" Chastity continued to keep her smile up.

Molina rubbed at the nape of his neck. "Yes. Would you mind if we spoke inside?

Chastity glanced below, her discomfort clear.

"Oh my, how impolite of me. Please come in." Chastity held the door as Molina walked into the foyer.

"Damn it," Jake said. "He walks right in."

Jake fumbled for his phone to call Terri. He moved himself across the street. Miles dragged noisy garbage cans and dumped them in the rear of the hauler.

* * * * *

Chastity walked past, and Molina followed her to the living room. The three Britt children sat on the velvety antique couch, well-behaved and well-disciplined. Seeing three young children sitting still with their hands on their knees surprised Molina. He guessed the youngest's age likely was around two.

"This is Shante, Elijah and Deshawn. I am their teacher. I must take them to our Ministry and school for their lessons today. Their foster mother had an important business matter to attend to."

The two older boys, on cue, said, "Good morning, sir." Deshawn gave a pleasant "Hi" of his own in his little three-year-old voice.

Children often proved challenging for Molina. He nodded his head.

"Could I get you a drink, Detective?" Chastity offered.

Molina declined and began asking questions. "Foster children, you said?"

"Yes. The children are in the best care with one of our parishioners," a proud Chastity said.

Molina went on, "I see that. They are well-mannered. What church did you say you belong to?"

"The Ministry of Salvation. My father is The Minister."

Molina whistled as he perused the spacious home. The collection of paintings on the walls rivaled any in a Manhattan art gallery.

"The Minister does well for himself," Molina stated. Chastity tried to talk, but Molina cut her off. "Who are the children's foster parents?"

Chastity became very uncomfortable. "I am not sure I can answer the question, Detective." She looked beyond Molina toward a staircase. "We believe it is best to mind our business as God has instructed us."

Molina knew the answer was coming but needed to establish a baseline, a border between truth and lies. With the keen perception of a seasoned law enforcement officer, he examined Chastity's behavior and eye movements. "Are there any other children in the home?" Molina asked, as pleasant as he could.

"No," Chastity spilled out before Molina finished the question. She glanced again at the staircase. Molina recognized she was lying.

* * * * *

Miles was tossing cans into his cart when the noise caught his ear: sharp voices, a scuffle. Jake's gaze snapped to a thin man yanking a blonde-haired girl by the arm. Recognition hit. The hardware store. The Elder.

He exited the brownstone's side door, dragging her down the driveway. Jake's pulse climbed.

The man led her past the cars, toward a detached garage crouched at the end of the lot. He glanced over his shoulder once, quick, like he was checking the street. Then the door swallowed them both.

Miles shrugged, assuming it was a father establishing rules. Jake felt a twist in his gut. Something was very wrong. He locked his eyes on that garage. Waiting. Listening.

As Miles continued to collect the other neighbors' cans and dump them into the truck's rear, Jake saw the man dart back to his house. The young girl could not be found. Jake's pulse quickened and he broke into a sweat. His instinct was correct, and now he was left standing by the edge of the driveway, anger and confusion rumbling within while he planned his next move.

"Come on, Jake, we're almost done. What are you doing?" Miles asked, following Jake up the driveway to the garage. "Jake, what are you doing? We should mind our own business. Let's get back to work."

The thin man in the black suit left the side door to the garage open in his haste.

"We can't go in there, Jake. Come on, man. We will get fired."

Jake ignored Miles's warnings but appreciated his partner following him into the garage.

"Miles, that was the freaky guy from the hardware store. The church boss."

Both gave glances when the child's cries arose.

"I'm scared. Please! It's dark. I'm scared!"

Jake and Miles both searched and failed to locate her in the garage. They found standard landscaping tools, a bicycle and a car parked inside. No signs of the girl.

The child sounded more desperate when she yelled out again. "Please, it's too dark!"

The burly garbageman flicked on his pocket flashlight and crept toward the car. He expected to see the child huddled in the back seat. Leaning close, he said, "It's okay," not sure if she could hear him or if the words meant anything to her at all.

But the Jaguar was empty.

The whimpers still floated in the air, thin and trembling. They crawled under Miles's skin. The wrongness of it all pressed in on him. If the man came back, Miles feared arrest and, worse, being fired. He turned to leave.

"Where are you going, you big oaf?" Jake whispered.

"We shouldn't be here, man."

"Are you scared, Miles?" Jake asked.

"Man, her father is just punishing her for being a bad girl. Come on, man. I don't want to get in any trouble."

"Miles, we have to help her, man. I think it's Hope. Terri's missing kid."

Miles now understood what was happening. It took him a minute. He studied the garage with more urgency and froze when a child's voice yelled out, "Elder!"

The haunting voice, its desperation climbing with every pained shout, startled the two men. Jake ran toward the sizable rolling toolbox behind the vintage Jaguar, from which the voice seemed to emerge. Miles crept to the toolbox and shined his flashlight behind it, though the beam disappeared into the sunlight filtered through the garage windows. The girl remained out of sight, yet her voice was very present, piercing the building's walls.

"Elder! Please! I'm scared."

"Do you think she's in the toolbox?" Miles asked his partner.

"No, Miles. I think she's under it."

Miles pointed his flashlight into the two-inch space under the box and bent down until his face hovered near the diamond plate. "She's not here either."

Jake, in his frightened state, maintained his common sense. "Miles, move the box off the diamond plate." The toolbox slid off the panel with ease. It was quiet now. All they could hear was the distant grumbling of their parked garbage truck. The two sanitation workers stared at the shiny metal flooring.

"Well, you are the big, strong one. See if it moves," Jake said. He still needed to walk Miles through the mystery. Miles flung the plate aside and uncovered a large hole. Rusty metal bars affixed to the hole formed a crude ladder. Miles aimed his light down. A child's glistening eyes stared back from the bottom. She screamed and ran away. Miles screeched at a pitch higher than Jake thought possible for the big guy. Jake couldn't make a sound.

"I found her! I found her!" Miles shouted.

Jake had to gather his wits for both their sake. "What did you see? Where did she go?"

"We have to find her," Miles said as he climbed down the hole.

"Now you're talking," Jake said.

"I've got to help her. She needs help."

Judging by the flashlight in Miles's mouth, Jake could see the hole was about eight to ten feet down. Miles disappeared into a tunnel. Jake followed.

Chapter 46

"Mrs. Devlin, I'm investigating a case of a missing child. There is reason to believe that this child was once the foster child of one of your father's parishioners. I am exhausting leads and learning anything I can about the child to locate her. We need to verify that she is safe."

Molina tried the approach of finding "the child safe." Finding "the bad guy and putting them in jail" never worked in urgent situations. Neither did the trigger words like kidnapping or criminal investigation.

"I can't help you. There are no missing children here. I mind my own business and work hard, like I'm supposed to," Chastity said, devoid of emotion.

Again, she looked at the staircase. Her hands shook. Molina, however, had little patience or political correctness. "Well, I heard you people were pretty fanatical."

"I think that you're being an insulting detective," a deep, drawling voice said. Jonathan Devlin slithered into the room, somehow undetected. "And you are?"

"Oh, I'm Detective Molina. I'm from the Missing Persons Unit of the NYPD. Are you The Minister?" Molina spoke confidently but felt uneasy. He didn't have a backup.

"No" was all Devlin answered.

"Who are you then?" Molina sought a different route to break the tense pause.

Chastity answered with a little more confidence. "That is my husband, Elder..."

Devlin cut his wife off abruptly. "Woman, please refrain from talking. I can speak for myself." He then turned to Molina.

"I am Jonathan Devlin, Elder of the Ministry of Salvation. This is our private home, Detective. If it is church business you wish to discuss, maybe the Ministry is the best place to do that. We are very private citizens."

"Yeah, I got that. But this is a police investigation, and I am afraid we have our own rules to follow. I need information on a missing child," Molina stated.

"I assure you there is no missing child here. These children are indeed well accounted for," Devlin explained, gesturing toward the Britt trio.

"Agreed. No one here is the child in question," Molina conceded.

Before Molina could say anything else, Devlin continued the conversation. "I can only assume that my wife explained to you that no other children are in this home."

"You know, Elder Devlin, what they say about the word, assume."

The room was again silent. Devlin gave his wife a crooked stare. Chastity looked at Molina, confused. The detective hit another question in a loud, clear voice.

"I'm looking for an eight-year-old girl. Blonde hair, blue eyes, thin build, about this high. Her name is Hope. She was the former foster child of Mr. and Mrs. Tanner, who were followers of this cult...sorry, church. Mrs. Devlin clearly stated she knows who I'm talking about."

Chastity came to her defense. "I didn't! No, I did not!"

Her counterargument did not directly address Molina's allegation. Instead, it resembled a desperate plea to her husband. Elder Devlin seemed to grow taller and thinner as he shot a death glare at his petite wife. He had reached his limit and was becoming more unnerved.

"Detective, you have insulted us in our home, and your demeanor appears hostile. I must ask you for your credentials and insist you leave at once," Devlin scowled as he clasped his bare hands before him.

Elijah's innocence shone like a beacon of hope. "Does that man mean Sarah-Prudence, Mrs. Devlin?"

Chastity stood stone-faced. She was afraid even to blink. It was exactly what Molina required to remain a little longer. Shante elbowed his brother.

"Elijah, mind your own business. You will get us all in trouble."

The Elder recognized the significance of the child's outburst. "Children, may I remind you that you are to be seen and never heard. Please go to the kitchen and remain seated at the table."

Molina knew he had the upper hand. While innocent small talk with young children wasn't his strength, pressing people to give up information, especially ones who weren't savvy enough to spar with him, certainly was. He was the alpha in the room now. He gladly stepped all over Elder Devlin's command to the young boys.

"Elijah, who is this Sarah-Prudence?"

The boy smiled. "She's my girlfriend."

"That will be quite enough, child! Do as you are told!" Elder Devlin shouted.

Molina continued. "Can you tell me where Sarah-Prudence is?"

Elijah shrugged his tiny little shoulders. "She's shy. She likes to hide."

"You, disobedient child." Elder Devlin moved closer. Molina stepped between them. The aggressive movements and the detective's protective stance put a scare into the boy.

The child then yelled out, "He's gonna kill me!"

Molina turned his head toward Elijah in confusion. "What?" the detective asked.

Elder Devlin again yelled, "Child, you must mind your own business!" The serpentine Elder reached out around Molina to grab the child's arm.

Elijah screamed in horror. "He's gonna kill me! Just like he killed the funny lookin' man!"

Molina broke Devlin's grip on the child's arm by jamming his thumb into a pressure point on Devlin's bony wrist. Elijah ran for it. He headed deeper into the house, down a hallway. Devlin looked menacingly at Molina, then stalked after the child.

Chastity screamed, "Jonathan, don't hurt him!"

Molina leaped forward to begin the chase. Something unexpected caught his legs, and he fell to the hardwood floor. It was Shante, the oldest Britt brother. "Mind your own business!" he shouted at a stunned Molina. "Go away!"

Chastity ran after her husband and Elijah. Deshawn sat and cried. Amid the frenzy, Molina stood up and grabbed Shante by his shirt. He lifted the kid right off his feet and brought him nose to nose. "Now, listen to me! You will take care of your little brother. Take him outside and wait there. Do you understand me?" Molina growled.

The anger registered in Shante's expression. He nodded his head in acknowledgment. Molina dropped him onto the couch next to the hysterical Deshawn. Shante started reciting a prayer. He hugged his baby brother and kept a watchful eye on Molina, who was running in pursuit down the hallway.

"Come on, Deshawn. We got to work hard and help The Elder. Then he will give us more ice cream." Shante took Deshawn by the arm and ran up the front staircase in defiance of Molina's instruction.

* * * * *

Miles swept his flashlight over the little girl curled up against the back wall of the short tunnel. She refused to look up, instead burying her head in her arms. Miles recalled how scared he had been of the dark as a child. The dark hole felt cool and damp, as most underground tunnels do. Miles wore his empathy on his sleeve as he perspired. He aimed at calming the child.

"Hey, kid, it's all right," Miles said in the softest voice he could muster. "You're not alone anymore. I, I, I'm afraid of the dark too."

Jake stepped behind his giant partner and witnessed a side of Miles that he never thought existed. Miles took a couple of steps toward the little blonde girl. She curled her knees up tighter inside her nightgown.

"Whatever you did, I'm sure your daddy loves you. Come on, we can go up together and talk to him," Miles said.

To their surprise, the child answered, "I don't have a daddy."

Miles had to reason with her. "I get it. You're mad at him for leaving you down here. I'm sure..."

The girl stopped him and said, "No. The Elder is not my daddy. He is hiding me. Nobody is to see me."

Miles sat down next to the girl. "Why would he do that?"

"You must mind your own business. You shouldn't be here. I'm not supposed to talk to strangers."

"Well. My name is Miles. What's yours?"

Her blue eyes flashed from her tears as she looked at Miles. She sat, lost in her thoughts. Then she spoke.

"Sarah-Prude..."

She stopped. Tears fell down her face.

"Please don't cry," Miles said. His voice quivered. He leaned his back against the wall. The child looked at Miles now as he wiped his eyes with his sleeve.

"Hope," she whispered.

Jake felt close to collapsing. Adrenaline flowed like a jet stream through his veins, and he couldn't talk. His shaky hands dropped his phone to the tunnel floor. He picked it up and tried steadying himself enough to call Terri. Miles heard her words but couldn't grasp their meaning. His sidelong glance revealed his confusion.

"My name is Hope," she clarified.

"That's a weird name," Miles said without thinking of its significance.

"Well, it's better than Sarah-Prudence," she retorted.

Miles agreed, and they smiled at each other. "Who is Sarah-Prudence?" he asked.

"It's what Elder Devlin calls me."

Miles was confused. It took little to do that. "Who's The Elder?"

Hope took a breath. It was time for her to save herself. Her past made such a decision incredibly daring, incredibly brave for a young child. She rejected both silence and obedience. Hope chose freedom. She spoke up.

"The Elder is a very bad man," she whispered. "Please help me."

"I will do anything to keep you safe."

"Promise?"

Hope looked up at the standing giant and a tearful Jake Johansson.

"I thumb swear," Miles said.

"Is that like a pinky swear?"

Miles smiled as he put his thumb out. "Yes, but thumbs are bigger." Hope locked her thumb to his.

"You smell," Hope pointed out to Miles as they walked toward the ladder bars.

"Oh yeah! You should smell my truck."

Jake finally spoke up. "Hope. My name is Jake. I am a friend of Terri's. She's been looking everywhere for you."

"Terri! She's here?" Hope shouted.

"Shhhh. We don't want the Elder guy to hear us. Let's go. We will call her once we get out of here." Jake showed Hope his phone. She followed Jake up the ladder. Miles didn't follow.

"Come on, Miles. We got her, let's go!"

Miles swept the beam of his flashlight through the tunnel, the light catching on a wooden door to the left. A rusty padlock hung on a corroded latch. He pressed his ear to the wood. Metal rattled inside. Gripping the lock, Miles yanked hard. The latch snapped with a metallic crack. The door groaned open, and a breath of sour musk and rancid meat stuck to the back of Miles's throat.

Light spilled into the tunnel. Electric light. A single bulb dangled from the ceiling of a square chamber, its sway casting long, swinging dark shapes. In the middle of the floor knelt a woman, wrists chained, a wooden box covering her head. When she shifted, the chains clinked, and Miles's blood rushed and thundered in his ears. He scanned the room. Someone was here. Watching.

His gaze landed on a folding table in the far-left corner. A man wearing a terrible toupee sat still as a stone gargoyle. He grinned without warmth, his right hand giving a stiff thumbs-up. His left hand lay on the head of a cat resting in his lap. The cat's eyes glowed in the light. The man never blinked.

Miles put on a superhero cape of his own. He streaked toward the corner, as if the motionless man were a cunning final boss who had set this trap deep in the bowels of a dark, dank cellar.

"What's going on here? What are you doing to her?"

The man maintained his eerie smile as Miles drew near. As he approached the seated figure, Miles realized why the man was silent: neither he nor the cat was alive.

Miles's superhero persona quickly disappeared, and he gave a quick squeal like a frightened kitten and jumped back. He then stepped back from the chained woman, feeling a bit embarrassed. Miles tried to pull the chains out of the floor. They didn't budge.

"Miles, what the hell, man? Something is going down in the house. There's a bunch of yelling. Hurry up," Jake said.

The woman in the headbox began wiggling and moving her head. Miles panicked and pulled harder at the chains. He was terrified as he ran to the nearby table and examined it closely. In the faint light, he could see keys resting inside a bowl. He held them up. They rattled softly in his trembling hands.

"Miles, come on! Hurry!" Jake was desperate.

Miles steadied his grip and tested the keys against the woman's restraints. The first, a thick iron key, was far too large for the tiny shackle lock at her wrist. He muttered under his breath, sifted through the ring again, and tried a smaller one.

This time, the key slid in. A twist. A click.

The chain around her wrists fell open, and the woman's hands froze at her sides as if unsure they were hers. A slight, muffled wince escaped from inside the headbox. She curled her fingers into a shaky fist, then loosened them again.

Now came the worst part.

Miles turned to the headbox. It had a different lock entirely, heavy and reinforced, with a keyhole wide enough to swallow a fingertip. He tried the small key again. Useless. The large key, though...that fit the shape.

Behind him, Jake pleaded.

In the corner, the dead man smirked in his chair.

The room reeked of old suffering.

The painted black wings on the woman's bare back looked as if they bled from her pores.

He pushed in the large key, turned hard, and the internal bolt snapped free. The headbox door creaked open. The woman inhaled a raw, ragged breath and forced her stiff body upright, rising to her full height for the first time in God knows how long.

She had a slim build and was short in stature. Her torn skirt floated lightly around her legs and bare, dirty feet. She dared not make another move. The voices and movements were different, but her survival instincts kept her obedient. Miles again found the large, peculiar-looking key and raised it to the locked box beneath her chin at the neck. The box opened halfway, revealing a padded interior and a young woman's face staring straight ahead. Light caused her to narrow her vision.

"Are you all right?" Miles asked.

"I am good, Elder. Thank you," she answered.

"I'm not The Elder. I'm Miles," he explained with his unique brand of dopey innocence.

Tears ran down the woman's dirty face, but she still forced herself to remain still and compliant. "I'm sorry, I'm sorry, I'm sorry," she repeated. "I must do as I am told."

"No, really, it's okay. You're safe. I won't hurt you. What's your name?" Miles tried the same tactic he used to befriend Hope.

"I am your angel. I do what I'm told. I work hard. I am your angel," the woman said.

Miles's eyes opened wide in shock. "Holy smokes! I know who you are. You're the girl on the news. You're that policeman's daughter. You're. M, Mon, Monica. From the news. Monica. Yes."

Monica Beame blinked and glanced at Miles, who offered her a warm yet concerned smile.

"Everybody has been looking for you. Come on. I have to get you out of here."

Monica collapsed in relief right into Miles's arms. She was weak, but she recognized somehow that her ordeal was over. The petite witch lifted her tired arm to Miles's mucky, hairy face. She sensed his kindness in his big brown eyes. She was Monica Moon Beame, after all.

"Thank you," she mouthed to her savior.

* * * * *

Molina realized he had run too fast down the hallway. He acknowledged his tactics were poor and slowed down to think. He kept his hand on his holstered pistol. The seasoned detective wanted to call for backup. However, he didn't want to give himself away or give the tall weirdo an excuse to hurt the child.

The house's first floor sprawled wide, hallways branching into shadowed rooms. A narrow staircase at the back curled up to the second floor. Little natural light slipped through, leaving the air heavy and the walls dim. Red and gold trim ran along the corridors, and every heavy wooden door bore a carved Christian cross. The place felt like a lavish mausoleum.

Molina turned corners, tested doors, each hinge groaning. There was a dense stillness, thick enough to muffle his footsteps, as if the house itself were ready to pounce.

He cleared each room as he arrived, nervous for himself and scared for the child's safety. Molina took out his mobile phone and began texting McColgan for backup. A woman screamed from the second floor. Molina sprinted up the stairs to investigate the source. At the top, he faced an unsettling stillness that surrounded him as he searched. Walking down the long hallway, he noticed the eerie resemblance to a haunted hotel. It felt nothing like a family home. The atmosphere made him uneasy and anxious.

Molina crept down the hall, every step measured.

The door ahead exploded open.

Chastity flew through it like someone had fired her from a cannon. Her feet were off the ground as her back slammed into the opposite wall with a bone-jarring thud. A painting crashed down, sliding over her and clattering to the floor.

Molina's pistol was in his hand before his phone hit the ground.

Chastity scrambled backward, eyes wide, mouth frozen in a scream that never came. Her left arm hung useless, throwing her off balance as she clawed away from the doorway.

Molina advanced, boots pounding, gaze locked on the dark opening she'd come from.

A dark shadow loomed at the end of the hallway like a harbinger of doom. A high-pitched giggle pierced the air. Elijah appeared, his small face twisted in terror, and a black-gloved hand covered his mouth and nose. Devlin stood behind the child. His smile hooked at the corners, tugging a chill straight through Molina's bones. His other hand clasped Elijah's neck, showing he was in control.

"Please, Jonathan? I beg you, husband. Please don't hurt him. He is a child. Please!" Chastity begged.

Devlin gave another of his signature giggles.

"He is no more a child of God than the abomination that you birthed out of your rotted womb."

"POLICE! DON'T MOVE!" Molina commanded.

"Don't say that, Jonathan! She is our daughter," Chastity cried.

Neither Devlin nor Chastity acknowledged the detective's first command. He yelled it again. Elijah stared at Molina, horrified.

Devlin snarled. "I made a mistake finding that beast for you. I was mistaken. She was to make our family whole. She only tore you further apart from me. I am the one who loves you. I am the one who should be the father of your child. You worship me. I am true love."

"Yes, Jonathan! Yes! Always! I love you," Chastity cried. Her husband was melting down, and she feared his next move. "Let Elijah go."

Molina stepped closer. "Goddamn it. Let the child go."

Devlin ignored both their requests and continued his rant.

"I should have foreseen the consequences of taking that disgusting pariah's offspring into my home. He haunts this family like a demon ghost, a worshipper of Satan. The dark angel Lucifer's temptation was sent forth to destroy you. To destroy our Ministry. To torture me. Me! God's one true knight! My love! My love! You, it was all for you. He could never love you like me. God himself could never love you like me."

"I know, Jonathan, you're my husband. Not Kevin. You ripped the mask off him. You showed me what he really was. Lust, that's all he ever wanted. He's a sinner. And me? I was nothing but a forgotten conquest in his indecent, godless life."

"You are a sinner!"

"I've paid, Jonathan. I've bled for my sins. I've begged before God. I've worked, I've prayed, I've given you everything I had left. You showed me love again. You said you forgave me. You told me you could love her, that you'd find peace, that you would be her father."

"I know I will never be that tainted offspring's father. Let her loose to go and find that ingrate who defiled you."

"Kevin doesn't even know about her. He's unaware that we conceived a child that night. Yes, I listened to him. I swallowed his lies. I was young. Stupid. But he ran, Jonathan. He ran the moment life started growing inside me." Chastity lost herself in her own words and then shouted, "He is not in our life."

"I know, my dear." Devlin giggled again. "I made damn sure of that."

Elijah tried shouting something from under Devlin's hand. Molina edged closer. "Let the child go, Devlin!" Elijah was becoming more frantic and trying to break Devlin's grip. Devlin then turned his attention to Molina.

"Or what, Detective? You're gonna shoot an unarmed man? Get out of my house. This doesn't concern you. Mind your own business."

Chastity interrupted, "Wait! You made sure of what, Jonathan? You made sure of what? He ran away from me! You said that! He ran away!"

Molina was tiring of the domestic banter between the husband and wife. "Come on, kid," he said to Chastity. "He obviously killed Kevin!"

Devlin's eyes narrowed in on Molina. His leather gloves creaked. Elijah's eyes bulged as he began kicking his feet. With a short, high-pitched giggle, Devlin squared his shoulders and tensed his muscles in anticipation of a neck-breaking twist.

There could be no hesitation.

A deafening, explosive blast thundered through the hallway.

Devlin stood still as a statue. The hole in his forehead appeared like magic. The red wall behind the tall, skinny Elder looked wet, but not significantly different. Elijah reached for his ears as he broke Devlin's grip. He ran back through the doorway. Chastity was holding her ears as well. She was trying to scream, but Molina couldn't hear anything coming out of her mouth. He could hear only an ear-piercing whine for the moment. The hallway seemed to tilt back and forth through his blurred vision.

As Detective Molina lowered his weapon, he started hearing Chastity's screams get louder and louder over the ringing. Devlin collapsed to the floor in an inhuman heap. Chastity crawled to her husband's side.

She grabbed him and repeated, "I loved him. I loved him!"

Then the new widow started hitting her husband's body with her fists while continuing to scream, "I loved Kevin! Kevin!"

Molina froze in the doorway. Elijah knelt on the floor of an ornate bedroom, sobbing. His brother Shante's head was cradled in his arms. The detective crossed the room fast and dropped to his knees. His fingers went to Shante's neck. No breath, no pulse. A tight, strange collar cinched his throat. Molina found a button on the device and slammed it. The lariat sprang open, but Shante remained still.

Molina started CPR, hands pounding against Shante's chest. He glimpsed a staircase, desk and phone behind the bedroom. Panic clawed at him, but he kept the rhythm. Compress, breathe, compress...driving air and life back into Shante.

"Hey, kid, grab that phone over there. Call 911. Where's the baby?"

Chapter 47

The scene in Columbia Heights was a spectacle of chaos and confusion. Dozens of people sprinted in all directions like scurrying cockroaches; their faces twisted with alarm. Fire trucks, ambulances and police vehicles scrambled together, creating a maze of flashing lights and blaring horns. Police officers and detectives in suits and earpieces rushed around to coordinate their efforts. The sharp sounds of police dogs barking and the thump of helicopter blades overhead added to the discord.

Amid it all, the putrid garbage truck stood out like a sore thumb. Detective Molina sat composed in the back of an ambulance, observing as an emergency medical technician inserted an intravenous line into Shante Britt's outstretched arm. Despite the overwhelming commotion, the young boy's eyes remained open, his gaze fixed on the sky above. To Molina's relief, Shante blinked several times.

"Are you going to the hospital with him, Detective?" the medical technician asked.

Before Molina could answer, Captain Scott Granai, Commanding Officer of the Missing Persons Squad, intervened. "Molina, I need you here a bit longer. Hutchinson will go with the child."

Molina looked to the medic and then to Shante.

"Shante is looking good so far, Detective. We need to get him to the hospital immediately," the emergency worker said.

Detective Hutchinson stood with Captain Granai outside the ambulance. A reluctant Molina made the switch. The ambulance screamed its siren as it sped away.

Captain Granai passed information to Molina. It involved Chief Beame, a girl and a body found in a garage. Molina heard the words, but they didn't compute. The emotion of this unexpected ordeal overwhelmed him. Granai's official descriptions dissipated into the truck exhaust, and Molina turned instead toward the front door of the ominous house. It was filled with torment. It fixated him.

A uniformed officer emerged carrying Deshawn from the house. The toddler appeared disoriented as he surveyed his surroundings. Molina ignored his captain and ran to them. The officer informed Molina that his K-9 dog, Angel, had found him in a closet and was beaming with pride while sharing the information.

"Molina! Detective Molina!"

A distinct voice was trying to get his attention.

Molina shook his head to focus. Chief Daryl Beame was standing at full attention in front of him. The chief had wet eyes as he gave the detective a slow salute, the ultimate sign of respect. Then, Chief Beame hugged him and said, "Thank you, Detective."

Molina struggled to speak and form coherent thoughts. He followed Chief Beame to the ambulance. A medical team, detectives and three others surrounded it: a garbageman, a blonde girl and Monica Beame on a gurney.

An overwhelming rush of emotions engulfed Molina. The magnitude of the event began to sink in. A deranged cult was brought to light, unearthing a missing child and his chief's abducted daughter. And he stood at the center of it. Molina quickened his pace and headed toward a group of civilians. He noticed McColgan trying to interview Chastity Devlin in another ambulance. Chastity appeared in shock, rocking back and forth while staring at her feet. Molina's thoughts cleared, and he ran toward the little blonde girl. However, a garbageman appeared before her, blocking his way.

"She needs some space," Miles Orsky bellowed. He was keeping his thumb swear.

Jake stepped in front of Detective Molina. They stared at one another. Jake spoke first. "You okay, Detective?"

"Yeah. You?"

"Yup, cleaning up other people's shit." The pair now shared a common understanding. They were definitely on the same team, the correct one. "How about my father's key?"

Molina reached into his suit pocket and tossed Jake the key with a half-smile. Molina knelt on one knee. "Are you Hope?" Molina asked as gently as he ever could.

She didn't speak. But she smiled and nodded her head yes.

"I know someone who misses you very much," Molina told her.

Molina looked up at Jake and asked, "Did you call her yet?"

"Not yet. Stupid phone broke," Jake said with his cracked phone in hand.

* * * * *

A bloody scream filled the room.

Fear, confusion, panic. Terri jumped up. She didn't recognize her environment. Something grabbed her bare foot, causing her to stumble as she attempted to kick it free. A white flash of pain erupted as Terri's knee met an immovable object. She felt herself spin in a circle. The screaming followed her awkward pirouette until she came to rest on a firm, spongy surface. She needed to focus. She needed to figure out what the hell was going on.

Her head defogged, and she took a breath. The source of the god-awful scream was a clock radio. She smashed a few buttons until the screaming stopped.

He needs a psychiatrist, Terri thought.

As her phone rang, Terri kept her head in her hands for a much-needed extra moment of calm. She looked down and saw "Molina."

"Ms. Sheehan, Terri, she's safe. I'm with her now," Molina said in a gentle voice.

Tears streamed down Terri's face as she tried to speak. She couldn't find the words to express her relief and gratitude, so she kept crying with the phone pressed to her ear.

Then she heard a small voice say, "Terri, I miss you."

Her heart swelled with love and longing. "I'm coming, baby. I'm coming," Terri replied through her sobs.

Molina spoke again. "You were right. I should have listened. We're at the Columbia Heights house. You were right."

Terri was overcome. She felt validated, vindicated and grateful all at once.

"It's okay, it's okay, it's okay," she tried to calm herself down. "I'm coming, I'm coming," she repeated, her voice trembling.

"Terri," Molina said her name softly, with empathy and understanding. However, he couldn't say much else and hung up the phone. Terri sat there for a few moments, frozen. She wiped her tears and savored a long, deep inhale.

"Jake!" Terri yelled through her sobs. "Jake, are you here?"

There was no answer.

In minutes, Terri and Mrs. Daschle zoomed through the streets in Terri's Jeep at Mach 10. They tried to call Jake but only reached his voicemail. Mrs. Daschle contacted Father Duffy and informed him of the situation, asking for any updates on his nephew. They encountered chaos at Cadman Plaza: news trucks, fire trucks, police vehicles, ambulances and curious onlookers. Despite the bedlam, Terri parked her car on the sidewalk. As they scanned, their hearts skipped a beat, seeing Detective McColgan from Molina's office. The situation intensified.

Terri made no introductions or small talk. "Detective McColgan, where is Hope?"

"Holy shit! Ms. Sheehan. You're here."

"Yeah, okay. Where's Hope? Where's Molina?" McColgan nodded toward another ambulance.

Terri made a beeline for it. She stopped dead in her tracks. Jake's humongous partner had his back to her as he walked to the truck. From between Miles Orsky's oversized legs, Terri could see little bare feet and a dirty nightgown walking ahead of the garbage man. It looked like they were going to board the medic unit.

Terri tried to yell out her name. "Hope!" Her weakened voice cracked. "Hope! I'm here. I'm here!"

The little girl stopped. She felt it even if she couldn't quite hear it. Miles almost tripped over her as he followed her like a loyal St. Bernard. Terri brought her hands together over her mouth. Tears poured but she made no effort to clear them. She was locked in on her little girl.

Hope peered around Miles's leg and tugged on his arm. He bent way down to listen to a message she had for her protector. Miles rose, grinning, viewing Terri. Hope stepped in front of him like a waking dream. Terri ran as fast as she could. She squeezed the little girl with every ounce of love and caring that only a true mother could give.

Mrs. Daschle found Jake standing near the reunion.

"Thank God," Jake exclaimed. "I was getting so sick and tired of all her whining about that kid."

Mrs. Daschle moved to slap Jake, but noticed him crying just as she was. She wrapped her arm around him as a true mother would.

Terri lifted her head to take a breath. Hope clung to her tight. In the background, Molina sat in the ambulance with a blood-pressure cuff wrapped around his arm. His eyes were bloodshot with exhaustion. The decrease in adrenaline left him spent. He smiled at Terri and nodded.

The moment of serenity was shattered. The Minister, the Cornings and some other Ministry members arrived on the scene. The irate Minister demanded to see his daughter. Detective McColgan tried to explain that his daughter was already on her way to Kings County Hospital. The Minister then began ordering everyone out of his home.

"I want to see a damn search warrant. Nobody should be inside my home. This is not a circus. You must all leave." The Minister was frenzied. "Lazaro, get these people off my property," he ordered the man, lighting a cigarette.

Jake looked down and recognized the smoker's red-laced Doc Martens anywhere. Terri stood and recalled where she had seen the dark-haired man before. The man named Lazaro realized what was happening as well. He turned to limp away.

Jake pointed at him. "Hey, remember me fuck-o? You broke into my house."

Terri added to the accusations. "You're the one who chased me. How's your hip?"

Lazaro kept hobbling away from the scene onto the street. Molina stood behind, watching with a smirk. The seasoned detective made eye contact with McColgan and gave her the nod. She grabbed Lazaro and threw him into a police car. McColgan locked the handcuffs on like a lightning strike. The cigarette never left Lazaro's mouth.

"Boy, I can't wait to fingerprint you!" Detective McColgan said.

Still livid, The Minister cursed at everyone in his path. He demanded to speak to whoever was in charge. A small, frail-looking man wearing thick glasses and a white collar spoke up.

"Oh, the man in charge would like to speak to you, too." Four other men of the cloth appeared. Father Benny again addressed The Minister. "You will need to speak to the police first and foremost. Then maybe the Internal Revenue Service. When you finish that, you will need to answer to us."

"Who the hell are you?" The Minister spat.

"We are the real clergy, I assure you," Father Benny said as he laughed.

Another priest looked deathly serious. "Minister, we represent the Vatican. We recommend that you cooperate with all the domestic authorities. Only then will we be able to discuss your standing with the Church and the Lord our God. If you fail in any way to heed our recommendation, then sanctions, both divine and earthly, will be ordained. Have I made myself clear?"

The Minister's complexion mirrored his watching supporters. "I follow nobody's authority except God's." Some followers gave a "Hallelujah" as witnesses. A younger priest then spoke.

"Okay, then we have been clear enough."

The four priests walked away.

The Minister seemed nervous. He wiped his brow and looked for somebody to yell at.

"That fella is a right eejit," Father Duffy announced as he stood next to Jake.

Jake jumped. He did not expect his uncle to sneak up on him. "What are they gonna do to him?" Jake asked.

"Ruin his life like they do to everyone that crosses their path," Father Duffy replied.

"Like they did to Keener?" Jake asked.

"Yes."

"Any word on that creep, Rufus?"

"Deceased."

Jake felt sadder than he had expected. "He died?"

"Yes. Jake. You tried, boy. You cared enough to try."

Jake drifted in his thoughts until Terri threw her arms around Miles. He opened his mouth to warn her about the state of those filthy coveralls, but it was too late. She squeezed him like a long-lost brother. Jake figured she was now fused to the big, smelly ogre forever.

Miles looked over. "Hey, Jake! Are you okay?"

"Yeah, Miles. I'm good now. Thanks for sticking by me, man. You really saved the day."

"We're a pretty good team, you and me," Miles said. "We both did it."

A familiar voice spoke to Jake now. "Somebody wants to talk to you."

Jake looked at Molina, who was standing in his entourage. The detective pointed at an ambulance.

Monica "Moon" Beame, once the Pinball Wizard, sat propped in the back of the ambulance, a faint smile tugging at her lips. Her father stood nearby, his voice firm as he gave orders to the uniformed officers.

Jake edged forward, his chest loosening with every step. She was alive. Breathing. Her eyes found his, and for a moment, the noise and flashing lights faded. Relief washed through him, warm and dizzying. She was here. She was still Monica.

She then spoke to Jake.

"I went looking for you. I assumed this was that other woman's house."

"Monica, I. I don't understand," he stammered.

"The day I saw you at work, I followed you both here. I thought she was taking you to her place. I went there to talk to her about us, but that's when he took me."

Jake felt sick but asked, "Did he hurt you?"

"Not in a sick, perverted way. I think he was planning to. He wanted to impregnate me or something."

"I'm so sorry, Monica. I never would, I never imagined that this would..."

"I'm glad you guys came when you did. Who knows what The Elder would have done to me if he found out I had an IUD?"

Jake struggled to grasp her point.

"Jacob Johansson, I'm sorry to tell you this. I've had some time to reflect on our relationship. Please don't view this as a break-up speech. Think of it as a liberation. I realize now that we are not compatible," Monica said, looking at Miles Orsky.

Jake set up another of his famous comments. He stopped himself.

"Okay, Monica, liberation, huh? Friends?" Jake offered his hand.

She was weak, but she reached out and gave a light shake. "Friends forever!" she affirmed. "But Jacob Johansson?"

"Yes?"

"Keep your girlfriend away from my superhero!"

Jake pivoted to see who she meant. His bulky partner in grime was still conversing with Terri. Terri pinched her nose while Miles talked.

"She's not my girlfriend, for God's sake!" Jake explained.

"That's too bad. When I first saw you together, there was a bubbly pink champagne energy around each of your auras," Monica sang in melody. "Keep her away from him anyway."

With a big smile, Jake yielded and said, "All right. You got it. That's a big thumb swear."

Jake stood alone while everyone around him kept busy. The cops and detectives were finishing up their official duties, Monica had gone to the hospital, and Terri prepared to board the ambulance with Hope and Miles. His partner still refused to leave Hope's side and argued with anyone who tried to separate them. Jake couldn't tell if Terri's eyes were watering from crying or Miles's pungent order. He kept watch and reflected on his own life. Nearby children innocently smiled and ran around the emergency vehicles.

Father Duffy walked up and summed it all up, poetic and accurate.

"When you stumble into shite..."

"Yup, belly flop!" Jake answered.

48

Mrs. Hitchcock wailed. The clock read 5:00 a.m. She always seemed to scream louder when woken up earlier. After yesterday, it was time for an undivided focus. Jake got out of bed and threw on his favorite New York Islanders sweatshirt and jeans. He was thankful he had kept his beer intake to a minimum last night with Uncle Duffy. Thus, the night ended soon, with no aftereffects.

Jake drove to the Hanover Place garage. He wished Terri were there with him, but she had more pressing matters. His Uncle Duffy had tried to talk him out of it. No, he needed to act. His father's legacy teetered. Revenge beckoned.

Jake opened the heavy door. The location grew familiar. Lights were activated with zero labor.

It was all gone. Nothing remained.

"No, no, no!"

Jake was dizzy with nausea. The gloves, mask, shirt, coat, gadgets, notes, books and papers were gone. Vanished. The place was bare except for a stool, the worktable and empty metal shelves. He walked out into the garage area. Even the vending cart was gone. Disoriented, Jake walked in a circle.

Should I call Molina? Did he have to confiscate everything? Why? Without a warrant? How was that going to help me now? I need that equipment to go after Captain Jay.

Uncle Duff didn't want him to do this. Could he and Molina have done this? Did they take everything out?

It didn't matter now. Jake glanced at his watch. The decision was made. The anger Jake felt fueled his vengeful agenda. Soon after, he parked at the Stanley Miller Nursing Home again. He sat in his car, trying to figure out his next move.

Jake thought back to his run-in with Ratner. The medication pickup was scheduled for today, Ratner had told him. It could occur at any time. Jake made up his mind and watched the door from his car. Several hours into his stakeout, Jake noticed three school-age children walking past the sidewalk near the nursing home. A guy on a bicycle nearly rode right through them. He didn't even make a move to slow down until he stopped at the front doors. The rude cyclist looked young despite his lumberjack beard. He wore an untucked button-down shirt and tight jeans, with his left pant leg rolled up. After adjusting his man purse draped over his right shoulder, the cyclist entered the building.

If what Ratner told him was the truth, Jake was waiting for a member of Captain Jay's group, the Squids. When the bushy cyclist exited again barely two minutes later, Jake knew he had his mark. He began following him in his car, a more difficult task than Jake expected. The cyclist weaved between cars, blew past stop signs and juked around pedestrians. Jake lost sight of him once, then again behind the steel skeleton of New York City scaffolding. He picked him up again when the man emerged into a crosswalk, where a yellow taxi honked its horn at the jay-biker. Luckily for Jake, a city bus slowed the man's pace, and he fell back within just a few car lengths. Now the arrogant gear-shifter dawdled, threw his bike down in the middle of the sidewalk and pulled out his phone. Jake pulled over to watch the man's next move. He was disappointed though. The man simply stopped to grab a bite while making a call. Jake realized undercover work can be quite tedious.

He hopped back on his Schwinn just as the digital clock in Jake's car struck noon. Jake was hungry and frustrated. He punched his steering wheel, cursing the rider. He contemplated running over the Tour de Snail competitor right there on Atlantic Avenue and extracting Captain Jay's location while he writhed on the pavement. But he'd have to keep up this slow-motion pursuit, even though his stops and starts in the middle of Downtown Brooklyn meant other motorists wanted Jake's head as their hood ornament. This revenge mission needed to reach a climax and achieve it fast.

The Squid leaped off his bike near an abandoned house in the Gowanus section of Brooklyn. Standing alone on the flat lot at the corner of 3rd Avenue and 3rd Street was a haunting red building. Stone-washed blocks edged the old concrete structure and its windows. Garbage and waste littered the barren, spacious property, which seemed out of place in the rest of the crowded neighborhood. A metal plaque in front identified the *New York and Long Island Coignet Stone Company Building* as an official New York City landmark.

The sloth on two wheels pranced toward the door. He knocked. Jake felt slight surprise at the opening door. The place looked deserted.

Jake was next up at the door. He realized he lacked a plan in case he spotted Captain Jay. Jake knocked anyway.

"Who is it?" a pleasant male voice asked.

Jake answered, "JJ. The horologist! I'm here to clean your clocks."

The voice said, "Oh! Wonderful!"

Another voice then butted in from inside. "I don't think we should open the door." Both voices began a civil debate about any further action.

After the brief tiff, another voice said, "I'm terribly sorry. You must have the wrong house. Nobody lives here."

Jake heard some light laughs and snorts.

"Tell your fucking boss I'm here, or I will burn this whole goddamn place to the ground with all of you in it," Jake said. He looked around the outside of the place. It was all stone and concrete. They might be a little denser than he was.

A falsetto voice came from behind the closed door. "Not by the hair of my chinny chin chin!"

Shit! Jake thought to himself.

He walked down the steps, picked up the rickety old bicycle and threw it through the boarded-up window. Two little kids were walking by. They stared at Jake the Barbarian, shaking their heads in disapproval.

"They stole my bike!" he said to them.

Although the plywood covering the arched window absorbed most of the impact, one pedal still broke through. The bike was left hanging, a wheeled wall ornament. The bearded Squid emerged from the door and looked outside. He stared at Jake in disbelief. "Hey, that's my bike! It's a classic, man." It was the most annoying voice Jake ever heard.

Behind him were three other bearded men looking over their melancholy mate's shoulder. Jake rushed at the door like a bull. Four tried shutting it, but Jake had a full start. He tripped on the top step and barreled into the half-closed door as he ran up. Two of the guys fell as Jake hit them. Jake was inside, but on the floor. Jake, the wrecking ball, tried to stand up as he heard multiple voices complain.

"Oh, come on, man."

"Is this really necessary?"

"What's your problem?"

Jake rose to his feet, bracing for a confrontation. The interior differed quite a bit from his expectations. Instead of a dilapidated space filled by junkies, with Brooklyn rats scurrying behind busted walls, the room was tidy, almost cozy, with nearly a dozen bearded men staring at Jake in silence. The ground floor opened wide and couches scattered across the space. A massive flat-screen TV hung on one wall, and a stocked bar glowed in the corner. The decor defied explanation.

In the far-right corner stood a knight in full armor. Its head was a balloon with a smiley face. Above an old Victrola hung a painting of a green rooster. The Victrola played a modern-day hippie tune. Neon lights bathed the bar in color. A fake palm tree stood beside the TV. A large stuffed penguin was propped against the palm tree. On the left wall was a wooden hockey stick crossed with a thin metal sword.

About twenty glass fish tanks divided the room. The tanks were of different sizes and sat on wooden pedestals. Each tank held random objects. There were no fish to be found. Or water. A sign on the wall read "Welcome to the Rabbit Hole."

A crooked staircase climbed to the second floor with a rounded railing painted like a barber pole. Dozens of mismatched clocks marched up the wall alongside it. Jake chuckled at the absurdity.

At the top stood a man with a bushy white beard and a handlebar mustache. A dusty captain's hat covered his head as his oversized brown shirt billowed around him, tucked into large trousers.

"Mr. Johansson. What a terrible surprise!" Captain Jay sang.

Jake stood stunned. His hatred consumed him, so he forgot about the ten men surrounding him. His fists were still up, at least.

"Forgive me if I seem rude, but I did not plan a party for you. I've been so disinterested these days," Captain Jay crooned.

"It's okay. There's a bar here."

"Yes. Well, come on up, and we can talk." Captain Jay walked out of view.

The Squids returned to whatever activities bearded men in tight pants typically engage in. Jake was sure that none of them were cutting any trees down. He skulked up the crooked stairs. The level above lacked the same spaciousness. Jake found Captain Jay looking out a rectangular-shaped window with his hands positioned at his back. Dry fish tanks lined the room from floor to ceiling.

"You found me. Now what?" he asked.

"I know everything. You killed my father. I know you killed that little girl."

"Oh, good for you," he said, lost in thought.

"What?" Jake screamed, ready to blow his top.

"I'm happy for you. It must have taken a lot of effort." Captain Jay kept his back to him. Jake thought about throwing him out the window.

"Ah, wasn't too bad," Jake played along.

"It seems that of all your efforts, you got some facts wrong."

"I don't think so."

"You see, Jake, I did not kill your father," Captain Jay stated. "I never take credit for something I did not do."

"Bullshit," Jake spat. "Don't tell me he died of natural causes."

"Oh, I don't lie. Your father's death was indeed enhanced. Put out of his misery, really," Captain Jay stated, smooth and melodramatic.

Jake clenched his fists. "If it wasn't you, then who?"

"The chef, of course, but you already knew that. You knew the answer all along, and you still accused me of killing your father. How can I ever trust you?"

"Call it whatever you want. You're still a murderer," Jake gritted.

"Yes. Yes, I am."

"I'm tired of this game. I'm taking you to the police, and you can take credit for whatever you want." The threat felt good, but Jake doubted he could make that happen.

"Once again, I find it difficult to trust that you will follow through with that plan. You see, Jacob, I have extensive life experience. I am an ardent admirer of existence and endeavor to embrace it fully. The key to achieving this is deceptively simple: take action without hesitation and avoid excuses. Refrain from accumulating possessions. Maintain your anonymity. Do not allow anyone to obstruct your path. Lead decisively, and avoid following others. Most importantly, be unwaveringly ruthless. Indeed, I have caused harm to others. Even took a few lives. I have found that collateral damage is necessary when cleaning a mess. Nobody's perfect. Even I make mistakes. But I own that fact. Then I fix it."

"You're not God," Jake growled. "You can't just take lives."

"God, oh God, right? God is a fabricated illusion. All religion is a fictional ploy to frighten people into following a leader. Someone of higher status. It keeps everyone in check. It serves a greater purpose, so don't get me wrong. If people hadn't believed in some omnipotent entity, there would have been a nuclear fallout years ago. Human beings are nothing more than animals. At the top of the food chain, but animals nonetheless. Without religion, it would be humans versus the planet."

"Bullshit!" Jake said.

"Humans would ultimately win by ending it all. In contemporary society, it's perplexing to observe individuals who, fueled by extreme beliefs, employ religion as a justification for self-destructive actions. This phenomenon sparked my curiosity about its underlying mechanisms. Unlike many, I navigate life with an awareness beyond the complications often associated with organized societal structures. I call it Me-ology."

Jake countered, "It's called Sociopath."

"I am perfectly fine with that, too," Captain Jay said.

"How have you gotten away with all this?"

"I hide in plain sight, or better put, I don't try to hide."

"Why do you blackmail everyone if you're not trying to hide?"

"Blackmail? No. I make deals. Blackmail is for money. Deals are how I get the things I want. I give as much as I take. I love helping people help me."

"Except if you don't get your way. Then you ruin lives," Jake pointed out.

"No, Jacob. If somebody does not hold up their end of the deal, I'm ruthless, simple and effective. It is their fault, period!"

"What about my father? He never made any deals with you," Jake shouted.

"Inconsequential, collateral damage. I needed a little extra cleanup on that one. I made some mistakes there. Besides, your father killed me first."

"Now you're Jesus?"

"Sort of, I guess. The Jypsy died at your father's hand. There was a resurrection, a baptism from the cold, salty water, a rebirth."

Captain Jay drifted off in his thoughts.

"So, you are The Jypsy?"

"No," the seafarer said.

"Um. You are not dead. You're standing right here."

"Rebirth is not complicated, my boy. Like a bone, it grows back stronger after being broken."

"I think my being here right now gives your theories a new perspective," Jake said.

"Yes, I suppose it does."

"How did you know who my father was and learn about the nursing home?"

"Ah, yes. That was a fortunate accident. You see, last year, I was taking my annual stroll to the water basin uptown. The place of my rebirth, so to speak. It keeps me grounded, you know. During the darkest part of the night was Penrod Johansson, with two different colored eyes and no mask, wandering about the bulkhead. He made absolutely no sense at all, even though I tried to speak with him. I mean, he was way out there, like a mindless zombie. I followed him back to the nursing home. Everything else was easy."

Captain Jay turned to face Jake. He still had his hands behind his back. "I need to take my medication now. Please follow me."

Jake watched the senior mariner exit, passing close. Jake could not comprehend how to deal with this situation, so he followed Captain Jay down the stairs.

"Ethan, did you get my medication?" Captain Jay asked as he stood in the middle of the room.

The bicycle rider got up off the couch and gave an unmarked canister to his perceived leader. The old man took the pill dry. Then, Captain Jay addressed Jake again.

"I guess you are wondering what's with all my Squids."

"No. I find them irritating. I'm more interested in the fish tanks," Jake said.

"Interestingly, you called them annoying. Such insight could be considered quite perceptive. Ultimately, the NYPD is effective in keeping the crime rate low. I have no affection for law enforcement agencies. It disheartens me to see them doing their jobs well. My quality of life would significantly improve if the city remained in constant disorder. Chaos can be viewed as an asset. During my recovery, I decided to start a movement, a social experiment, if you will.

"I posted an advertisement on Craigslist targeting wealthy young men eager to immerse themselves in urban life. In exchange for their commitment, I offered free housing and meals. Their only requirements were to wear fitted clothing and grow long beards. I asked them to visit underprivileged neighborhoods and to spend their parents' money at local businesses. My theory was that introducing a bit of affluent America into struggling areas would create some chaos for the police. A way to inflate their statistics with more participants.

I aimed to feed squids to the 'sharks' lurking in the ghetto. I couldn't have been more wrong."

"How so?" Jake was a little intrigued.

"Instead of chaotic turmoil, these audacious individuals thrived in the badlands of Brooklyn. They spent more of their parents' money than I had anticipated, even recruiting more friends into their lifestyle. It was as if this phenomenon were multiplying uncontrollably. Before long, I found myself igniting a different kind of movement, a more refined one. Coffee shops and trendy bars proliferate in Bed-Stuy, Park Slope and Crown Heights. Politicians call it gentrification, a concept that has gained significant popularity. Wealth, specifically, their wealth, is what the neighborhood craves. It represents mere affluent idealism. I believe it is a matter of time before the original Brooklynites act. As they are marginalized and financially pushed out of their communities, they will strive to reclaim their land. I may still find my chaos after all."

"Why are you doing this *Scooby Doo* bad-guy bit? Why tell me all of your diabolical plans? Sophomoric Dick Dastardly stuff, no?"

"You see, young Johansson. Legacy. Legacy is the fallback."

"I'm not following."

"You may beat me, pure and simple. I'm old and not as spry as I used to be. So, if I lose, at least my name will have a legacy. You, of all people, should understand, being the son of a street hero."

"God, that makes sense to me," Jake huffed in disgust.

"Until then, I get to enjoy some bloody violence right here under one roof. And maybe I come out on top. Ladies? If you please."

Ten Squids surrounded Jake, who looked around for somewhere to escape.

"Are you serious?" Jake yelled as he twisted his fists and twirled in a tactical circle.

"Mr. Johansson. They don't stand a chance against you," Captain Jay snickered.

Jake looked at Captain Jay with a squinted eye of confusion, and then the bike rider, Ethan, punched Jake in the face. It didn't hurt Jake that much, but Ethan let out a yelp and shook his hand in pain. Another bearded wonder stepped up and kicked Jake in the shin. Jake punched him in the face. Blood splattered out of the shin-kicker's nose. The guy started whimpering, "Why did you do that?"

Two more stepped in and swung their semi-closed fists. Jake dodged by standing there. They missed. He reached out and tossed one into the other. They collided and dropped clumsily to the floor. Three more now stepped closer. The one in the middle directed his partners to flank Jake on either side. It might have worked, as they landed many punches, but unfortunately for them the blows were friendly fire. Jake had easily slid away from their maneuver. Then came the guys with weapons: one had a yellow plastic bat, the other held a liquor bottle.

"Now we're talking," Captain Jay squealed with delight.

Jake head-butted the guy with the plastic bat. He held his red, splattered face and screamed, "I'm going to sue you!"

The Squid with the glass bottle proved more challenging. Jake had to bob and weave to avoid the blows. He grabbed the bottle brawler's sweater and pulled it over his head. With the man neutralized, Jake landed three punches to his chest.

"That's not fair. That's not fair!" the Squid coughed.

A blond-bearded, green-eyed male then called Jake a "racist corporate drone."

Jake punched him, landing a blow to the face, and the bottle fell to the floor. From there, the battle royal continued. It seemed like ten hours of nonstop scrapping. Only Jake emerged without leaking blood. Aside from some scratches to his face, body and hands, Jake's only genuine concern was getting a bald spot from having his hair pulled.

"Well done. Well done, Mr. Johansson. I never doubted you for a second," Captain Jay praised.

Jake was exhausted. He hunched over and breathed heavily.

"Good. Bumfuzzled and fatigued," Captain Jay noted.

Jake looked up. "Bumfuzzled?"

"Yes. It means confused."

"The only thing I am bumfuzzled about..." Jake bent down again to catch his breath, "... are all the fish tanks with no water."

"Ah, yes. You must get that from your father; attention to insignificant details. If you must know, I do not write things down. They are permanent and absolute. Each tank represents a file cabinet, an organization of things to do, or a reminder of things I have done or am presently doing. The various articles in each tank have abstract meanings. They are a diorama of life. I fill and empty the tank as I like. Take this one."

Jake looked over at the ten-gallon tank near the staircase. Inside were one blue-colored Christmas ball and one green one. That was it.

"This is my favorite so far," Captain Jay purred. "Guess what this represents?"

"You are avoiding my question. Why is there no water?" Jake persisted.

"The Fade, Mr. Johansson. Penrod Johansson's eyes. Your eyes!" Captain Jay hissed in a striking change of demeanor.

"Fuck you!" Jake said.

Captain Jay continued past Jake's curse. "Your father's eyes have sat in this tank for many years now, waiting for the moment I get to empty this chapter. No more eyes, no more Fade, no more Johanssons. I'm tired of thinking about it."

Jake edged toward the grimacing captain. The small, fragile sailor tossed the two Christmas balls to the side. Jake was surprised he didn't hear them break.

"Mr. Johansson, this is Miro."

Jake swiveled to his left. Standing next to a long purple couch was a massive man. Jake, at six foot two, wasn't exactly short, but this guy was enormous. He had a blond buzz cut and huge muscles. Not an ounce of fat. Jake swore he saw smoke come out of the Goliath's nostrils. Miro held a ball in each of his baseball mitts. Then he crushed them into dust and smiled. Miro had the most prominent, whitest teeth Jake had ever seen. The perfection of his bright choppers mesmerized him. Jake glanced downward.

"Are you wearing a romper?" Jake asked the dental titan.

Miro looked down at his blue Hawaiian-print one-piece. He gave another great big smile.

"Hey, Miro, maybe you can tell me why Captain Nemo here doesn't want to tell me why there is no water in these tanks." Jake looked over the crossed arms of Captain Jay. "What? It's bothering me," he said.

"This will be pleasantly terrible to watch," Captain Jay stated in a much deeper octave.

"You are a creepy son of a bitch, Vascones," Jake scowled.

Miro took a thunder-like step toward Jake. Captain Jay raised his hand to signal Miro to pause his attack.

"What did you call me?" The sailor's voice settled into a lethal calm that made the room smaller.

"What? I called you by your name, Vascones, Jayson Basco Vascones!" Jake made the name of evil sound so innocent.

"Never say that name out loud. Ever."

Someone struck a nerve. Jake strummed the chord. "Jayson Basco Vascones?"

Captain Jay seethed. He pushed the empty fish tank over. It crashed hard. Shards of glass slid in every direction across the wooden floor.

He stared at Jake like he was trying to rip his gaze through the back of his skull. "Before Miro ends your family's name. There is something you should know."

"You hate water. Right? It's water? You hate water?"

"I am your grandfather," Captain Jay whispered.

Jake, in full panic mode, yelled out. "What? Are you fucking kidding me?"

Captain Jay smiled under his waxed handlebar mustache. "Yes. I'm totally messing with you."

Miro smashed an empty fish tank over Jake's head. The pain was not so bad yet. Blood ran into Jake's eyes. The red obscured the view of Miro's giant basketball fists cocked to smash Jake's face.

"Come on, little girl," Miro taunted. The beast picked Jake up like a feather and slammed him against every wall.

"Wow, I made a Rorschach blot!" Miro bragged. "I see a loser!"

The other fish tanks exploded into tiny razors whenever Miro hammered Jake through their glass panels. The colossus raised Jake up by his neck and flattened him to the ceiling. Then he let gravity slam him down onto another fish tank. Jake tried to get up, bruised and bloodied.

"Batter up!" Miro slammed the palm tree into Jake's stomach like a Louisville Slugger. "Oh, I think he's gonna cry! There's no crying in baseball!" Miro continued his assault on Jake's body and dignity.

The Squids! Jake forgot about the Squids. They each took turns punching, scratching, slapping and clawing. Jake was in desperate, primal survival mode. He swung at any dark blur he even sensed. Sometimes he got lucky and punched the penguin. Miro kicked Jake square in the buttocks with his size 18 work boot. Jake almost crashed straight through the window's wooden cover. It held. And Ethan's bicycle was no longer stuck.

"Is anyone up for a little bowling?" Miro laughed as he grabbed Jake by his belt and carried him like a rag doll. Broken piles of furniture, glass and strange decor were everywhere. The room was unrecognizable and destroyed. Walls were splashed with Jake's blood. Miro swung Jake behind him and slid him forward across the floor with tremendous force. Jake's body cut right through the mess, leaving a thick streak of blood. Jake lay about ten feet from Miro. The Squids positioned themselves for something. Everyone laughed and pointed. One of them poured alcohol over his oozing cuts, and Jake screamed out in pain. *At least it washed my eye out*, he considered amid the burning. He could see a little as he lay bleeding from everywhere.

Jake sprawled out on the floor, knowing he faced death, but his life didn't flash before his eyes. His focus remained on one thing: survival. He searched for any means to stay alive. To his left, on the floor, he saw the sword that used to adorn the wall. It was a weapon made of sharpened steel, designed to kill. On his right, he saw his passion, his love, his outlet when life got tough.

Father Duffy's voice played in Jake's memory bank.

Ah, but don't be thinkin' too hard now. Just go with yer heart and if you always use yer God-given talents, you will always succeed. That's why the good Lord gave it to ya.

Jake reached to his right side. He picked up the old wooden hockey stick and used it to stand up. Miro laughed. The Squids laughed harder. Jake wobbled on the stick.

"It's over, little loser. Lie down and give up. Captain Jay will then slit your silly throat and end your misery."

Miro's cackle revealed those tremendous, freakishly white teeth. Jake heard a knife slide out of a sheath from behind him. He reached into his pocket and dropped the stress stone onto the floor. Miro the Giant kept laughing. Jake flicked the blade of the hockey stick fast and hard. It launched the stress stone like a spinning rocket into Miro's grinning mouth.

The hulking behemoth's pearly whites shattered. Blood poured onto the floor like a faucet until Miro brought his hand up to his mouth. The enormous brute fell to his knees, holding some fragments of his chicklets. He stared at Jake in disbelief. In a secondary motion, Jake swung the stick behind him and knocked a knife out of Captain Jay's hand. Jake body-checked the old man right through a sheetrock wall. Jayson Basco Vascones collapsed to the ground, covered in chalky dust. Jake ran forward and brought the wooden hockey stick down on the back of Miro's massive skull. The giant fell unconscious. The Squids couldn't run out of the front door fast enough. Jake slid down the unbroken stick to his knees.

Jake lifted his eyes toward the ceiling. "Got him, Dad."

He then lay down on the floor. He was feeling very sleepy.

49

Jake did not know how long he'd been on the ground. A pair of polished black shoes appeared at his feet, and someone called his name. The faint smell of peanuts drifted in. Then Father Duffy's face came into focus.

"Jacob. Jacob. It's me, lad. It's me."

Jake's adrenaline at the sight of his uncle woke him up. Father Duffy helped him up to a sitting position. Jake's swollen eyes were black and blue. They were barely open.

"I always said those old wooden sticks are so much better than the graphite ones," Jake said, delirious with pain.

"Ah, it's grand, lad. Ye'll be all right." The priest helped Jake stay up.

Terri stepped into view. She was horrified.

"It hurts worse than it looks," Jake told her. "How's Hope?"

"She's doing better today," she said between sniffles.

"You should be with her. Not here," Jake said, short of breath.

"I know, Jake. You are important, too. You stuck by me."

"God. I don't want her to go all missing again. You'll be impossible to deal with."

Terri laughed through her sobs. "She's in good hands. Mrs. Daschle is standing watch. She's got her hairspray."

The sailor began moaning and cursing under his breath. Sing X squatted and looked over Captain Jay.

"So, this is Jayson Basco Vascones. Captain Jay. The former Jypsy," Sing stated.

Vascones tried to lift his head. The old, broken man tried to spit, but only drool dribbled out.

Sing X whispered in the fallen sailor's ear. "I would like to pick your brain about a thing or two."

Vascones mumbled. Whatever it was, it sounded a lot like "fork do." Then, he began rambling in Spanish.

"What's with all the broken fish tanks?" Sing X questioned, taking in the bizarre decor.

Jake chuckled and winced. "He's afraid of water."

"Oh!" Sing X exclaimed. "Noted. I guess I'll have to waterboard this motherfletcher." Without another word, Sing X dragged Captain Jay outside by one foot.

Vascones screamed, "No! No! Not water!"

"How did you find me?" Jake coughed.

"Sing X had some friends track your broken phone," Father Duffy explained.

Jake felt for the phone in his pocket. It felt more crushed than before. Despite the pain, he couldn't help but be curious. "How did you get in touch with X-Man? That guy can be impossible."

"Not for L.O.L." Father Duffy looked at his bruised and battered nephew. "Is anything broken?"

"Yep."

"Do you think you can stand?" Father Duffy asked.

"Nope."

"I guess we should get you to the hospital," Terri added.

"Yep."

Father Duffy grabbed hold and threw a big forever hug onto his nephew from his knees.

"I love you," Jake whispered.

His uncle didn't let go.

50

Chapter

One Month Later

Cook began crooning to "Singing in the Rain."

Peeing in my pants

Just peeing in my pants

What a wet, warming feeling

I'm chafing again.

Jacob sat on the edge of Cook's bed, waiting for him to finish in the bathroom. "That's it. That's my story," Jake concluded as Cook sat back down in his chair.

"You should write a book," Cook said between bites of an apple he held in his mechanical claw.

"I was thinking more like a comic book or graphic novel."

Cook took another bite. "You're an adult. Write a damn book," he said, spittling chewed fruit at his guest.

"I'm too lazy and can't spell," Jake said. "It's never going to happen."

"Whatever happened to the big bad giant?"

"Uncle Duffy called an ambulance for him, too. The big dope says he doesn't remember a thing. The police figured the Squid pansies must have beaten him because there were so many of them. They didn't buy the beards' story that they were beaten by anyone smaller. Only two of the Squid schmucks initially cooperated with the police. The rest protested opposite the abandoned Rabbit Hole. Their parents will likely sue each other."

"Your eyes are looking better," Cook commented.

"Yeah. My ribs still hurt. I'm missing my hockey season."

"Glad you are alive, Jacob. I like our chats." Cook threw the apple core into a garbage pail.

"I promise to come still to visit," Jake stated as he walked to the door.

"Good. Now, don't go on being a hero." Cook picked up another apple with his claw.

"Speaking of heroes, I still don't understand how my father's illness all ties into this. I can't wrap my head around it."

"Jacob, he was very sick. I believe that. He didn't speak much. Sometimes, something would prompt him to mumble, but he usually came into my room and stared at the floor. I told you that."

"Yeah, thanks for being so patient with him," Jake said.

"I felt bad for him. I knew he wanted to talk, and I wanted to listen. Good people are like that when it comes to trauma. Firemen, policemen, E.M.S., doctors, nurses and other first responders love hanging out with their peers. They go to bars and social events to unwind and swap stories."

Jake inserted his thoughts aloud, "Like priests and rabbis at Pontiff's Pints."

Cook glanced sideways and continued, "They share stories to realize they aren't alone in facing daily horrors. They can reassure each other that they're not losing their minds. They can also refer one another to seek help when necessary. Your father was a unique kind of hero. No one else was quite like him. What he witnessed and accomplished is a tremendous burden for anyone to bear alone. And when someone fails, it ultimately breaks them."

"But he wasn't alone. I was there. Uncle Duff was there!"

"Oh yes! Tell a priest you might have killed someone. That's always a toughie," Cook said. Sarcasm oozed.

"He didn't kill Vascones, though!" Jake felt his temper rise.

"He thought he did. That counts. He also saw a little girl he was trying to save murdered. That is more than enough trauma to break any man. War! New York City street violence! The World Trade Center attack! Watching your mother die! Should I continue?"

Jake felt sick. "He, he, how could anyone go through so much?"

"Jacob, he did. And he would do it again, every single time. He did it for you, for people, for the city he loved. He did it because nobody else would. He did it because he could. He did it because he didn't know any better. He was a genuine hero."

Alex McCloskey opened his father's door and walked in. "Hey, ya, Dad!" Cook's switch flipped.

"Fill-er up! Un-leaded, please and don't forget the windows."

"Okay, Dad. Fine," Alex dismissed.

"Good to see you again, Mr. McCloskey," Jake said. "I was just leaving. Your father is doing well today."

Cook stayed in character. "Hey, my mufflers are making strange noises; it sounds like rrrrr rrrrr rrrrrr. This damn convertible is not going anywhere."

Alex McCloskey looked at Jake. A scowl covered his face. "What kind of doctor are you again?" There were no pleasantries.

"Proctologist," Jake answered staring back at Alex's condescending eyes. "Mr. McCloskey has been complaining about pain in his ass for a while now."

Alex stood nose to nose with Jake. "I think you may have other patients to attend to."

Before Jake could drop another wisecrack remark, Cook made another unpredictable statement. "Alexander, it's all right. He's all right."

Alex's eyes filled up. "Dad? You said my name!"

"No shit, Sherlock. I named you."

"How? What's going on? You said my name."

"Yeah. Yeah. Doc Johansson's a real winner and a good listener, too. He is leaving now. See you later, Doc." Cook waved a pretzel cigar in his mouth.

Jake took the cue and walked out with a swift parting wave of his hand. He eavesdropped on only a tiny part of the father and son's conversation as he walked into the hallway.

"Dad? You know it's me?"

"Yes, Alexander, of course, I know it's you, my crazy, overprotective son. I love you very much and I need to tell you something. I probably should have told you this a long time ago."

"Yes, Dad. I can't believe this! I'm listening!"

"Please stop trying to save me. This place is treating me well. Don't wear yourself down over me. I know I haven't been easy. I've been selfish, drowning in my own self-loathing for years. Couldn't keep on being the person I used to be.

"But the truth? I love that you never give up on me. I count the days until I see you and the kids. And, believe it or not, I've even grown fond of that nutty, pretentious wife of yours. I hate feeling cut off from you."

Cook took a pretend puff of his pretzel. "Now, tell me about my grandkids. And your flaky wife."

"Was it the ginkgo biloba? Was it the hypnosis tapes? It may be the..."

"Alexander!" Cook shouted. "Are you listening to me?"

"Yes, Dad! I'm here! I'm here!"

"What I am trying to tell you is, I think I'm ready to..."

Alex interrupted his father. "It was the new biofeedback therapist. I knew it. I can't wait to rub it in Anna's face!"

"Alexander McCloskey!" Cook yelled.

"I'm here with you, Dad. What are you trying to tell me?"

"Where's my fucking fish?"

* * * * *

Jake walked next door to his father's old room. Somebody's grandchildren were playing in the hall. Jake looked back and smiled.

God, to be a kid again. Things were just less complicated when you're a kid.

He found Ratner inside, talking with a familiar bald man with bright blue eyes. Jake's eyes widened in recognition. Horror-struck, Jake's heart stopped. The room spun. Jake felt his life force ripping out of his body, like a scene from *Alien*. A wooden wheelchair plagued the room, and the scowling Dame Bernice shot daggers at Jake. That didn't frighten him. The Demon Cat of Flushing sat on his hind haunches, statuesque on his tray. It licked its chops at Jake's fading soul.

Jake hid behind Ratner.

"Everything all right, Mr. Johansson?" Ratner asked.

"What the hell is that monster doing in here?"

The bearded, bald man answered in apparent disgust.

"That is my mother!" Arnold Pfeiffer said.

"Not her," Jake pointed out, ignoring Pfeiffer's unexpected presence. "I was referring to the cat."

Pfeiffer eased up a bit.

"Lord Humphrey? He wouldn't hurt a fly," Pfeiffer said as he petted the purring feline. "Besides, he's on a leash."

Ratner changed the subject.

"Look, Mr. Johansson, he's looking great today, showing symptoms of delirium and extreme agitation. I see some promising signs of post-traumatic stress disorder, and vitals are remarkably excellent," Ratner said while examining a chart.

Captain Jay lay semiconscious in a hospital bed. His eyes were wild with confusion.

"Our goal is to keep him alive long enough to wish death. Then keep him alive some more," Ratner continued.

"You're a sick man, R," Jake said.

"It was my mother's idea," Pfeiffer said, patting his mother's hand.

At that moment, a woman wearing a white nursing uniform walked in. Ratner looked up and said, "Oh, great. You're here." He glanced at his watch. "Right on time."

Jake's eyes opened wide.

"Jake, this is the special care nurse I hired to care for Mr. Vascones. Jillian Kidd, this is my friend Jacob Johansson."

Jacob and Jillian smiled at each other and shook hands.

"We are all at peace now," Jake said.

Dame Bernice Pfeiffer brought two fingers to her eyes and pointed them at Jake.

Epilogue

2 Years Later

M rs. Daschle answered the knock at her door.

"Theresa, my dear. Hello. What a delightful surprise," she greeted. "Oh, and Hope, it is so wonderful to see you too, sweetie."

Hope gave Mrs. Daschle a great big hug.

"Come in. Come in."

"Sorry to come over so late. Hope wanted to see Jake before we leave for vacation," Terri said.

"Oh, nonsense, dear. It's only eight o'clock. I'm a night owl, you know."

"We can only stay for a minute. We have to visit with Chastity, too. She was transferred to a residential hospital here in Brooklyn." Terri looked at her watch. Mrs. Daschle smacked her forehead.

"Damn. Jake ran out. He got called in to work at the last minute. He said something came up. He didn't call you?"

Terri looked disappointed. "That's so typical. You know Jacob, he can only focus on one thing at a time."

"I'm sure he will call soon as he settles that brain down," Mrs. Daschle added. "He's out saving the world again."

Hope sighed. "Oh, man. Can we call him?"

"Yes, of course, on our way to see your mother," Terri said.

Terri then turned to Mrs. Daschle. "Now that Chastity is in a residential hospital setting, she gets court-ordered, supervised visits every other weekend. But I try to sneak her over a couple of extra times. It seems to help them both. Chastity is making real progress. She would never have gotten through this if it weren't for her aunt and uncle."

"How are you doing with that promotion?" Mrs. Daschle asked.

"Great. A lot less work. Lots more money. When I was in the trenches, I complained that Arden Friel didn't work hard because he was too busy barking orders. I didn't believe it was true. I'm so glad the trials and lawsuits are over. Friel got what he deserved. I heard he's delivering porta-potties or something. Lucky he's not in jail like his Minister."

"Well, now that all the legal obligations have been met, maybe Jacob will finally get that ring he promised you."

Hope clapped her hands in approval.

"Mrs. Evelyn Daschle, are you hinting at something?" Terri asked.

"Girl talk, dear. I know nothing, I solemnly swear. Oh, by the way, an old client of mine has a beautiful single daughter. She is newly divorced and ready to get back on the scene." Mrs. Daschle then covered her mouth with her hand and whispered the rest. "Her husband left her for a man."

Nothing got past Hope. "The man was gay?"

"She's getting too old," Terri stated.

Mrs. Daschle continued, "Anyway, do you still talk to Detective Molina? I haven't seen him in such a long time. He would be perfect if he were still single."

"I saw him a few times after his retirement party. He and Jake hung out for a while, but then he stopped calling or answering and disappeared. It's been a while since we've seen him, too. We tried to be his friend, but I guess he couldn't. It's okay. We will always be grateful to him."

Terri stood up to leave. Hope followed suit.

"Well, we better go. Gotta get to JFK for our red eye after seeing Chastity," Terri said. "I'll call Jake on his phone. I miss him already."

Mrs. Daschle hugged them both. "I am going to miss you two. Especially at Sunday dinner this week. Colin won't have Hope around to laugh at his silly jokes."

"It's only for two weeks. I have been promising Hope a Disney vacation forever." Hope flashed an enormous grin. Mrs. Daschle returned a warm smile.

"I can't wait to see you at Miles and Moon's wedding," Mrs. Daschle said.

"I know we are so excited. Hope and I picked up our bridesmaid dresses yesterday."

"Two weeks!" Mrs. Daschle exclaimed to Hope.

Hope gave a thumbs-up. "Miles better take a shower. He thumb-swore."

* * * * *

Jake stood at the corner of West 49th Street and 9th Avenue. It drizzled outside, and the streets were almost empty at 2:00 a.m. He tried to blend in with the surroundings while sipping his third cup of coffee. Suddenly, he noticed a young African American girl walking opposite him. She appeared intoxicated as she struggled to keep her balance in high-heeled shoes. The girl was wearing a cocktail dress and looked as if she were walking home from a glitzy affair. Despite her intoxicated state, the girl appeared happy about something, twirling her wristlet purse and smiling.

A new love. A new promotion. Maybe she won lotto, Jake thought.

On the West Side tonight, the streets dimmed into an uneasy stillness. Jake's pulse quickened as he searched the area for a cab he could offer her. As he was about to abandon hope, he spotted two men trailing behind the girl. They advanced in unison, the silence thick enough to chew. Jake's instincts compelled him to react, and he ducked behind a parked truck, his heart racing.

One man, clad in a black flat-billed baseball hat and a black quilted jacket, veered off, crossing the street without a glance. He fixed his eyes on the girl, oblivious of any cars. The two men maintained a distance from the stumbling girl, yet their pace quickened, a predator's rhythm as they moved in sync.

Jake followed them, his breath shallow, adrenaline coursing through his veins. The shadows swallowed him as he trailed them for blocks, undetected, heart pounding in sync with their footsteps. They were closing in, almost upon the unsuspecting girl, and an imminent threat charged the air around Jake. It was about to go down.

The lone girl stumbled across West 41st Street, looking both ways before crossing. A knucklehead in a black hoodie darted across the street without a care, and as the girl passed the Bikini Bar, the attackers struck. Out of nowhere, the hat guy grabbed her from behind, covering her screaming mouth with his hand. Fear gripped her, and she struggled, but escape was impossible. No one could help her.

The man in the hoodie grabbed her legs. Both growled at her to shut up as she wiggled her body, trying to free herself. Hoodie reached up her dress and began pulling down her underwear. Jake exhaled and grabbed Hoodie's arm, then punched him square in the groin. The victim kicked her legs free while Jake lunged for Hat Guy. He ran across 9th Avenue and into a construction area under the bus ramps. Jake looked to Hoodie Guy, who was limping away in the opposite direction. The screaming victim was so confused that she stayed put and screamed.

"Go inside the bar. Call 911. I'll be back to help you," Jake told the girl.

Jet fuel filled Jake's arteries as he raced toward the towering construction fence. His heart throbbed, drowning out the sound of his footsteps. Hat Guy had a tremendous head start, but Jake knew he couldn't give up. When he finally reached the fence, he didn't hesitate for a moment. With a surge of energy, he scaled the fence in record time, his fingers gripping the cold metal bars.

Jake slipped through to the other side.

Darkness ruled the lot. The yard stretched wide with payloaders, truck trailers, shadows stacked on shadows. No lights. No sound. The chilly night air in his lungs.

He kept low, sliding between hulking machines. Each step silent. Each breath measured. The chain-link fence at the far end glinted under a sliver of moon. Hat Guy's only escape.

Nothing moved. Nothing breathed. The silence crawled over his skin. He was ready to call it.

Sneakers. Two of them. Sticking out from under a tarp in the far corner.

Jake closed in. One step. Then another. Eyes locked. He lunged.

The impact hit hard and fast. All in the shoulder. Bone crunched. A grunt burst from beneath the tarp. The hat spun to the ground.

Jake wrenched the man up. Hat Guy was dead weight in his grip. He was faking unconsciousness now that he was caught. Jake dragged him across the gravel. The cuffs bit down around the man's wrists, chaining him to the inside of the fence.

No need to toss him over. Let him hang there. Let him wait.

"Miss, you okay?" Jake asked the young lady outside the bar. A few protective patrons surrounded her. She nodded her head, but she was still shaking.

"What's your name?"

"Nikki."

"Nikki, did you see where the other one went?" Jake asked.

She pointed east along 41st Street. Jake immediately ran to see if he could catch the second criminal. Rushing past a dumpster, he spotted Hoodie sitting against a wall with his feet sticking straight out. Jake checked his pulse, which felt normal, and then dragged the punk back to the scene.

* * * * *

All was quiet on 9th Avenue after the police cars and emergency vehicles left. An African American gentleman wearing an oversized bubble jacket and a beanie appeared on the corner. He surveyed the area and found an unmarked brick space on the wall beside the dumpster near the Bikini Bar. Sing X spray-painted his signature calling card. A masked figure stepped out of the shadows.

Sing X looked him straight in his dual-colored eyes. "Man, it sure feels good to have you back. Two rapists. Not a bad night."

The Fade grunted and nodded in agreement.

Sing X gave an examining eye.

"You're a little shorter than I remember and I think your eyes are um, backward. I'm just saying."

Blue light danced across The Fade's fingers as the Hero of the Streets shrugged his shoulders. He turned and faded back into the shadows.

* * * * *

The following day, Colin Duffy sat at his desk, reading the newspaper.

Rookie NYPD officer foils attempted rape of Broadway actress

By James Fanelli, New York Post Contributor

NEW YORK CITY — Police have arrested two men in connection with the attempted rape of a 22-year-old actress who was walking home early Sunday morning after celebrating her debut as a Broadway lead.

At approximately 2:00 a.m., the suspects, identified as Devin Thomas, 28, of Jersey City, and Corey Edwards, 26, of the Bronx's Mott Haven neighborhood, allegedly attacked the woman near 9th Avenue and West 41st Street. Both men have extensive criminal records and are also under investigation for at least three similar incidents in the area, authorities said.

According to police, Officer Jacob Johansson, a rookie assigned to the Midtown North precinct, spotted the suspects following the actress. When the men attempted to assault her, Johansson intervened, subduing both and placing them under arrest without further injury to the victim.

Thomas and Edwards were held overnight at the Special Victims Division for questioning. Charges are pending.

Johansson, whose quick actions likely prevented a sexual assault, is being hailed as a hero by the department.

Collin Duffy sat back with a proud smile.

"Just like his father."

The End

Acknowledgement

I wish to express my deepest gratitude to the individuals whose guidance, support, and encouragement made this book possible.

To my wife, Liz, whose patience, strength, and love have sustained every chapter of my life. To my children, Tiana, Thomas, and Zachary, whose light and imagination continue to inspire my work.

To my parents, Wendy and Everett, whose steady faith in me has been both anchor and compass. And to my brother James, whose support has never wavered. To my extended family, thank you for shaping this journey in more ways than words can fully express.

To my Aunt Terri, who believed in me long before I learned to believe in myself.

To my closest friends and longtime companions, thank you for your encouragement, perspective, and belief in my creative path.

To my colleagues in the NYPD and the Special Victims Division, as well as my brothers and sisters in law enforcement and emergency services: your integrity, courage, and humanity have influenced my writing more than you may ever know. You have shaped the way I see the world and the stories I tell.

In memory of Sgt. Paul Tuozzolo and Sgt. Alex Baez, your service, sacrifice, and legacy endure.

To my bandmates and creative collaborators, past and present, thank you for reminding me that art takes many forms and that expression is a gift meant to be shared.

To the faculty who helped shape my voice, my work ethic, and my love of learning: thank you for the doors you opened. A special acknowledgment to Dr. Merman of Suffolk County Community College, your influence reached further than you could have known.

To my professional team:

Paul Dinas and Phil Carlucci, whose editorial expertise transformed this manuscript into its strongest form. Your guidance, patience, and dedication elevated each page.

And finally, to the readers, thank you for giving this story a life beyond my own.

About the Author

Ev Newman is a retired New York City detective who spent more than twenty years inside the pressure cooker of the Special Victims Unit, where he specialized in child abuse investigations and learned exactly how heavy a human story can get. These days, he trades squad rooms for the open stretch of the Great South Bay, patrolling its waters and pretending he finally has time to breathe.

He lives on Long Island, where he was born, raised, grilled, seasoned, and occasionally overcooked by life. A die-hard New York Islanders fan, he has endured enough heartbreak to qualify for sainthood or padded walls, depending on the season.

Ev writes stories cut from scars, pieces of himself hammered into fiction because that's the only way they'll stay still long enough to talk. Fade is his debut novel, though "debut" is a loose term; he's already completed several more full-length manuscripts, proving this is not a hobby, a phase, or a midlife experiment. This isn't a late-in-life detour. It's the road he was built for, finally cleared of traffic.

When he isn't writing, he's still making noise: shouting at hockey games, singing with a local rock band, or scribbling down a twisted plot on the nearest workable surface. His house is full of teenagers, guitars, and the kind of chaos that makes reality impossible to ignore.

www.ingramcontent.com/pod-product-compliance
Lightning Source LLC
Chambersburg PA
CBHW032004110726
47901CB00004B/958

* 9 7 9 8 9 9 9 4 3 6 9 1 7 *